SMOKY BACON CRISPS
Finding the edge of life

Dave Mearns

This book may be purchased in hard copy or as an e-book,
both through Amazon.
ISBN 978-0-9933784-0-9 (Paperback)
ISBN 978-0-9933784-1-6 (eBook-Kindle)

Also by the same author:
Shadow State
ISBN 978-0-9933784-2-3 (Paperback)
ISBN 978-0-9933784-3-0 (eBook-Kindle)

Publisher:
Dave Mearns (info@davemearns.com)

Cover and book design:
Paul Drummond (www.pauldrummond.co.uk)

ACKNOWLEDGEMENTS

As well as thanking my daughter Tessa for her role as chief editor, I want to acknowledge some of the people who have been especially useful in the research for *Smoky Bacon Crisps*. The staff of *Computer Division* in Stirling verified the section on hardware, even to the extent of revealing that they too resorted to a soldering iron at times. Margaret and Lesley who command the self-service checkouts in my local Tesco were not exactly models for my *Mhairi* and *Irene*, but they were certainly the inspiration. Alec Watt, the gentleman bookmaker, never knew that he was part of the research for the book, but he was patient in dealing with my many queries over the years. I would certainly recommend him to Scottish racecourse punters... other things being equal of course. My Gaelic language consultant was Donnie Mackenzie, former President of Stirling Gaelic Choir. I also want to acknowledge the young woman I spoke with on the Passport Agency telephone helpline. She showed extreme professionalism and patience through my long list of what must have appeared bizarre and even suspicious questions. I was a little afraid that she might have referred my call to the police as 'possibly terrorist related'. Finally, I need to emphasise that all people and events in this book are fictional. There are references to specific roles within Police Scotland. I have no information about the actual incumbents of these roles and this fictional narrative should not be associated with them.

Dave Mearns

April 2013 (Revised edition, October, 2015)

CONTENTS

ACKNOWLEDGEMENTS   i

1. TOUCHING BASE   1

2. MEETING   6

3. THE FUNERAL OF ROBERT ALEXANDER   10

4. NEW BEGINNINGS   13

5. DONNIE'S UNDOING   17

6. ROY'S REMEMBRANCE   24

7. RETRIBUTION   26

8. HENRY'S MAGIC   34

9. SHOPPING   40

10. CHRISTMAS PLANNING   46

11. CHRISTMAS EXTRAS   50

12. RECONNECTING   56

13. TIDYING UP THE YEAR   66

14. SPRING HAS SPRUNG   74

15. BLACK HOLES, LOVING AND LONELINESS   81

16. A BOYS' DAY OUT   85

17. DISCOVERING ANTHONY   99

18. POLITICS   102

19. CULTIVATING   108

20. A GIRLS' NIGHT IN   114

21. THE LEAVING OF ANTHONY   117

22. EXILED   121

23. TWO OF A KIND   128

24. REUNITED   132

25. A SATURDAY AFTERNOON 138

26. CULTURED 143

27. BODYGUARDS 148

28. MAUREEN 152

29. TO THE NORTH 154

30. ROSIE 161

31. THE UNACCUSTOMED WALKER 163

32. AONGHAS OF ASSYNT 167

33. REFLECTIONS 177

34. MAUREEN RETURNS 182

35. THE PASSPORT OFFICE 185

36. HENRY'S NIGHTMARE 192

37. THE INTEROGATION 200

38. CONFUSION IN THE CULLODEN 205

39. THE POWER OF SILENCE 208

40. MUCH ADO ABOUT SOMETHING 215

41. BETWEEN THE LAW AND A HARD PLACE 223

42. TELEVISION STAR 229

43. PREPARING 232

44. A BRIEF MEETING 238

45. DINGWALL'S REVENGE 241

46. FIGHTING BACK 247

47. THE DEFENCE DOES NOT REST 250

48. NOTHING IS THE SAME 255

49. THE GATHERING 258

50. ROY'S SPEECH 274

51. THE PENSIONERS MARCH 280

52. AFTERWARDS 290

53. COMING TOGETHER   296

54. NEWSNIGHT   305

55. A DISTINGUISHED VISITOR   311

56. MEETING UP   318

57. MOVING ON   331

1. TOUCHING BASE

Nothing had changed in the last year. The workers still flooded out the factory gates at exactly 5.00pm, fanning out in an undeclared race to the end of Leven Street and the buses as well as the pubs beyond. There were more women than there would have been in times past, but still they all headed for the buses, leaving the two nearest pubs in Dumbarton Road to their men-only traditions.

Roy Fox had never been back to the factory gates in the year since his retirement. Work was something that had defined him for most of his life but it had been time to move on from that definition. He felt contented with his memories of himself as a working man. He had only reached the level of supervisor, a single grade above the shop floor, but he had been good at his job and popular among the men who worked under him. His retirement doo had been one of the best and he had left with an unseen tear in his eye.

The first winter had been fine, with every morning reminding him that he had been released from the routine of a working life. Spring and summer saw Roy immersed in his allotment, finally with enough time to do it justice and also to help a couple of still working cronies to keep their plots in order when wives would object to not seeing them at weekends. Even autumn was OK, with clearing and re-designing the plot for the next year taking priority. But this second winter was a different matter. Roy's regular 7.00am rise was thrown into question when it would be into darkness and what was the point getting up when all there was to do was to go to the corner shop for the morning paper?

Roy had found it hard when his wife Sheila had died nine years earlier, but he still had his work to structure his life. If Sheila had been here they might have done all sorts of new things given his release from work. But she wasn't and he had cried about that this morning as he had done on many mornings. He was facing the loss of his past and also of his future. That was what had led him to sheltering from the steady drizzle in the shop front at the end of Leven Street.

In the second wave of released humanity he saw Billy Burnett, one of his long time mates at work. Billy returned his gaze, gave him a big smile and a wave from across the street, but carried on round the corner with his friends to the pub. Roy pulled himself back from taking a step across the road to join Billy. He knew how that would work out, with Billy welcoming him warmly, introducing him to his new friends and asking him how he was getting on. The conversation would embarrassingly dry up after five minutes and Roy would make an excuse to leave. Better to let everyone keep their respect and let go of the past. Roy went back to his flat to make some dinner, watch TV and wait until a decent hour to go to the pub.

*
**

Donnie Anderson was trying not to drink too much because the doctor had told him it was bad for his one remaining kidney. He was determined just to have a couple of pints in the evening and absolutely nothing during the day. Most days he walked the country or the streets. In the summer he would use his bus pass to go somewhere in the country and walk home, often twenty miles or more, and in winter he set out early to walk the city streets trying to find new routes every day. Three months ago he had reached sixty five years of age and officially was retired from unemployment, for that had been his status for most of the last thirty years. In fact he was elated when he made that transition because he felt that there was now no question of him being a 'scrounger'. Overnight, the constant guilt about not working and living off benefit had been lifted from him. He now had some status; he was a retired gentleman.

But he still had his days like today – days when he slowed down long enough to catch up with his feelings – days when the fear and the panic and the crying came back – days when he wanted to die and just have peace from it all. If he could kill himself that might also make amends to the other people he had hurt in his life; people like his wife Susan who could take no more of him and had left twenty five years earlier with their fifteen year old son, Donald.

Donnie had never fitted into life. At school he would try to make friends, but he would try too hard and, instead, he was always the first to be bullied. Only Donnie knew the revenge he would eventually exert on a long list of bullies. Donnie was a dangerous victim.

Today he was on one of his walks. He reckoned that seven hours would be a good time and the pace was keeping him ahead of his feelings. A couple of people who knew him had waved but he couldn't stop…he mustn't stop…he must keep going…fast. But the crying caught up with him at the furthest extremity of his walk, as he reached the cemetery behind St. Mungo's Cathedral. He sat on one of the benches holding his head in his hands. Two women passed by tutting at "that man being drunk and it was only lunch time." He considered growling at them or worse, but he was better at controlling himself these days. His mind went for a wander round his life and didn't like what it saw. He got two buses home and went to bed.

**

Henry Doncaster sat opposite his forty-eight inch plasma screen television. The table in front of him held two lap tops which he operated independently with left and right hands. His computing set-up, including ultra-high speed cabled broadband, had cost nearly six thousand pounds, but it was more than paying its way. With access to all the horseracing and betting websites, Henry was taking on the bookies. Indeed, with the advent of the internet 'Exchange' websites, he was as much a bookie as a punter. Today was like any other in that it had begun at 7.00pm the evening before as he studied the fields for the next day's races, looking at the corners of the market in which he specialised: an experienced Brazilian jockey, a claiming apprentice jockey and three stables whose horses he knew nearly as well as their trainers and a lot better than their owners. At 9.00pm his homework was complete and he would go briefly to the pub to be home in time to get a proper night's sleep before the real work began on the betting sites at 7.30am. With the major bookies declaring most of their prices by 9.00am, his travail was generally complete by 11.00am. Today he was slightly later because he had caught up on a late change that involved a senior stable jockey switching to the lesser fancied horse in a race and leaving an apprentice to ride the favourite. That had involved additional betting on the lesser horse and serious betting against the favourite before other punters became aware of the revealing change. With a satisfied sigh he closed his laptops and stretched. He might or might not watch the races that afternoon. Watching was not hugely important to him; the real buzz was the dexterity of his work in the morning. Perhaps, he mused, the time was coming close when he would make the ultimate step of taking control of a market. He had been working it out for some time, noting subtle betting patterns that showed how a big player was silently controlling hundreds of betters and layers. Maybe soon... perhaps next week he would pick a small market and take it over.

Henry was a gentleman geek; indeed he would readily agree with that stereotype. He lived alone and, apart from two months with Mary when he was twenty-eight, he had always lived alone. It was not that he failed to get on with people; he was friendly and carried an understated confidence that appealed to others. It was simply that Henry was attracted to problems more than to people. His working life had involved organising the logistics for a distribution network. He had created a system where several companies could share his logistics website and dovetail their journeys with each other.

His employer had made millions out of his work, but paid him a pittance. If truth be told, money was not important to Henry; it was solving problems that really appealed. Henry had decided to retire two years previously, aged sixty-two. When that time came he informed his company that, as well as his normal pension, he would allow them to pay him a lump sum five times greater than they had expected. His employer's initial incredulity was quickly followed by a cheque when they realised that Henry had charge of the encryption for the logistics website.

Henry decided that a balanced life must include a short walk in the park in the afternoon before a spot of shopping for a nice meal that early evening.

2. MEETING

Men are not very good at meeting. They can be in a nodding relationship with each other for years without communicating further or even knowing each other's names. Such were the relationships between Roy, Donnie and Henry, all 'regulars' at the Culloden Bar. Roy was first to arrive, promptly at 9.00pm, nodding to a couple of 'friends' whose names he did not know and taking his usual place seated at the far side of the bar, facing the door. He loosened the button on his Harris Tweed jacket, took off his old flat cap faded from twenty years of washing, folded it once and placed it on the bar. Without him needing to order, Maureen, the bar manager, poured his usual pint. Maureen was the archetypal Scottish bar manager. Attractive, always well dressed and looking about five years less than her actual forty-nine, her presence was commanding. She rightly took pride in running a smooth operation where the junior staff knew their roles and performed them dutifully, not in fear of Maureen's retribution, but in fear of letting her down. The pub would open twice a day at the exactly appointed times and there was never trouble at closing. Maureen never shouted 'time'; she simply tinkled a small silver bell five minutes before closing and the locals immediately supped up and even cleared the tables, returning debris to the bar and bidding Maureen a good night. Though she had managed the Culloden for fifteen years, none of the regulars knew anything about Maureen, except the fact that her mother had died last year, occasioning her first non-holiday absence.

Maureen's main assistant, Rosie, was a tall, elegant twenty-four year old woman of mixed race. Her mother's side were of African-Caribbean origin and had lived in London for three generations. Rosie's mother had broken with tradition by falling in love with a Glasgow man. The only good thing to come from that relationship was Rosie.

Henry strode in at five past nine with his expensive long

brown trench coat thrown open as always and his Racing Post under his arm. If truth be told, there was nothing in this ninety page daily publication that Henry did not already know, having studied it online since 7.00pm the evening before. He took it to the pub simply to have something to bury his head in if anyone showed the temerity to break the unspoken rule and initiate conversation. Like Roy, he sat at the bar, but in the middle of its long stretch, facing the gantry and far enough away from Roy such that only an informal nod to this other 'regular' was required. Again, like Roy, he took off his hat and placed it on the bar. Henry's hat was an exquisite brown fur felt Fedora, hand made by Christys' of London. Again, Maureen had his usual half-pint in front of him before he had opened his paper. "Thanks Maureen," he acknowledged.

"Missed you last night Henry," she replied.

Maureen knew the names of some of her regular patrons. She knew those, like Roy, who had been regulars when she had started fifteen years earlier because she had taken the step of introducing herself and fervently remembering all the names. She did not do that with later arrivals simply because you never know which newcomers will become regulars or when that will be deemed to have happened. Henry was one of those, but he had identified himself last year when he had said that he was 'sorry for her loss' on her return from cremating her mother. Maureen had been touched by that. Others had respectfully nodded to her or even doffed their caps in the traditional Scottish mark of respect for the bereaved, but Henry had been the only one to actually speak to her.

"I got engrossed with my work last night and it was nearly closing time when I realised," explained Henry.

Maureen smiled. She would have loved to ask him what work he did at home every evening, but she too knew the rules.

Donnie's entry, at a late 9.30pm, resembled his personality. He pushed the door ajar and furtively looked inside; then entered while still holding the door ready for a quick exit as he scanned the whole bar. Feeling safe from whatever prospect he had imagined, Donnie let the door close and moved towards the bar. Maureen sighed as she poured his pint; who on earth was this total stranger she had known for twelve years? Donnie paid for his drink without comment and took it to the corner far away from the television where the English Premier League football game was entering its final phase. Maureen had the owner of the Culloden take an expensive subscription to get the top English games rather than the less expensive Scottish fixtures because she did not want trouble from opposing factions of fans. Sometimes newcomers would complain, but soon they joined the regulars in becoming aficionados of the English game.

When Maureen tinkled her silver bell at five minutes before the 11.00pm closing, she did not know that this would ring the changes for so many people. Like Pavlov's dogs, the tinkling bell initiated the familiar conditioned response in the dozen or so regulars still present. They supped up, cleared their tables and started to leave. The last three, last only because Roy and Henry were always diligent to leave no clearing up to Maureen and Donnie because he was in the toilet, gathered at the bar to bid Maureen good night. Maureen pointed to the far end of the pub where an old man sat peacefully with his chin on his chest and a nearly full half-pint of beer in front of him.

"Old Robert has fallen asleep again. Give him a shake and I'll put a half behind the bar for him tomorrow."

Donnie, keen to do anything for Maureen whom he loved as he had loved many women unsuccessfully in his life, went over to Robert, shaking him gently.

"Time to go home Mr Alexander. Just leave your beer; Maureen will put one up for you tomorrow."

It is a Scottish tradition to be especially respectful of the oldest member of any community, hence Donnie's use of 'Mr Alexander' rather than 'Robert'.

Robert Alexander did not rouse. Donnie became agitated and with agitation always came fear for Donnie.

"I can't wake him...he won't waken up...please waken up

Mr Alexander…please!"

In the past Donnie often had had to beg for his fear to be relieved.

Everyone ran over, but even though she had to come round the bar, Maureen was first. She knelt straight in front of Robert Alexander, staring into his face and feeling his cheeks with the soft palms of her hands. Robert would have enjoyed that, had he been alive.

"Call the ambulance and the police, but I know that he is dead."

Roy and Donnie looked to each other blankly and Henry took out his iPhone.

3. THE FUNERAL OF ROBERT ALEXANDER

No one knew the person who had been Robert Alexander. He had been a regular at the Culloden for as long as anyone could remember, but no one knew who he was. Social Services traced his address to a single room rental which they paid as part of his benefit. The rental paid left Robert with his old age pension and slender needs. His single room revealed riches of an old television that could access only four channels, a double ring electric cooker of ancient origin and a single bed. There was no telephone because Mr Robert Alexander knew no one and was known by no one.

There is a tradition that the living are responsible for the dead in the order of their relationship with them. So, there being no appearing relatives of Robert Alexander, the Culloden took responsibility for his funeral. The decisions were difficult, but Maureen asked the regulars to take part. The logistics were put in the hands of the Cooperative Funeral Society, a business of high repute in the community. There is an old saying in Glasgow that "everyone departs this world via the co-op". But there was a question to be answered: should he be buried or cremated? Different people had alternative opinions, but Roy helped the community to come to the right decision when he observed, "We don't know if Robert has any relatives or not, but if they do come forward later it will be better if they are given the choice of leaving him buried or cremating him". The regulars of the Culloden contributed an impressive £800 to bury Robert. The owner added £200, Social Services contributed an unspecified amount, and the Cooperative Funeral Society quietly absorbed their deficit – they knew that they were part of the community. The result was a hearse and one car to follow. Maureen declared that those present in the pub when Robert was found should go in the car; that was Roy, Donnie, Henry and herself. Some others had brought cars and they were quickly filled by the regulars. At the graveside there was a respectable gathering of some fifteen people. Roy stood beside Henry who was stood beside by Donnie. Standing shoulder to shoulder they looked an odd trio with Henry at six foot four, Roy five foot ten and Donnie just failing to reach the five and a half foot mark. The minister, who did not really know if he was relevant, because he did not know if Robert had religion or which it was, did his best job.

"We are gathered here today to mark the death and celebrate the life of Robert Alexander".

Roy felt his insides nearly come outside.

"Why can't we do better than this? This man lived within our community for at least thirty years and we can say nothing about him!"

He looked round him, at Henry and Donnie and said, "This is not right."

Neither acknowledged, but both understood.

The funeral party appropriately retired to the Culloden where the owner had supplied sandwiches. Understandably, Roy, Donnie and Henry gravitated together. Maureen attended to her overall responsibility but she too favoured the three.

Roy initiated the inevitably difficult question. "It is terrible that we could not do better by him. What does this mean? Does it mean that any of us can pop off and we do not know each other well enough to bury us properly?"

Donnie endeavoured to develop the discourse. "That's the way the world is; you are in it and someone rubs you out of it, so you are history."

"No, Donnie...there must be more to us than that," said Roy.

Donnie lost his breath. People rarely paid him enough attention to use his name. He could say nothing...he was not accustomed to sustaining a discussion. Henry rescued all concerned from the possibility of further encounter.

"Roy, you are absolutely right. It is up to us to do whatever we can for Robert and 'wha's like him'."

The latter reference to the writing of Robert Burns escaped no one; it was their collective responsibility to look after their slender community. Donnie nodded as though he understood, but Henry and Roy smiled because they did understand. Maureen observed all this at a distance from which she would not be expected to hear, but she had heard so much that she had to retire quickly before the frog in her throat reached her eyes.

4. NEW BEGINNINGS

Nothing would ever be the same anymore; that is a wonderful epitaph for any man and perhaps Robert Alexander might have appreciated it. Certainly, the futures of Roy, Donnie and Henry were forever changed. No longer could they live in relational isolation, believing that they did not need people, but atrophying under the pretence. They were facing the dreadful prospect that they might need each other.

None of the three entered the Culloden in the next seven days. Roy was the first. As he came in, Maureen pondered on whether to say something. She wanted to say how pleased she was to see him and how the past week had been hell. She wanted to say that she had overheard their conversation after the funeral and how that had made her feel. Maureen found herself tripped up by what she was feeling. There was no 'attraction' to Roy, Henry and especially to Donnie, yet she felt so 'connected' with them. Maureen resorted to her first default position; she poured Roy's pint and passed it to him without a word. Roy nodded and supped his beer, but then he did a dreadful thing; he looked at her, straight in the eye. Maureen caught her breath; this was either a moment to withdraw or the opposite. She chose the opposite.

"I guess we are all affected by Robert's death...and by what it has raised in us."

Perhaps Jean Paul Sartre would have defined this as an inescapably 'existential' moment. In terms of Glaswegian philosophy it was a 'grounder'. A 'grounder' is an encounter offered by the other where it reaches us so fundamentally that we cannot but receive it. Roy replied, "True, Maureen...that night we found him dead...I keep replaying it in my mind... and finding that he was connected to no one. When we saw him in the pub we would all say, 'Hello Robert', but we would pass on by. I never sat down beside him and made any effort to get to know him."

"That's more or less what has been with me too...it was difficult for me to come in here the day after the funeral," said Maureen.

Roy looked at her. "Yes, I did the same again, didn't I...I couldn't face coming in here but I didn't think of anyone else but me...I didn't think that I might have responsibilities to anyone else."

Roy paused, wondering if he was going to say the next bit.

"Ever since my wife's death I have not really thought about other people...I have not felt that I should include consideration of anyone else."

Maureen needed to end the conversation, but she also needed to honour it.

"It's nice that you came in and that you talked to me," she said with a smile and the tiniest touch of his arm as she turned away to serve a new customer. Roy smiled too; it was nice to meet another human being.

It had taken Roy a week to return to the scene of Robert's death and what that had raised in him. Both Henry and Donnie took one day more. Roy was already established in his normal position at the far end of the bar when Henry entered and paused to look around. When Henry typically arrived shortly after 9.00pm he would be fresh from having worked his wonders arranging the very best early prices on his equine investments for the next day. Relieved of that concentration he would normally enter the bar in high spirits, but not this evening. His expression was serious, reflecting the amount of thinking that he had been doing in the past days. In Glaswegian parlance he had 'given himself a good talking to'. Throughout his life Henry had talked to himself. In his one brief 'living together' relationship his partner, Mary, had asked him about this. He had passed it off wrapped in the defence of humour, "Because the conversations are interesting," almost biting his lip as he uttered the words because he knew that he was not allowing Mary to see him. The reality was that Henry talked to himself because he was too used to managing his life on his own. As a child of parents who were frightened that youth of his age would 'lead him astray' and who endeavoured to keep him away from others, he had become expert in being entirely in his own world. In adulthood he had not sought out others and where they happened to get through his defences he seemed to have ways of getting rid of them…like Mary. The later life he had created also reflected his considerable skills of pure self-reliance. The logistics website, where only he had authority, and his current absorption in the on-line betting world were dramatic examples of how good he had become in keeping his life invulnerable to other people. The conclusion of Henry's days of self-reflection was his decision that he was not a 'lost cause'; it was possible that, even at sixty four years of age, he might for the first time let others in to his life. That was a profound conclusion and marked this serious entry to his first testing place, the Culloden. Scanning the bar, he soon picked out Roy Fox and strode forthrightly towards him.

"Good evening, can I buy you a drink?" uttered Henry for the first time in his life.

"No Henry," said Roy without rebuff. "I like to keep total control of what I drink and that gets messed up if we buy each other drinks…but I'll take a pack of smoky bacon crisps."

"Maureen, a half pint for me and two packs of smoky bacon crisps; fresh ones mind!" said Henry in mock seriousness, to be met by Maureen's pretend scowl and smile. Her friends were meeting.

Donnie's journey over the past days had reached the same conclusion as Henry's but by a much more tortured route. He had none of Henry's fundamental self-esteem, so the discomfort he had felt like the others had been experienced, not as a challenge, but as huge pain. Probably he had felt Robert's friendless death more powerfully than the others because it could easily be him. He knew that he did not engage with others and would likely die alone, but he would have to revise his whole way of looking at himself and the world if he were to change things. He would have to conquer his fear of people or at least defy it, in order to risk really meeting others. That was the breakthrough he got that gave him the possibility of change – perhaps he did not need to conquer his fear – perhaps he could simply defy it. With a huge breath of courage Donald Anderson entered the Culloden.

"Pack of crisps Donnie?" queried Henry as Donnie approached.

"Yes thanks, smoky bacon".

"We have decided not to buy each other drinks because it can get out of hand, but crisps are fine," explained Henry.

For the rest of the evening our three gentlemen got to know each other gradually, in the way that men do. Although they were all engaging in unfamiliar territory, the conversation flowed well. As well as the content of their conversation, they achieved other unspoken objectives, like assessing each other's humour. Since humour is a fundamental dimension of men's serious communication it needs to be assessed in each other and experimented with in conversation. By the end of the evening they knew each other's humour well enough to use it with confidence. So, when Roy said to Henry, "See you tomorrow...if you are still alive," Henry knew that this was Roy telling him that he understood him well enough to know that such 'gallows humour' would be OK with him. Neither Roy nor Henry would use such humour with Donnie because they could both sense that Donnie was too close to his own death. Instead, Roy looked Donnie in the eye and said, in a quiet, respectful voice, "Look after yourself Donnie." This message also carried a hidden component if Donnie wanted to hear it; that his new friend knew that he was in trouble and was genuinely concerned about him. Thus, in their conversation the men met each other more profoundly than any witness could appreciate.

5. DONNIE'S UNDOING

This was one of Donnie's favourite winter walks. He had taken two buses to Kilsyth and picked up the Forth and Clyde Canal tow path that would take him most of the eighteen miles home. It was a great walk on a sunny, frosty winter's day. The canal was superb for walking ever since it had been renovated and re-opened as a special project to celebrate the millennium. Prior to that reclamation it was thirty six miles of broken locks with debris filled pools of stinking water. Generations of children had been warned, "Don't go near the canal in case you fall in and get drowned." The result was that the canal carried associations of dread for the population. But with its locks repaired, closures re-opened, bridges raised to allow navigation all the way across the country and rubbish (including 56 cars) removed, it had become a source of pride for the people of central Scotland. Now it was enjoyed by thousands of walkers, cyclists and canoeists, not to mention people in canal boats and yachts who would use it as a traverse from the East of Scotland to the West in spring and returning at the end of the sailing season in autumn. Anglers too enjoyed its coarse fishing for more than twenty species of fish in waters so pure that even the delicate mayfly nymph could survive. Old men would lean over its many bridges and reminisce on the years before its closure in 1963, when Dutch herring boats would use it as a way to access the rich fishing of the Scottish west coast. "Aye", mused one such worthy to his crony. "The herrings is gone, but we've goat oor canal back."

Now within two miles of home, Donnie was pushing himself to make it before darkness, but it was a forlorn hope. Perhaps he should not have had that stop for a pint in the 'Stables' pub near Kirkintilloch. That had slowed him down in more ways than one. It had been against his rule to have a beer during the day, but he had been fuller of the joys of living than usual and had lost his discipline for a moment. Now he was feeling his feet. He wore his favourite shoes, but realised that he needed proper boots. Most of his walking was on tarmac and the shoes were fine for that, but the canal path was a rough grey cinder that was hot on the feet. In his walking meditation he tried unsuccessfully to work out how he could find the £80 for proper walking boots.

"Nearly there now" he assured himself as he passed the only 'sail by' fish and chip shop in the World. It was virtually dark as he went through an underpass and was caused to pause.

"Whit's yer hurry grandad?" came the voice, followed by a titter of laughter from two others.

He dimly made out three shapes blocking the path a few feet in front of him. He could only stop – to turn and run would have been suicide – they had fifty years on him. He remembered that sometimes you can get out of this kind of situation by humouring the opposition, so he slipped closer to the vernacular and tried.

"Hi lads, how are youse doing?"

"We is poor, grandad and youse is gonna help us oot," said the ringleader.

"I'm just a pensioner son; I've got nae money," appealed Donnie vainly.

"Bet you've goat mair than us," was the retort as the shape moved towards him and into better light.

"I know who you are…you're big Malcolm Jamieson's boy," said Donnie in recognition and hope that it would make a difference.

"That's sumthin you'd maybe better forget," came the threat.

A cold shiver spread over Donnie as he realised that it may not have been clever to show that he had recognised the thug.

"Sorry son; I mean you no hairm."

The three thugs laughed at him and the ringleader intensified the threat.

"I'm sure you dinnae mean us hairm old man, but maybe

it's youse that is getting hairm. Can you see whit this is?"

Donnie looked at the ten inch kitchen knife that was being waved in front of his face. "I've got about £12...you can have it," conceded Donnie beginning to search his pockets, as much in the hope that it would distract the boy. He took out a ten pound note, two pound coins and a fifty pence piece, handing them to the boy who pocketed the cash.

"An the watch as weel," commanded his assailant.

"But it was my grandfaither's," begged Donnie.

"Slash 'im Malky," squealed one of the lesser thugs.

"Yeah Malky...dae it," urged the other.

Donnie quickly removed his grandfather's watch and handed it over.

"See if he has any mair," commanded the leader.

The two smaller boys humiliated Donnie in the searching of his pockets.

With an intonation of disappointment one of them declared, "He's got nuthin else, except a pack o' Polo mints."

Donnie once more in his life felt the humiliation of being assaulted. 'Assault' does not necessarily involve physical harm; it is more about the power the assailant exerts over you. In earlier times he might have found ways of taking later revenge against these three. That was the way he had survived a lifetime of abuse to retain a modicum of self-respect. Donnie now could feel his anger rising to meet his fear. That had always been the dangerous combination he had had to fight against in his life. He had flashbacks to being beaten at school with the voices of the bullies in the background urging the leaders to play football with his head. He also had images of his father and of another time ten years later when he had been in the army and had been stripped and beaten. Sometime later he had caught the main perpetrator unawares, and what he had done to him would probably never be known. Donnie did not understand that violence in him, but he knew to beware it and never ever to talk about it.

"Shoes aff," instructed Malky Jamieson.

Donnie bent down, half expecting his head to be kicked into the canal, and with cold, fumbling, useless fingers he tore at his laces, breaking one of them in the desperate effort to get his shoes off. He handed them to the boy.

"Chib him noo Malky," implored one of the smaller psychopaths.

"No need," said Malky. "This old man knows whit he gets frae ma faither if he squeals. It'll take 'im some time tae get hame onyway," he added, tossing Donnie's shoes into the canal.

The three of them laughed while Donnie felt his humiliation more deeply. The leader turned and one henchman made to follow, while the other hesitated.

"Can we no cut 'im, Malky?".

"No need" was the response and the three disappeared into the darkness laughing.

Donnie had what may seem to be a strange initial reaction that is only comprehensible to those who know abuse from the inside. He had an initial feeling of gratitude towards the fifteen year old Malcolm Jamieson. Donnie knew that he had been in more danger of death from the two henchmen. In fact, Malcolm Jamieson had saved him from them. That realisation did not deter Donnie from fantasising on how he could gain huge revenge on Malcolm Jamieson. The need of the abused for retribution that will preserve a minimal self-respect is so strong that it will sometimes take what seems to outsiders to be inappropriate revenge on the perpetrator, or, even worse, on other victims. Society at large has never understood the dynamics of abuse.

It took Donnie three hours to get home, partly because the rough track cut his feet and he had to rest, but also because he kept stopping to lie down, roll around in the dirt and cry. His crying was not only about his hurt; it was about his struggle within himself to control his anger. He knew the revenge he could take, despite his age, but he desperately wanted to get away from that part of his history. He got home at 7.30pm and slumped on to his bed.

*
**

Two days later Roy and Henry were concerned that they had not seen Donnie. Roy initiated the conversation.

"I don't want us to miss anyone else like we missed Robert. I know that Donnie will be fine, but I don't want to take that for granted."

"Agreed brother," said Henry as though they were part of a fraternity, which perhaps they had come to be.

"Let's go round to his place," he suggested.

Thus the other two friends arrived outside Donnie's flat. They had purchased six cans of beer as an excuse of introduction. There was no immediate answer to their bell ringing, so they kept on ringing. This is important in the friendship of men – that they are not put off by an initial non-response – that they keep 'knocking on our door', without breaking it down of course.

After looking through his spy hole, Donnie opened the two Chub locks. Roy took the initiative, in the fashion that men do.

"Donnie, we missed you at the pub and we felt like a party, so we've brought a wee carry-out. I hope that is OK with you."

The way this is expressed by Roy recognises that none of them can say that they are concerned about Donnie, but it makes it difficult for him to decline this mild invitation of social contact.

"Come away in lads; I had a nap and slept in," lied Donnie.

"Aye, the sleeping sickness gets us all when we get on," joked Henry.

Both Henry and Roy noticed that Donnie was gaunt, unshaven, and had patches of dried mud on his face. They also saw his eyes...his crying eyes. Women would be more direct with each other in this situation, but men have to negotiate the 'men need to appear solid' imperative, so they have to be circumspect in their support of each other. Henry reasoned that Donnie might speak more easily with just one of them present. Also he judged that Donnie had probably not eaten for a while.

"Look guys, I'm starving and the chippie is doing a 'buy two get one free night'. Suppose I get us some fish suppers."

"Great idea," said Roy, impressed by his new friend's inventive untruth.

Donnie looked blank and eventually whispered, "Yes, that would be nice...I'm hungry." Roy and Henry could see that Donnie was in a bad way.

Henry made sure that he was away for half-an-hour, only purchasing the fish suppers five minutes before returning.

"Donnie's had a difficulty," was the way that Roy understated Donnie's story on Henry's return.

"Then our friend needs the best of attention," added Henry as he opened three cans of beer to accompany the fish suppers. He did not look for plates, knives or forks because everyone in Glasgow knows that fish suppers should be eaten in their papers. No attempt was made to speak further about Donnie's difficulty. Donnie had confided and that was a lot for one evening. Men have a need to be careful not to push too far, because men are experts at recoiling; men know that about each other.

When they were walking home a couple of hours later, Roy gave Henry all the detail that Donnie had given him. "Bastards," was Henry's response. Roy told him a story about his grandfather. "When he was eight years old my grandfather was horsewhipped by a forty year old 'gentleman' who thought that he had upset the horse that drew his carriage. The whipping was severe to the extent that my grandfather lost a lot of blood and was scarred for life. Twenty years later my grandfather stopped the same gent in the street, and asked him if he recognised the scars. Then he took out a horsewhip and had his revenge. He had waited twenty years to a time when the power between them was reversed, with him twenty eight years old and his assailant sixty". Henry found it a powerful story and nodded meaningfully, though he could not quite work out its relevance to the present situation.

6. ROY'S REMEMBRANCE

Roy stood with the posy of flowers in his hand. He had put on his best suit, white shirt and a carefully chosen tie that his wife Sheila had given him on his last birthday before her death. He had polished his old but good black dress shoes in which he used to dance with her. It was 9.30am and he was standing by her grave on the minute of the tenth anniversary of her death.

Their daughter, Emily, had phoned him from Canada at 7.30 that morning. She knew that he would be going to meet her mother and she wanted him also to speak for her. Emily seldom returned to Scotland, not because she was uncaring but because she cared too much and could not handle the distress she felt when she was too close to the loss of her mother. "I am still so sad that she was not able to be at my wedding," she had cried down the phone that morning with Roy sweeping back his tears and trying to speak only when he thought that he could stop his voice from breaking.

"Emily is doing very well in Canada. John has got promotion and now does not have to be away from home so often. That's good for Emily and for little Paul and Clara." Roy went on to give Sheila a full account of her grandchildren whom she had never met.

"And I am doing pretty well. I am not drinking too much and I have even begun to make new friends; men, mind. One is called 'Henry'. He is a very intelligent man who used to handle a company's 'logistics'. I do not quite know what that is. Now he is retired and does things with the horses. Again I do not quite understand it, but he seems good at it. Anyway, we get on well and I look forward to meeting him most evenings after nine in the pub. By the way, although I go into the pub most evenings I only go in at nine for a couple of hours and I never have more than two pints. My other new friend is 'Donnie'. He is quite different from Henry – in fact all three of us are different – that's what is unusual about our getting on so well. I think that Donnie has had a troubled past. You have to be careful not to startle him because he gets frightened easily. He seems to have lived alone most of his life and he is not used to being with people. But when he is with Henry and me it seems to be really good for him. I think we are really important for him. I like them both and it seems important for all of us that we have made friends, though I do not quite know why. Part of me feels that it is good to make these new friends and another part of me feels guilty about making friends with others after you. Sheila, you were always my best friend and you always will be my best friend. I wish that I could believe in what you believe; that we will meet again in the 'ever after'. I dearly wish that I could share that with you…that I could be with you…my bestest friend." Roy had to stop then because he was crying and could speak no more. He went home to spend the rest of the day alone in contemplation, as usual on these anniversaries. He did not go to the pub that evening. At 11pm he took off his dress shoes, still new tie and best suit, tidying them away in the wardrobe for another year. Roy went to bed to be with his bestest friend.

7. RETRIBUTION

Roy was in the pub an hour earlier than usual on the day after his meeting with Sheila because he was lonely. A young man of about 30 years of age dressed in an expensive dark suit and sporting a mop of ginger hair came over.

"Can I sit with you Mr Fox?"

"Certainly Nicholas, how are things with you?"

"A lot is good and, as always, some is bad," replied Nicholas, looking Roy straight in the eye.

"I suppose that is in the nature of your business, Nicholas".

Roy returned the young man's eye contact.

"Yes, it is. And how are you Mr Fox?"

"Well, you catch me at a difficult time because yesterday was the tenth anniversary of my wife's death."

Nicholas responded quickly.

"I remember her…I was only about fourteen and newly in the senior team. She brought our sandwiches after a game. I remember, her name was…was it 'Sheila'?"

Roy found himself stiffening with feeling. How could this young man remember the name of his wife after all these years and only from a single meeting?

Nicholas supplied the answer.

"She was really nice…I was the youngest in the team and I had been pretty beaten up in that game, although I scored the winner. She washed my cuts and bruises and put five plasters on me. My mum said that she must be a very nice person."

Roy could almost hear no more, so choked up did he feel. The day after he had been with Sheila this young man was commemorating her as well as any person could.

"You were good you know," said Roy, changing the subject away from his tears.

"You mean, at football?"

"Yes, you were good."

"Because I had a good coach," said Nicholas, honouring his

football mentor, Roy Fox. Roy added, "You were always better than the others who were two years older than you. You know that I had scouts watch you in three games?"

"And I played bad in those games...I couldn't hold it together."

"You were 'sent off' in two of those games. What was that about?"

"I don't know...it was as though I was close to becoming something else and whenever that has happened in my life I've blown it."

"That sounds difficult to understand," said Roy.

Nicholas smiled, "That is Roy Fox to a tee; anyone else would judge me, but you would just like to 'understand'.

"Well, I wish the world would just make an effort to 'understand', or even just to 'respect' each other," said Roy, his feeling state persisting but being displaced away from his wife. "One of my best friends, an old man of sixty-five was mugged last week, probably by one of your team...a young punk called Malcolm Jamieson. My friend, Donnie Anderson, was threatened near to death. They took his money, his grandfather's antique watch and they threw his shoes in the canal. Worse than that, they humiliated him."

Roy, surprised at how much feeling he had about Donnie's humiliation, told the whole story to the former star player in the youth football team he had coached for fifteen years.

When Donnie and Henry arrived together, Nicholas took that as a signal to leave.

"Nice to speak with you Mr Fox...you were important to me...you were different to me than other people...and I guess you still are."

Nicholas slipped out, nodding only slightly to the arriving Donnie and Henry.

"What are you speaking to him for?" Donnie posed the rhetorical question.

"Do you know who he is?" added Henry.

"Yes, he is Nicholas Andrews. I have known him much of

his life," replied Roy with irritation.

"He's not 'Nicholas', he's 'Finn' said Henry in annoyance. Do you not know what he is?"

"Yes, I know what he 'is', but I also know **who** he is... probably better than most."

"He is only the most violent gangster in Glasgow," said Donnie, trying to keep his voice just short of a shout in case anyone else heard.

Henry added, "Some people think that 'Finn' is his real name, but it's not; it's because he takes delight in taking his victims apart with a 'Finnish' filleting knife. He is the most feared person in Glasgow; he cuts people up for fun."

"That stuff is exaggerated; if you really know him he's a different person," said Roy, not expecting to persuade his friends.

"Well I would prefer not to 'really know' him," ended Donnie.

"Fair enough," said Roy. "Whose turn is it to buy the crisps?"

**

The next evening young Malcolm Jamieson was drinking in his local pub. The fact that he was considerably under age was of no concern to the publican; of more concern was that Malcolm Jamieson senior should not be roused. Young Malky had consumed six pints thus far; enough to reinforce his image among those present, but too much for his fifteen year old body. He made his wavering way to the toilet. After he entered, a 'body built' young Adonis took position at the door of the Gents. He stood tall in a dark suit with hands folded in front. On his hands he wore black gloves made of thin leather and fastened with press studs at the wrists. He always wore those gloves when he was working; they protected his hands from unsightly damage. Another customer made to enter.

"It's full," said Adonis.

"Whit dae ye mean it's full; it can't be full," retorted the punter whose drinking had lost his reasoning.

Adonis reached down, firmly grabbed the man's balls and lifted his body six inches off the floor.

"I said, it's full...better use the 'Ladies' now that you're equipped for it."

"OK mate," said the punter in a higher octave and moved away.

A moment later Adonis made way for Finn to enter the toilet. He took position at the wash basins, waiting for his victim to complete his task at the urinals further down the long, thin room. Young Malcolm finished his business and made to leave.

"Remember to wash your hands," said Finn.

"Fuck you bastard; dae ye know who yer fuckin talkin tae?"

"Indeed I do; I am talking to young Malcolm Jamieson, a cowardly boy who may die tonight."

Finn's words were expressed without emotion because emotion only dilutes terror.

"Who the fuck are you?" Young Malcolm's words still retained a modicum of bravado, but his spine tensed to experience his fear.

"This should introduce me."

Finn withdrew a twelve inch thin bladed knife from its tan leather sheath inside the back of his trousers.

"I waited until you had finished because it can be so messy when someone pees all over you."

"Shit, you're Finn," said Malky.

"Precisely; and you probably know what I do to people... with this."

Finn moved up close to the terrified boy, pinning him against the wall and speaking within three inches of his face with the blade held between them. He spoke slowly, rolling the long thin knife from side to side, letting it glisten in the light.

"This knife is of the finest steel. It is made thin so that it can be inserted under the bone to cut the flesh from it. The Finnish steel takes an edge like no other knife. I can cut out internal organs as easily as a surgeon with his scalpel. Or we could remove an easier external organ. You choose." Young Malcolm begged for his life and his body parts.

"I'm sorry Mr Finn. Please don't cut me, please, please!"

"I am told that you too have a knife. Where is it?"

"In my back belt sir," snivelled Malcolm.

Finn reached around and removed the knife. He held it up disdainfully between finger and thumb in the small space between them.

"You call this a 'knife'; this is a pathetic toy."

He tossed Malcolm's knife into a urinal.

"Now where were we? Yes, I was just about to start removing some parts of your body. You can limit it to one, simply by choosing which. You could choose a kidney. That will be messy, but in many ways a good choice because you will still have another one. Then there is the prostate gland. Please choose that one – I would love to experiment – I haven't done one of them yet. Of course there is always the other organ I mentioned...Ready to choose, or shall we just do all three?"

Malcolm Jamieson felt fear that he could never have contemplated. He sobbed for his existence or even for a quick death. He shit his pants.

"Oh pooh!" said Finn, "Let's get this over with; the smell is terrible. Would you like me to tell you what you are going to do?"

"Yes sir...please sir." Malcolm shook uncontrollably such that he could hardly get the words out.

"Well the first thing you are going to do is to treat older people with respect. Do you know what I am talking about?"

"Sorry sir, I've nae idea," denied Malcolm.

"OK. I see that we have to refresh your memory," said Finn, lowering his knife from Malcolm's throat to his groin and flicking the tip such that blood seeped through Malcolm's trousers.

Malcolm screamed loudly enough for the whole bar to hear, but no one moved. Adonis smiled at them in a fashion that reinforced their decision.

"That old man...at the canal," screamed Malcolm quietly but quickly.

"Good boy!" said Finn. "You just managed to save your tadger, for now anyway. Do you know that I have a collection of them at home? They are preserved in formaldehyde, but they don't look too good. Let me tell you what you are going to do. You are going to buy a box which you will give, publically so that there are witnesses, to Mr Donald Anderson in The Culloden, along with your sincere apology. You must address him with respect as 'Mr'. Into the box you are going to put £12.50, Mr Donald Anderson's grandfather's watch, and an expensive new pair of black dress shoes, let's say, size eight. The shoes will cost you at least £90 and you will put the receipt into the box so that I can check on you and he can exchange them if the size is wrong".

"But the watch is in the pawn and I've got nae money," offered Malcolm in apparent amnesia about the future status of his organs.

"That is absolutely fine dear boy, because I am going to help you out; that is what I do after all."

Finn slipped a small wad of six twenty pound notes into Malcolm's top pocket.

"Usual rates – 20% per week compounded. Nothing happens for four weeks, by which time it's up to £250 and you either pay or you really choose which parts of your body you keep. Ask your father if you should pay or not. Another thing...if anything happens to any old man in the area I am going to hold you personally responsible. I will not be concerned whether you were actually responsible or not. Do you understand all this?" "Yes," whimpered Malcolm.

"Yes what?"

"Yes sir."

"Now go and clean yourself; you do not want to let others

smell you like this, do you?"

"No sir," said Malcolm and retreated into a cubicle.

Finn tidied his knife away and swept out, picking up Adonis on the way out.

"Arrange for Malcolm Jamieson senior to get a 'reminder' to keep him in place. Have it done tonight," he instructed.

*
**

Three days later Roy and Henry were chatting at the bar when Donnie entered in his usual way, holding the door ajar as he paused to scan the pub before going on to meet the other two.

"Smoky bacon?" queried Henry.

"Thanks," confirmed Donnie.

"Why do you stop at the door and look around the whole bar before you come in?" asked Roy.

"Do I...I didn't realise that I did," was Donnie's innocent reply.

"You do it every time," probed Roy further.

"News to me," said Donnie in a fashion that could only terminate the exploration.

Roy smiled and shook his head. Donnie really was a crazy kid.

As Donnie ordered his pint and attacked his crisps a figure came through the door. Donnie stiffened as young Malcolm Jamieson came towards them. He slipped off his bar stool to give him at least a chance to evade attack.

"What is it?" asked Roy.

"That's him...Malcolm Jamieson...the thug," replied Donnie, nodding in the direction of the ever nearing figure.

Roy jumped off his bar stool and stood between Donnie and the boy. Maureen had radar for anything going wrong in her dominion and made to come from behind the bar.

"Stay back Maureen, this thug won't be a respecter of women," commanded Roy. Maureen was paused by such chivalry and stayed back.

The boy stopped ten feet short of Donnie and Roy, judging that to be the best 'public' distance.

"I want to apologise to you Mr Anderson, I should not have done that to you the other night," he began.

Donnie was confused, mainly by the fact that the thug was speaking proper English rather than his previous vernacular.

Bringing a box he was carrying up to chest height, the boy began to take things out of it, speaking as he did so.

"Here is the £12.50 I took from you, and this is a new pair of shoes to make up for the ones I threw in the canal. They are expensive ones mind and the receipt is in the box in case they are the wrong size. And here is your grandfather's watch...I wound it up. I'm sorry that I took these things from you and if you are ever in difficulty with anyone else here, let me know and I'll sort them out."

The boy put the box down on the bar and hurried out rather than expose himself to further embarrassment. The whole bar stayed in silence, unable to make sense of what had just happened.

Henry broke the silence. "What on earth was that about?"

"I don't know, but I have my suspicions," said Roy.

Donnie had not heard their offerings.

"Look at this receipt – it's for £90 – I'll be able to exchange them for good walking boots." Maureen concluded the disjointed dialogue with her own observation.

"Well one thing I noticed was that Roy Fox was my 'knight in shining armour'."

The whole bar looked at Roy who blushed profusely.

8. HENRY'S MAGIC

At precisely 3.45pm Henry closed the laptops in front of him and switched off the television. He had performed magic; for the first time he had taken over and manipulated a horse race market. It had involved four laptops instead of his usual two and various interventions over the past seven hours in relation to twelve multinational bookies and the main betting 'Exchanges'. He had used a total of sixteen of his betting accounts, all with different logins and passwords. His coup de grâce as far as hiding his identity was concerned was to engage proxy network access in order to hide his Internet Protocol address and route some of his playing through Canada, The Netherlands, Romania, Switzerland and South Africa. His disguises had given him a couple of precious minutes before the big bookies realised the kind of 'run' he was putting on them. The choice of the 3.45 race had been a good one – it was a small enough market to be influenced by his betting and laying (taking other people's bets). He was experiencing a strange mixture of feelings. Of course there was elation and satisfaction; rightly so, because the operation had taken considerable planning and no little nerve to pull it off. There had been a critical point where he could have dropped out of it with a small profit when it looked slightly shaky, but he had stuck with his strategy and invested more, so that the market had swung down again. As well as the joy and elation there were other feelings. He knew that he had done nothing illegal or even 'improper'; everything he had done was part of legal bookmaking practice. Yet, he felt slightly uncomfortable. He had intentionally manipulated a market to his advantage, but thousands of other punters would have come in on the back of his moves assuming that they were based on inside knowledge about the horse's actual chance of winning. They, as well as the big bookies, would have lost money, much of which was currently zinging down the ether to some of the twenty-four bank accounts he used for these ventures. He also felt a strange self-consciousness, as though others were looking at him, which they patently were not, or talking about him which they certainly were. In a few minutes time the trainer of the horse he had chosen for the venture would be wondering who he was while she faced interrogation by the race course stewards on the 'unusual betting pattern in the 3.45 race'. His dominant feeling was of 'power'; the little man had put one over the big boys. He remembered this feeling from his work days, where he alone had known how the logistics worked. Henry decided to put on his best suit, take an early evening walk to an expensive city restaurant, have a meal of extravagance and then a long taxi ride rather than a bus pass job back to the Culloden to meet his friends.

*
**

"But it doesn't feel right," argued Roy from their usual corner of the Culloden. "We should be using the corner shops, not the supermarket."

Donnie countered, "But they have great stuff Roy. Every time I go I find things that I've never heard of. Like last time I came home with 'escargots'. I think it was French. I had no idea what it was, but I followed the instructions and it tasted great."

"Did you find out what it was?" queried Roy.

"No, what is it?"

"Never mind Donnie, it's nice you liked them."

Donnie looked somewhat suspiciously at Roy but the conversation was put back on track with his friend's next argument.

"Supermarkets are big, impersonal places; no one gets to know you or even remember you, whereas the corner shop is friendly and is concerned about you."

Donnie retorted, "My corner shop isn't friendly. They look down their noses at me every time I go in, whereas my ladies at the supermarket remember me and are very friendly."

"Your 'ladies'?" queried Roy.

"Yes, Mhairi and Irene - they supervise the self-service checkouts. I tried the self-service once when the normal checkouts were busy. I made a bit of a mess of it; I kept forgetting to zap things before I put them in my bags and I zapped some things twice. But they took me in hand and helped me through it. They're great fun."

"Zapped?" queried Roy.

"When you put the shopping up in front of the scanner, it 'zaps' it," clarified Donnie. "Oh," said Roy, none the wiser.

At this point in a discussion characterised by increasing confusion rather than clarification, Roy and Donnie were temporarily saved by Henry's arrival. Unlike Donnie's furtive entries, Henry swept expansively into the pub, with coat flowing open to reveal his good suit. He strode confidently across the bar raising his fur felt Fedora to Maureen as she pulled him a pack of smoky bacon crisps and Roy produced the coins in payment.

"So what's with the good tin flute?" queried Roy.

"It is in celebration of my supreme intelligence," said Henry.

"Well we all know that you are a genius Henry, but what have you done now?" probed Roy, genuinely believing that Henry was one of the most amazing people he had ever met and enjoying the fact that they were friends. But in these circumstances it is important for men to continue to appear to put each other down; that is a dimension of the way men show their regard for each other.

Henry paused, desperately wanting to tell the story to his friends, but seriously doubting whether they could understand it. Taking a deep breath he attempted the impossible. "After a lot of research I decided to take control of the betting market in the 3.45 at Wetherby. My chosen target was a horse called 'Chancer'.

"That's a right name for a horse!" interrupted Donnie.

"Yes it is, but the horse is irrelevant in a true betting coup," obfuscated Henry in retaliation.

Donnie bowed his head in pretended submission.

Henry continued, "To cut a seven hour story short, I organised bets and lays such that I could only win."

"Give us more detail for I am a simple peasant who would like to understand from the master," urged Donnie in well-placed sarcasm.

Henry looked down on Donnie with familiar suspicion. "Essentially, I placed sizeable bets on Chancer to win at 12:1 thus influencing the market to reduce his odds. Then I layed him when his price reached 3:1 in such a way that my book was perfectly balanced."

"Do you understand a word of what he has said?" asked Roy of Donnie.

"Brilliant!" said Donnie to Henry, completely ignoring Roy. "It must have been difficult to work out how much you had to lay to get the perfect balance."

Henry looked long at Donnie and expressed exactly what he was thinking, "You amaze me Donnie."

At this point Roy raised his hand as though he was in a school classroom. "Did Chancer win?"

Simultaneously Donnie and Henry raised their eyebrows in disbelief at the naivety of this question. Each looked to the other and shook their heads in tandem.

"Explain it to him Henry."

Henry obliged. "In fact, I don't know if Chancer won or not; I switched off the television just as the race began."

Roy, by this time thoroughly confused, shook his head. "But how do you know if you have won or not?"

Donnie offered help, though, in fact, it did not actually help poor Roy. "Henry created the perfect balanced market in which it did not matter whether Chancer won or lost. In either case Henry would make more or less the same profit."

"I see," lied Roy for the umpteenth time in his life.

Henry looked at Donnie in unprecedented admiration.

"Donnie, you really do understand this stuff, don't you?"

"Easy," said Donnie, "it's like on the Stock Exchange."

"What do you mean?" enquired Henry.

"Like on the Stock Exchange, where a group of movers 'seed' the market. They inflate the price of a stock by buying it heavily. Others think there is a good reason why the stock price is going up and they also buy in. That raises the price even more and the movers simply choose their moment to sell and take their profit. You couldn't lose as long as you had enough capital and the nerve to hang on, always presuming that you had chosen a horse that wouldn't become a 'drifter' in the market for other reasons." "Donnie, you have become my soul mate."

Roy shook his head. "Can anyone explain what we have been talking about?" he begged. Donnie tried unsuccessfully to help Roy. "Basically, Henry bet the horse heavily at an average of 12:1. That pushed the price of the horse down and other people thought that it was being bet for a good reason, like maybe the trainer knew that it would win, so they also bet it, right down to 3:1, at which point Henry 'layed' the horse; that means he took other people's bets at 3:1. So, think about it Roy, it's like selling someone something for £12 and buying it back from someone else for £3. Henry could only win."

Henry looked at Donnie with incredulity. "How do you know this stuff?"

"Years ago I used to mark the board in a bookie's shop but he said that I was crap at that and he would try me behind the window."

Henry nodded. "Taking the bets and working out the pay-outs?"

"Yes, that stuff was easy; they would bet five horses with cross trebles, four timers and accumulator and I would work out the pay-outs."

"Without a calculator I presume?" asked Henry.

"What's a calculator?"

"You are, dear Donnie," declared Henry with a beaming

smile.

9. SHOPPING

No one really knew how they had actually decided to go to the supermarket the next day, but they were all at the bus stop at the appointed hour.

Donnie addressed Henry. "Did Chancer win?"

"In fact he did not, Donnie, so lunch at the supermarket is on me."

"Because your book was slightly imbalanced against him?"

"Precisely, my dear boy."

The three gentlemen trooped on to the bus, placing their senior citizen passes on the sensor and declaring the supermarket as their destination.

"Time for the weekly shopping then gents?" queried the bus driver, adding, "It'll be the fillet steak I imagine?"

"It'll be the pie and beans as usual," quipped Roy.

The sparring continued from the driver, "No, you guys have got it right good. My taxes pays for your big pensions and in return I'll be made to work till I'm eighty for mine!"

To this Roy added the clean ace, "Any more cheek from you and you won't make it till you're forty!"

Bus drivers and also butchers generally make cheery adversaries in banter.

They struggled their way to the back of the bus to reach the one long line of seats where the three of them could sit together.

Henry looked around him. "There are only two people on this bus under sixty".

"Yes, it is the bus passes that keep the buses going" suggested Roy.

"I heard they were thinking about doing away with them," added Henry.

Donnie was shocked. "What! I won't be able to get to my walks without my bus pass." Roy re-assured him. "Do not worry dear Donnie; they are not going to take our national bus passes away."

"Why wouldn't they?" asked Henry.

"Because they know what would happen," began Roy. "The whole of the pensioner army would rise up against them. Flags would be made and uniforms issued. Pensioners would be supplied with stout sticks and steel zimmers if they could not manage the sticks. Along with associates from south of the border, two million pensioners would march on Edinburgh. The television news would carry film of pensioners with bleeding heads passing out during interviews and being presumed dead. The younger people, incensed at the brutality and knowing that they too would sometime become pensioners, would join the march to the Parliament building in Edinburgh and pull out the Members of the Scottish Parliament to be pilloried."

"And I think that I know who would be the Ché Guevara of this revolution," said Henry. "I will be pleased to serve," replied Roy, humbly bowing his head.

The supermarket reached, the three began the painful process of stretching old sinews that had become accustomed to the seated position. Passing the driver on his way out, Roy had one final stab. "Very well driven driver. We will look out for you on our way back."

But the driver had sharpened up to elevate himself to the standard of the pensioners.

"Remember to stand well back from the kerb in case you find me!"

Donnie, considering that they were now entering his territory, took the initiative and led them to the trolley park, suggesting the smaller model. "The big ones have a life of their own; the wheels are all shot; but the wee ones are newer. Besides, they're 'pensioner sized'."

Entering the store, Donnie observed that it was busier than he expected. "I suggest that we go our own ways to get what we want; then meet back here in fifteen minutes and I'll take you through the checkout."

Henry was minded to point out that he often came to this

supermarket and knew fine how to go through the checkout, but he stayed quiet in order to give Donnie his place.

Twenty five minutes later Donnie and Henry were waiting at the appointed place, indeed they had been waiting some ten minutes.

"Let's go and find him; he has probably crashed his trolley and been taken to hospital," suggested Henry.

They decided to stay together in the jungle search on the grounds that they might lose more men if they split up and were ambushed. Eventually they found Roy, not on the ground floor food hall, but up the escalator among the kitchenware. Roy had a frying pan in each hand and appeared to be comparing their weights. He smiled as they approached. "This is a great place you brought us to Donnie; the bargains are tremendous!"

Both Donnie and Henry stared open mouthed at Roy's trolley which was brimming full of every conceivable kitchen utensil.

Roy pondered, "I can't work out which of these frying pans to take. Perhaps I will just have them both," and he plonked them into his trolley.

"Roy, let's think a little," implored Henry.

"Aye, screw the nut," was Donnie's linguistic equivalent.

Henry began to take Roy through it. "Remember the OAP Law".

"What's that?" enquired Roy.

Henry explained. "The Old Age Pensioner's Law is, 'Don't buy it if you might be dead before you use it'."

"Yes, you're right," conceded Roy. He put one of the frying pans back but picked up another utensil. "What's this when it's at home?"

"It's a Wok," said Henry. "It's for making stir fry."

"I like stir fry," said Roy conclusively.

"But do you MAKE stir fry, Roy?" challenged Henry.

"No, I get it from the Chinese...but if I bought a Wok I MIGHT make it," argued Roy, as much with himself as with

Henry.

"OK," conceded Roy, catching Henry's expression. "Maybe I'll leave the wok...it's a bit heavy anyway."

"Shall we go through the rest of your trolley with the same discipline in mind?" enquired Henry.

Roy sighed. "I suppose so."

After ten minutes negotiation the items in Roy's trolley were reduced from fifteen to four. Four had been disqualified because Roy did not know what function they served and six on the grounds that he could not explain when he would use them. The ice cream maker was given up without negotiation.

"Perhaps we should help you with your food shopping now. Shall we make a list?" suggested Henry.

Donnie aided the proceedings with the offer, "I'll go and put our two trolleys in lock-ups; this could take some time."

Under Henry and Donnie's supervision Roy's food items were collected, though he was noticed to surreptitiously add five that had not been on the list. No punishment ensued and Roy escaped with his cream cakes, portion of roast chicken, shallots, his much reduced bottle of whisky and even his cider vinegar. They put Roy's trolley in a lock-up and enjoyed a well-deserved lunch in the cafeteria; a lunch financed by Henry's excess winnings on his horse that had lost.

"Time to check out," announced Donnie, taking the initiative once more. "We'll go to the self-service check out. Maybe we'll meet Mhairi and Irene; you'll like them".

Roy and Henry wondered if this was perhaps the main purpose of their visit to the supermarket. Arriving at the self-service checkout area, Donnie continued in charge. "It will be easier if we check out one after another; that way I can give you help if you need it."

As Donnie began to zap his items a voice beside him rang out, "Mhairi, call security; that old reprobate is in again!"

Donnie turned round with a smile on his face to greet Irene, one of his 'ladies'. At this point another 'lady', presumably Mhairi, skipped up to join them.

She started with a mock reprimand to her colleague. "Irene, that is no way to speak to one of our customers...especially one of the old and infirm ones who is simple minded."

"Wow" thought Roy, "these are ladies you can spar with."

Donnie endeavoured to exert his authority. "Now ladies, you have to be on your best behaviour, for I have brought two other gentlemen customers." He proceeded to introduce all concerned.

Irene immediately sussed out Roy and Henry as well as the difference between them, so she addressed Roy. "I'm pleased to see that Donnie has got care assistants to take him out; we have been very worried about his wanderings."

Roy's giggle exploded.

Mhairi continued their normal routine. "Now Mr Anderson, have you worked out what you are spending today?"

"Nineteen pounds and eighty-six pence" declared Donnie immediately.

"Well let's see how it works out" continued Irene, with Mhairi smiling warmly in the background.

Donnie processed his shopping with particular care not to make mistakes. The total came to £19.86.

Irene continued the panto, "Mhairi, see here that Mr Anderson has done it again. I told you we should put him forward for Mastermind. But then again, he hasn't yet mastered putting his clothes on...his flies is not done up!"

In horror Donnie looked downwards and then, also in horror, he realised that Irene had got him good and proper, for his flies were intact. Everyone laughed; even Henry for whom this banter with women was unknown territory.

Donnie shook his head and said, "Irene, you'll be the death of me."

"Hopefully!" she replied quickly before he realised the opening he had given her.

The bus ride home was uneventful. It was not the same driver as earlier and Roy thought about taking him on in the usual manner, but he could not have matched Donnie's ladies, so he just enjoyed the journey. Life was becoming different for him, though he could not quite understand what had caused the change. Henry was also inside his own thoughts. He had not really understood the banter with the ladies – indeed he had felt nervous and embarrassed about it – yet it had seemed OK with everyone else. He realised just how much he had isolated himself from other people. Perhaps the first thing he had to do was to lighten up with people. While Roy and Henry reflected during the bus ride, Donnie fell sound asleep. In his dreams, he smiled at his ladies.

10. CHRISTMAS PLANNING

Maureen's initial question was innocent enough. "What are you boys going to do over Christmas?" Yet it caused all three to pause and play the same tape over in their heads. Roy was first to declare himself. "I don't usually do anything at Christmas. In fact, with everything closed, it can be a bit boring."

Maureen expressed surprise. "You don't have any family to go to at Christmas?"

"No, I only have my daughter Emily and she lives in Canada."

Maureen extended her interrogation. "What about you Donnie?"

Donnie averted his eyes; he did that when the conversation was difficult.

"Same with me," he proclaimed in the 'clipped' tone of one who wants to say no more. Maureen disguised her probing as curiosity. "Do you not have any family, Donnie?" "No," he said. "I mean Yes... well, 'yes and no' I suppose. I had a wife but I haven't now. And I had a son as well, but I haven't seen him for twenty-five years." Sensing Donnie's discomfort Maureen turned towards Henry who anticipated her question.

"Those two may seem to be loners, but I am the expert in it. I have absolutely no one and I never have had anyone."

"No brothers or sisters even?" queried Maureen.

"Well I do have a sister, but we haven't met since my mother died five years ago."

"Why not? Did you fall out?" continued Maureen, finding it easier with Henry than Donnie.

Henry said timidly, "No, we just didn't keep in touch. Well, I didn't keep in touch. My sister wrote to me a couple of times but I forgot to reply."

Maureen sent no particular message through her face but Henry still heard it as 'Henry, you ass – get your act together in this life!' He replied to the unvoiced message, "I could have done better."

Maureen reckoned that she had stirred things up enough and that she might leave the three of them in their present state of flux. She moved off to serve another customer and employed her usual bar manager's skill of listening unobserved to the distant conversation between Henry, Donnie and Roy.

"Maureen touched a tender place there for me," began Henry.

Roy nodded in agreement. "For a few weeks I tossed around the idea of phoning my daughter and seeing if I might visit them at Christmas. But I took so long to make a decision it was too late."

"Why too late?" asked Henry.

"By now it would be impossible to get a cheap flight" Roy replied.

"Not necessarily," said Henry, "There are some websites that specialise in late bookings; flights that people have cancelled. If you are flexible about dates it is often possible to get better deals late-on than earlier, even at Christmas."

"But it's too near the time now; it would be an enormous upheaval for Emily," argued Roy.

Henry smiled at Roy. "You sound like me, Roy. I am an expert in making excuses for not taking on new things."

"But...but..." began Roy, finding himself empty of rationalisations.

"Worth a phone call to Emily?" queried Henry. Then he tried bargaining. "If you phone Emily, I'll write to my sister Amanda."

"You are a pig Henry Doncaster," agreed Roy offering his hand in the traditional way that deals are cemented. "I bet that you had already decided to write to Amanda!"

Both Henry and Roy had the same new feeling; that it was nice to hear the other use the name of someone they loved.

Donnie knew precisely what was now going to happen. He thought about making an early exit, but it was too late.

"How about you, Donnie?" broached Roy.

"Me, what?" said Donnie in feigned ignorance.

"How about making contact with your son?"

"Donald...he'll be forty now...he wouldn't want to know me after all this time."

"How do you know?" challenged Henry, "You're just assuming that; why don't you at least give him a chance?"

"I just **know.** I wasn't much of a father and he was old enough to know that," said Donnie, becoming flustered by their persistence. People did not usually persist with Donnie; he was generally able to keep them away from him.

Roy continued, "But he is twenty-five years older now. He is a man of forty, probably with children of his own."

"Yes, he has two sons," added Donnie.

Henry sat straight up on his bar stool using his full six foot four inches to exert authority. "Donald Anderson, do you mean to tell me that your son has been in contact with you?"

Donnie adopted an appropriately small voice. "Well, he sent a Christmas card a few years ago. He lives in Argentina; it had his address on it."

"So you sent him one back, or wrote a letter to him...or phoned him?" probed Roy on behalf of the prosecution, while all the time knowing the answer.

"No," came the small voice in admission.

Henry and Roy left a long and loud silence so that Donnie could hear himself.

For the time being the discussion ended there; all three of them ordered their second drinks of the evening and small talk resumed. There was no further pressuring of Donnie who seemed relieved by that. Towards the end of the evening Henry offered to help Roy to look into flights so that he was properly informed before he phoned Emily. Donnie stayed very quiet throughout the rest of the evening, more in thought than anything else.

Maureen re-visited the group. "I forgot to tell you that early this evening I had a man in here asking about Robert Alexander. He was Robert's brother; he hadn't had contact with him for years and had heard that he had died. He was most upset and was asking about us looking after Robert. I told him what we had done and where he was buried and I said that you three would likely be in later if he wanted to ask more, but he had to go away. The last thing he said was that he was sad he had not made more effort to stay in touch with his brother."

The three men heard this story powerfully and left in silence.

11. CHRISTMAS EXTRAS

Roy had a computer and thought that it might be connected to the internet, but when Donnie and Henry visited Roy's flat for the first time, Henry declared Roy's system beyond redemption. "Roy, you are obsolete...I'm going to help you to become functional again by getting you a decent set-up for almost no money, but for the sake of speed on the present project let's go round to my place to do some surfing."

Roy was grateful that he did not have to ask what 'surfing' was, and pleased too for this first opportunity to visit Henry's flat. Donnie, nearby but not apparently listening until this moment, joined in. "Can I come too? I'm interested to see your set-up Henry."

"Delighted to have you Donnie," said Henry with enthusiasm.

This was another of those moments Donnie had been experiencing more often recently – someone saying words to him that he could not remember hearing before – warm words that seemed genuinely felt.

Both Roy and Donnie had the same initial reaction on entering Henry's flat. This place made their flats look like untidy hovels. Nothing was particularly new, but the carpets looked fresh, the kitchen clean and tidy, and the whole place must have been dusted recently. On this last point Roy made a mental note that his once monthly peremptory dust around the flat may be insufficient, while Donnie tried to remember if and when he had ever dusted. When they entered the main living room they gasped at the forty-eight inch flat screen television that dominated one wall of the room. Six feet in front of the screen was a long narrow table with a large swivel chair in front of it and two partially closed laptops on top. On the wall to the left was a desk top PC and monitor with another smaller swivel chair in front and two more closed laptops strewn on the table beside the PC. Also on the table, as far away from the PC as possible, was a coffee maker and one cup. To the side of the PC table was a single small armchair.

"This is my 'operations room'," declared Henry. "From here I try to outwit fellow betters from around the world."

"That TV is bigger than the one in the Culloden," judged Donnie.

"And you have **five** computers in this room," added Roy in awe.

"Yes, but the real asset is unseen; it is the ultra-high speed broadband."

"Can we put the TV on so that we can see it?" asked Donnie in the tone of a small boy seeing the best toy of his life.

"Certainly," said Henry, pressing one remote and then another.

Soon a football game emerged, but Donnie was not as impressed as he had expected. Going close up to the screen he observed with disappointment "The picture isn't that great."

"Oh, I know why that is", said Henry, doing more business with the remote until the picture was sharp enough to see the blades of grass. "I don't normally have it on 'high definition'."

"Why ever not?" queried Donnie.

"Because there is a 2.2 seconds delay on HD, and a lot can happen in 2.2 seconds when you are betting on a horse during a race," explained Henry.

Roy kept being amazed at what he did not know. "You mean you can actually bet **after** the race has started!"

Henry nodded. "Yes, amazing isn't it, but I don't do it often because some people are at the racecourse with their iPhones and they have faster information."

Henry moved to the PC table, sat in his swivel chair and booted up. Roy joined him, standing behind the chair, thinking about the many new experiences he was having now that he had friends. Donnie sat in the large swivel, staring at the huge television screen.

Twenty minutes later Henry closed down the PC. "So there we have it; a big range of prices, but if you can go next Tuesday you can have ten days, coming back just before Hogmanay, for a brilliant price. That last website specialises in late deals, often re-selling cancellations, but the problem is that their prices change rapidly; there is no guarantee that the deal will be there tomorrow."

"I'll phone my daughter this afternoon. I'm worried that ten days is asking a lot of her," said Roy, getting up to move towards the door.

"It's nice that you are phoning her," said Henry with a smile, a gentle touch on Roy's shoulder, and a little feeling of regret for his own isolated life.

"Donnie, we're going." Roy shouted back to his friend still totally immersed in the television.

Donnie followed Roy out, shaking his head. "That's some TV Henry."

"Let's watch a football game on it together sometime soon Donnie," invited Henry. "Brilliant!" agreed the small boy Donnie.

Roy guessed that it would be late morning in Vancouver as he sat down beside his telephone table. He had thought about pouring a small malt whisky, but tutted at himself in rebuke and made a cup of tea instead. As he sat by the phone he wondered why on earth he was so scared. Why should he be scared? All he was doing was phoning his daughter whom he loved and whom he knew loved him. How far had he isolated himself since Sheila's death that he felt fear in reaching out even to someone who loved him. In the past the fear would have been enough to stop him but he knew that he was going to make this phone call. He dialled the long number written on the paper in front of him. Emily answered the phone and Roy began, "Hello darling, this is your dad."

Henry was also doing something he found difficult. He was sitting at his PC to write to his sister Amanda. Henry knew why he had 'forgotten' to respond to Amanda's earlier letters. He knew that he had felt uncomfortable 'forgetting'. He thought that he would only have to forget once, but she had written a second time, some months later, and it had been difficult to forget a second time. He loved his younger sister Amanda. He remembered one day when she was little. She had kept falling in the snow and she giggled to him every time. He had smiled back at her then and he was doing it again now, all these years later. How could he have cut this lovely person off, so abruptly, and twice? Why could he never depart from his comfort zone and simply be with other people? He had been doing that these past weeks with Donnie and Roy, but now it was time to try to make up for his earlier mistakes and that was much more demanding. He switched off his PC to take up a pen and some stationery.

"Dad, it's great to hear you" exclaimed Emily, "Is everything all right?"

"Yes, darling, everything is great, except one thing and that is I would dearly love to see you and John and Peter and Clara," replied Roy with a calm confidence that surprised him.

"But I don't think we will be able to come over any time soon, dad."

"I was more thinking that I might come to see you, if that was alright?" said Roy.

"Yes, yes, yes, dad – that would be great – I stopped asking you because it sounded like you felt it was too far or something. Oh yes dad, it would be just lovely to see you. John often asks about you and Paul and Clara have only seen you once. Can you come for Christmas?"

"I would love to darling," said Roy.

Henry had finished his letter, sealed it immediately, affixed a first class postage stamp and placed it on the mantelpiece in his full view. Doubtless there would be times before he posted it when he would want to tear it up or at least 'revise' it. Putting the stamp on it helped, because he would not want to sacrifice the first class postage. As he looked at the envelope on the mantelpiece, he felt his vulnerability creep back over him. He realised that there was only one thing for it and got up to put his coat on. At this point the phone rang and he jumped in fright; this must be the first time in a month that his phone had rung. It was Roy, bubbling with joy as Henry had never heard him, and asking if he could get that website back up to book his travel to Vancouver.

"I will do that very thing Roy, but first I have to post a letter. Come round to my place and bring a credit card. I'll be back by the time you get here."

There was just a slight pause on the line, and Henry continued, "Don't bother about the credit card Roy; we'll do it on mine and you can settle up later."

"Thanks Henry," said Roy.

Donnie was trying to write the first personal letter of his life. He started twelve times before he got three sentences. An hour later he scrapped those three sentences and the various attempts he had made to build on them. The next two sheets of writing paper were soaked with tears and had to join the waste bin. He rose and went to the bathroom, stood in front of the mirror over the wash basin and looked into his face. He spoke to himself. "Donald, you have to stop pretending. You have pretended all your life. It is time to do it different. You don't have much life left, so let's try to not pretend."

Donnie returned to his table and wrote a five page letter in half-an-hour.

Donnie arrived early in the Culloden that evening hoping to ask a favour of Maureen. "I've written a letter to my son," he began, holding up the letter and its envelope, "But I've never written letters before and I wonder if you could read it to see if it's OK."

Maureen found herself taken aback as she realised that Donnie was probably not making a slip in his choice of words; it was quite conceivable that he had 'never written letters before'.

"It's just a first try," said Donnie as Maureen began to read his letter.

She had only read the first two sentences when she said to Donnie, "I'm just going to take it into the kitchen to read it properly."

On her way to the kitchen she asked Rosie to cover for her. Fifteen minutes later Maureen re-appeared. She had obviously been crying and had made the mistake of thinking that she had successfully wiped away the evidence without use of a mirror and forgetting that her mascara was not waterproof. She reached over the bar, handing the letter back to Donnie.

"Donnie, you take that to the Post Office at nine o'clock tomorrow morning. You tell them that it is Air Mail to Argentina. You pay the postage and you leave it with them. Donnie, it is the most beautiful letter I have ever read."

Donnie was somewhat taken aback, but he managed to say, "Thank you Maureen."

12. RECONNECTING

Amanda Smallwood was surprised to receive the old fashioned vellum envelope with her name and address printed in capitals. Who sent such things in these days of Email? Even the postman was respectful over the delivery, bringing it to her at the door rather than leaving it in the post box beyond the fictitious 'dangerous dog' sign at the end of the drive. She went inside, poured a cup of coffee, and opened the letter. Immediately her eyes filled as she scanned the handwriting ending in "I love you sis" and signed by her brother. 'He's an incompetent vagrant' her very competent husband, Derek, had once offered as 'support' when she was grieving Henry's failure to respond even to her second letter. In her husband's world Henry would indeed be 'incompetent' but to Amanda he was her only big brother and from being a very young girl she knew that he loved her. It was just that he just was never able to show it. Amanda read her brother's letter:

> Dear Amanda,
>
> I want to apologise to you for not replying to two letters you sent me after mother's death. In fact, I really want to apologise to you for my whole life. As I sit here writing, I am remembering you as a very small girl walking and falling in the snow, with huge giggles and full of life. This image reminds me of my own inability to relate with anyone. For me that goes so far back that I do not remember. I love you dearly and I have always loved you although I am sure that I have never said that. I so wish that when we were younger I could have told you that, but I had to remain separate from everyone else.
>
> As you know, our parents had 'high hopes of me'. I italicise the phrase because that is what

it was for me – something alien from me. I could not live up to what they wanted me to be. Father wanted me to take over the family business and had clear ideas on what I needed to do that. I hated boarding school. Early on, aged six, I thought that it must have been a mistake that I had been left there. Then I thought that I must be really bad to have been sent there. Later I lost the guilt and got angry at some of the things that happened there, not to me but to others. I told our parents, expecting that they would feel the same as me about these horrible things and take me away. Instead, mother went into a flutter and father told me that I was a liar. And so, I stopped being angry and went 'underground'; I made myself impervious to others. I established a life inside my head and stayed there. I am still pleased with the way I got myself expelled, aged sixteen, by sending a ten page letter to The Times. Of course they did not publish it, but their enquiries came back to the school. It was a dramatic but effective way to break free from the school and from father's expectations. He didn't even argue when I said that I was taking a job instead of finding another route towards University. Father never valued the line of work I got into, which is precious since he sold armaments to the highest bidder. That was fine by me because by this time I had stripped myself away from the family and everyone else. I worked within one company for most of my life and liked it. I was completely lacking in ambition; I think I was scared that ambition would drag me back into father's world. I know that I could have left my company, copyrighted the systems I had created and made a fortune. But that would have been dangerous because it might have led me back into his world. Instead, I stayed in my splendid isolation; indeed I revelled in it.

I was attracted to women but the last thing I wanted was any kind of relationship. I especially remember Mary; I know that you liked her too. I really did love her; perhaps I still do in a pathetic kind of way. But I fought that feeling and eventually I drove her away. I remember the tears in your eyes when you confronted me about that. I knew that you were right, but of course I hid that.

At work people presumed I was gay. I got lots of anonymous fag Email about their fantasies. But that was all fine by me because it meant everyone stayed away from me.

In all these years of my life I loved you, but I even stayed away from you. I'm sure I actively snubbed you when I would come home during school holidays. Sometimes I got furious at our parents when I thought they were not listening to you, but, hell, I never showed you any of that. I loved Andrew, whom I thought was your best boyfriend; I even forced myself to smile at him a couple of times.

I watched you become your own person. You wanted to be a dancer and you were not going to be put off that. I remember you hiding your bleeding feet so that mother would not see. I saw you being warm and effusive with father; perhaps you felt just that, or maybe you were more skilful and less destructive than me about getting what you wanted. I remember when you found that you could not have children. I sobbed in my bed that first night and kept saying, "It's not fair", but I never said anything to you.

I very nearly intervened when you were to marry Derek, but I stopped myself when I realised that this is exactly what father would have done if he disapproved of a suitor. Becoming my father has always been a really scary thought. But I wish I had said something... just to you; at least it would have been the first time that I would have showed that I cared for you. When Derek became managing director of our family firm I had a strange mixture of feelings. First I felt that I was definitely 'off the hook' from that expectation; and secondly I was jealous; it sounds irrational. My only good feeling was gladness for you; that this might bring two of your worlds together. You still had that third world – your dancing – and that is how I remember you because I think that I saw you most fully when you were dancing.

It is only in these past few months when, despite my seclusion, I seem to have made new friends that I am remembering that life is about more than the defences I created all those years ago. Most particularly, our life should be about the people in it.

I love you sis.

Henry.

*
**

Roy had managed the twelve hour flight without difficulty; indeed he had enjoyed meeting the two people berthed with him in the adjoining seats. They were going to visit their daughter who had recently given birth to their first grandchild. Roy noted that he could have done that, twice, some years earlier. Nonetheless, he disembarked in the same positive spirits that had been with him for some time.

John Edwards, his wife Emily and children Paul and Clara met him as he pushed his luggage trolley through the final sliding doors. Emily and Clara were bouncing up and down in glee, Clara with the excuse that she was four years old and Emily in pure joy that her father had finally come to them. Paul bore the serious expression of an eight year old who already needed to be a little concealed, but John wore a generous smile that his son would eventually learn.

Christmas came and grandad's presents of Nintendo DS's were received with amazement at how cool he must be to think of them (Henry had offered advice). Now, as the children played with their presents next door, Roy, Emily and John stayed at the dinner table. Roy took the initiative. "It has taken me a very long time to get over Sheila's death. In fact, that's not right, because I have not gotten over her death. But I have got beyond her death enough to realise that I need to continue my own life."

Roy was speaking very seriously and this impressed Emily and John. How would it be for either of them if one died? For the first time they were seeing their father/father-in-law as being ahead of them in life – a nice thought for both of them.

Roy continued. "Recently I have taken a different turn on life. I have two dear men friends, Henry and Donnie. In many ways life has been more generous to me than to them. Yes, I have suffered a grief that neither of them has, but that is only because they have both felt so many earlier troubles that they could not engage or sustain relationships. Yet they are both struggling to defy their histories in that regard. And their struggles have led me finally to appreciate what I have, rather than what I have lost. I want to thank you both for being so patient with me that you could receive me here after so many years of neglect. Sometimes it is important that the elders thank their kin."

Both John and Emily were taken aback by Roy's gravitas.

Can you really meet your father in this kind of way? Wow! What does this open up? Emily tried first in her typical down-to-earth fashion. "Dad, I'm gobsmacked by the way you are talking, but I love it. It's like you are opening up ways that we can **really** talk, rather than just 'small talk'."

Roy instantly knew what she was talking about. "We spend most of our life in small talk and that is OK, but we need to be able to not do that when we choose."

Roy listened to himself with interest; this was different stuff he was coming out with. Was it OK? It felt OK, so he continued. "We have only so much time in our life, so we can waste it or we can do the best we can with it. I have recently switched from the first to the second."

"And I'm pleased to hear that Roy, and hopefully to meet you there," said John in a way that made his wife love him even more.

*
**

Donald Anderson was intrigued to get a letter from Scotland in handwriting he did not recognise. He turned the envelope around in his hands trying to unravel a mystery that could easily have been solved by opening it. The handwriting was unsteady, as though the author was unfamiliar with writing. The date stamp was two weeks earlier. It had probably arrived at the hotel just before Christmas and now it was December 27th. He cursed the Argentine postal system which had a reputation for losing and delaying international mail.

Donald was enjoying his breakfast on the patio beside the pool of the Forcadell apartment hotel in the desirable San Isidro locality within extended Buenos Aires. Donald's property development business kept a permanent penthouse apartment in the hotel for executives or clients. His family home was some thirty kilometres to the north, in Tigre, a popular residential area within the extensive delta region of north - eastern Argentina, bordering Uruguay. After the Argentine economy collapsed in 2001, with the peso depreciating from 1:1 to 3:1 in relation to the US dollar, Donald and his two associates had become involved in the stuttering property market. Their external finance was welcomed as well as the jobs they created. The fact that Donald and his British colleagues were fluent in Argentinean Spanish helped them gain acceptance despite the Islas Malvinas affair. But it was their underlying business plan that had opened all doors to them. Their model was that for every ten highly desirable homes they were allowed to build, they would additionally construct twenty social housing units donated to the locality. The 2001 collapse had hit the working classes and much of the professional middle class, but there were many other more wealthy people who had seen the collapse coming and had liberated their money in time, largely at a cost to their compatriots. The property market, constructing expensive gated communities, was booming in this sector, so the provision of free social housing hardly dented the developers' profits.

Unable to solve the question of the provenance of the letter, Donald opened it and began to read.

> Dear Donald,
>
> You sent me a nice Christmas card a few years ago and I didnt reply. I would like to invent a nice reason for that but I would be lying and Ive done enough of that in my life. The reason I didnt reply is that I am a coward. I was scared to talk with you in case you judged me for letting you and your mother down all those years ago. So I did what I have always done in my life. I buried my head in the sand and cut myself off. I am sixty five years old and only recently have I begun to find some courage in life. This is the first time I have written a personal letter in my life. I dont know how to do it but here goes.

When your mother left me and took you with her I was glad. She said that she could not try any longer to live with me. I was glad because I was exhausted trying to live with her. Im not saying this well because I dont have good words. What I mean is that I was trying really hard to be a person someone else could live with. I was trying to work out what would be the things a good person would do and then try to do them. But I kept making mistakes. I would buy Susan your mother expensive presents when we were struggling with no money. Then I would completely forget her birthday. She would say that I never told her that I loved her and so I told her. I was stupid. I had no idea. I still have no idea. She was right when she said that I didnt get it and I maybe would never get it. The day she left I bought a bottle of whisky and got drunk at home. I felt great. Like a huge weight had been taken off me. I remember thinking that I had forgotten to say goodbye to you. But I didnt even feel bad about that. Ive thought about you sometimes in these last twenty five years and what Ive thought is that you would probably remember very little about me or our about time together. Thats because I was never there. I mean I was there but I wasnt really there. I was never OK with being with you. I was never OK with being with your mother. Ive never been OK with being with anyone. After leaving school I went into the army because I couldnt find anything else to do. The army was good for me and it was bad for me. It gave me something to take up my whole life but it brought some evil out of me. In the army some recruits are picked on and that was me just like in school. I have never understood why I was always picked on. I was small but I wasnt a weakling or gay or anything and it was usually them that got picked on. Recently Ive thought that it was because I was too keen to make friends and sucked up to people like a weakling but Im not sure. Anyway to cut a long story short I got beaten up bad by six of them one night. I made it much worse by fighting back. I always did that. I had an operation and they took one of my kidneys out. I remembered the six of them and I got five of them while I was still in the army. The army threw me out but hushed up the damage I had done. Three years later in civvy street I did the ringleader real damage. I was questioned about it but the police let me go. If the army had put my previous stuff on record I would have been sunk. The thing is that I dont feel bad about that stuff. Maybe Im bad because I dont feel bad. Maybe the real thing is that Ive never cared about anyone. I didnt even care about my wonderful wife and son. Susan stayed with me much longer than she should have. She wasted so much of her life with me. When she left I remember saying to her that she was doing the right thing. I didnt only mean that it was the right thing for me I also meant that it was the right thing for her to escape while she still had a life to have. Recently I have made two friends at the Culloden. That is totally new to me. They are both much brighter than me but we get on fine. They pay me respect. I have been thinking different. A long time ago I got a hold of my anger so that is not going to happen again but recently I have also been feeling other things. I dont understand them but I think they are why I am writing back to you a few years too late after your christmas card. Maybe twenty five years too late. I am sorry for the hurt I caused you and your mother. If you could pass that on to her with my love that would be nice.

Donald Anderson.

Young Donald Anderson stared at these five pages of tightly written script with no paragraph breaks or punctuation beyond full stops. It was the last sentence that particularly stayed with him, *If you could pass that on to her with my love that would be nice.* He looked at his father twenty-five years later; hell, forty years later. When he was young he had been confused by his father who had let him down so often. There was the time that a scout for a professional football team was coming to watch him play for his school team and his father had forgotten to come. The game had been one of his worst and a young boy had to grow up fast enough to see his future disappear into his past. There had been the time that he and his mother were leaving and he didn't really understand why. He just wanted his father to say that it would be OK and that they could all stay together. And there were all those years when he had hated his father. The Christmas card marked the end of that long phase; young Donald Anderson had become enough of a person in his own right that he was no longer a prisoner of his past.

Donald phoned his secretary to ask her to re-schedule his appointments for that day. Then he called his wife to say that he was coming home because he wanted to talk with her about a letter he had received from his father. Young Donald Anderson had learned at least one thing from his father – to talk with his wife about his feelings.

13. TIDYING UP THE YEAR

"OK, I am getting the hang of it now," said Roy with perspiration running down the creases in his face as his unaccustomed fingers punched the remaining life out of the faded keyboard.

"See what a little motivation does to your dedication!" exclaimed Henry in pride at the effort his friend was putting into his computing lesson.

The motivation for Roy was the discovery that some computing skills could help him to keep in contact with Emily, John, Paul and Clara without needing expensive phone calls. "You know, Roy," said Henry, "Within a few years all old people's homes will need to have an IT consultant because every resident will expect to be online. Also, surfing and Skyping will keep the residents mentally fitter."

"Sounds like you could have a lucrative business idea there Henry," observed Roy.

Henry shook his head. "No, not for me the world of work dear Roy, for I am a retired gentleman."

Donnie stood behind them wondering if he should get a computer, but decided that a telephone might be a higher priority.

While Roy had been in Canada, Henry visited his IT suppliers, a small local shop called "COMPUTER GLEN" run by Amjad and Mohsin. Most purchasers used the major suppliers when buying their hardware, but Henry preferred a small local outlet where the staff offered a personal and skilled service. A few years earlier Henry had 'interviewed' Amjad and Mohsin for the position as his IT providers. Amjad and Mohsin did not know that they were being interviewed; to them Henry was simply an elderly gentleman who had popped into their shop to ask some questions about his antiquated system that was giving several problems. They were happy to help and, untutored in the hard sell or even the soft sell for that matter, they made no attempt to push purchases. Near the end of the half hour they were still not losing patience but they had begun to wonder about their initial assessment of the elderly gentleman, so sophisticated had his questions become. Henry closed the session by giving them a detailed specification of hardware they could procure for him. At £5,750 this was the largest single purchase Amjad and Mohsin had yet received. Since that day they were Henry's IT suppliers and consultants. Henry strode into COMPUTER GLEN in his usual confident manner.

"Good morning Mr Doncaster," was Amjad's greeting.

Hearing the name, Mohsin came out of the back shop with a soldering iron in his hand. "Old fashioned technology I see in your hand Mohsin," was Henry's pretend jibe.

"Old Mrs. Robertson can't imagine getting a new PC after spending ten years learning her present one, but we can't get spares for it, so here I am trying to mend it with a bit of soldering," explained Mohsin.

"Only you two would take that on," was Henry's praise. He was always careful to praise both of them because he knew how competitive they were with each other.

"What can we do for you?" asked Amjad.

"You can do me a big favour; you can put together a second hand system: PC, keyboard, mouse, printer and web camera for as close as you can get to free and advise on the cheapest broadband offer my friend can purchase."

Amjad and Mohsin nodded. "Come back on Thursday and we'll look at what we've dug up," offered Amjad.

Henry had smiled as he left the shop on the Thursday. As he had expected, "as close as you can get to free" turned out to be entirely free. Amjad and Mohsin had pieced together bits of old systems that worked well enough, but had been replaced by owners keen to keep up with the latest technology. He had also noticed that the 'free' mouse and camera were still in their packaging. Amjad or Mohsin would later take the hardware to Roy's flat at Henry's behest.

Roy said "Let's leave it there for today. It's Hogmanay and I need to clean the flat." "Like, you clean it once a year, whether it needs it or not," joked Donnie.

Roy scowled at him. "I have been raised in the Scottish tradition of clearing out the old year before the new one starts. Yes, the flat gets a good clean whether it needs it or not." "Maybe I should do that too," said Donnie, more to himself than the others.

"Now don't you be doing anything drastic Donnie Anderson, for if you are cleaning your flat you might not be recognising it again and you will be losing all the things you have tidied up," teased Roy, slipping into the Gaelic sentence construction of his Western Isles childhood.

Henry interrupted the banter. "OK, suppose we give you both the considerable time you will need for a project of such epic proportions and meet at the Culloden at ten; it will be open until after the bells anyway."

'The bells' is Scottish shorthand for midnight on New Year's Eve when various bells would be sounded to mark the New Year. In fact, in Glasgow's more recent history, the main sounds used to be the fog horns of the many ships on the Clyde.

The assignation thus agreed, the three dispersed to the seasonal task. Donnie first called at the corner shop to get advice and to purchase appropriate cleaning substances. The advice was important because previously he had attempted to polish his dinner table with caustic soda. Roy liked this old tradition, remembering his mother moving his father about their island croft as she tried to clean around him. With a frog in his throat he also remembered the way that Sheila had busied herself every Hogmanay evening; perhaps he would think of her as he worked. Henry opened the door of his flat, looked around and sighed. Everything was clean and tidy; no improvement was possible. He decided that he would bake; that seemed to be a kind of equivalent.

Around ten o'clock they arrived one-by-one at the

Culloden. Donnie was first, making his habitual furtive approach towards the door and nearly jumping out his skin in fright as young Malcolm Jamieson came out of the shadows towards him.

"Hullo Mr Anderson; ur ye gettin oan OK?" was the greeting.

"Yes Malcolm, just fine," replied Donnie realising that his fear was misplaced.

"No one's been botherin ye roon here?" interrogated Malcolm.

"No, everyone has been fine," assured Donnie, puzzled at the enquiry.

"Mind tae let me know if onyone gies ye grief and I'll sort them oot proper," reminded Malcolm.

"Right...Yes..." replied Donnie, unsure as to whether he should really be encouraging Malcolm to 'sort out' some unknown person.

"Thanks Mr Anderson, and a happy new year to ye when it comes."

Young Malky paused, then completed what he wanted to say. "If ony yin asks if I've been lookin oot fir ye...like a ginger heided bloke...will ye tell them I hiv?"

"Yes Malcolm I will, and a happy new year to you too," said Donnie, entering the pub thoroughly confused.

Right behind Donnie came Roy, whistling as he strutted down the street. When had he last walked so sprightly and how long ago had it been that he had whistled a merry tune? As Roy settled beside Donnie and accepted his packet of smoky bacon crisps Rosie came up to them.

"Roy, a man came in just after opening time tonight. He checked that we knew you and then he gave us £100 to 'put behind the bar for Roy Fox and his two friends'."

Roy and Donnie looked at each other.

"Was he a ginger headed man?" asked Roy, ignoring Donnie who was choking on his crisps.

"No," said Rosie, "He had dark spiky hair and a body...I mean...**what** a body..." Rosie salivated. "He must be a body builder...basically he was a hulk."

"Let me know who he is once you've had your first date with him!" chirped Roy, to which Rosie scowled and swept around to another customer.

"Well," said Roy to Donnie, "That's a mystery...but it seems that we are into free beer for a while."

Donnie, shaking his head, said to Roy, "Who are all these blokes with ginger hair?"

Roy looked at Donnie quizzically, as he often did, and chose to ignore the question that made no sense.

At this juncture Henry swept into the pub carrying what appeared to be a large tray covered with a cloth. He immediately caught Maureen's attention and addressed her in a whisper. "Maureen, I have rather gone overboard with my baking and I thought that it might be nice for the evening to allow people to help themselves, but I wanted to check with you first, because it might affect your crisp sales."

"It's a lovely thing to do this special evening; thank you Henry," confirmed Maureen. Henry removed the coverlet to reveal a remarkable array of more than a hundred cakes of different varieties. He offered first choice to Donnie and then Henry before announcing the free goodies to the company.

Roy told Henry about the £100 gift for their beer into the new year.

"Do you know who he was," asked Henry.

"Not a clue," replied Roy.

"But we're looking for a gang of men with ginger hair," interposed Donnie.

Now Donnie had two people looking at him quizzically.

"Do either of you know who is that young man across the bar?" asked Roy, nodding to a man of about twenty-five years of age.

Both shook their heads, with Donnie adding "He first appeared the day after you went to Canada. He stays about an hour then leaves. He never talks with anyone."

Roy observed, "He looks very shy."

Donnie nodded, "Yes, maybe he's trying to be here."

"What do you mean Donnie?" enquired Henry.

"It's like he wants to be here but it's difficult for him. I'll find out."

Donnie raised himself from his bar stool, picked up the cake tray and moved round the bar. Reaching the young newcomer, Donnie extended a hand in greeting. "Hello, my name is Donnie Anderson. Have a cake."

The others watched this in silence from the other side of the bar. They had never seen Donnie this way; he was usually much more backward in coming forward.

The young man was clearly startled and for a moment looked as though he might flee the pub. But he stayed, uncomfortably, took a cake and shook Donnie's hand. He tried to speak. "My name is Anthony...Anthony Mason."

"Nice to meet you Anthony," said Donnie. "My friends and I have noticed you coming in these days so I thought I would say 'hello'."

Donnie pointed across the bar to Roy and Henry who waved back as Anthony looked towards them. Anthony nodded to them but quickly looked away in a nervous kind of way. Then he struggled to speak, stuttering nervously. "My mum and I have just come here."

"Where were you before?" asked Donnie.

"Lochinver...we stayed in Lochinver."

It was as though every utterance Anthony made had to be an intentional, forced act. There was nothing spontaneous in his speech.

"It's probably very different here," said Donnie.

Anthony looked at him. "Yes, there are so many people in Glasgow. In Lochinver I know most of the people, but I don't know anyone here."

"Yes, I've lived in Glasgow all my life and I still don't find it easy," said Donnie in truth and without humour.

"In Lochinver I went to the pub every evening, so I thought that I should come here," added Anthony.

Donnie nodded and took care to leave most of what he was thinking unspoken. "The three of us are the same; we would probably be sitting alone in our flats if we didn't come in here most nights."

Suddenly Anthony looked at his watch and made to leave. "It's my time to go now; it's nice to meet you," he said in hurried speech.

"You're not waiting for the bells?" queried Donnie.

"No, my mother will be expecting me," Anthony explained.

"Well, it has been nice to meet you Anthony and a happy new year when it comes to you and to your mother," concluded Donnie.

"And to you too," said Anthony, but pausing before adding, "I'm sorry, what was your name again...I forgot."

"It's Donnie, Donnie Anderson."

"Thank you Donnie Anderson," said the young man as he departed fast out the door.

Donnie explained the encounter to Roy and Henry in as much detail as he could remember.

"Sounds like a weird bird," assessed Henry, making Donnie feel uncomfortable.

"He's not 'weird' Henry; he's frightened. He was 'trying' to be here. He had given himself an hour; or perhaps his mother had given him an hour. If he could last that hour things might be OK. It was really difficult for him to be here; I don't know why, but I could see how difficult and also important it was for him. It was good that he asked my name at the end. He wouldn't have registered it at first because he was so frightened, but he asked for it again. That's a good sign; like he was really trying."

Henry looked at Donnie, "How do you know all this stuff?"

"Easy," said Donnie, "I've been there."

By now it was just after 11.00pm on the last evening of the year and Maureen scanned her crowded bar. Everything was under control; the punters were enjoying themselves and were well-behaved despite drinking a bit more than normal.

Rosie was expert as usual and the two newer bar staff were doing what they had been told. She had been watching the way the staff worked quietly and fluently together, noting that every single customer was being served precisely in the order they presented themselves. Yes, everything was tidy in her queendom at the end of another year. Maureen barely heard the phone ring in the kitchen. She answered it and came to her three gentleman saying "Donnie, it's your son on the phone."

14. SPRING HAS SPRUNG

'Don't step on the ground until April. Ignore what the southern garden books say; in Scotland the first of April is soon enough for the start of the season.' As he stood surveying his allotment on the last day of March, Roy remembered the words of his five years deceased gardening mentor, Bobby Devine. When Roy's place on the Council's allotment waiting list had come to the front fourteen years previously he had immediately gone to visit his new responsibility. Bobby Devine worked the next plot and greeted the new gardener unusually.

"Well I hope that you are a good gardener, for you are taking on a great responsibility. That is the best plot in the whole site. I had to stop some of the rogues here from stealing all the soil in the plot before you arrived. Old Ronnie Kerr worked that plot for forty years and the soil is the best. It is said that he buried his relatives in it to improve the fertility, but I don't think that is true."

Roy immediately realised that his plan to watch and copy what the other gardeners did in order to cover up the fact that he had never in his life worked a garden, was probably not going to be possible, so he decided on honesty as the best policy.

"I'm afraid that I have never had a garden in my life before," he confessed.

Bobby Devine's eyes opened wide in delight. "Well you have come to the very best place. I will be delighted to help you get started."

Roy thought that the teacher might get more out of this arrangement than the student, but he also knew that there were times in life when the best status to have is that of apprentice. Thus began a nine year relationship in which, no matter how much he learned, Roy was forever the apprentice. Roy smiled as he saw Bobby Devine once again in his mind's eye.

Winter had taken its toll on the appearance of his plot, with the overwintering leeks looking drained, and the purple sprouting broccoli having lost its battle against marauding pigeons. The local pigeon fancier must have wondered why his birds came back heavier after their exercise flights. Roy had contemplated a campaign involving a borrowed air rifle and using the shed as a hide, but a collection of expensive dead racing pigeons on his plot might be difficult to explain. The day was warm and some digging exercise was a tempting prospect, but Roy knew Bobby Devine's rule and the fact that he was still the apprentice, so he promised his ground that he would be back to tend her tomorrow.

*
**

The flat racing season had just started with the 'Lincoln', a race with twenty horses spread across the width of the track and coming down its straight mile like a cavalry charge. The Lincoln was not a betting race for Henry, because, for most of the horses, it was the start of the season and their form was imponderable. But Henry watched it on his large screen partly in celebration of the start of the season and partly because, of course, it was run at 'Doncaster'.

Henry had completed his accounts for the jumps season to the end of March. This was a way of closing out on the jumps and switching to his much preferred flat racing where his knowledge and profits were always higher. Nevertheless, his figures for the first thirteen weeks of the year showed a profit in twelve of them. As well as his normal betting he had undertaken only one or at most two 'market management' exercises each week because they were very demanding of nervous energy. On two out of these eighteen manoeuvres he had merely broken even, while fifteen had been successful and one had failed. In this last case he had undertaken his usual ploy of betting heavily on a horse in order to lower its odds so that he could later sell it to other betters at the lower odds.

But no matter how hard he bet it down, its price kept rising. Finally he realised what he was up against and sold his stock at a bearable loss. Obviously there was insider dealing in the market; someone knew that this horse was not going to win today. Later he had watched the race out of interest and sure enough the horse ran and jumped well over the first fourteen furlongs only to go back down through the field in the last two furlongs. Henry wondered how the horse had been slowed. It would not have been drugs which were far too risky nowadays. Perhaps it had been one of the of the old fashioned but simple tactics, like taking the horse for a ten mile walk during the night before the race or hobbling a front leg to a back leg so that the horse had had to spend most of the nightly hours standing on three legs. Greyhounds were much easier to slow; all you had to do was to throw them a meat pie just before the race. Henry did all his sums, totalled the profit for the first quarter of the year and permitted himself a satisfied whistle. He then wrote a cheque for £200 to the 'Injured Jockeys Fund'. Considering his financial position, he regarded it as amoral to retain his winter fuel allowance for that year.

*
**

Donnie was also in good spirits on that last day of March. Apart from two weeks when there had been thick snow, he had been able to keep up his walking regime three or four days a week. He now reckoned that he was the world expert on Glasgow walks with associated bus services and he wondered if he should write a book on the subject. Every now and again he would be startled by a now familiar shape jumping out of the shadows and a small voice asking him if he was 'doin all right'.

Donnie had spent regular time with their new acquaintance, Anthony Mason. He had been surprised at his assertiveness with Anthony on Hogmanay. It wasn't like him to take that kind of initiative. But he felt a kind of responsibility towards

Anthony; like he might understand Anthony better than others, so he should look out for him.

The phone call from Donald on Hogmanay had taken him aback. There had not been time for that old fearful, guilty part of him to intervene and find an excuse not to take the call. So, he had just talked with the son he had not met for twenty-five years. The only sticky part was when Donald asked him if he had spoken with 'mum' at all.

"No, I haven't," mumbled Donnie.

"Why have you never made contact with her?" asked Donald in genuine curiosity. Donnie paused, "I felt so guilty that I didn't think that I had the right to interfere."

Donald kept it going, "Maybe she wouldn't see it as interfering; maybe you could send her a card on her birthday, like I sent you a Christmas card."

"Yes…" said Donnie with a pause.

"It's the sixteenth of April dad; I'll send you her address," added Donald helpfully.

"Ah… yes," came the embarrassed acknowledgement.

Donnie had carefully noted down the fourteen digits of his son's Buenos Aires phone number as dialled from Britain. He explained that he did not have a phone at home but had been thinking of buying a mobile and he would use that to phone. Donald had offered guidance.

"Calling Argentina from a cell phone would cost you a week's pension dad. Text me and I'll call you back."

"OK son, I'll do that," said Donnie, wondering what a 'text' was, but feeling sure that Henry would know.

They had ended the call with Donnie feeling feelings he could not remember in his life, feelings that had to do with his son repeatedly calling him 'dad'.

*
**

Maureen was testing the mechanism that received payment and in return released the balls on to the green baize surface of the new pool table that the Culloden's owner had hired at a reduced trial price for the first six months. It was well situated in the alcove at a back corner of the pub. In a previous existence of the hostelry this had been a separate room, so it was nicely secluded. Maureen was not thinking of seclusion for the sake of the pool players; she was more concerned with seclusion from the older regulars who would undoubtedly scorn the concept of a pool table in what they considered to be their private territory.

Henry did not disappoint her presumption. "A 'pool table'! Dear Maureen, why do you desecrate a sacred place like the Culloden with one of them and the riff raff they encourage."

Maureen had prepared a counter for him.

"Henry!"

She declared this first word of her response and delayed in the way a schoolteacher might pause the process to demand attention and the concession of authority. She continued, "You must be aware…" again a short pause to get her adversary off balance and thinking about what he should be aware of… "that we have young people who are also regulars here. I think it is good for a pub to represent its whole community. It is good for the young people to have things here for them and it is good that the pub is also a welcoming place for its elder citizens. Do you not you agree?"

This last challenge was much too good for Henry. There was nothing for him to say except a timid, "Yes."

Roy offered his appraisal, aware that it would nail down his friend's coffin, but being amused by that possibility. "I think that you are quite right Maureen. We are the local pub, so we should represent the young people as well as us geriatrics."

Roy had cast a glance in Henry's direction as he uttered the last phrase. Henry grunted but did not respond further, realising that he had been conclusively defeated.

Roy, by now enjoying his ascendency, added, "In fact, Maureen, I would dearly love to avail myself of our latest acquisition. I used to play a fair game of snooker and pool is a simpler version. OK..." he said, looking at Donnie and Henry, "Who will take on the master?"

Both Donnie and Henry looked away but in the ensuing pause a small voice piped up.

"I will," said Anthony Mason.

All the regulars followed the players to witness The Culloden's inaugural game of pool.

In Scottish parlance there is the phrase, '*some games you win, some games you lose, and some are rained out*'. This epithet from Scottish philosophy encapsulates the whole of life, but it does not describe what happened to Roy. It does not describe total annihilation. After Anthony's 'break off' Roy narrowly missed a challenging pot on a red ball. Thereafter Anthony sank all seven yellow balls and then paused to check the house rules for the end game.

"Is it last pocket for the black ball or any pocket?"

Suddenly Roy saw a slim opportunity for survival. The question reflects different customs in the culture of pool. Sometimes the final, black, ball may simply be sent into any pocket, but in another iteration of the game it has to be sunk in the pocket in which you sank your last coloured ball. This latter version is less commonly played, but it carries the interesting prospect that the player who is behind might come back from the dead simply by making sure that the white cue ball is left in a position from which it will be impossible for their opponent to sink the black ball in the required pocket. Roy looked at the table. It would be easy for Anthony to sink the black in the top left pocket, but his last yellow had gone into the bottom right pocket. Roy declared the rule of the house.

"Last Pocket."

There were noticeable sighs from the half of the bar who understood the significance of this ruling, and continued blank expressions from the others who were also watching proceedings. Anthony surveyed the table for some time, with the cognoscenti agreeing that the shot was impossible.

Nodding his head to acknowledge to himself that he was satisfied with his calculations, Anthony smoothly struck the cue ball on to the black ball to project it just to the left of the top left pocket, such that it struck two cushions, came back down the table and glanced off one of the red balls that rested to the right of the bottom right pocket. Slowly, losing its momentum and having nothing to appreciate its significance in the world of Physics, the black ball dropped into the corner pocket. The whole pub erupted in cheers and Maureen's pool initiative was embraced. Roy scowled, smiled, and warmly shook the hand of 'the master'.

15. BLACK HOLES, LOVING AND LONELINESS

It was a simple thing to do, to insert the envelope with the birthday card to Susan into the post box. Donnie had strained to make himself do it but he had failed. Instead he had crumpled up the envelope and tossed it into the waste bin. He had gone home and broken his rule not to open his whisky bottle in the middle of the day. Now it was virtually finished and he was well gone. In his drunken state there was the mixture of confusion and clarity that is difficult for the sober to understand. There were also the feelings to which normal consciousness usually denied awareness. It is so easy to cut yourself off from people in your life; all you need to do is to not respond and they go away. Donnie felt chilled by this thought; chilled in the knowledge that this is how he had led his life. It was a different thing to reach out to another person; that made you vulnerable to their rejection. Donnie's sadness, with normal defences now anaesthetized, took him into his past.

Donnie's life had been defined by rejection and from a very early age. His earliest memory of his father was of him smiling over the cowering four year old and taking off his belt with ultimate cruelty. The feelings of all his subsequent beatings by an array of people followed on from this. He had smiled to his father in hopeful defence, only to feel the full force of the belt across his eyes. The sixty-five year old Donnie screwed up his eyes in the memory of the pain and he cried out in fear and also in hate. He rolled on the carpet in his flat and whimpered. He had whimpered all his life and no one had ever come to save him. His mother could not save him then, for she had already been beaten unconscious by the fists.

Donnie was in the same black hole into which he was always sucked when things went wrong for him. The final fantasy was always the same. He was standing over his father's body with a mush of brains and blood replacing the head and holding a two pound hammer. That wasn't the reality...or was it? Donnie did not know any more; he had not ever known. So he just lay there and did all that he could do; he whimpered until sleep set him free.

*
**

Roy was on his weekly Skype to Canada. He had talked with Emily and John. He liked that he got on so well with John; he hadn't really expected that, but they talked well together. He could tell that John respected him but he was impressed with how openly John spoke with him. Roy felt that he always had to be ready for that openness, so that he could respond in kind. Perhaps John was doing the same. Or maybe Canadian men were different from Scottish men; no bad thing, he thought. Then he had spoken with Paul and Clara together, both vying for the central position on the camera. He had also told them the latest chapter of 'the story'. One time he had made up a bedtime story about two adventurer children exploring the Amazonian rain forest and this had become a compulsory part of the weekly Skype. Indeed, Roy found himself 'googling' to find information about the various parts of the world the adventurers visited, because he knew that Paul and Clara would be googling to check the veracity of the storyline. He had even constructed a tale set in Vancouver. Suffice to say that Roy had to maintain his good record to date and that required homework. For the last part of the weekly call Emily always returned to talk with him alone.

"Dad, have you never met anyone else?" she asked.

Roy choked up and could not speak.

Emily continued, "I mean, mum has been gone a long time and she would want you to be happy; she said that to me before she died."

Roy tried to respond, but as he did so, he knew that it was not sufficient.

"I am happy darling; I am happy in myself and now that I have more friends I am happy with them."

But Emily was his wife's daughter and she would not be so easily deflected.

"You know what I mean dad."

"Yes, I know darling, but I just can't," was Roy's right response.

"Yes, I know dad, and I love you for that. I love the way you still love my mother. But that does not mean that you have to stop your life; you can do both."

Emily looked straight into his eyes and Roy looked straight back. He had no idea what he was going to say, so it just fell out.

"But I can't. You see, your mother is still inside me, and that is loving for me. I would hate to lose her from inside me."

Emily paused so that she could take in what her father had said.

"I understand dad and I love you."

*
**

Henry felt alone and lonely. This was bad for Henry. He was used to being alone, but not lonely. Most of his life he had been alone and that was familiar to him, but there were times like this when he also felt lonely and it was a deep loneliness. It was a loneliness that would not be dispelled by a jovial interchange with his friends in the Culloden. It was a loneliness that could only be faced. He was sixty-four years old and he had never had a person really close to him. He had never taken a really big risk. He thought, 'You can live life just by staying in control and that gives safety, but is it really living? Perhaps 'living' means going to the edge of life.'

Henry made himself a cup of tea and sat down to stay with what he felt. What might his life have been like if he could have gone to the edge? Might he have had a life-long partner and children and grandchildren? Sure, it was too late to rewrite your life at sixty-four, but why had he not done it forty years ago? Why had he been so stuck on this course all his life? Henry was aware that in this moment he was doing the very thing he had always done; he was thinking about his life, but he was not feeling his life. That was how he had done it and he was still doing it. He picked up Amanda's letter to him, the letter he had started to read and which had thrown him into his desolate state.

> Dear Henry,
>
> You sent your letter just after I had left for three months practising my Spanish in South America.
>
> I am crying as I write this letter. I am crying with happiness, with sadness, with loss and with love, especially with love for my big brother. I feel like that little girl in the snow, looking at my big brother whom I love and who I know loves me. And ever after that moment he could not be there for me. I kind of knew why he could not be there for me but I was always the little girl and I could not find a way to ask him why he could not show me love. You would always smile at me, but also dismiss me. I cried about that. I am pleased to say that I still cry about that. I often thought that I should just dismiss you so that I would not feel hurt any more, but I was not able to do that.
>
> I love you Henry, and I want to be in your life.
> Amanda.

Henry put Amanda's letter down. He thought about Roy and Donnie as well as himself. What a Pandora's Box had been opened by these departures from safe seclusion. Then he thought about his little sister and this solid sixty-four year old did what he had not done for fifty years. He sobbed.

16. A BOYS' DAY OUT

"It was a long winter," concluded Roy as he supped his pint.

"I'm sure winters get longer when you get older," added Henry, also supping.

Donnie looked at them both. "You are a pair of grumpy old farts, aren't you?"

Henry sometimes wondered about the down side of his friend finding his confidence. "Not grumpy, just realistic," asserted Roy.

"That's what grumpy old farts say," countered Donnie.

"Language, Donnie," scolded Henry.

Undeterred, Donnie continued, "It doesn't change the fact that you two are in danger of becoming grumpy, boring old men."

"And you are not, of course, Mr James Bond?" queried Roy sarcastically.

But Donnie was on top form. "Only if I hang around pubs with you guys."

"What do you suggest, dear Donnie?" asked Henry also with a touch of sarcasm in his expression.

Donnie thought for a moment. "Remember that film...I can't remember what it was called...where two old guys made up a wish list of 'things to do before we are dead', and then they started to do them."

"Well, I have always wanted to go to New Zealand," said Roy.

Donnie bounced up and down in his seat. "Me too; I've always wanted to go there." "Moi aussi," added Henry, "But it was always a funny prospect to go that far on my own. Shall we go next week?"

The others chuckled and Roy offered more detail. "I think three weeks there is a minimum; a week on North Island and two weeks on South Island."

Donnie added, "We can get the government to send our pensions over."

"Of course," said Roy, warming to the fantasy, "It is a very long flight for old gentlemen who might get deep vein thrombosis so we will have to fly First Class!"

They all chuckled at the fantasy and added various embellishments.

Donnie brought them down to earth with a suggestion. "OK, seriously though, how about we do some different things this year: you know, things we haven't done much before... but realistic things?"

"Maybe some things that are challenging and some that are just good fun," suggested Roy.

Henry seemed in pensive mood. "It is difficult to do new things when you are just by yourself. I think of lots of things to do but then, when the time comes, I don't bother or there is a horse I want to track or some other reason not to do anything new. Perhaps it would be different if we were doing the things together."

Roy found another reason not to act. "But how could we find things that would be new, or a challenge, or fun for **all** of us?"

"That's not the point," explained Donnie, "We would each choose something that we would do as a group. It might be new, or challenging or interesting or whatever, for that person, but it might be old hat for one of the others. But we would still do it."

Roy was warming to the idea, but Donnie's previous insults still required retribution. "OK, let's do it, I'll choose first. I want us to go to...let me think now..."

Henry interrupted. "Roy Fox, you are a very bad man, you are trying to think of something that will be terrible for our Donnie."

Roy humphed at being found out while Donnie caught up on the discussion, choosing the moment to seek advantage. "Thank you Henry," he said in an authoritative tone and scowling in mock fashion at Roy. "Since it was my idea and you both are obviously in agreement, it seems right that I should choose first. Let me see what I will choose...

Yes, what I would love to do that I have never done before is to go for a day to the horse racing."

Henry raised an eyebrow in surprise, but it was Roy, with a big smile on his face, who spoke first. "Great idea Donnie; I think it is forty years since I was at the racing. I remember that I came away winning that time."

"And later you gave it all back through the betting shop I suppose," suggested Henry. Roy lowered his eyes in concession.

"OK, let's go racing, but let me look after the two of you in case you make a bad habit out of this," offered Henry.

"Yes boss," said Donnie with his biggest smile.

The next evening Henry had come prepared with the necessary research.

"There is a race meeting at Ayr on Saturday, but I don't like Ayr, especially on a Saturday, There are too many drunken young yobs there for the show they put on after the racing. Also, Ayr is not good for concessions, they make you book a week ahead if you want the 'seniors' tickets. Hamilton is a good track if you avoid evening meetings – yobs again – but it only starts next month. So, I would suggest the Musselburgh meeting a week on Wednesday. It's a long way to travel but the busses are good. Also they have a 40% reduction for us geriatrics; all we need to show are our bus passes.

The others nodded with big smiles.

"Musselburgh is a nice wee place, I remember going my holidays there one time," quipped Roy.

"It may have changed in the past hundred years," insulted Donnie.

Roy pretended to punch him and Donnie loved it.

Henry thought that it was time to make a teaching point.

"OK, I feel kind of responsible for you two going into the kind of world I frequent, so I want to give you one big lesson before we go."

"OK teacher, what is it?" asked Roy.

"I want to teach you the difference between 'betting' and 'gambling'."

"Same thing I would have thought," said Donnie from his 'disdainful pupil' persona. "Not at all," retorted Henry, now proudly in charge of proceedings, "Betting is a noble tradition where you wager what you are willing to lose on an event where you have used some skill in coming to your judgment. Whether your bet wins or loses, it is just harmless sport. You do not 'chase your money'."

"You mean bet more the second time to try to win back what you lost the first time," said Donnie.

Henry scanned him with considerable suspicion. It sounded as though Donnie knew far too much about 'chasing his money'. He returned to his lecture.

"Gambling, oh I can hardly utter such profanity of a word..."

Henry was now in that part of himself that could be a bit of a drama queen.

"Gambling is a depravity that has ruined countless men and their families. A gambler looks to luck rather than skill and learning. He would bet on two rain drops running down a window. He would bet on a single number from 1-36 on the roulette wheel even though he knew that, with the zero on the wheel, his odds were 36:1 and the pay-out was only 35:1".

"35:1 sounds good to me," said Donnie.

Henry looked at him through narrowing eyes wondering if Donnie was taking the piss or if he really was stupid enough to think that betting at 35:1 on a 36:1 contingency was 'good'. He decided not to be deflected by Donnie's delinquency or imbecility, and escalated the narrative.

"Of course, the most stupid gamblers of all are those who play the National Lottery." "Hey, steady on, I play the lottery sometimes," protested Roy.

"Precisely," retorted Henry with the semblance of a

snigger.

"I can feel another lecture coming on," wisecracked Donnie to defuse the situation at least temporarily.

Henry obliged. "The lottery gives back just over 50% of its takings in prize money. It is like playing roulette where half the numbers are the Casino's. So Roy, Donnie, which of you normally intelligent men will give me a £20 note on the promise that I will give you only £10 in return?"

In the perfect knowledge that his interjection would get him even more firmly buried in logic, Donnie protested. "It's not the same. In the lottery you have the chance to win huge."

Henry applied the final put-down. "Yes, dear Donnie, you have a one-in-six million chance to win three million!"

"Three million still sounds a lot to me," whispered Donnie loudly enough only for Roy to hear.

Henry did not know what Donnie had said but gave him a big scowl just in case it was merited.

**

Wednesday of the following week found our friends on the journey to Musselburgh. This involved three busses: one into the city centre, another 'express' bus to Edinburgh, followed by a local bus to Musselburgh.

Henry took up the conversation at the start of the journey. "Right, I have printed three copies of the relevant pages from the Racing Post website. This will give you all the information you need to work out which horses you want to bet on in the seven races. You need to work it out for yourselves, but perhaps you will pay particular attention to the fact that the 'going', that means the condition of the ground, is 'heavy'. Now, that is unusual for Musselburgh because its sandy coastal soil drains readily. You might also pay attention to the race distances and whether the horses have successfully travelled that far. You might want to look at other variables, like previous trainer or jockey success, but that is up to you.

The most important thing, the thing that will distinguish you as proper 'betters' rather than degenerate 'gamblers', is to work out what your budget allows you to bet on each of the seven races and stick to that.

The journey took hours, but the boys were in great spirits for their day out, switching from bus to bus in delight at the free travel and Roy's exchanges with the drivers, especially on the bus from Edinburgh to Musselburgh where he risked their very existence by raising the Glasgow/Edinburgh narrative.

As he zapped his bus pass, Roy quipped to Henry, in calculated hearing of the bus driver, "Oh look Henry, this Edinburgh bus accepts a Glasgow person's bus pass!"

However the Edinburgh driver was particularly sharp. "Yes, but only on this bus service...because it goes to the crematorium!"

Now it was Roy's turn to humph in apparent defeat and move down the bus, but he was already preparing his rebuttal.

It was such a simple thing to do when you have all the time in the world, to take three busses across the country for a day at the races, but all of our men felt it as an adventure. Roy and Donnie behaved like little boys on a really fun outing together and even Henry, who had been at countless race meetings, was in delight at going there with his two friends.

Donnie spent much of the journey immersed in the Racing Post and as they approached Musselburgh he made his declaration. "OK, I have got the winners of the seven races."

Henry smiled and waited with interest to discover what his friend, expert in number as he was, had detected in the pile of data available to him.

Donnie continued. "I have decided, from looking at previous performances, that the heavy 'going' is the most important factor, so I have eliminated horses that have not proved they can do well on 'heavy'. I have decided that the second most important thing is the distance of the race. I have eliminated horses that may be struggling to make the distance of the race because the heavy going will make that even more difficult. I have ignored other variables, like horses that have previously done well at Musselburgh, because the heavy going will change the track appreciably. This analysis has led me to conclude that there are only three horses that can win the first race; four for the second, third and fifth; two for the fourth and sixth; and only one horse can win the last race."

Henry simply looked at Donnie; this was a man who had never in his life been at a race meeting, yet his method of analysis, based only on reading some pages of the Racing Post, sounded coherent.

The journey to Musselburgh ended with Roy addressing the driver. "Thank you driver, for a reasonably competent performance. Of course, there were glitches, but I am sure that the inspectorate will take these up with you upon receipt of my report."

Roy judged his disembarkation leap perfectly, landing on the ground just as the bus accelerated violently from the stop. He smiled back at the driver to mark the latter's defeat.

Once inside the racecourse it was Donnie who was wide-eyed in delight as he surveyed the horses. "They are beautiful...I didn't realise how beautiful they were."

Henry was curious. "Tell me Donnie...tell me how you see them as beautiful."

"Look at their limbs Henry, look how slender they are... how can they carry their weight... they are built purely for speed... they are magnificent... look also at the muscle build, and these are only two year olds. See that the three I picked for this race all have better muscle build than the others."

Henry agreed with Donnie's assessments, but he was especially pleased to see the respect that his friend had for the pure beauty of the animals.

In the betting ring several bookies appeared to know Henry. One of them, with his board naming him as 'Alec Watson', was declaring loudly to prospective betters, "We take money... pounds or euros."

The bookie nodded to Henry as they approached.

Henry doffed his fedora in greeting and made a pronouncement to his friends. "I have a rule that says Alec Watson is an honourable bookie especially deserving of custom and, other things being equal, we should place our bets with him. Of course, if another bookie is offering a better price, you bet with them."

Alec Watson shook his head and smiled. "Thank you Henry, but please take your winners elsewhere!"

Henry bowed in appreciation and respect.

As they moved on, Roy needed an explanation. "He...Alec Watson, I mean he actually seemed to like you, even though you would be up against him."

Henry was delighted to explain the essential ethic of bookmaking. "We are not 'up against' each other; in fact we are married in harmony. We each create a construction of a race. Neither of us knows how closely our constructions are to reality until the race is run. Then we celebrate and commiserate, each in our own part, but we are in a shared venture together. You will notice that when the bookies pay you out your winnings they invariably say 'thank you', albeit through clenched teeth if your win is big. Remember also that the bookie is always honest."

Roy needed further clarification. "You say 'honest bookie'... surely not!"

But Henry was firm, "Surely yes. You will always be able to trust a bookie, for they are coming from a reputation that says they can't be trusted, so they have to go the extra mile to prove that they are trustworthy. The bookmaker's word is their bond."

"So what have you gentlemen decided you can afford as bets on each of the seven races," enquired Henry.

Roy had decided. "Five pounds on each race and I have already decided on the winners." There was a slight silence thereafter, but Henry had to ask the question. "And on what criteria did you make your choices Roy?"

"It was easy. There is 'Margaret's Boy' in the first… my mother was 'Margaret'. There is 'Heilan Hame' in the second, after our Highland croft. There is 'Big Jugs' in the third…"

"OK Roy, I think we get the picture…" interrupted Henry and turned to enquire of Donnie, "And what is your stake on each race Donnie?"

Donnie hesitated because he knew that Henry might not appreciate the answer. "Well, it depends."

Henry regarded Donnie with his expected suspicion. "Depends on what dear Donnie?" "Depends on how many horses I think stand a chance."

Henry glowered at Donnie, a tactic that usually brought the latter into order.

"OK," wilted Donnie, "five pounds…usually."

Henry did not remove the glower, but added his own information. "For my part I will bet £10 on each race."

Donnie picked the wrong one of his three for the first race; one of his other choices stormed home at 20:1. Roy and Henry also lost, as all did on the second, third and fourth races. In the paddock for the fifth, Henry offered a slight wave to one of the jockeys, but with no obvious acknowledgement.

Roy challenged Henry. "So, what goes down Henry? Do you know that jockey?"

Henry admitted the offence. "Yes, I know him; well…it **feels** like I know him. His name is Lucas Santos. I have won a great deal of money on the back of his skill since he came over from Brazil as an apprentice several years ago. But he doesn't know me, except perhaps as someone who waves at him when he is at Scottish meetings."

Roy probed further. "So why do you take an interest in him?"

"Because he is simply the best, especially over sharp tracks at distances that require sectional timing. He can comfortably race off a weight of 110 pounds and is pure muscle for that weight. He is also a 'natural' horseman, seemingly knowing when to drive the horse and, much more skilful, when to take the lead from the horse. I've been making a fortune off him for nine years, but six years ago I made the mistake of Emailing one of the TV racing channels to draw attention to his expertise and questioning why he wasn't getting more and better rides. That Email cost me plenty because other betters then became aware of him."

"So you'll be on him in the next race then," Donnie suggested.

"No, the conditions are against him and I don't think that his price will represent value," answered Henry.

"What horse is he on?" asked Roy.

"Sheila's Pride," replied Henry.

"Oh, yes, that's mine," said Roy.

With a smile Henry said, "Of course it is, Roy."

Roy had the first winner of the day when Sheila's Pride stormed past three other horses in the last furlong to win by four lengths. Roy was jumping up and down long before his winner passed the line.

"Right, let's go and get my winnings. Donnie, I had £5 on at seven to one – what do I get?"

"You get £35 profit plus your stake back; look for £40".

But Henry intervened. "I have a custom that, while the bookies are getting their pay-out list organised, I first go to the winner's enclosure to thank the horse."

"Yes, let's do that," agreed Roy and swept off with the others following in his wake, cutting through the crowds like an important person, which of course he was. Somehow getting right to the rail at the winner's enclosure, Roy proceeded to thank the horse in glowing terms and very publically, now and again pausing to tell those around him that he had been 'on' the horse and that was because it had the name of his wife. The racing fraternity are generally a tolerant lot, and he got nothing but nods and smiles. Donnie was smiling too, but Henry was red with embarrassment and looking around to see if he might be recognised. The jockey turned towards the commotion, spotted Henry and nodded to him.

"Nice ride Lucas," said Henry.

"Thanks," replied Lucas Santos.

Twenty-five minutes later Henry was still gobsmacked. "He nodded to me...he must have recognised me...he spoke to me."

Roy observed, "Dear Henry, you have repeated that twelve times already...by the way, did I tell you that I won £35 on the last race...thank you Sheila...she would have enjoyed coming racing."

"Shut up you two," demanded Donnie, "I've doubled my stake on this race that's just about to start."

Roy looked at the starting boxes as the race began. "I completely forgot to bet on this one; I hope that 'Canadian Dream' doesn't win."

"I forgot to bet too," said Henry with amazement that even he could make such a slip. "You two are just star struck," said Donnie, shaking his head.

It would have been nice if Donnie's horse had won at 10:1, but it was passed just before the line. Donnie stamped his foot. "It's not fair; I've had three seconds and three thirds." Henry consoled the annoyed child, but in an adult way. "You are right to be disappointed, Donnie, because you have picked good horses at big prices all afternoon and just been pipped every time. That happens, but stay with your good logic and things will balance out over time."

Donnie grunted, but secretly he was pleased to receive praise from Henry.

The 'lucky last' is a designation of the final race that is perpetuated by punters and bookies alike. The punters raise it to prominence as the final opportunity to get their money back while the bookies see it as a wonderful opportunity to add value to the day by taking advantage of punters trying to get their money back.

"What have you picked for the last race?" asked Henry of Roy.

"Donald's Delight".

Turning to Donnie, Henry asked, "Is that also your choice for the lucky last."

"No, of course it isn't; it's got no chance," replied Donnie.

"So what have you gone for?"

"The winner," replied Donnie firmly.

A five furlong race takes barely a minute to run and in that time the full range of emotions is felt by the assembled company. Roy was still cheering Donald's Delight as it passed the post last by a considerable distance. Henry, somewhat embarrassed by his lack of success on the day, had chosen the favourite, 'Countonme', which was clearly living up to its name as it took the lead inside the final furlong only to be caught on the line by a complete outsider, 'The Avenging Angel'. Henry never expressed frustration on a racecourse or even in private in his racing office, but he let himself down by exclaiming, "How on earth could that horse win this race?"

Donnie supplied the answer. "Easy...it was the best horse in the conditions."

Henry turned to him. "Donald Anderson, do not tell me that you picked The Avenging Angel to win this race."

"Of course I did. According to my calculations the race was set up for him. He hadn't run for over a year but previously he had done well on heavy going and also after a lay off. Another thing I took into consideration was that it looked as though his change of stable was from a poor one to a strong one, so something was expected of him. Easy!"

Henry was stupefied; how could Donnie have absorbed all this from the Racing Post on their bus ride. "So how much did you have on him, £5 or £10?"

Donnie was a little slow to respond because he knew that Henry would not approve, but he also felt somewhat cocky. "I had £20 on him at 40:1."

Henry was speechless with a range of emotions. He was horrified that Donnie should have quadrupled his stated bet, but he was again in amazement at the ability of his friend. Donnie obligingly filled the silence. "Besides, you told me to bet on him."

Henry went purple. Now that is an over quoted descriptive, but when your very concept of reality is cast against you, there is a genuine possibility of pulmonary failure. Henry burst. "What on earth do you mean? I would never have picked that horse!"

Donnie helped his friend to understand his own wisdom. "You reminded me that every one of the six previous winners had come from my list of 'possibles'. Now in the last, I had reduced that list to only one possible... there were good reasons against all the others...even the favourite."

This last reference to the favourite, which Donnie knew that Henry had bet, would have represented a dangerous confrontation to a lesser friend, but Henry was not that man. He looked at Donnie and a lot went through his mind in just a few moments. He had always liked Donnie, but, if truth be told, he had not estimated him very highly in their early meetings; his repeated use of the term 'Dear Donnie' was evidence to that. It would be very difficult for him to treat Donnie as an equal, but he also recognised that the challenges Donnie had faced in these past months were much more demanding than his own. He tried to represent all his feelings in his response. "Donnie, I am constantly in admiration of you. You are a difficult person to read and I keep making mistakes; I keep underestimating you. But you are right and I am wrong. However, please also accept my experience on this present situation; your 'doubling up' is a very dangerous policy and I am worried that you will take your winnings to the betting shop and lose much more than you have won."

Donnie looked at Henry, perhaps for the first time as an equal. "I don't think that it is likely I will fall into that danger, for I will be asking your opinion on any bets I might make. In any case, I am thinking that this might be a good moment at which to retire from horse race betting."

The smile that Henry gave Donnie was as warm as either had experienced as transmitter or receiver and quickly had to be countered lest the basic law of male encounter be violated – that men should not openly offer each other spontaneous and simple affection.

Donnie provided the counter. "Of course, you might not be a good choice of consultant, because by my reckoning Roy has won £10 today and I have won £770, while you have lost £60! Never mind, I'll buy your fish supper, you loser."

17. DISCOVERING ANTHONY

Anthony's skill at the pool table had secured his status among the Culloden regulars who would nod to him on passing, but it did not really integrate him into the community in any significant way, perhaps because he still took up his regular isolated position at the bar and rarely approached anyone, except occasionally Donnie's group. Donnie was the only one who would approach Anthony, as he did this evening when Anthony arrived. "Hi Anthony; you're late tonight."

This caused Anthony quickly and anxiously to look at his watch.

"Only two minutes mind," added Donnie, smiling.

"I'm usually dead on 9.00."

"Regular as clockwork," agreed Donnie, still smiling.

"Maybe I'm getting sloppy," joked Anthony.

"That would be good; I wonder what you would look like if you became **really** sloppy!" Anthony continued the fantasy. "Maybe a long haired hippie."

"Wearing sandals and smoking dope," continued Donnie.

"Yeah man, far out," said Anthony in a long drawl and with a beaming smile.

"Too much man," said Donnie shaking his head as they both laughed.

Donnie noticed that exchanges like this were possible now but would have been unimaginable when Anthony had first arrived in the Culloden. Donnie had no idea what Anthony's condition would be called, but he had a sense of how it was for him.

He decided to take a risk. "Joking aside, you do seem much more at ease these days Anthony."

Anthony looked Donnie in the eye and paused a while, wondering if he could respond or if he could not respond. Finally, and with the semblance of a stutter, he replied, "I'm more relaxed in here and I'm more relaxed with you and with

Roy and Henry...but I'm not relaxed out there." Anthony nodded in the direction of the door.

"It's still scary out there?"

To Donnie's surprise, Anthony continued. "It's been scary for me as long as I can remember. I keep it under control by having my routines, but if someone messes them up I get panicky and things fall apart."

Donnie kept it going. "How do people mess you up?"

Again Anthony looked directly at Donnie, wondering if he could continue. "Well, last night I was coming here and some boys shouted names at me...I had to run home."

"I noticed you weren't in last night," said Donnie, secretly seething inside and wondering about the rightness of allocating a punishment task to young Malky.

"It happens more in cities than in the country. I like living in the country; there are more people like you and Roy and Henry there. People in the country don't mind so much that you are different."

Donnie seriously hoped that he wouldn't cry, but he did feel sad, so he said that.

"It's sad that people treat you bad."

Anthony replied quickly, "You get used to it...no, that's crap, you don't get used to it." Anthony looked down and Donnie stayed silent. "My mother wanted us to try the city again because she can get good work here. We work out things that I can do regularly each day; coming in here from nine to ten every day is one of them. It must be just one hour and one pint, then I go home and we talk about my day. I've talked a lot about you...she likes you a lot. I love my mum."

"She sounds nice; give her my best wishes," said Donnie with a resumed smile.

"I will tell her that Donnie Anderson fancies her!" said Anthony with a mischievous expression.

Donnie's smile widened. "You are a rogue, Anthony Mason!" he said, returning the compliment of using his full name.

They both laughed and carried on talking for the rest of Anthony's hour, deliberately extending his stay until two minutes past ten to compensate for his late arrival. During those last two minutes they counted out the seconds on their watches in a ritual whose significance they both understood.

When Anthony left, Donnie walked slowly and pensively round the bar to take up his seat beside Roy and Henry.

"So, what have you two been talking about all this time?" asked Roy.

"Oh...just things," replied Donnie such that Roy and Henry knew that the subject was now closed.

"Pack of crisps anyone?" enquired Henry.

18. POLITICS

"I was looking into our New Zealand trip." Henry filled the silence that normally marked the end of their evening greetings and the argument over whose turn it was to buy the crisps. "I think that we need a full three weeks in South Island. I was googling it this afternoon and there is so much to see. I think that we should fly in to Christchurch, hire a motorhome and initially head north to the wine country."

Roy picked up the fantasy. "Now you're talking my kind of holiday. We park up in a vineyard and get blootered for three weeks."

"No, Roy, we make a half-day visit and then work our way towards the west coast," corrected Henry.

"Isn't that where the gold mines are?" asked Donnie. "I'd like to pan for gold."

"In fact you can do just that; there are places you can buy your pan and get stuck in," added Henry.

Roy found that all the ideas could be accommodated. "So, we buy a massive carry-out from the vineyard, pop over to the west coast, buy Donnie a pan and watch him collect our gold while we lie in the sun and get blootered. Then we sell the gold and buy a bigger carry-out!"

Both Henry and Donnie gave Roy one of those looks again. Henry continued to develop the theme. "Once we get down the West Coast we can work our way round to Milford Sound in the Fjord area. It's supposed to have beautiful scenery there; wonderful walking too."

Donnie pricked his ears. "Then we had better get you boys fit. I was thinking that one of the new things we should do this year is to go walking and camping."

A silence fell over the group with Roy trying to think of something to change the subject and Henry wondering whether Donnie's sudden death might be seen as justifiable homicide.

Donnie was not going to let it go. "Seriously guys – it would be good for you two to get some exercise – there is nothing better than walking the hills."

"I get plenty exercise at my plot," said Roy.

"Me too," added Henry, causing both to turn to look at him, but declining to add the obvious challenge.

"Anyway," continued Henry with alacrity, "it's not your turn to choose Donnie, for you picked the horse racing."

Donnie's glum expression marked his acceptance of Henry's logic and gave space for Roy to make the winning move. "I was just thinking about what I would choose. I've been interested in politics for ages but I've never been to a political meeting in my life. I thought that it would be a different thing for all of us to go to the hustings and it might be interesting, particularly with the Scottish Parliament by-election coming up in our constituency."

Henry was not wildly enthusiastic about this idea, but it represented nirvana compared to the prospect of walking and camping, so he responded with inflated enthusiasm. "What a good suggestion Roy; it is not something I would have chosen to do on my own, so it fits our project well."

Donnie was less enthusiastic. "But we could never agree on which party meeting to go to; you two voted for different parties last time and I didn't vote at all."

Roy considered the problem and quickly came to the solution. "You are quite right Donnie. With politics we always need to be fair about things; we will go to three different party meetings!"

Donnie wanted to kick himself, though he would have preferred to kick Roy, but he had to accept the hole that he had conspired to fall into, so he just sighed and nodded his submission.

Roy looked at Henry, "OK Henry?"

"OK Roy," agreed Henry with a glum face.

Roy continued with the initiative, "Henry planned the last one, so this is down to me. I will find out the times and places of the three meetings; that will be the Liberal Democratic Party for me, though the swines let me down badly last time, and the Conservative Party for Henry."

"Now you just wash your mouth out with soap Roy Fox! You know fine that I have never in my life voted Conservative; it would have given my father too much pleasure. Anyway, there are none in this constituency; they gave up after their office got burned down…twice. Mine will be the Labour Party."

Roy nodded and turned to Donnie. "And what Party will you choose?"

"I don't know; maybe I'll see if the Monster Raving Loony Party is standing in our constituency."

"How appropriate," added Henry.

The next Wednesday evening found that the attendance at the Liberal Democratic Party hustings in the school hall was swelled by three senior gentlemen sitting in the back row. The candidate was being introduced by the local Party Chairwoman and Roy found himself crunching his teeth, something he often did when he was irritated. He looked around the hall; no one else seemed to be showing any feeling, so he swallowed his irritation and turned his attention to Mr Robin Fairweather, the candidate. At twenty-five years of age Robin Fairweather was young, even for the Lib Dem Party. This was his first Scottish Election, though he had previously stood for the local council and had done quite well, coming second to the sitting Labour councillor. In the present by-election Robin Fairweather might have stood a chance, with the longstanding Labour member having suddenly retired under a cloud to do with expenses. However, unfortunately for Robin Fairweather, his Party, at British level, had formed an alliance to support the Conservative Party in power. That was not going down well in Scotland where the Lib Dems were now polling at 7%.

Robin Fairweather regaled the assembled audience of seventeen including four stewards, a journalist from the local paper and the school janitor, with details of his impeccable background and the hard work he had been doing for the community. He skilfully put down all the other parties in turn and then shifted to the policies of his own party. He presented the policies well, though Roy judged it as 'slick' in the derogatory sense of that term. Now, it is not really possible simply to 'swallow' one's mounting irritation and expect it to dissipate. Roy was finding the steam seeping out through every pore. "He's a slick bastard," he whispered to Henry and later to Donnie. "He's one of those typical 'career politicians' – they can be from any party – they all sound the same and they care not a jot for anyone but themselves."

"Yes Roy," said Donnie, declining to mention the fact that he had been quite persuaded by Mr Robin Fairweather.

Suddenly and apparently from nowhere as far as the audience was concerned, Roy exploded. He stood up, pointed at Robin Fairweather, and at the top of his voice he shouted, "YER A TORY – YER NUTHIN BUT A TORY!" Everyone looked round at Roy to stare in silence at the militant.

Roy sat down; the people turned to face the front again and Robin Fairweather made a fatal mistake. Judging that this old gent would not be up to much, he decided to take him on by responding to the criticism and by that means to show off his ability. He looked at Roy and collected himself to begin the execution.

"I am sorry you feel that sir." If you are going to destroy someone publically, it is best to be polite. Robin Fairweather continued. "If you look at our Scottish policies compared to those of the Scottish Conservative Party, you will see that they are diametrically opposed. Take for instance..." Robin Fairweather spent the next five minutes comparing the Lib Dem and Tory Party policies on education, health, social services and finance, concluding with, "So you see, the Liberal Democratic Party is quite opposite to the Tories."

At that moment Robin Fairweather might have saved himself if he had quickly moved on, but he decided to savour his victory by leaving a tiny silence that should have marked

Roy's submission. Instead, it gave Roy a further opening. Standing up for the second time he shouted "SAYING YOU ARE DIFFERENT FROM THE TORIES HASN'T STOPPED YOU GETTING INTO BED WITH THEM!"

Robin Fairweather elected to ignore this last interjection, mainly because he knew he was angry and to respond from that emotion would not be clever. "Moving on to look at what the Liberal Democratic Party can offer this community…" In this part of his presentation Robin Fairweather was showing his local knowledge and making sure that the journalist from the local paper was getting every word. At the end he made the mistake of looking in Roy's direction.

Roy accepted the unintended invitation, stood up and bellowed "I STILL THINK YER A TORY!"

Henry lowered his head in embarrassment while Donnie tried to suppress a giggle.

Robin Fairweather would have liked to have severely injured Roy at that moment, but all he could do was to ignore him and begin his summation. "So, as I have said, we propose to use the extra ninety million pounds that we will get from the additional corporation tax income on the back of the recovery to aid essential services. Education will get forty-five million, Social Services fifteen million, and Health thirty-five million."

Donnie pounded Roy's ribs with his elbow. "He's said it wrong; that adds up to ninety-five million!"

Roy stood up and for the first time added a smile to his eye-contact with Robin Fairweather. Perhaps at some level of awareness Fairweather knew that he was doomed, though not exactly how.

Roy executed the political waif when he thundered, "YER A TORY THAT CANNY COUNT!"

Most of those attending, including the janitor, burst into laughter and more damning for Robin Fairweather's political future, so did the reporter, Sam Hunt.

The Chairwoman had had enough and bellowed to the

stewards, "Throw those troublemakers out."

The four stewards moved towards the elders, as Henry sat holding his head in his hands while Donnie took off his coat and jacket ready for a fight. Roy pushed past Henry and moved down the row towards the stewards, holding his head high and greeting the first. "If you will be so kind as to make way my man – my friends and I would prefer to leave with dignity."

Roy strode out closely followed by Henry still with his head bowed and Donnie looking slightly disappointed as he put his jacket and coat back on.

19. CULTIVATING

Donnie was sitting in a posh tea room. He had finally written to Susan and he had mailed the letter. It was not a long letter but it was an honest one. This time he did not need to check it with Maureen; he knew it was OK. Susan had replied briefly but warmly, suggesting that they meet in the tea room and giving her phone number.

Donnie made sure that he was there ten minutes early and Susan was careful to be five minutes late.

"Hello Donnie," she said as she came up behind him.

Donnie whirled around, knocking the fine china teacup off the table to its destruction. "Hello...you're...you're older," he said as clumsily as with the teacup.

Susan laughed loudly. "Donnie Anderson...you don't change...of course I'm older you twit."

Donnie was embarrassed but he could also see the funny side of it, so he smiled as he explained, "For twenty-five years I've seen you in my mind's eye the way you were the day you left."

"You're older too," said Susan, "but you're not in bad shape for sixty-five."

"I walk a lot and I don't drink much...usually."

"Let's have some tea," said Susan as she sat down.

*
**

Henry was also having tea with a beautiful woman, his sister Amanda, at her home. She had been careful to choose a time when they could not possibly be surprised by her husband's return. Derek was in China trying to seal an armaments contract. She and her brother had reviewed the last five years of their lives and their lost relationship. Henry was making sure that he did not fall into his old pattern of being glib and using humour to hide. He had promised himself that he would be real in this relationship, no matter how bad he felt. Amanda had never seen her brother like this, talking like an adult to her as an adult. It was exciting and she hoped that they wouldn't lose it. She made sure that she was just as open as Henry. "You know, speaking with you like this reminds me of what I have never had in my marriage."

Henry helped by staying silent.

Amanda continued. "You have talked about being alone and I have also been alone, with Derek. He has always provided well, but he has never been able to be there for me emotionally. Soon I became like that with him too, and we stayed in that unspoken agreement too comfortably. Some things would awaken me like a couple of frantic affairs, as well as trips like my last one to South America. On this trip I decided that I was going to leave him. I am not going to stay stuck any longer. Of course, I should have done it years ago, but that is no reason not to do it now. Really, I just came home to set this in motion and then I am going back to Bolivia. I have been helping with a school in Cochabamba and I am back here to put together the finance to really make a difference to it. Father was careful to make sure that the shares in the business came to me and not to Derek, even though he was managing director, so I am a very wealthy woman."

Henry was aware of the mixture of feelings inside him so he stayed true to his purpose and let them out. "I feel like I'm crying with happiness and sadness at the same time. I am so happy for you. I am so happy that you are grabbing your life back again."

"And your sadness?"

Henry looked at her in the way one looks at one's lover. "... Sadness that I have just found you in my life and I am going to lose you."

"Why are you going to lose me?"

"Bolivia is a long way away from Scotland," replied Henry, logically as always.

Amanda took a deep breath in mock frustration. "Henry, I

can see that you are a bit green about this 'living' thing. You have not yet realised that everything you do in life is a choice. Sometimes we think that we do not have choices, but that is only because we have forgotten that we do. Come with me to South America."

*
**

Roy was in his allotment planning the later seeding, as he talked with Sheila. "I think we will do well with the carrots this year Sheila; I am going to plant them in a top layer of fine sand, for I have realised that our soil is too loamy for them. A thick loamy soil is good for most things, but not for carrots. Also, I think we should get rid of the asparagus. It takes up too much room and whenever we get a good head of shoots for picking some terrorist is coming and stealing them. Paul Brady came at dawn one morning and found the culprit clearing out all the asparagus plots; he reckons he sells them on his market stall. And then there is the strawberry beds, but we are organised for them. They all come on in the same three weeks so we are organising an 'allotment watch' with two of us on, in shifts, every night. That will keep the strawberries safe. We are also talking about electrifying the fence around the allotments, but the police might not be too happy with us electrocuting the thieves. Anyway, I am looking forward to seeing how these celeriac will do this year. Bobby Devine always said that we had too short a growing season up here to get decent sized celeriac, but there is a new variety that is supposed to be more suited to these northern climes."

*
**

Donnie was enjoying meeting Susan. She was completely different from twenty-five years earlier. She was much more confident, self-assured and surprisingly relaxed considering this potentially difficult meeting. Donnie couldn't help wondering whether the earlier cowed person completely lacking in self-confidence and perpetually anxious was as a consequence of living with him. But he was determined not to get sucked into his black hole, so he stayed positive.

"It was nice that you wrote to Donald; he sent me a copy of your letter," said Susan, intent on making this meeting something more than a tea party.

Donnie explained honestly. "I was also pleased that I wrote. I found it difficult. I started many times and then I gave myself a good talking-to and wrote it straight off."

Susan nodded. "That's how the letter sounded. Donald was over the moon to get it; he thought that he would never hear from you again."

Donnie was feeling his courage. "I have been trying to change the way I am."

Susan was intrigued by this. "What do you mean, Donnie?"

Donnie took a deep breath; he was not sure that he had the words for this. "I always thought I was no good and I was always very frightened... worse than that, I could be violent."

"You never hit me," said Susan with considerable feeling.

"No I did not – it was not that kind of violence – that kind of violence comes from the bully and I was not the bully."

Susan was way ahead of him. "No, I suspect that you were the bullied."

Donnie looked into Susan's eyes. "How do you know? I never spoke about it."

"Donnie Anderson, I have had twenty-five years to think about the man I loved who could not love me and I eventually worked it out."

Donnie was still looking into Susan's eyes and his own eyes opened to cry, something he had only ever done alone in his life. Susan reached her hand forward and placed it gently on top of his.

*
**

Henry was in a tailspin; the rear rotor blade had sheared and his helicopter was spiralling down towards inevitable destruction. How could he respond to his sister? She was so clear – for her it was simple – you just made choices for your life. But for him it was different; his present life was defined by his past. Yes, it was limited, but he enjoyed it; perhaps he enjoyed it <u>because</u> it was limited and he only ever had to meet challenges that he had set up for himself. He never had to go outside of his box. Recent times with Roy and Donnie had been stretching him, but Amanda's challenge was so much more.

"So, what about it Henry? It would be a 'family' thing done with the family money." Henry had only one word in response. "But...but...but..."

Amanda helped him, "Yes Henry, there are always 'buts' in life... but we have a choice over whether we let them rule us."

Henry put up his hand, in a way to ask her to pause, and he explained what was going on in him as well as he could. "You are so much further on than me...you are so free, while I am nervously holding open the box in which I contain my life. I look at you and the simple way that you, rightly, point out that we have choices over our life and that terrifies me."

"I understand that. It terrified me for most of my years with Derek. OK, how about we discuss it, but as a fantasy?"

"I don't understand." said Henry, but immediately scolding himself for his lie. "No, I do. You mean we could talk about the South America thing but as though it was a fantasy, so that there was no pressure on me actually to do it...yet."

"Precisely Henry Doncaster; you are such a brave coward."

They shared a smile and Henry voiced what both had been feeling. "You know Amanda, our relationship has completely switched around; you are now the big sister and I am the little brother."

Amanda nodded. "Is that OK for you?"

Henry took time to respond. He looked at Amanda and he looked inside himself. Finally he began to nod slowly. "Yes, it is, for I have stayed still while you have grown up."

"It feels nice being a big sister!" said Amanda, smiling broadly and shaking her upper body in the manner of a child experiencing glee.

"It feels nice to have a big sister," said Henry with a big smile. "I'd like to do our fantasy, but remember that you have to look after your little brother."

Amanda was not going to let him off with that manoeuvre, so she threatened him. "Watch it little brother or I'll bash you!"

*
**

"So, this is the last job for today Sheila – there is just enough time to plant a couple of rows of tatties – no point in doing more because I don't eat many. This year we have got 'first earlies'. We are a bit late in planting them but they should still be ready in late July. I remember Bobby Devine's new potatoes; they were so sweet and tender that we would eat a few raw as soon as they were picked. We would sit together beside the tatties and have our tasting. Then he would thank the plants. He said that the art of cultivation was to have a relationship with your plants – a relationship in which they grew out of your respect for them."

20. A GIRLS' NIGHT IN

Maureen tinkled her silver bell with the same delicacy as always, but there was none of the usual warm humour in her voice. She just wanted these men (they were nearly all men) to be out of here as soon as possible. Henry noticed the difference in her and she noticed him noticing. While others cleared up he stayed seated and looked at her with concern as she stood tall behind her bar. She avoided meeting his eyes because she knew what they asked. She knew that Henry understood her better than most men. He would have been nice to have had as a father, or even an older friend, but he was on the other side of the bar and that was where he would stay. Henry's sensitivity to Maureen was an unusual experience for him; he did not exactly see himself as the empathic type. But in his recent meeting with Amanda he had been surprised at how much caring he could feel and even express. Something was happening to him and he liked it. His empathy for Maureen was so good that he was able to communicate his caring and also his respect for the distance she needed. He finished his beer, took his glass round the bar, laid it in front of her, looked her straight in the eyes and said, "Good night dear Maureen."

"Good night Henry," she said with the only warm smile she could afford that evening.

Maureen had asked Rosie if she would stay behind after closing that evening without telling her what it was about. Rosie busied herself nervously with locking up. Maureen had never asked her to stay behind at evening closing time before. Now and again they would spend some time together after lunchtime closing, just chatting like girls, and recently they had had an afternoon shopping trip downtown. Despite the age difference they got on well; they were like sisters together. But what was this about? Had Maureen found some huge deficit in the till and was about to face her with it? The rational part of Rosie dismissed this idea, partly because she knew that she was utterly honest with Maureen. She liked her too much to be otherwise and she knew that Maureen knew that. Besides, Maureen kept such a firm grasp of the accounts and the stock that an illicit deficit could never be created.

Maureen went behind the bar and sighed. "Rosie, I am pouring myself a quadruple gin and tonic and I'm being light on the tonic, what can I pour you?"

"Half the gin and double the tonic would be about right."

Maureen smiled as she poured; she really liked Rosie. "Let's get out of here; the kitchen is our space."

Maureen lifted their glasses and left the bar with Rosie following her.

By this time Rosie was sure that this meeting was not about her but about Maureen, so she took the initiative. "Maureen, I am concerned for you; what is going on?"

Maureen looked back at her. It felt unusual to want to confide in someone who is both your employee and so much younger than you, but the differences felt smaller than that. However, it was still difficult for Maureen to speak directly. That was nothing to do with Rosie or their relationship; it was to do with the fact that Maureen never confided in anyone. So, she began indirectly. "I am going to have to be away quite often in the next few months and I would like you to be bar manager at those times. I'll make sure that there is extra part-time staff and that you are paid as bar manager at those times."

Rosie could be as firm as Maureen; perhaps that was why they liked each other. "Of course Maureen; it goes without saying. But, as your friend, I would like to support you in whatever this is."

Maureen understood that she had to meet Rosie's caring. She wanted to meet Rosie, but it was rare for her to be vulnerable with anyone. She took a deep breath and began. "I found two lumps in my breast and a mammogram has confirmed them. Other tests have led the consultant to suggest that I come in for tests under anaesthetic. I do not know what I am going to find when I wake up."

Maureen only barely made it to the end of this disclosure as she filled up. She was looking at Rosie with wide open tear filled eyes disclosing a person as vulnerable as they can be. Rosie responded as her best woman. Saying nothing, she got up from her seat, moved around the small table, knelt beside Maureen and hugged her as well as any human being could.

It was a long hug. It was a hug that was so much better than words. It was a hug that could not be misinterpreted like words. It was a hug that cemented a relationship at its present depth. As they came apart both looked into each other's eyes. Both were crying, both were sad, both were happy, both were together. The details would follow, but the support of one woman for another would prevail, no matter what. Such is the love of women.

21. THE LEAVING OF ANTHONY

"From my research I think that early January is the best time to go," declared Henry with authority.

"Go where?" asked Roy.

"Go crazy like Henry," quipped Donnie.

"To New Zealand of course." Henry was undeterred.

"You're not still going on about New Zealand!" Roy shook his head.

Henry continued. "Early January is the middle of their summer and seems the most reliable for weather; though it is relative – parts of South Island get two hundred inches of precipitation a year."

"What's 'precipitation'?" asked Donnie of Roy, by way of making fun of Henry.

"Rain to you and me, or snow."

Donnie continued. "It'll be like being in Scotland. Why travel so far to get rained on?" Henry continued to ignore the objectionable child. "Also, the sand flies might not be so bad at that time."

"What are…"

Donnie nearly asked his question before Henry interrupted him. "Think of them like giant midges, Donnie."

"Then it's definitely like Scotland."

"Not really, Scotland does not have a huge range of venomous snakes and spiders like New Zealand." Henry squinted to see Donnie wriggling in horror at the thought.

Roy intervened. "Henry you are being very bad with our Donnie again, for you know very well that New Zealand has no such poisonous snakes and spiders."

Donnie held up a clenched fist in pretended threat to Henry.

Roy changed the subject to one that might be more problematic. "What do we do about the other political meetings that we said we would go to?"

There was a silence that reflected the embarrassment of all

concerned and the fact that their expulsion from the political meeting had not since been discussed. Henry broached the important question, "Do we have to go to the other two just because we said we would?"

"Of course we don't," replied Roy with alacrity.

"But I enjoyed the meeting; I thought the guy made a lot of sense," said Donnie, hiding the mischievousness behind his intervention. "Anyway, we made a firm commitment to go to three; it wouldn't be fair not to hear the other two. Mind you, if Roy is coming we maybe better 'tool up'."

Roy suppressed his smile; he could see that Donnie was being mischievous so he continued the drift in a serious tone. "I know a ginger-headed block who could get us tooled up."

Henry, his anxiety making him miss the ironical nature of the conversation, blurted out, "What are you saying – that we will take weapons to political meetings – are you both mad?"

"No, just you Henry!" said Donnie as he and Roy laughed together.

Finally Henry caught up and smiled. "That's another one I owe you two."

Roy thought that it was time to seek to close an embarrassing chapter in their recent exploration of new experiences. "Suppose we put it to the democratic vote? Who votes that we suspend our decision to go to the other political meetings?" All three raised their hands as one.

As they completed their plebiscite they became aware of a disturbance in the back corner of the pub, at the pool table.

"Go to fuck you dumb bastard; we dinnae play wi retards," was the expletive from one of the young players, followed by another.

"Yeh, go hame to your mum you dipstick."

A third youth tossed a coin to Anthony saying, "Take your money back lamebrain; no numpties allowed on this table."

Anthony had put his coin on the table in the accepted way to indicate that he would pay for the next game of pool against the winner of the present game. However, the present players were not regulars of the Culloden and had no awareness of the high standing Anthony held therein. They only knew him from the way he was treated in the neighbourhood.

The first continued the assault by turning his cue around to use it as a club.

"Put him over the table, haud his legs apart and I'll batter his balls; we dinnae want retards spawning retard kids."

At this point a shape flew across the room, dived on to the ringleader pinning him to the table top and, picking up a pint glass, broke off its top on the edge of the table. The terrified ringleader knew what was going to happen as the broken tumbler was held high above his face. He screamed for mercy, "Naw mister, dinnae gless me!"

As he ran over, Roy bellowed, "Donnie, don't do it! Don't Donnie. Give me the glass!" Donnie stayed still over his victim pinning him so firmly that he had to look up at the sharp edges of the tumbler held above his face. Donnie paused for a long time then stood back freeing the young man and putting the remains of the tumbler into Roy's outstretched hand. Anthony was sitting against the far wall of the pub near the door sobbing.

Maureen was the first to speak, addressing herself to the young man who had nearly lost his face, "You were violently assaulted in front of twenty witnesses; shall I call the police?"

"Naw missus, dinnae bother," was the predictable reply.

Maureen continued, "All three of you are banned for a week for your terrible insults. If it happens again you will be banned for life."

The reply was also predictable. "Dinnae bother missus, we willnae be back. This pub's crap onyway."

The three louts left and Maureen turned to Donnie. "That was the worst violence I have ever seen in this pub. Donnie Anderson, you are banned for two weeks. Go out through the kitchen."

Donnie nodded, saying, "Sorry Maureen," and left.

No one noticed that Anthony Mason had left the Culloden

for the last time.

22. EXILED

The next two weeks were unusual in that Roy, Henry and Donnie were more isolated from each other than they had been since they got together. Maureen too noticed the difference with no sight of Donnie or Roy and only twice seeing Henry who had apologised for his non-attendance at the Culloden.

"I'm sorry that I haven't been in Maureen. It doesn't seem fair to deprive you of my custom when you are the one that has done right in this affair. I just wanted to pull back from it all for a while. Both Roy and I are having no contact with Donnie during these two weeks, but it wouldn't seem right for the two of us to have regular meetings without him."

Maureen took it in her stride, as was her way. In any case she had more important things in her life at this time.

*
**

The days were becoming long and Roy passed much of his time in his allotment. Everything was coming up in the order that was expected and he maintained his usual dialogue.

"I never understand why the carrots are always the slowest, but they are getting going now and looking healthy in their sand. I've planted them between two rows of garlic because the smell is supposed to keep the carrot fly away. I don't use much garlic, but I'm sure that Henry can make good use of it in his cooking. The tatties are coming along fine in the mound that used to house the asparagus. They say that tatties is good because they break up the ground, but I am thinking that it is the gardener that is breaking up the ground with all his digging."

As well as Donnie's jibes about fitness, Emily had been asking Roy about his exercise. She went every day to her gym and each week she would tell him how much good it was doing her and that he should do the same. The thought of himself prancing up and down in a leotard in front of other men and, horror of horrors, women, made him feel ill, but he promised to go for the odd walk now and again. He started early one morning, about six o'clock. One advantage of not going to the pub in the late evening was that he could get up really early. He chose the canal for his walk, chiefly because he had heard Donnie say that he didn't walk there anymore. He really did not want to meet Donnie for a little while after the Culloden incident. The canal proved to be a good choice; at that early hour it was empty of people and the wildlife was surprising. He had no idea that there were so many foxes, mink, weasels, herons, deer and even an otter in this little ribbon of countryside woven through the metropolis. He found it easy to go out the next day and the next, walking a little bit further each time. After ten days of this he reckoned that he was doing ten miles a day. However, after a careful check on a map in the library, he reduced the estimate to four and a half. Still, he felt good about himself and reported proudly to Emily.

*
**

Henry was even more absorbed than usual in his horse racing enterprise. His accounts showed a profit so large that it startled him. Some of his banks were phoning him to point out the large sums he had in his current accounts and to suggest more lucrative areas for investment. He declined to inform them that he had already found a particularly lucrative area for investment! He was especially pleased with his adopted jockey, Lucas Santos. Having studied one jockey for so long he felt that he knew his riding better than anyone else. He knew that he was particularly strong in front running middle or long distance races over tight tracks and he was regularly picking Lucas's most likely prospects backed by the largest bets he had ever placed. An increasing nuisance to his activity was the tendency of some bookies to cap his bets. While the general public believes that punters can never win against the bookie over the longer term, the bookies know that this is a myth. Also, bookmakers prefer to take bets from losing punters than winning ones, so many of them operate an electronic surveillance of betting patterns to identify those punters who tend to do too well and they 'cap' their bets according to a formula. For example, they might not accept the punter's £100 bet but instead offer him one of £4.65. Their thinking is that it might create bad publicity to cut off a customer, so they insult them into going somewhere else. When this started to happen to Henry a few years previously he had felt flattered, but now it was becoming a nuisance. Of course Henry had numerous ways round such impediments, with slightly different versions of his identity holding accounts with the same bookie. He knew that they could identify users through their internet protocol address, so he had his five computers running through different proxy IP addresses. The accounts with the bookies had a range of logins, and no two accounts with a single bookie went through the same bank account. To bypass the capping Henry had had to open more routing accounts in banks in Croatia, Gibraltar and Malta. He was amused with the last two because Gibraltar and Malta were the registered homes of a number of the largest bookies and exchanges. Nowadays he could not hold all these details even in his very good mind, so he had created an electronic log book stored on his PC with an automatic back-up to a spare hard drive and linked to remote storage 'cloud' systems based in Finland and Labrador. Recently these cloud systems, with their huge storage facilities, were being homed in cold climates to reduce the massive cost of the air conditioning systems required to cool them. Of course, this electronic log and storage system was the beneficiary of Henry's exceptional encryption skills. His final security measure was to remove from the darkest recesses of his PC's hard drive any references to the random number generation system he had used in the creation of the encryption system. As he removed the last citation he said to himself, "The Pentagon would be less secure."

His remaining problem was what to do if he died. Previously he had not been concerned with this question because he had no friends or causes but things for him had been changing rapidly. He thought about Amanda and her Bolivian project, reckoning that they would be better recipients of his assets than dormant accounts which governments would eventually plunder. So, he spent some time in these two weeks constructing his last will and testament. Apart from the legal jargon of the will leaving all his estate to Amanda, there was an appendix giving details of all his banking and betting accounts. This appendix consisted of a single sheet of paper filled with rows of numbers. The will carried the instruction that, in the event of his death, his lawyer would be presented by another party with the encryption code to apply to the appendix. The will included advice on a selection of secure companies that could be contracted to apply the code.

Henry made an appointment with his lawyer to lodge the will and to check on its legality. Visiting his lawyer was a rare experience for Henry, but one which he always enjoyed. Mr Findlay Macsween OBE, of *Macsween, Dickenson and Macsween*, had been Henry's lawyer for ever. Indeed he had been the family's lawyer, a fact that had created some difficulty at the point when Henry had rebelled. Henry had consulted Mr Macsween on matters to do with separating himself from his father. This resulted in Henry's father putting pressure on Macsween; basically threatening him with losing his position as the family and company lawyer. Findlay Macsween's instant response had been to resign as the family and company lawyer.

Henry pushed open the large oak and glass inner door to the Victorian terraced building that housed Macsween, Dickenson and Macsween. The receptionist recognised him immediately and came forward carrying a broad smile to the reception hatch. "Good morning Mr Doncaster. Mr Macsween is expecting you and says that you should go right on in."

Henry was impressed that his lawyer would always give

him an appointment the day following his phone call. He tried to remember when he had first met Mr Macsween; it was in these offices but it was a very long time ago. Mr Macsween must be a good age, he thought.

Findlay Macsween was indeed a good age; in fact he was eighty years old and had been retired for twelve years. His only remaining client was Henry Doncaster, a young man whom he had known and liked for many years. He remembered the distasteful time around Henry's father and recalled being pleased to be free of the unpleasant man. He enjoyed the infrequent meetings with Henry and the fact that it brought him back into his old office. Whenever Henry phoned for an appointment the receptionist would immediately inform both Findlay and his son Stewart. She would then move any of Stewart's appointments out of what was now his office and into the small, spare office. If Stewart had the temerity to complain, or even to sigh, she would look at him with that diminishing expression she had perfected and say absolutely nothing. Within seconds Stewart would nod his head and say, "Of course." Thus it was that Findlay Macsween rose from behind his desk at Henry's knock and came to the door to greet him.

"Good morning Mr Macsween," said Henry as they shook hands.

In those moments Henry always felt like the young man who had first come to see Mr Macsween all those years ago.

"Good morning Mr Henry," replied Findlay Macsween, as if to confirm the memory.

The next day, at one of his now regular tea parties with Amanda, Henry gave her two sheets of paper; one with a lot of numbers on it and the other with the name and address of Mr Macsween. Amanda had never met Mr Macsween, except perhaps as a child when he had visited her father. Henry asked Amanda to keep the first sheet very safe, not at home but preferably in a safety deposit box, and to destroy the second sheet after memorising its contents. Amanda was amused. "Henry, this 'read and destroy' thing is straight out of a movie; are you a gangster?"

Henry paused. "No...at least I don't think I am."

*
**

Like Roy, Donnie had also been walking, but for him it was more obsessive. During these two weeks he walked every day and for many hours. He set himself a target of covering one hundred miles in each of the two weeks and, with a couple of days to go, he was already exceeding that figure. As usual in the summer months he was going beyond the city, using his bus pass to take him to one point or bring him back from another. Donnie had exchanged his expensive unused dress black shoes for a stout pair of walking boots. Having 'walked them in' on local walks, Donnie was now striding out across country, using ancient communication paths and deer stalkers' tracks. He blessed the Scottish Parliament's 'right to roam' legislation. This 'wild walking' was so much better than sticking to the roads; this was real freedom.

He had not thought much about that last evening at the Culloden. He knew that it was a different thing for him than it would be in the eyes of others. They would be horrified at what he had done, while he was pleased with what he did not do. He remembered his thoughts as he had held the glass above the young yob's face. He remembered realising that he had a choice. He did not have to bring the glass down, so he had stopped. He remembered his huge anger but also that, in the end, he had controlled it. He knew that many years ago he would not have had a choice over his actions. It would be impossible to explain to others this difference and how significant it was for him, but explaining it to others was not important to someone as separate from others as Donnie.

Two days before his exile was to end Donnie received a small package in the mail, a package from Argentina. He had spoken on the phone with Donald several times, though Donnie was not very good on the phone. It was not the technology that was the problem because Henry had been careful to help him buy only the most basic model of mobile phone. It was simply that he had never become accustomed in his earlier life to communicating with another person using a telephone. He tried as hard as he could but kept leaving silences in the wrong places. Eventually he would become frustrated and swore at the instrument, which amused his son greatly. Donnie read the letter that Donald had included in the package.

> Dear Dad,
>
> Angela and I would like you to visit us for a couple of weeks in Argentina. You haven't met Angela – she is adorable – and our sons, Mark (15) and James (14) are curious about their grandfather. What we thought would be nice is to spend just a few days in Buenos Aires; enough to see some of the history of the place, and perhaps we can go to the horse racing in San Isidro; I know you enjoy that. But then we would fly down to San Carlos de Bariloche for the rest of the time. We have a house there, by the lake, in a little community called Llao Llao. It is in the foothills of the Andes with wonderful scenery and marvellous walks. Angela is keen to join us on the walks, but the boys say that they will 'pass' that bit. It's funny how young people don't like walking (or maybe they just want the house to themselves!)
>
> Anyway, I've enclosed a return air ticket. If the dates on it don't suit we can easily change the ticket. Text me and I'll phone you back.
>
> Love,
> Donald and Angela.

23. TWO OF A KIND

Donnie hovered in a shop entry down the street from the Culloden at lunch time closing. Maureen and Rosie came out together; he thought it funny that they linked arms and smiled as they walked towards where he was secreted. He jumped out as they approached and nearly sent them to their maker. Rosie screamed at him, "Donnie Anderson you are indeed a crazy man for you have terrified us out of our wits!"

"Sorry Rosie, sorry Maureen, I didn't mean to frighten you. I just wondered if my two weeks was up tonight or tomorrow night."

"Tonight," replied Maureen without expression and the two women continued down the street.

Donnie was pleased with that decision and he fairly skipped up the street and around the corner where he too was subjected to a near death experience as young Malcolm Jamieson jumped out in front of him.

"Sorry tae frighten ye Mr Anderson, I wis just checkin that ye wis OK. I heard about whit happened two weeks ago. Those were bad men ye took on. The leader is Billy Kyle – he is pure bad, man. I can't help ye wi him because he's too big fur me, but I've been lookin oot fur ye so that I could tell Finn if you wis goin tae get done. Finn would gut 'im fur sure. But the wurd is oot that Billy goat done by a pensioner, so he can't show his face roon here. The wurd is that he's gone tae Edinburgh, hivin help him. I heard that the Culloden banned ye fur life. Wid ye like me tae burn it doon?"

Donnie put on his most responsible voice to give his answer. "No Malky, I am looking forward to going back to the Culloden tonight, so please do not burn it down." Then Donnie paused and made a surprising suggestion. "I'm going to the café for a bacon buttie and cup of tea; fancy one?"

"That would be great Mr Anderson; I'm fair starved so I am."

As they walked together down the road Donnie wondered what had possessed him to invite Malky along. Maybe it was to do with him being pleased that his exile was over and that he could meet his friends again. Perhaps it was also that he could see some of himself in Malky. At the café Donnie ordered mugs of tea plus two rolls and bacon for each of them: wee Malky did indeed look hungry but it wouldn't have been right just to order two rolls for him.

From the way Malky began the conversation it was clear that the urban telegraph had made Donnie into a folk hero and there was street cred for Malky in being seen with him. "The wurd is that you done over Billy Kyle real good; that you would have glessed him but he peed his pants and you let him go. His two mates called him a lassie and widnae hing oot wi' him onymair, so he had to go or somewan wid hae done him. The wurd is that you were a commando during the war and can still do the business. I'm right sorry aboot whit I did tae ye Mr Anderson."

Donnie was interested in the story as it had developed, with all the embellishments gained in the re-telling. Only one part had some truth in it; the nature of his violence had been trained by the military, though to have been a commando during the war would have pushed him far into his eighties. Donnie thought that it was not necessary to factually correct the story, but instead he asked Malky a question that surprised both of them. "Malky, what are you going to do with your life?"

"Dunno," replied Malky in the accustomed fashion.

Donnie decided that a different track was required, so he spoke about his own life.

"Why I'm asking is that you remind me of how I was when I was young. I never had any idea what I was good at so I drifted. Eventually, the only possibility seemed to be the army. But after that I just drifted again. I drifted all my life."

"I would like tae be like you Mr Anderson; you're cool fur a pensioner."

"But isn't there anything that you think you might do in your life?"

"Well, I dinnae want tae turn oot like ma da," revealed Malky.

Donnie was surprised at this. "What do you mean?"

"Well ma ma disnae know if he's goin tae come hame deid of a night," answered Malky, perfectly seriously.

"So you want something else for yourself?" continued Donnie. "What might you do?" "Weel I've nae education; I'll be leavin the school later this year with nuthin tae ma name. An there are nae joabs."

Malky paused and looked at Donnie. "I thought that I might try tae join the army. Ye dinnae need ony qualifications, ye jist need to be sixteen. They say ye need to be fit, which I am; and that ye might not get in if you've goat convictions, which is OK because I've never been caught."

"Maybe the fact you've never been caught shows that you're bright as well!" said Donnie with a smile.

"No me; the last thing I am is bright," said Malky, scoffing at himself.

Donnie was quick to challenge. "Just because you don't do well at school doesn't mean that you can't be bright when you find things that interest you. Is the army what you really want to do?"

"Kind of...I mean I think that I would be OK for it; I can look efter mysel OK. And my uncle said that you can learn a good trade in the army."

Donnie noticed that Malky did not speak in the same pronounced dialect when he was talking about his hopes. He pondered and nodded. "Yes, that's right; there are more chances to learn a trade in the army than in civvy street nowadays, but you still have to stick in and show willing or the trade you learn is potato peeling. I speak from experience!"

They both laughed and finished their bacon butties.

"Thanks Mr Anderson; that wis rer."

Donnie smiled at his new friend. "Pleased you could join

me. You're not a bad lad Malky; I remember that you held off those other two from doing much worse to me at the canal that night."

Malky looked pleased. "Aye, one of those is pure mental; he did a guy right bad jist efter that time. I dinnae hing oot wi him onymair."

Donnie concluded the meeting with what he most wanted to say. "Malky, if ever I can offer you any advice with the army or anything else, just ask me...but don't jump out of shop fronts!"

"Thanks Mr Anderson," said Malky as they went their separate ways.

24. REUNITED

Donnie was earlier than usual on his return to the Culloden that evening. He entered in his usual way, nodded nervously to Rosie who was washing tumblers and made his way around the bar to their usual spot to await Henry and Roy. Rosie opened the door to the kitchen to inform Maureen of Donnie's arrival. Maureen came out and crossed over to Donnie. "Donnie, will you come into the kitchen? I would like to talk with you."

Donnie wasn't expecting this and was tempted to flee as he had regularly done when sent to the headmaster's office for a flogging. But he quickly grew up, nodded to Maureen and worked his way round the bar to the kitchen door. No one in the pub paid any attention to this event because the happenings of two weeks hence were by now part of ancient history and well forgotten.

Maureen gestured Donnie to sit at the small table and went over to the sink. "I'm having a cup of tea; would you like one."

"Yes, Maureen, milk and two sugars please," replied Donnie, very nervous and trying not to show it.

Maureen made the teas, put Donnie's in front of him and sat down at the table opposite him. She stirred her cup slowly and said, "I need to understand what happened two weeks ago or I won't be able to feel safe with you around."

Donnie did not expect to be asked to explain; he knew that Henry and Roy would listen if he had chosen to speak, but they wouldn't demand it of him. He had forgotten about Maureen and that women were more direct. Donnie began, in stumbling fashion, wondering vainly if Maureen would let him off with an apology and a partial story. "I suppose it looked pretty bad; I'm really sorry Maureen... that I did that in your pub."

"Apology accepted Donnie, but it's not enough."

Maureen was firm; could he get off with giving just a little bit more? Donnie lowered his eyes. "I just got really angry with the way they treated Anthony... I've always liked him." He raised his eyes slightly but found that Maureen's were unchanged by his paltry efforts thus far. He fell into silence because he had nowhere else to go. Maureen also stayed silently waiting. Donnie, feeling trapped and panicky, suddenly had the image from months ago of himself standing in front of his bathroom mirror in his struggle to write to his son. He said to himself firmly, "Just do it Donnie." He looked up and directly at Maureen. She could see the difference in his face; it was like there was an adult there now. She kept silent.

Donnie, still looking directly at Maureen, began to show himself. "Can I explain what was going on in me and where it comes from? You're right, that's the only way you will have a chance to understand it."

Maureen nodded and stayed silent, grateful that she and Rosie had talked about how they would approach this; she knew that Rosie would not enter the kitchen.

Donnie took a deep breath, paused, and began to tell it exactly the way it was. "When the yobs were calling Anthony names I wanted to smash them, but I held back because I knew that Anthony faced this every day of his life. It would have been bad for him to get it in the Culloden because he felt safe in here, but he could manage it on his own. It was when the leader wanted to do him physical harm that I had to intervene. Part of that was about me; it was like me going to be pinned on the table and have my balls smashed. But it wasn't just about me; there was a cool part of me that just wanted to protect him. I reckoned that if no one stopped them, the leader would really do it." Donnie paused before moving into very private territory. "It's the next bit that would be difficult for others to understand. One of the things they teach you in the army is that if you are in danger you must not piss about; you must go in with immediate and huge violence. It must be immediate before the other person gets their act together and it must be huge in order to remove their threat completely. You must take them out in that first moment, or they will get you. All that talk about only using 'reasonable' force to repel an attack is pure crap – the police know it's crap; even the kids in the gangs know that it's crap. That was the zone I was in; that is why I was so violent. Henry or Roy might have been able to talk the lad out of it, but I don't have those skills. There is one other thing and it's very important to me..."

Donnie paused; Maureen was still looking with the same expression. He could not detect judgement in her face, so he could go on to his most personal territory. "I'm not sure if I can explain it well, but I'm really pleased that I didn't glass him. I mean, I'm not just pleased because it means that I'm not in the jail right now; I'm pleased that I had the control to stop." Donnie paused, looked down, and said slowly, "I haven't always had that control."

Maureen was brief in her response. "Thank you for explaining it to me Donnie; I understand better now. Let's go through to the bar."

When Donnie left the kitchen he found Roy and Henry already on their bar stools, munching crisps. Neither of them greeted him.

"Can I buy you guys some crisps?" he asked lamely.

They both held up their packs to indicate sufficiency, but neither of them spoke. Donnie was upset; he had not expected that they would 'cold shoulder' him. He sat on his bar stool feeling very alone, while Roy and Henry munched.

After a while Donnie asked Rosie for a pint, at which point Roy said, "The least you could do Donnie Anderson is to buy our pints for we is fair thirsty after two weeks!" Henry added, "Well, Roy, it may not be possible for young Donnie to buy us pints because all the tumblers might be broken!"

"You are two bad men!" said Donnie with relief and a smile.

Their conversation that evening was more animated than usual because they had a lot of catching up to do. Donnie was delighted to hear about Roy's walks, but Henry kept quiet, afraid that expectations in that regard might pass to him. Henry told them about the stage he had reached with his betting genius, but, unusually, he also spoke about his meetings with Amanda; even talking about some of the new thoughts he had been having, including Bolivia. He was pleased that they listened to him without cracking jokes. Roy was best. "It sounds as though entirely new things are happening for you."

"Yes, it's like my life is opening up rather than closing down."

Roy, and also Donnie, nodded their heads in understanding.

Donnie had the biggest news as he proudly read Donald's letter aloud to them and showed them his air ticket.

"So how do you feel about the trip?" asked Roy.

"Great," said Donnie and paused. "A bit scared too."

Roy nodded knowingly. "Yes, it's a big thing."

"Yes, to go half way across the world to meet grandsons I've never seen, a daughter-in-law I've never seen and a son I abandoned twenty-five years ago."

The pause in the conversation marked its solemnity. Donnie's feeling of fear was heard but it also had to be played down; men do it that way.

"There is only one possible solution," said Roy gravely and with a shaking of his head. Henry understood immediately. "Yes Roy, there is only one possible solution to such a predicament."

Donnie looked from one to the other, not knowing what he was missing. In a flash Roy grabbed the air ticket, held it aloft and announced, "I will have to be going in your place!"

Donnie jumped up and down trying to retrieve his ticket, but he had none of the athleticism of his previous visit to the Culloden.

Rosie looked across at them and scowled, saying to Maureen, "Men are such boys."

"And the more so, the older they get," added Maureen. She went to the kitchen and returned with an envelope, saying to Rosie "And tonight the boys are going to have to learn another lesson about their inadequacies."

Rosie looked at the envelope which she recognised and

said, "Too true."

Maureen crossed the bar to the trio, who were by now in uproarious laughter, and handed the unsealed envelope to Henry, saying, "This was left by a friend of you three."

Henry took out the letter. He scanned the few lines it contained, took a big sigh and shook his head. "It's from Anthony, dated a week ago. I'll read it."

> Dear Donnie, Roy and Henry,
>
> I wanted you to know that my mum and I are going back to Lochinver tomorrow. I am really pleased about that. It is so much better for me there than in the city. I remember you said that you might come north and do some hiking. It would be great if you came to Lochinver. We know someone who has a caravan. They don't rent it out because it's not too good, but it's available for you. I remember Henry wasn't too keen on the camping and the caravan is much better than that. I'm not too sure where we will be staying, but I will be in the public bar of 'The Crannog' most evenings from 8.00pm. You could phone me there or just drop in. You are great friends to me. My mum sends her love to Donnie.
>
> Thank you,
> Anthony.

Rosie looked to Maureen and asked "Which one of us is going to tear them limb from limb?"

"Your turn Rosie," said Maureen. "I'm tired and it looks as though you might enjoy it more than me."

Rosie nodded. "Too true; I like destroying men."

Maureen looked to her and smiled. "Maybe we should talk about that some time."

Rosie gritted her teeth saying, "Yes, but don't blunt me

now," as she crossed the bar to destroy some men.

Rosie, for her age, was a formidable woman. Henry looked at her crossing over to them and thought thus. She began her disassembly of the men in a quiet yet threatening tone. "So, you will have read your friend's letter. You will have read that he and his mother have had to flee the city. You will realise that this means his mother has had to give up her job yet again to take her son to a place of safety. You will notice the date of the letter, which is a week after Donnie's incident. I want to ask you some things. Which of you 'friends' sought Anthony out after the incident? Which of you 'friends' talked with him and his mother? Which of you 'friends' tried to help his mother hold their life together in the city that gave her the only chance of a job? In fact, which of you 'friends' have even given him and his mother a thought in the past two weeks? Thank you gentlemen for doing no more than is expected of men; to think only about yourselves." Rosie stomped off.

Another silence fell over our small group, but this one was not engineered and it was not a joke. Eventually Roy said, "Of course, she is right."

25. A SATURDAY AFTERNOON

Early Saturday afternoon was an unusual meeting time, but Henry had invited Donnie to watch the early soccer game on his big screen and thereafter to help him work out what was needed to get a passport for his Argentina visit. The game was between Manchester United and Liverpool and, as they supped their cans of beer, the two discussed their ideas on the result.

Henry was clear. "It has to be a decisive victory for Man U. Look at their home record this season, ten wins, two draws and no defeats, with twenty eight goals for and only seven against. Also, Liverpool has been bad this year; I'll say 3:0 for Man U."

Donnie pondered, "I can see where you're coming from Henry, but there is more to it. If you look at the recent form, Man U have been winning, but losing a goal a game. Also, these games are like local derbies; there is seldom more than one goal in it. I'll say Man U to win, but only by 2:1"

Henry also nodded in understanding of Donnie's logic. "OK, shall we each venture a fiver on our predictions and I'll look for the best odds available online?

"Done," agreed Donnie.

As the start of the game approached, with the players warming up, Donnie drew his seat up to within five feet of the four foot screen, such that he had to move his head from side to side to follow the play. He turned around to Henry who was on his PC and, with a boyish smile, he said "It's as good as being at the game!"

Henry smiled. "And you've got good odds of 11/1 for your 2:1 prediction, while I've got a skinny 9/1 for my 3:0".

The key moment of the game as far as our two punters were concerned came early in the second half when Liverpool scored to equalise Manchester's first half goal. Henry groaned as his bet went down while Donnie did a jig in the limited space between him and the television.

"Told you Man U would lose a goal!" scoffed Donnie as he sat down.

Henry slumped down beside him and they both cheered on Manchester to score again which they did with virtually the last kick of the game, at which point they did a jig together. Donnie's £55 winnings would go into one of Henry's accounts, so he counted out £55 cash into Donnie's hand as he said, "Good stuff Donnie, that was a well thought out prediction. Now, shall we look into this passport thing?"

"Have you never had a passport before?" asked Henry.

"I don't think so" answered Donnie but with doubt in his voice. "I don't remember having one."

"So, you've never been abroad in your life?" continued Henry.

"No...well only to Germany with the army," said Donnie.

Henry pondered on whether members of the armed forces needed passports for military service at the bases in Germany. Perhaps the bases were regarded as sovereign territory; but they would still go off base at times; surely they would have needed passports? Perhaps the military held the passports centrally in case someone lost their passport, or 'lost it on purpose' if they wanted to stay home.

Henry beckoned Donnie over to sit beside him at the PC. He flexed his fingers in preparation for his favourite sport of surfing. Twenty minutes later Henry was not pleased with the conclusiveness of his results. It seemed that there was no such thing as 'military passports' for UK service personnel. These existed in the USA perhaps, thought Henry, because 81% of American citizens do not have a passport. He always shivered when he remembered that statistic; it was frightening to see that a country with so much international influence had so little international experience. His surfing appeared to suggest that British military personnel did not require a passport for most European visits on duty, though there were some other opinions. Henry reckoned that in Donnie's much earlier times it was even less likely that a passport would have been required for the bases in Germany. Donnie added weight to the conclusion when he pointed out that the army issued Travel Warrants, so passports were probably not required.

Henry laid out the position. "It's a pity that we can't prove you had a passport previously, because it will make this a 'first application' and that's a bit more complicated."

"How so?" asked Donnie.

"As well as filling out a form you will have to have an interview." Henry paused on the last word, accurately expecting a groan from Donnie.

"Why would they want to interview me?" he asked.

"To make sure that you are who you say you are; a genuine British citizen who is not dead." Henry sniggered as he said the last part.

Donnie protested. "Of course I'm British...well Scottish, and of course I'm not dead!" Henry was ready. "Ah, but you might indeed be dead dear Donnie."

"Then I would not be able to punch you the way I'm just about to," said Donnie rocking his fist in front of Henry.

Henry thought that it was the time to clarify Donnie's existence. "What they are concerned about is that this person applying for the passport might have gone to a graveyard and picked out the details of a seven year old child who died in 1953 and whose name was Donald Anderson. So here are you, applying for a passport in the name of Donald Anderson when you are, in fact, Osama bin Laden!"

Donnie brought up the second fist. "But I'm not, I'm Donnie Anderson; anyway Osama bin Laden is dead."

Henry tilted his head. "Are you sure about that? They buried him at sea pretty quickly and they didn't show photos. No, I think that Osama bin Laden may now be Donnie Anderson."

Donnie went into a tantrum, shaking his head and his still clenched fists.

"Mmmh, perhaps this behaviour would not go down too well at a Passport Office interview. I think that I should come with you to the interview in case you slug the interviewer."

"Thanks Henry," said Donnie lowering his fists. "I promise to be on my best behaviour." "Mmmh," said Henry, not too convinced.

Henry's googling brought them to the *Identity and Passport Service*.

"It appears that we can complete the application form on-line; shall we do that?" "Definitely," agreed Donnie, getting ever more anxious about this whole process.

Henry brought up the first step which was a page of warnings, while the next few steps sought information about the applicant. Donnie had difficulty remembering his postcode, but Henry's postcode directory helped with that. Things started to get difficult at the seventh step, asking for details about Donnie's mother. After some effort Donnie remembered her date of birth, but he had no idea about her place of birth.

Donnie expressed his frustration. "Why on earth do they need to know where my mother was born? She's been dead for twenty years!"

"I imagine that they are trying to track your identity through your mother's; so if they find her in the records it should lead them to you. Where do you **think** she was born?" Donnie shrugged his shoulders. "Probably Glasgow; I don't know."

"Ok" said Henry, "let's put 'Glasgow' and we can sort it out later."

A worse difficulty arose on the eighth step, looking for the same details about Donnie's father. They had to complete all fields in order to progress, but Donnie had absolutely no idea of his father's birth date. Henry tried gentle facilitation, "Do you remember celebrating any birthdays of your father?"

Donnie looked at him as though he was daft. "Celebrate… my father? Are you kidding?" They decided to enter a wild guess so that they could move on. Step nine was the last one that required new information. In vain hope Henry relayed it to Donnie. "I don't suppose you know the date your parents were married; maybe you have their marriage certificate?"

Donnie once again looked at him as though he was from another world. "No, but I know the date the bastard died!"

Henry stayed calm. "Quite so Donnie, but it doesn't ask for that; perhaps we need to invent another date and clear it up later. They'll send you a copy of the application form for you to check and return. We can enclose an explanatory letter with it. It's good that you're not in a hurry for this passport Osama."

Donnie raised his threatening fist once more.

Getting to the end of the form after seventy five minutes of sweat from Donnie, Henry announced, "Ok, the last step is to press this icon to send the application. Be careful to press it only once mind or we will get too many passports!"

With some ceremony Donnie pressed the button, only once. Henry raised his eyes to the heavens scared to imagine the repercussions of their dodgy application.

26. CULTURED

"Ok, when are we going then?" said Roy to the bemusement of the others.

"Going where?" asked Donnie.

"Going camping and hill walking of course. That's my choice and I've been practicing for it."

"Fine by me," said Donnie.

Henry groaned; now that both Roy and Donnie were into walking it seemed inevitable that he would be drawn into physical exercise, but perhaps he could stall the process a little more. "Now Roy, you and Donnie have already had choices; perhaps it is my turn?" Roy paused to gather his counter argument. "But my choice didn't work out; we aborted it after only one political meeting."

"And we all know who caused the aborting Roy," said Henry, adopting his most authoritative tone and raising himself on his bar stool so that he could more effectively look down upon Roy.

Roy conceded. "Ok, but can I go ahead and plan the trip for the future?"

Now it was Henry's turn to have to accede to this reasonable request. "Ok by me, but we should work out the basics first, like where and when we are going and for how long...and whether we are actually 'camping', or perhaps staying in a nice hotel?" Donnie had to quell this possibility. "I couldn't afford a hotel. I suggest we contact Anthony and take him up on his caravan offer."

"But caravans can be very damp," said Henry with his nose slightly turned up.

Donnie smiled as he terminated Henry's feeble attempts. "So you would prefer a tent in the rain?"

Roy settled the issue. "So, shall I contact Anthony at The Crannog and set things up? How about we go for five days at the end of the month? I can hire a wee car from Ashok's garage;

he does low cost rentals. Donnie nodded enthusiastically and Henry just nodded.

After a second round of crisps Henry returned to the matter of his choice. "So, are we agreed that it is my choice next?"

"Yes Henry," concurred the innocents.

Henry nodded and neither Roy nor Donnie liked the way his mouth turned up at the side in the form of an ill suppressed smirk. "Well I have put considerable thought into this. Following our quest I wanted to pick an experience that you two might otherwise miss in your lives."

Already this was not sounding too good, thought Roy and Donnie. Henry continued, "I wanted to pick something that would expand our consciousness – something that would give us an altogether different narrative for our conversations – something that would be...uplifting."

By this time Roy and Donnie were looking at Henry with the deepest suspicion.

"I have investigated the possibility and found that there are tickets available in the cheap seats and with geriatric reductions for tomorrow evening. I will reserve them online tonight. If we meet here at 6.30pm that will be time enough to get the bus there for the 7.15pm start. Smart dress without being formal will be fine. Is 6.30pm OK gentlemen?" "Er... Henry...you haven't actually told us where we're going," observed Roy.

Henry smiled broadly at both of them. "To the opera, gentlemen!"

Maureen, she with the extremely acute ears, suppressed a laugh at the other end of the bar and slipped into the kitchen to tell Rosie. Forgoing her tea break Rosie came out to gloat. As she moved across the bar she could see the withered frames of two formerly proud men as they contemplated their next humiliation. The shoulders were drooped and the eyes lowered. Every now and again the mouths would open and close like fishes, always failing to find words that could express their shock. The old minds were trying to think up excuses: perhaps the recurrence of an old illness, or the sudden death of a long dead relative, but to no meaningful avail. These were two totally defeated men, a sight for Rosie to savour. She could not resist just one little barb. "How are your arias, gentlemen?"

*
**

The bus was faster than expected and the three entered the theatre before 7.00pm, which was just as well because there were stairs to climb; in fact there were a lot of stairs to climb.

"Are we not there yet?" pleaded the sixty-five year old child Donnie before they were half way up.

Henry rebuked him appropriately. "So the one hundred miles a week walker cannot manage a few stairs."

Roy did not object because that would have meant speaking which required breath that was currently unavailable. Once they reached the top of the upper circle they had to go down some twenty steps to row B then make their way to the middle seats. Donnie looked over the heads of the people in the front row and gasped at the drop.

Henry disappeared back up the stairs, giving Roy and Donnie the chance to moan about their predicament. On his return Henry explained, "I was just ordering our beers for the two intervals."

Roy was confused. "But if you order them now they'll be flat by the time the intervals come."

"No Roy, they pour them just before the interval and leave them out for us," Henry explained.

Donnie was shocked. "But if they leave them out someone could snaffle them."

"Oh no Donnie, not at the opera," assured Henry.

Donnie went quiet, wondering how many drinks he could snaffle if he got to the bar sharp at the interval.

Roy had not noticed the orchestra in the pit below the stage until the arrival of the conductor was applauded. "Wow" he said, "It must cost a bob or two to have such big band; why don't they save money and use taped music?"

The woman sitting in front of Roy turned all the way round to glower at him. Roy reckoned that he had said something bad.

When the first male singer began, Roy made his second major mistake when he whispered to Henry, not quite softly enough, "That bloke's pants must be too tight; he's singing as high as a lassie."

They lady in front turned fully round once more. Henry whispered to Roy at an undetectable level. "He's meant to sing like that; he's a countertenor."

"Oh," said Roy in his usual way when something is not really explained.

Roy and Donnie made it to the break without falling asleep; Roy because he was terrified of the prospect of falling on top of the woman in front of him and Donnie because he found it interesting. They retired to the bar for their drinks and some further explanation from Henry.

"You are doing well staying with this opera. Orlando is more difficult than, say, a Mozart opera like The Marriage of Figaro. Handel's style, with its Baroque aspects, is not appreciated by all opera goers. You will see that tonight is first night and it is by no means full."

"The English subtitles help," said Roy too loudly again. "I wouldn't have understood the Italian singing."

Donnie kicked him none too softly. "Roy, they are singing in English!"

"Oh," was Roy's only reply.

Henry continued. "In fact, it is an excellent production; much better than I expected. The conductor has done wonderful work with the orchestra because they will not often play this stuff. Orlando is doing a good job of acting the man going in and out of madness and his singing is exquisite, and, while Angelica is a bit one-dimensional, the soprano Dorinda is perfection.

Roy's record was not too good this evening, but he persisted. "Why do they have the two main blokes singing so high? It sounds weird."

Henry was more positive than he often was in relation to Roy's observations. "Good question Roy. In fact, that high male voice was prized for its beauty in Handel's day. Today we call that the level of the 'countertenor' but some male singers can go even higher; to contralto or even alto. So prized was that high male voice in Italy that there even were those boys who would make the ultimate sacrifice in order to maintain their art; they were called the castrati."

Roy quivered. "Does that mean what I think it does?"

"Yes Roy," confirmed Henry.

Roy and Donnie did not feel well.

Roy did better through Acts two and three, with only one occasion that required the woman in front of him to turn around; when he clapped not quite at the end of an aria. Donnie gave his appraisal on the bus on the way home. "I liked the singing, especially Dorinda; she was also the best actor along with Orlando. It took me till half-way through to get used to the countertenor voice, but then it was OK; very beautiful in fact, especially Orlando's. But I'm not sure about the storyline; it seemed a bit weak, with Orlando loving Angelica but being pretty shell shocked and Dorinda loving Medoro, but Angelica and Medoro having it off together."

Henry nodded. "Agreed Donnie, but you have to remember that it was from nearly three hundred years ago; it's bound to seem a bit weak to us now."

"But Shakespeare was from more than four hundred years ago Henry, and there is nothing weak about his storylines."

"True, dear Donnie, true," Henry agreed. "What do you think Roy?"

The lack of reply led them both to turn round to find Roy with his head buried in his chest, sound asleep.

27. BODYGUARDS

Maureen was in a flap. Maureen was never in a flap; she was far too much in control of her business and confident about her ability to sort things out to ever be in a flap. But that control and confidence was not possible in relation to what was going on in her body. She was desperate to know and she was desperate not to know. Since last Wednesday she knew that tomorrow, Tuesday, was her hospital admission date. She had had her last outpatient meeting with the consultant. He had helpfully moved it to a morning, outside

his normal clinic, so that both Maureen and Rosie could attend. Rosie had been tremendous; just to have someone there who could listen more easily than you and who could remind you of your list of questions was so supportive. But she also felt Rosie's support emotionally; Rosie had been someone with whom she could cry when they came back to the Culloden.

Roy was rarely in the Culloden at lunch time, but it had been a warm morning and his walk had been the longest ever, still short by Donnie's standards but Roy was pleased and a cool pint shandy plus a pie would be a good reward before heading back to his allotment. Besides, he had brought two nice punnets of huge strawberries for Maureen and Rosie, a small step in his campaign to win back their favour after the Anthony matter. Maureen had thanked him for the strawberries, not as openly as he had expected, but better than Rosie whose thanks resembled a stifled growl. Maureen was clearly distracted and Roy felt brave after his good morning, so he asked her. "Is anything troubling you Maureen, you look distracted."

Maureen looked back at him and decided that it was OK to give him problem number two, but not number one. "Thanks for your concern Roy. I've got a problem with the security firm that normally picks up our weekend takings. Their men are on strike so they can't come. We've had a big weekend, what with the sunny weather, and I'm way over the maximum our insurance allows us to keep in the safe. Rosie and I are going to have to take it to the bank ourselves this afternoon."

Roy's offer was instantaneous. "I'll come with you; the more we are, the safer the money will be."

"With respect Roy I think any villains could easily brush aside two women and a pensioner."

Roy nodded and came up with an idea. "I know how to sort it; I'll have something fixed by closing time." He took out his new mobile phone.

Come closing time Roy was well finished his pint but still seated in his normal position at the bar. His phone rang and he spoke briefly before closing it. "We are all set when you are Maureen," he said.

Maureen was unsure. "Roy, is this safe?"

Roy nodded confidently. "Trust me Maureen. This is as safe as it gets in Glasgow."

Rosie grunted, not specifically at Roy's assurance, but at the generic concept of trusting a man.

With the pub empty of customers apart from Roy, Maureen went to the kitchen to open the safe. Until recently Rosie would have known not to follow because Maureen had kept her unaware of the combination. Long ago she had explained to Rosie that this wasn't about not trusting her, it was about keeping her safe from intimidation. But this had had to change with Rosie now deputising for Maureen as bar manager, so she followed her into the kitchen.

As they came out of the kitchen with Maureen carrying a small holdall, Roy went to open the front door ahead of them. Out in the street the sunlight blinded them for a moment until they recovered, at which point both Maureen and Rosie yelped, Maureen with fright and Rosie with lust, for standing on the pavement right in front of them were Finn and Adonis.

"Good afternoon Mr Fox; good afternoon ladies; where are we headed?" asked Finn, while Adonis eyed up Rosie in every aspect.

Roy answered. "Good afternoon Nicholas; we are going to the Bank of Scotland round in Telfer Street."

"Fine Mr Fox," said Finn waving his arm graciously to invite them to go first.

The short walk was an interesting experience for many of the participants. Roy, Maureen and Rosie walked in a line ahead with Finn and Adonis following closely. Soon Rosie dropped back to walk beside Adonis. Maureen whispered to Roy. "Is that who I think it is? Is that Finn?"

"Yes," said Roy, "We are safe as houses."

Maureen laughed. "We are taking a bag of cash to the bank escorted by Glasgow's most feared gangster. I can't believe it. But you're right; no one in the city is going to take on Finn. Is it true what they say about him... about his violence?"

They had just crossed the street, so Roy skipped behind Maureen to be on her other side. Roy answered. "These things are all very much exaggerated. Both sides exaggerate them. Nicholas would exaggerate them to make others fear him more and the others would exaggerate to show how brave they had been in standing up to him. Then those who hear the stories further exaggerate them; that's how these urban myths develop."

"But I suspect that he's more dangerous than an 'urban myth' Roy."

"Perhaps Maureen, perhaps, but he's safety itself for us!"

They had crossed another street and Roy skipped behind Maureen again.

"Roy, why do you do that; why do you skip behind me every time we cross the street?" Roy looked surprised. "It's just what a man does when he is walking with a lady; for the gentleman always has to be at the road side."

"Why?" asked Maureen in genuine curiosity.

Roy looked at Maureen, surprised that this was new to her. "In case one of the horses that pull the carriages should rear up, then the gentleman can shield the lady of course."

Maureen, despite all that was going on for her, gave him her biggest smile. "Roy Fox you are my best gentleman!"

With the bank reached and Maureen, Rosie and Roy entering the doorway, Roy paused to wave back to Nicholas. "Thank you for your assistance Nicholas."

"Any time Mr Fox, any time," replied Nicholas.

Rosie and Adonis waved a temporary farewell to each other.

28. MAUREEN

Maureen was not in the Culloden this evening. She was getting ready for her hospital admission the next morning. The consultant had taken her through a range of scenarios on her last outpatient visit. She had liked the way he had begun the discussion.

"We will be in an unusual situation in surgery. As your physician I will want to represent your wishes in everything I do. That is always what I want to do as a physician. But our difficulty will be that you are unconscious and we will not be able to talk together. Before we go into surgery I want to understand you and your wishes as fully as possible so that I can have that dialogue in my head as we are together."

Even Rosie had liked this statement from a man; the last phrase 'as we are together' seemed especially loving.

The meeting had been unhurried as her surgeon explained what would happen and talked with her about various scenarios. At one point she had become distressed at a scenario and said, "Oh God... then just take it off."

Her surgeon had paused and said, "This is so difficult for you Maureen; I can understand your exasperation and your distress, but we must try to make sure that the decisions we come to will be ones that you will feel OK about years from now when you are not exasperated and distressed."

Much later Rosie told Maureen that she had never expected any man to have such empathy; hell, she had never expected a man to have any empathy at all. They had laughed as they cried.

In the end the surgeon had said that, while they had made no firm decisions for most of the scenarios, he had a sense of who Maureen was as a woman and that he felt he could represent her in theatre. Maureen had ended the meeting by asking him if she should not have a glass of wine the evening before. His response was that he would positively prescribe three glasses of wine that evening; in any case the surgery would not take place until the day after her admission. Then he said what seemed to be a strange thing. "Don't be surprised if you think about a lot of things the evening before you come in. This is a huge thing and you might find yourself thinking about your life."

Now, as she had got all her things together for the next morning and sat down over her prescribéd three glasses of wine, she understood what he had meant. As soon as she stopped busying herself with preparations she found her feelings. These were not the same feelings she had been having over the past weeks. There was none of the frustration, the anger, the sadness; or the worst, the fear of losing. No, these feelings were different altogether. They were feelings that did not have proper feeling names. They were feelings like 'significance' – a sense of things that had been and were significant in her life and things that were not. This new construct totally re-ordered her life. Some things that she had previously seen as defining her life, like her relationship with her father, seemed to have lost significance while other things, in a variety of relationships that she had previously seen as transient, were now coming from the background into the foreground. These brief moments were being appreciated rather than dismissed. There was Paul and their short time together. OK she was probably right to 'dump' him as unreliable in the long term, but she did not have to deny her love for him. Then there was her wanting to be a singer. Yes, it had been 'sensible' to let that go as a career prospect, but, hell, the whole of life is not about being sensible. Singing for her had been about love – the most important love of all - the love of herself. She did not cry; she laughed. She had not lost something; she had found something. She may be going to lose her life, but she had also been given the perception to find it.

Maureen poured the second of her three prescribed glasses of wine and continued her most private evening.

29. TO THE NORTH

"But Maureen has been missing three days now and we are concerned about her. Can you not tell us anything?"

Roy had been sure that he could get something out of Rosie, but he was having no success. He tried again. "Can you not even put our minds to rest that she is OK?"

Rosie glowered at him. "If I did that then I would be telling you something about her and I've already said that I am telling you nothing!"

Roy wondered if there was a bit of the islands in her; well if there was, he might as well give up because there would be no way past a made decision. He went back to Donnie and Henry.

"She's a hard one that Rosie," he reported.

"I like her," said Donnie, "but she frightens the hell out of me."

"So," said Henry, "I've been thinking about my next choice for us; our trip to New Zealand."

"Will you shut up about New Zealand!" interrupted Roy. "It's Sutherland we are to be going to and I've got everything fixed up. I rang Anthony at The Crannog the evening before last. He was very pleased to hear from us and he phoned me back this afternoon to confirm that he has fixed up the caravan. There is to be no charge for it but we can contribute towards the gas. We should bring our own sheets and towels. It is a four berth caravan so there is plenty of room for us. We'll get the keys from him at Achmelvich, just north of Lochinver; that's where the caravan is. There are lovely beaches evidently. I've booked the car as well; a 2003 Nissan Micra. Ashok says that it was a great wee car in its day; the first of the Micra hatchbacks he says. He gave us a special deal on it." Henry did not voice his thought that Ashok must have been pleased to find anyone willing to rent the old banger.

"So," continued Roy, "I will pick you up from your flats just before ten on Monday morning. I will have got a little food to get us started and perhaps a few cans of beer. Remember to bring your rain gear in case we get a shower or two. Henry, that does not mean an umbrella! Also of course bring your walking boots. Henry, do you have walking boots?"

"I've got good trainers," offered Henry.

Both Roy and Donnie shook their heads.

"I'll help you to buy decent boots Henry," Donnie offered. "It's important to get ones that fit just right."

"And I'll bring extra plasters," said Roy, sharing a knowing nod with Donnie.

*
**

As they ascended the long hill just north of Ullapool, the 2003 Nissan Micra Hatchback slowed down as it had done on every hill since Glasgow. Roy's seat was as far forward as possible and he resembled a jockey urging his mount onward as he perched over the steering wheel. This driving position was not a matter of Roy's choice, rather it was a function of his earlier excesses; for the small car was completely filled by the three men, their bags, bedding and six boxes of groceries, not to mention four dozen cans of beer. When Roy had picked up Donnie all he had got was a shake of Donnie's head but when Henry joined the party his reaction was predictable. "Good gracious Roy; what have you got in the car; we are away for five days, not weeks."

Addressing Henry, Donnie added, "We should have remembered about Roy and shopping."

They made it to the top of the Ullapool hill, but only just. There had been a previous hill, just before Inverness, that was not so steep but very long. That time the little car had not quite enough horsepower to make it. Tantalisingly it came to its exhausted stop at a point where they could see over the top, but not reach it. The queue of holiday traffic had built up behind them and the cacophony of continental horns needed musical direction. Because they were on the actual brow of the hill it was difficult for the traffic to pass and the queue had built up. They found that the embarrassing solution was for Roy to slowly roll the car one mile backwards down the hill with Donnie and Henry outside the car directing vehicles around it. The final humiliation had come with the radio traffic announcement, "There is a five mile northbound tailback on the A9 just south of Inverness. Southbound traffic is also affected."

The reward for reaching the top of the Ullapool hill was the view of outer Loch Broom and the Summer Isles, appropriately bathed in sunshine. In better spirits for the view and the sunshine they motored north to the limestone fed green of the scattered hamlet of Elphin, then swinging to the west along the north shore of Loch Assynt, almost to Lochinver but branching north towards Achmelvich.

As they approached the campsite Roy said excitedly, "Donnie, Henry, just look at that beach; it's as good as Anthony said."

Then Roy fell silent, for the beach reminded him of his childhood home on the West of Harris with its beautiful white sand beaches.

Anthony was waving enthusiastically beside a caravan; a van that looked quite smart thought Henry with surprise. As they extricated themselves from the too small tin can Anthony greeted each of them with exaggerated handshakes. Roy muttered something about being sorry that they had missed him before he had left Glasgow, but he quickly realised that those times were gone from Anthony's consciousness. Anthony was 'here and now' in life and that was the way he should be met.

Anthony was diligent as their host. He showed them all the details about the van and pointed out the camp site facilities. Roy picked up a nest of five plastic buckets. "Why so many buckets? Are they for gathering mussels?"

"They could be," agreed Anthony. "There are good mussel

beds at the wee loch just south of here, Loch Roe. But the buckets; well it sometimes rains here, and they can come in handy for the leaks."

Henry's brief optimism about the 'smart' van dissolved. Also, he also did not trust Anthony's choice of the word 'sometimes'.

Anthony concluded his introductory speech which Donnie suspected he had rehearsed well. "Make yourselves comfortable my friends. It would be nice to see you at the Crannog this evening. I will only be there from 8.00 pm, but they have excellent bar meals if you come earlier. I have gathered the Ordinance Survey maps for the area and will give them to you this evening. I have also asked Jock to come along. It is said that Jock is part of these hills and they are part of him. It is said that Jock cannot die because the hills would die. No one knows how old he is but he tells stories from before the war."

They bad farewell to Anthony and settled into their new home. Roy was the only one to have been in a caravan before so he immediately reserved his bed, followed by Donnie. They had claimed the two forward single bunks on either side of the fold-up table. Henry protested. "But there is no bed for me!"

Roy looked at Donnie and they both shook their heads as Roy, slipping more firmly than usual into the speech of his childhood, said, "Ochone, ochone Donnie, would you look at our friend here; for he is lost if he is taken out of his nice flat in the city. He can do those fancy computers and things but he cannot work out where is that other bed."

"Don't tell me," demanded Henry as he scoured the back of the van, finally releasing a catch and nearly being flattened under the dropping double bed. "Well, at least mine's bigger than yours," he declared in a weak effort to restore some authority.

Henry and Roy cooked dinner together, though they were more at cross-purposes than 'together'. Roy kept throwing more and more food into the mix in an attempt to justify his shopping excesses, while Henry was much more circumspect, at one point observing, "Roy, we already have pork chops and also lamb chops, I don't think that we need sausages as well. Anyway, where are the potatoes? I can't find them."

Roy blushed. "I forgot the potatoes."

Henry looked in disbelief. "You mean you bought all this food and you forgot the potatoes!"

An hour later, having made the best attempt they could to dispose of huge plates of pork and lamb chops covered with baked beans, they headed into Lochinver for their 8.00pm meeting with Anthony. The Crannog was everything that Anthony had claimed for it. Built close to the pier it had certainly known better times when the fishing fleet was much larger. But it gave an immediate appearance of warmth and friendliness and presented an easy mix of tourists, fishermen and locals. Anthony gave them a wave and finished his game of pool with two fast and accurate pots, the latter being one of those complex shots off two cushions that had taken him only a second to compute and execute. His opponent looked at him in disbelief, mumbling "good shot" to which Anthony shook his head and said "lucky one."

Anthony greeted his friends warmly and took them to a table in the corner where his own half pint of beer already rested as though to reserve the space. In their accustomed manner they each bought their own drinks while Anthony hosted the smoky bacon crisps. "He was surprised by your last pot," said Roy as much in question as statement.

Anthony smiled. "Yes, I finished him off too quickly."

"You don't let them know how good you are, you hustler," added Roy also with a smile. Anthony explained, "They would soon stop playing me if they knew...but I let myself go a bit when we play against other pub teams...I have the reputation of 'rising to the challenge'."

Roy, Henry and Donnie looked at each other and smiled at Anthony. Their thoughts were all varieties on the genius of their friend who throughout his life had been bullied for being 'simple'.

Anthony took them through the two maps that covered their area, marking out walks that covered beautiful landscapes but would not be too tough for Henry, the unaccustomed walker. At this point the door of the public bar opened and the locals fell silent, looking at the figure in the doorway. He stood in his Harris tweeds that would have been new some sixty years previously but had only now reached perfection. The hardy cloth is such that it comes to a point where it no longer deteriorates; it has taken on the person and can only die with them. In his left hand he held his crook, the same one that he had carried on the hill all his life and which had genuinely been used to pull lambs from rivers in spate. He was of medium height and muscle but he had that wiry build that characterises someone, man or woman, who has spent most of their life outdoors in the Highlands. But it was his face, especially his piercing blue eyes of Viking heritage, that attracted the attention of the visitors, as he scanned the bar switching his gaze from face to face giving each attention but not responding to those who nodded back or raised a glass to him. Finally he scanned Roy, Henry and Donnie, spending a long time looking at Donnie.

Anthony moved across the room to greet Jock and take him to their corner. At the same time the barman came forward with what appeared to be a very large glass of whisky and a small jug of water, placing them in front of Jock. No mention was made of payment. Anthony introduced Roy and Henry, saying some things about each of them. They were both surprised that Anthony had previously paid them such good respect that he could remember considerable detail. Jock looked to each of them as they were introduced, saying nothing and showing no response except his clear attention. As Anthony switched to Donnie, his introduction was more personal. "Jock, I told you about the friend who protected me from the thugs in Glasgow; well this is him, Donnie Anderson."

This time Jock looked even more piercingly at Donnie who

shivered slightly. "Nice to meet you," said Donnie timidly.

The thirty minute conversation that ensued was awkward because Jock did not do any of the usual things that people do to make others feel comfortable, yet he seemed to effuse such an aura of gravitas that the few things he said were especially considered, particularly his detailed account of the weather they could expect for the next three days. Nearing the end of the meeting Roy, still trying to make small talk, said that this was the first time that any of them had been to Lochinver and it seemed to be a beautiful place. Jock turned to look at Donnie. "But **you** have been here before," he declared. Donnie returned his stare, briefly searched his memory and shook his head, saying, "No...never." Jock also paused and closed the contact with, "It was a long time ago...no matter." Raising himself, Jock collected his crook and, without saying farewell, he moved to the door and out into the night.

Donnie shivered.

30. ROSIE

Adonis had been as good in bed as expected so it was especially surprising to Rosie that she had ended their relationship. It had been clear to her that she should end it, though she did not know why. Perhaps all the stuff with Maureen had been affecting her. Even now, as she was hurriedly locking the Culloden after the lunchtime opening, she was preoccupied with her friend. She would visit Maureen twice a day, after the lunch time and evening openings. She told no one about these assignations, though she had tried to explain to Adonis her need to spend an hour at the close of the day with her friend. Probably he was no different than most people in finding these late meetings strange, but they were precious for Rosie.

Maureen had shared her life with Rosie more deeply than is possible with close friends or relatives. She had never experienced that moment of hesitation when we wonder if disclosing the next thing will be too difficult for the other to hear or too difficult for us to hear them hear. She had told Rosie every detail of the meeting with the surgeon after the operation. She had told her about his hesitation, almost stumbling, when he had described the conversation he had had in his head during his work. "I did as I said I would and I kept you in my mind during the surgery. There came a critical moment when I had to decide on the mastectomy. The biopsy had come back positive, but we knew that the lymph nodes were clear. The easy route would be the mastectomy, so I had our conversation. I heard different parts of you; I heard you shouting, "Just take it off then!" I also heard you crying; that part didn't want to give up but thought that she was not strong enough to hang on. I also took part in the conversation. I told you about the safer route, the mastectomy, and how the other choice could more easily lose you your life. I told you the detail of how we would work to protect you if we did take that more risky choice. On your behalf I made the risky choice. I hope that I chose wisely."

Striding purposively down the road away from the Culloden Rosie felt guilty that she had left the washing up for the evening session. 'Maureen would never have done that,' thought Rosie. But then she smiled, 'Of course she would...if she was hurrying to meet her friend.'

The first part of the route to Maureen's flat covered the same ground as that memorable walk to the bank where she had used the opportunity to hit on Adonis. She smiled as she remembered herself flirting expertly. It felt so long ago that she had done that and she smiled at her skill. Perhaps she could still allow herself to exercise that skill in the future, though the beneficiary would have to have something more to offer than a beautiful body he knew how to use.

So, what had changed in her and why? The 'what' and the 'why' seemed to come together in seeing how she was with Maureen. She did not have good words for it yet; it was like she felt herself as a woman more than as a girl. The girl could gorge on Adonis, but the woman needed more. The girl would not have been able to dump Adonis but the woman could do that easily. The girl might grudgingly give her time to support Maureen but the woman welcomed the opportunity.

There was another part of it as well; it was to do with seeing herself differently in these encounters with Maureen and, perhaps for the first time in her life, liking this woman called Rosie.

She reached Maureen's tenement block and rang the bell for her flat. "Come on up Rosie," beckoned the disembodied voice down the intercom as the door lock clicked open.

31. THE UNACCUSTOMED WALKER

Henry had almost enjoyed their first day walking, were it not for a third degree blister developed early in their walk up to Loch na Coire Ghuirm by Eas a Chual Aluinn, the highest waterfall in Britain. They had lain out flat to peer over the edge to see the water tumbling vertically for more than a thousand feet. An hour's uphill walk later they had reached their final destination at the high corrie under the summit of Glas Bheinn, some 2,500 feet above sea level. Jock had directed them to the 'Loch of the Green Corrie'. "It is certainly the best loch in these parts but the trouts there are very wise. They see the fishers coming up the hill and decide if they will stay hidden for the day or come up to have some sport with them. They are good fish of a two pound average, growing fast in the limestone fed loch. If you catch one you will be a good fisher... or a lucky one."

Throughout the walk Roy and Donnie had tried to look after Henry in that male unspoken way. But Henry was hard to look after, only telling them about the blister when it was well developed. Donnie had scolded him. "You should have told us about it before it got so bad. We would have rubbed it with lavender and camomile oils and it would have disappeared entirely. Now we will have to give it the 'second skin' treatment."

Henry had no idea what 'second skin' meant, but he held his foot out trustingly for Donnie to apply what turned out to be a special plaster.

"There," said Donnie. "That will make it fine to walk on for the next few days. Now I'll massage your feet with the oils so that you get no more blisters."

Henry was not at all accustomed to having a man, or even a woman for that matter, massage his feet, but then again, he was not accustomed to anything they were doing in this holiday.

Roy and Henry fished but Donnie decided to climb to the summit of Glas Bheinn. All got what they wanted from the day, with Donnie waxing lyrical about the views from the summit, Roy telling and re-telling the story of the two and a half pound trout he had caught and Henry relieved to find that Donnie's plaster and oils had worked very well indeed.

*
**

The torrential rain of that evening and the morning of the next day served to explain the five buckets, with that being the precise number of leaks in the roof of the caravan. One bucket had to be balanced on part of Henry's bed but his complaints fell on deaf ears as it was pointed out that he could easily sleep on the other side of the double bed. The rain relented at lunch time allowing them to pick one of Anthony's shorter walks, up the river Kirkaig to the falls by which it exited Loch Fionn; a perfect choice as the rain had filled the powerful river.

In the Crannog that evening they enjoyed a fresh seafood meal that would have graced London's finest restaurants. At precisely 8.00pm Anthony entered, along with Jock. This seemed to surprise the locals; perhaps it was rare for Jock to come in so often. This time Jock had his dog at heel; a collie that looked as wise but a tad more friendly than his owner. Anthony introduced the dog as 'Spot' and the five men sat down together. Jock's extra large whisky and jug of water arrived as usual without question of payment, as well as a bowl of beer for Spot.

This time Jock was positively effusive as he looked towards Roy. "I heard that you got a good fish out of the Green Lochan. Did you catch it along the trench on the west side as I suggested?"

Roy's affirmative response led to a long discussion about fishing between the pair, with the others tuning out. Suddenly Jock ended that discussion and turned his chair to face Donnie who felt the same shiver as previously.

Looking Donnie straight in the eye Jock picked up a new topic. "So tomorrow is your last day and you will have somewhere special to go to?"

Donnie knew that Jock expected the answer to come from him, but he tried to divert the attention by looking enquiringly at the other two.

"Anywhere I can catch another fish!" declared Roy.

"Anywhere that's not too hard on my feet," offered Henry.

Jock was not to be deflected. "And you Mr Donald; what would be your wish?"

Donnie had no particular answer in mind but he found himself saying, "I like walking up mountains and there is that big one out the back that has a strange shape."

Anthony understood the description. "That will be Suilven."

"Yes," said Jock, "Of course it will be Suilven."

Turning to Roy, Jock offered more information. "And on its north side it has Loch na Barrack, perhaps the second best loch in the area."

Turning lastly to Henry, Jock continued, "And most of the walk to the loch is along a good track and the real ascent is only if you are going to the top of the mountain."

"The loch will be far enough for me," declared Henry.

Jock turned to his new fishing friend Roy. "Many people hear about how good is Loch na Barrack, yet they come home empty handed. The secret is not to go near the edges, for the fish lie under the banks and the vibrations from your walking will tell them that you are there."

Roy nodded knowingly as the second best fisher in the pub should do to the master.

Jock turned sharply back to face Donnie, so sharply that Donnie jumped again. Jock opened his mouth as though to say something important, but then paused and simply said, "I will be interested to hear from you tomorrow night Mr Donald."

Spot rose in time with Jock's leaving and occupied that space in the crook of his master's left knee as all good dogs should.

Donnie wished that he could stop shivering.

32. AONGHAS OF ASSYNT

Donnie slept fitfully, full of dreams that were memories or memories that were dreams. Yet he awoke fresh at 6.00am and started to prepare breakfast for the company. At 6.30 the table was set with toast, butter, marmalade, Roy's cornflakes with full milk, and Henry's plain yoghurt. The cooked breakfast for all three was on its plates in the warmer. Donnie turned the radio up loud, but still the two pretended to sleep, so he pulled the covers off them.

"Go away, I'm asleep!" protested Roy vainly trying to pull up the non-existent covers. Henry adopted the policy of continuing to ignore Donnie, but that could only escalate proceedings. Donnie lifted Henry's bed bucket and stood over him; still Henry pretended to ignore him. Dramatically Donnie tipped the bucket over and Henry dived out of bed to avoid the torrent of water. Well, it would have been a torrent of water had it rained during the night, but the bucket was empty. Henry came as close to swearing as he ever could while Donnie laughed at his success in fooling the normally clever Henry and Roy laughed because it had turned out worse for Henry than for him.

*
**

"My, that was a good breakfast you made this morning Donnie" said Roy as he downed the last portion of bacon.

Donnie nodded and added, "We will need a hearty breakfast if we are going to climb Suilven. It is a fine day for it."

Henry thought that the ground rules needed to be re-established. "Remember that Roy and I are only going as far as the fishing loch."

Donnie nodded. "Yes, that's fine. I'll leave you there and go on up to the top."

Roy joined in. "You're sure you want to do that? It looks

steep."

"It looks worse than it is; it's just a hands and feet scramble in places, not real climbing."

"How do you know?" asked Henry.

Donnie paused, genuinely unsure. "I don't know... I must have heard about it from someone...sometime."

Suilven can be approached by tracks from the East, the North or the West. There is also a beautiful route from Loch Sionascaig to the South, though that approach is little known and a glance at the map would suggest that the way is blocked by the large Loch Fionn. However there is a narrows in the loch that is fordable with water only up to the waist. But our travellers were committed to the main tracks, so they only considered the other three directions. They discounted the route from the East because it was the longest and also involved a long drive. Roy observed, "It looks as though the track from the North is shorter than the one from Lochinver to the West".

"Yes, but the track from the west follows the river and is very beautiful," Donnie replied. "How do you know?" asked Henry.

Donnie looked at him but had no reply.

So, they set off from Lochinver in good spirits on the estate road starting behind the posh hotel. Roy was irritated. "These estates think that they own the place."

"Well, maybe that's because they do own it," said Henry.

But such logic only provoked Roy further. "These lands were stolen from the people hundreds of years ago and given by English monarchs to prominent supporters. Some were already Lords and others were bequeathed the title as well as the lands. The Lords found it more profitable to have sheep than people, so the resident poor had their homes burned and were sent to the boats. When they got on the boat they did not even know whether it was going to Canada or Australia".

Henry felt moved to add to the discourse, but soon regretted it. "Yes, the 'Clearances' was a difficult time; there are stories about it in my family history."

Roy jumped in immediately. "And I'll bet we won't be needing to be asking which side they were on!"

Henry bowed his head in submission and made a mental note to make no further mention of his landed family history.

Donnie shook his head. "You two should get up to date. The owner of this estate sold most of it to the local community; he only kept the bit back at the posh hotel."

"Yes," said Roy, "The best bit!"

At the junction with the track from the north, they sheltered from a heavy shower in Suileag bothy. Donnie set up his Primus stove and made what all agreed was the best cup of tea in the history of mankind. When the shower abated they went outside into the screaming blue sky to view Suilven in all her majesty – a gigantic sandstone rock whose geological origin had been in the North American continental plate. It rose almost vertically from its shoulders and was capped with a round westerly summit that gave the mountain its 'sugar loaf' nickname. The clarity of the air after the shower made it feel that the mountain was right in front of their noses. Even Henry gasped at the experience, while Donnie sat down on a rock and cried softly.

Roy sat down on the rock next to his friend and asked after him. "How is it with you Donnie?"

Donnie tried three times to say something in response but he could not find words that were right. In the end that was more or less what he said. "I don't know...I just found myself crying...I don't know why."

Now their journey to the mountain took them over a bridge across the river and off the track. It was fifty minutes of difficult terrain and several inclines before they reached the face of the mountain and the lochans that guarded it. Roy and Henry set about making up their rods and lines while Donnie brewed more tea and ate all but one of his sandwiches. He emptied his pack of all but essentials, keeping his waterproof jacket, the one remaining sandwich, a bar of chocolate and two small bottles of water. Though Scotland is full of natural drinking water, none is retained at the tops of mountains. He wrapped his non-essentials in a plastic bag and weighed it down with a stone. Roy watched Donnie's deliberate preparations out of the corner of his eye. It was as though Donnie had been climbing mountains all his life; he seemed to be so natural with it all.

All three were ready at the same time. They stood in front of each other and did not fill the space with inconsequential chatter. Donnie broke the silence. "I'll go on up then." "When should we expect you back?" queried Henry.

"I don't know how long it will take," answered Donnie.

"But how will we know you are all right?" continued Henry.

"You'll be able to see me up the whole of the steep bit." Donnie pointed to the middle of the mountain. "I'll be following that crack to the top plateau. Anyway, it's not the kind of mountain that you fall off; it's not a vertical climb, up that route at least."

Donnie set off and the others watched him for a time as he followed the track round boulders and gradually steepening in the fold of the mountain. They were both impressed at how well he moved. In their silent observation Roy breathed deeply and remembered that while this place was not his Islands, it was at least the Highlands, and he felt at home. Henry's mind passed by lots of things, but paused to recall his first experience of fly fishing at six years of age. His father had given him a rod that was fitting for his size, but the task of teaching him was delegated to the head ghillie.

Donnie was quickly in another place. The wetness from the earlier shower had dried in the hot sun and he was racing up the mountain. As one sure foot went down the other was raised to win new ground. In steeper places he found his hands working effortlessly in coordination with his feet. It was as though he could tell at a glance what hold would be firm and what might not. At times he found himself choosing a steeper route in preference to one where the sandstone had been crumbled by two hundred years of other climbers. He did not stop for rests because he was too excited to be tired. With his ascent half completed he briefly turned round and gasped at the height he had gained above the patchwork quilt of lochans below. He could make out Henry and even the gossamer thread of his line as the sun reflected off it. On the other side of the lochan he saw Roy casting his line while lying on his stomach.

Roy was determined to out-fish Henry once again, as he had done at the Green Corrie, though he had already admitted to himself that his Green Corrie fish was more attributable to luck than skill. That fish must have been suicidal to chase his fly as he was lifting it out of the water. Looking across the lochan at Henry, Roy had to admire his beautiful casting. Even into a slight breeze Henry left a long enough delay on the back cast to shoot the line forward so that the leader kept going straight beyond the end of the fly line, rather than fall in a crumpled heap which it did anytime Roy was casting into a breeze. At times when the breeze was stronger Roy noticed that Henry was employing the 'double pull' to extend his line more powerfully. Roy sighed; he could never match that skill born of a landed family. But what Roy had in his favour was his hunting instinct. Trained initially in catching fish by children from the travelling community, Roy prided himself on being able to catch fish in unlikely places and by improvised means. At this moment he was working on getting his flies to land softly and drift under the bank of a small promontory diagonally to his left. He would have been in plain view to the fish if he had been standing or even kneeling, but lying on his stomach, though uncomfortable, was the mark of a hunter. Roy noticed the one inch baby frog that nearly jumped across his nose and remembered the story an eighty-six year old Highland woman serving in the Kylesku Hotel had told him about her grandfather who would fish with a small frog as bait at this time of year. Perhaps the frog could be a follow-up tactic in a part of the lochan out of sight of Henry.

Henry was paying the same amount of attention to Roy. He knew that Roy had been lucky with his fish the other day, but it would have been churlish to point that out. Instead Henry had adopted his common competitive tactic of pretending to be unconcerned with competition. In reality he was trying as hard as he could. Observing Roy's prone position he recognised its merits but his heritage simply could not allow him to stoop so low. Instead he was combining every ounce of quiet skill and determination in order to cast long into parts of the loch not normally reached by the average angler.

"Yes!" came Roy's scream, so loud that it not only crossed the loch for the benefit of Henry's ears, but also informed the rest of Sutherland. Henry's heart sank as he saw Roy's rod bent by a good fish. Perhaps such a heavy fish might get off, thought Henry, but he immediately scolded himself for his lack of grace and looked to the west at the approaching storm clouds.

Donnie heard a version of Roy's shout a thousand feet above, but he paid it no heed. With the sweat pouring down his face and his fingers covered in cuts from the stone, he was striking out in fervour for the top. He was a crazy man, almost running up the steep incline and crying because he could not go even faster. In the midst of his obsession he did not see the sky darkening, nor feel the sudden ten degree drop in temperature that introduced the weather front. He did not even feel the hailstones except as unwelcome obstacles to his hand holds. Then he made his first climbing mistake and such a basic one. He moved his left foot a microsecond before his right hand hold was secured. The slide was only a few feet as he leaned his whole body surface on to the crumbled stone in the search for friction.

Donnie lay in that position screaming in frustration and pounded by the hail already turning to equally cold rain. He lost the sense of time and the censoring of mind. For the first time in fifty years he recalled the fact that he had been to Suilven before. He remembered himself soaked and painful, screaming in frustration and aged fifteen. It had been the last day of a holiday in the Highlands and he had set off early, on his own, to climb the mountain that had drawn him all week. It was this mountain; it was Suilven. He had walked up the same Glencanisp track and it was pouring rain, but he was not going to let it stop him; he had to climb the mountain. He had taken the same turn to the south at the meeting of the tracks without stopping for rest and in the perpetual rain. When he had reached the lochans he had carried straight on to the incline. The crack was the natural route for water to come off the mountain and he was climbing in a waterfall. Then the sole of his rotten shoe completely tore off. He did not have walking boots, only city shoes. He had screamed in abject frustration as he was screaming now. Tearing off the remaining upper part of his broken shoe he had flung it off the mountain and tried to continue without it. Fifteen minutes later he could not bear his bleeding foot so he had slithered down the mountain and hobbled painfully back to Lochinver.

Now, fifty years later, he was not going to miss the mountain again. The scrambling was difficult in the wet and having remembered his past he was not as blindly driven as before, so his progress was slower, more deliberate and more secure. But while his earlier amnesia had rendered him impervious to the pain, the cold and the exhaustion, that was not the case now. Now he had consciousness and he could feel every frailty in his sixty-five year old body. But he could see the top of the ridge just twenty feet above him and, with that encouragement, he forced another effort. The last few feet were as near the vertical as he had been and he felt the first flicker of fear that needs to be a mountaineer's constant companion. Straining every sinew he was trying to extend his arm above him towards the final edge when he felt it grasped by something very large and very warm. In one flowing motion he was pulled to the top and on to his feet.

"Well, that was one of the most courageous pieces of climbing I have seen in a very long time," said his helper, standing in front of him. "And it was also a skilful climb for you had all the moves of a young man," he continued. "I am pleased to meet you, though you are very late. My name is Aonghas (Angus)."

For a moment Donnie wondered if he was dead. He certainly could be dead. Perhaps he had lost his hand hold on that last steep section. If he was dead, then who was this in front of him? At just over six feet in height with a bushy brown beard and dressed in old grey kilt and plaid, he supposed that this might be God, or perhaps Saint Peter. But the teeth were wrong; a lot were missing and the rest were brown. God would not have bad teeth. Donnie's next step in the search for logic was more chilling for he remembered a number of his previous actions on this earth and realised that it may not be heaven he was going to and therefore this might not be God.

"Hello," began Donnie with appropriate temerity. "My name is Donnie".

"Yes, of course it is Dòmhnall; for you are 'the mountaineer of Assynt'," replied Aonghas.

"It wasn't really mountaineering to get up here, just a bit of scrambling," said Donnie in qualification of his new title.

Aonghas was not to be put off. "Nevertheless, it is 'the mountaineer of Assynt' that you are and that you have always been, though you are a little late."

"What do you mean, 'a little late'?" Donnie queried tentatively.

Aonghas looked Donnie up and down, and with a sigh in his voice he continued, "Och, it's just that I expected you when you were a boy. But never mind, it's nice to meet you and to see you climb. Well, and you would have climbed many mountains harder than this if you had come earlier. Anyway, what is past is past and what is to come is to come. Now you just sit there and have a wee rest. This cloud will clear in a moment and you will have wonderful views when you go on to the summit."

With that, Aonghas turned on his heel into the mist and

towards the summit. Donnie could still make him out as he went along a path and through a gateway in the wall. 'Wall?' queried Donnie of his senses. 'What is a wall doing on top of a mountain? And what is that gap that looks like a gateway?' The thought of 'the gateway to heaven guarded by Saint Peter'...or whoever guarded the gateway to the other place... was too much for the exhausted Donnie, so he laid his head down to have a little sleep. Perhaps when he awoke there would be no wall...there would be no gateway... there would be no mountain.

*
**

"So, after I had a little sleep I followed Angus along the track to the summit. There <u>was</u> a wall, and a gateway; the old iron gate was lying beside it. But when I got to the summit...there was no Angus. I searched around the top but there was no place he could have gone."

Donnie ended his telling thus and looked at his Crannog audience. Roy and Henry had heard it before when a dishevelled but exhilarated Donnie had slithered at speed down the mountain towards them. They had been looking forward to telling him of their fishing expertise that had led to a final tally of two fine fish each and with Roy arguing that another big one he lost at the landing net should also count. But Donnie had only wanted to recount his own tale. Of course they had to interrogate Donnie's reality, with Roy inquiring how much whisky he had taken up with him and Henry asking if he had hit his head at any time.

The rest of Donnie's Crannog audience consisted of Anthony, Jock and an even older man called Duncan who had come along with Jock and who only spoke the Gaelic. When Jock had entered with Duncan at his side, the contingent of locals all stood up in apparent reverence and surprise at Duncan's arrival. Of course, the same large whisky had been put in front of Duncan as well as Jock.

Roy was the first to break the silence following Donnie's story. "What's that about there being a wall on top of the mountain; you don't get walls on top of mountains!"

Jock looked at Roy. "On top of Suilven you do. It is a dry stone wall that continues in bits and pieces down the south side. Landowners used to mark their boundaries with iron fences but Suilven has a stone wall. Imagine the poor estate workers being told to build a stone wall over a mountain."

Jock then began the serious interrogation of Donnie's tale. "Tell me the actual words that Aonghas said to you."

Donnie paused to remember. "He said that my climb in the conditions had been courageous...and that I had all the moves of a young man. He said that he was pleased to meet me though I was very late. He kept saying that I was late."

Jock and Duncan exchanged glances but said nothing.

Donnie continued. "He called me 'the mountaineer of Assynt' more than once, but I said that that made no sense, because it wasn't even a real climb."

Jock, with some impatience in his voice, challenged Donnie. "What were his **exact words** about you being 'the mountaineer of Assynt'?"

Donnie tried harder to remember. "He said, 'Nevertheless, it is the mountaineer of Assynt that you are and that you have always been, though you are a little late'." Then he went on to say that he had expected me when I was a boy and that I would have climbed many mountains harder than Suilven, if I had come earlier."

Jock sat back in his seat, as did Duncan. Leaning over towards his friend, Jock whispered in the Gaelic, "Tha mi smaoineachadh gun do thachair e ri Aonghas a Asaint." (*I am thinking that he has met Aonghas of Assynt*). Duncan nodded and added, "Agus bho'n rud a thuirt Aonghas ris, 's e mo bharail gu bheil beath' an duine bochd air dhol seachad air." (*And from what Aonghas has said to him I am thinking that the poor man has missed his life*).

33. REFLECTIONS

Roy was poaching his 'first earlies'. The real benefit of an allotment is not the amount of fruit and vegetables you grow, but the quality. These early potatoes are sweet and their skins are so fine that they do not need to be peeled. Roy had discovered that it was not necessary to dig up whole plants in order to harvest his earlies. It was possible to 'poach' one or two from each plant. He would slip his hand into the loose soil of the earthed-up plant and gently feel around the roots until a specimen of sufficient proportions was located. He could then pinch the tuber off the root without otherwise affecting the plant. Indeed, Roy had a theory that this poaching technique actually encouraged the plant to put more energy into growing the remaining offspring.

"So, Sheila, we are going to set up an experiment. We are going to do all our poaching from this row and leave this other one untouched. We are going to keep a record of the weight of potatoes we poach. Then, when we later dig up the whole crop, we are going to compare the weight of potatoes we get from each of these two rows. Then, of course, we will have to add in to the tally of the first row the weight of potatoes we have previously poached from it. Sheila, I see you raising your eyes to the sky as though I am talking gibberish. I suppose it is a 'boy's thing' that I am on about again, but you wait until my experiment on the poaching of potatoes is mentioned in Alan Titchmarsh's gardening programme."

After his poaching, weighing and recording, Roy moved to his carrots. "Ochone, ochone, the carrot fly is beginning to appear again. The garlic did not work; perhaps the carrot fly is partial to garlic! Give it a couple of weeks and the crop will be decimated. When that carrot fly gets into your soil you can never get rid of it."

Thinking of the carrot fly took Roy on to a consideration of his friend. "It's like Donnie; something got into his soil a long time ago and he has never been able to get it out. He tries all sorts of things, but the disease is deep in his soil. But he is also a strong man; he is never giving up. He is like a terrier; he hangs on no matter what."

Thinking of Donnie took Roy to Henry. "Henry is different; Henry lost something a long while ago and he can never get it back. Henry is living his life with something missing at his centre." And from Henry, Roy's reflections had to come to himself. "And so am I living with something missing at my centre."

**

Henry was enjoying one of his by now regular afternoon teas with his sister. "So, I have started it," said Amanda with a forced coldness in her voice. "I have told Derek that I am leaving him."

Henry nodded; he knew that his sister would not have been deflected in her resolve once her mind was made up. "How did he take it?"

"Like a spoiled little boy," declared Amanda. "He had absolutely no idea it was even on the cards. He shouted a lot and said that I could not leave him, but there was no semblance of love in it. It was as though I was a possession that he was in danger of losing. Eventually he said that I was not going to leave him; it was him that was throwing me out and that he had another relationship anyway. I said that that was OK but it would be better if he gave it to me in writing so that there was no misunderstanding."

Henry looked bemused. "That seems a strange thing to say; why did you ask him to put it in writing?"

Amanda smiled. "Oh my dear brother, you are such an innocent in this world. I have spent the last few weeks separating all my assets so that he will not be able to get his hands on them, but if he puts in writing that he is throwing me out and that he has been having an affair, I will have a good basis for a claim against **him**."

Henry shook his head and smiled. "Do you think that he will send the letter?"

"If he does it quickly while he is still in his 'spoiled little boy', then he will. But if he talks to his lawyer first, he won't."

Amanda's analysis was succinct, but then she changed the subject. "Anyway, I don't want to talk about me, or far less about Derek, I want to hear about you. Are you coming with me to Bolivia?"

Henry suddenly faced the kind of challenge that contact with Amanda had made him aware was possible. He could talk around things without showing himself, or he could speak as honestly as he could and trust that their relationship would take it. He went with honesty.

"I am scared by your question. Immediately I realise that it raises the fundamental difficulty I have with living. I suppose, really...I am scared of living...of going to the edge...of doing things that might matter. Instead, I make a game out of living. I live through the game I make of betting. I get lots of excitement from that every day...a huge array of feelings... big personal challenges...and a considerable sense of achievement. But it is a 'game'...it does not mean anything...I don't even do anything with the money I make. I just 'collect' it in the fashion of the stamp collector gathering stamps. The game can give me that sense of living at the edge, but it is not real. I could stop it one day and invent another game the next. Your question, 'will I come to Bolivia', faces me with my question...can I come out of playing games and live for real?"

"And can you?" asked Amanda, desperately trying to suppress all the feeling she had behind this question. Henry must make his own decision.

Henry paused and that gave Amanda her answer. "Poor Henry...poor dear Henry...of course you can't...not yet anyway. I love you so much that I keep pushing you, but I will always love you anyway."

Henry looked at her and his eyes filled so that he put his

hands up in front of his face. Amanda came off her chair and moved round to hug him and caress his hair. The tearoom looked on at the lovers.

**

Donnie had established a new regime in his life built around discipline. Instead of his former approach that required jobs to be left until a month after they should be done and then forgetting most of them anyway, his new regime required him to make a list of jobs with expected completion dates. Some jobs were daily, like washing his dishes; others, like laundry, were weekly; while paying bills was monthly. Another monthly activity was to write to Donald. It would not be too many months before they met and Donnie did not want to leave the whole job of finding out about each other until then. Donald had picked up on his father's initiative and typically would send his own letter a week after receiving his father's. As Donnie began to write, his reflections were not of past events but of his present experience.

> Dear Donald,
> It seems strange to think of a man of sixty five years changing but that is certainly happening to me. We were both surprised by my writing to you but that was just the start because I am finding that a lot is different in me. I seem to have grown up a lot. All my life people told me to grow up. It is a stupid thing to say to anyone but they were right about me. Every time anything went wrong I would become a child again. I was usually a hurt child a scared child or an angry child. Often I was all three. Recently I have not been like that. I have been more like a grown up. When something goes wrong now I think of how I can fix it. Or when I feel something

difficult I address it rather than just retreat. I am also more organised like I keep my flat clean and do my washing regularly. I even painted a room last week. One of the things I have found about being an adult is that you have more feelings more real feelings. A lot of the feelings I would have like feeling sad or angry or guilty were not real feelings. They were places to hide. They were places to hide from what was really happening there and then. Hiding meant that I didnt really have to face anything and nothing could change. I was like the mountain climber who would always quit when things got difficult. Now I am a mountaineer who looks for another route when things get difficult. It feels funny to grow up. Also its not all good. Some things hurt more now.

34. MAUREEN RETURNS

"Rosie, the last thing I want to do is to 'make an entrance' like some second rate movie star."

Rosie rearranged her face into a dismissive expression, which she would never have dared to use in her earlier relationship with Maureen. "Maureen, right, let's get this straight; you are not going to slink in there like you are apologising for coming back. The Culloden is your queendom and you are going to stride in there like the monarch that you are. You are going to be more than you were not less than you are. You are not a 'second rate movie star'; you are our first rate bar manager. Besides, they are all expecting you and they are all wanting to treat you like their first rate person."

"But I don't feel 'first rate' at all," protested Maureen.

Rosie was undeterred, "We have talked about that before; how being away for a time and having a big operation can dent your confidence. Even your doctor warned you about that. But if you give into those weak feelings you will just make it all the longer before you get your confidence back. Now, let's go over again how you will handle the half hour that you will be in there. Do you remember what we planned?"

"Yes Rosie," said Maureen, not really believing that Rosie would let her off with such a cryptic response.

"So, take me through it once more," commanded Rosie.

Maureen sighed and repeated what they had rehearsed.

Rosie had decided that Maureen should make her big entrance at 8.00pm but only stay until 8.30. This would cover her re-entry, but minimise the possibility of questions from the customers. The next day she would be on the lunchtime and evening shifts with Rosie as usual and her absence would be regarded as a thing of the past that merited no further comment. Rosie had also spoken with the regulars, telling them about the 8.00 to 8.30 slot and threatening them with severe injury if they dared to ask Maureen anything about her absence.

At the appointed time, with Rosie behind the bar glancing nervously at her watch, Maureen entered from the back room. She was made up to the hilt and wearing the kind of new outfit that automatically makes a woman feel like a star. As she opened the door she had donned as big a smile as she thought she could maintain for the half hour. But that smile was nearly shattered when she came through the door to find the bar full to bursting. Even punters who came only a few times a year were there to honour her. The bar and every table were decorated with fresh flowers brought by customers and there were three gigantic platters of cakes baked by Henry. The assembled company belted out 'three cheers for Maureen' and one of the younger regulars, who was said to have won a gold medal at the 'Mod', the annual festival of Gaelic singing, gave a rendition of Burns' *My Love is Like a Red Red Rose*, after which his five year old daughter presented Maureen with a bouquet of red roses. Maureen remembered her mascara and resisted tears.

She spent the half hour going round the company, having at least a word with everyone; generally asking them a question to pre-empt them questioning her. Rosie saw everything without once seeming to look. She had a lump of emotion in her throat because she knew the bravery of her friend. She knew that it would be a long time and many tests before Maureen might get the 'all clear'. She knew that her friend was enduring this uncertainty every day. She knew that Maureen was living a continual nightmare of checking every sensation in her body. She knew that the worst moments were those mornings when Maureen woke up and, for a few seconds had forgotten her nightmare; only to remember again.

"So Maureen is back with us" said Henry to acknowledge the event.

"Yes, and she has survived breast cancer to do it," replied Roy.

"Is that true? I didn't know that," chipped Donnie.

"No, and you are not supposed to know it either. So you had better forget that you know it in case you accidentally let Maureen know that you know it," instructed Roy.

"I understand boss...I think," added Donnie in mock humble fashion.

35. THE PASSPORT OFFICE

"You mean that you sent it back without checking it...and you didn't correct the bits that we made up...or enclose a note about them?"

Henry was coming out in hot flushes at the thought of imprisonment. Donnie had just informed him that he had received a letter from the Passport Office asking him to come for an interview. He further disclosed that, a few days after Henry had helped him to complete the on-line passport application, they had mailed him a hard copy of his completed form with a request that he check and return it to them. Donnie had simply returned it and sought to justify that to a horrified Henry.

"But I still didn't know the right answers to their stupid questions; I didn't know where my mother was born, or my father's birthday, or when they were married. I thought we were going to sort that out at the interview."

In his pause for thought Henry considered possibilities like simply withdrawing the application. But Donnie would still need to get a passport to go to Argentina. Anyway, they would have already investigated the facts in the application and found the errors, so they would likely involve the police. Perhaps if Donnie were to die before next week's interview it would leave Henry in the clear, but that seemed just a bit harsh.

Henry concluded, "We'll just have to come clean with them at the interview. I'll do the talking. I'll explain that we couldn't just leave those fields blank because the form did not let us move on without them being completed. I'll tell them that we meant to explain it in a covering letter when we returned the hard copy, but we forgot. I'm sure that I can talk them round; I'm good at that."

On arrival at the Passport Office they encountered their first problem when they met the receptionist. She was not to be 'talked round' by Henry.

"As I have already said sir, there is absolutely no possibility that you can join Mr Anderson in the interview room. The interview is an entirely private event."

Henry had not panicked all morning – yes he had been a trifle anxious and a little tetchy with Donnie a couple of times, but now he was panicking. The thought of leaving Donnie on his own with the interviewer certainly merited panic.

He tried another tack. "But there must be circumstances when a helper is allowed in the interview room; what if the applicant is a minor... or if he has learning difficulties?"

The receptionist was savouring this rare opportunity for revenge on at least two members of her hated public. She looked at Donnie as she answered Henry. "Excuse me sir, but this man is definitely older than sixteen."

She tried to reduce her sneer to a minimum without much success.

Henry was blubbering by now. "OK, but what about the 'learning difficulties' example; surely they are allowed a helper in the interview?"

Henry realised from his adversary's widening smirk that there was some hole in his logic, though he felt briefly encouraged by the start of her rejoinder.

"Indeed they are sir, indeed they are..."

She looked at Donnie as she delivered her killer blow to Henry. "Your friend with learning difficulties could certainly have had a helper with him at the interview, but that would have had to be agreed in advance and the disability evidenced."

Henry bowed his head in abject defeat and took his seat alongside Donnie in the waiting area.

Twenty minutes after the scheduled time for the interview Donnie was called. Henry tried to regain his functioning and offered guidance to Donnie. "Just tell them what happened; that we had difficulty with the on-line form filling. Tell then that I'm out here and can explain."

Donnie nodded and followed the receptionist's directions

towards the interview room. He felt strangely unflustered, certainly compared to Henry. In the past he would have been so scared that he would have run down the corridor in the other direction, out into the street and on to the first bus to anywhere. Yes, he was not looking forward to this interview business, but he was not really frightened by it. He wondered what had happened to his fear. He knocked on the door and was kept waiting too long before being ushered in. Walking towards the suited interviewer behind a desk, Donnie said, "Good morning," and offered a handshake that was ignored.

An hour later Henry asked the receptionist if the interview usually took this long.

"No, not at all; this is a very long one," she answered, delighting at the squirming victim in front of her and imagining a similar fate for the other one.

Fifteen minutes later a suit came into the reception area and spoke quietly to the receptionist before moving across the room to Henry.

"Mr Doncaster, will you come with me?"

Henry recognised the conscious use of power in the complete lack of clarification to accompany the question. There was no indication of where he was being asked to go to, and for what, or by whom. Yet, Henry also knew that there was some justification for his being treated with such minimal respect so, without comment, he followed the suit out of the room and down the corridor. As he entered the interview room he could smell what had been going on. He could smell Donnie's re-emerged fear. The suit moved behind the desk to sit beside Donnie's interviewer while, without the courtesy of an invitation, Henry pulled a straight backed chair from the side of the room and settled down beside a sweating Donnie whose frightened darting eyes had returned. Both suits sat with their thumbs on the desk and their fingers tucked underneath the edge. Henry wondered if there were panic buttons located under the edge.

"My colleague was having a little trouble with this interview and we thought that you might be able to clarify some points," began the suit who had escorted Henry.

Obviously this suit was the boss of the other suit, so Henry reckoned he could forget the other one and concentrate on the boss. He was interested to see his anxiety decreasing now that he had the possibility to exert some control on the situation. Henry was good at 'cool' in difficult situations; after all, his betting exploits demanded considerable cool every day. He decided to give boss suit his place and his power, while not losing his own. They just had to do some 'business' together.

Henry smiled and nodded. "Yes, I'm sure that I can clarify things. You must have found the application 'unusual'."

This wording was intended to be a disarming beginning in so far as it acknowledged there was a problem with the application, so that boss suit was given that victory right away. But Henry's use of the word 'unusual' was a considered one. It reflected his attempt to define the reality of the event. In any conflict setting the victor is usually the one who succeeds in defining the reality. So, 'unusual' acknowledged the difficulty but in a fashion that did not ascribe wrongdoing, whereas words like 'problematic' or 'concerning' would have added wrongdoing to the definition of reality.

Henry continued, "Basically, I was helping Mr Anderson with the online application. Hah! I was helping him because I thought I knew more about online stuff! In fact, as it turned out, I didn't know as much as I thought…"

Henry was pleased with this start because, straight away, he was accepting all the responsibility and defining it in terms of his lack of ability, rather than wait for the suits to define it in terms of criminality. Henry knew that this opening statement was critical. If he could get it all out before they interrupted he could present them with a gift wrapped package that they could accept as an explanation and which emphasised their superiority over these incompetents.

Henry continued, "We had some blanks in Donnie's memory of his parents' dates and I couldn't work out how to enter these on the online form. I couldn't leave them blank because they were required fields and when I tried to enter something like 'don't know' it did not accept that as a date. I'm sure that it was my stupidity; I'm not that good with computers myself..." Junior suit shot a sideways glance to his boss, but the boss ignored him and stayed looking at Henry. Henry noticed the weakness; obviously they knew that there were problems with the on-line process. Someone of lesser skill would have gone on the offensive, blaming the inadequacies of the online process. But Henry knew that aggression is dangerous when you are in the less powerful position. It is too easy for the opposition to counter with even greater threat. Better, Henry thought, to give the suits the opportunity to hide the website inadequacies by accepting these customers' self-definitions of incompetence and see them conveniently out of the door.

So Henry continued, "What I meant to do was to enclose a letter of explanation along with the hard copy of the form when you sent that to us. When, only the other day, I realised that Donnie had sent the hard copy back to you without our explanation I was horrified and thought that the only thing that I could do was to come along today to explain."

Henry sat back, still looking squarely but deferentially at boss suit. He knew that he had already beaten junior suit, but bosses sometimes feel the need to show off their power, especially in the presence of their underlings. These next few moments of silence were important to allow boss suit to accept the terms.

Suddenly Henry became aware that Donnie was about open his mouth. That certainly must not happen, so Henry firmly exerted as much force as he could on his heel that was positioned nicely on top of Donnie's toes. Donnie must have got Henry's whole message because he took the pain without making a sound.

Boss suit spoke. "You have given us a great deal of trouble Mr Doncaster."

Henry interrupted. "I am sure that I have sir; I was thinking while I was in reception that you have probably spent a lot of time trying to trace Donnie's identity through these inaccurate entries on the form. I am truly sorry for that waste of your staff's time and your own."

Surely boss suit must accept this grovelling, but Henry thought that it might cap things nicely if he could introduce a new element which would help boss suit to agree the way out. "There is something else that is relevant, something that Donnie would be reluctant to raise himself. But I am sure that he can trust your discretion. Donnie has difficulty with questions about his father. While you or I would certainly remember our father's birthday and our parents' anniversary, anything to do with Donnie's father has been blocked out long ago."

Henry bowed his head slightly and softened his voice, "Blocked out by his father's continual beatings of him and his mother. Eventually Donnie joined the army to get away from his father."

Surely this was game, set and match, thought Henry, ignoring Donnie's glaring at him. Boss suit looked at his junior who nodded back as though he understood the unvoiced question.

"There is another way we can get enough information to confirm Mr Anderson's identity; we can get it through his army records."

Henry kicked himself for never thinking about that, but did not forget to close the meeting. "Of course... brilliant... I'm really sorry that we have wasted so much of your time."

Donnie spoke for the first time to give the suits the date he entered the army and his ID number.

Henry looked at Donnie. "How on earth do you remember those?"

"A soldier never forgets his date and his number," replied Donnie.

Henry and Donnie left the building.

"They were OK when you came in but they were really hard on me before that," complained Donnie as they walked to the bus stop.

Henry could not believe his ears. "And did you not see **why** they became OK? Did you not see my genius in disarming them?"

Donnie thought for a moment and said, "No."

36. HENRY'S NIGHTMARE

Lying in bed, Henry felt pleased with himself as he thought about the Passport Office event a couple of weeks previously. Obviously, in retirement, he had not lost any of his sharpness, though recurring dreams about the receptionist were disturbing. He continued to be unsettled about his last meeting with Amanda. Her challenge to him about radically changing his life had met an honest response and she had accepted what he had said and loved him nonetheless. Yet, did he have to be so scared to leave his comfortable but predictable life? Would it not be exciting to cash in and move on, with Amanda, to Bolivia? Wasn't such a challenge just the kind of thing he needed? The rational side of Henry noted that he knew absolutely nothing about Bolivia, so he googled it on his bedroom laptop to be displayed on his smaller thirty-six inch bedroom monitor on the opposite wall. A later page led him to earthquakes in neighbouring Chile and he followed that through to previous seismic events in Christchurch, New Zealand. Henry deemed this to be important research for their fantasy trip and was surprised to learn about 'liquefaction' and also how some people had survived quakes by sheltering under tables, beds and such things. Around this point surfing gave way to dreaming and it was difficult to know the difference.

Henry awoke to the sound and the vibrations of his building collapsing in an earthquake. Remembering the advice, he dived under his bed. The crashing continued and intensified until it was right inside his room.

A voice rang out above the earthquake. "This is police armed response. Come out with your arms in front of you immediately!"

Henry wondered if his television was still on and whether a movie was getting mixed up with the earthquake. At this point he found himself being dragged out, feet first, from beneath his bed. The movie must, somehow, have taken over his room;

perhaps this was a 3D trial transmission he wondered vainly.

The human brain always seeks to make what sense it can of its experiencing. That is what Henry's brain was endeavouring to achieve in those first moments of his arrest. After being dragged from under his bed Henry tried to struggle to his feet. Perhaps there is an instinct in the biped to achieve the standing position when under threat. If so, that instinct was contraindicated in Henry's present circumstances as he felt two small pricks in his chest heralding fifty thousand volts through his body.

Though fifty thousand volts sounds a lot, the amperage generated by the Taser is small and death is only rarely the result. But it did give the sixty-four year old Henry quite a turn, with his eyes bulging, his tongue lolling about and his legs feeling like jelly and crumpling underneath him. He passed out as much with emotional as electric shock.

He awoke in another dream. In the dream the bells were ringing. What bells? The bells of doom? He was in a small space, lying on a minimal bed with no covers. He was wearing a one piece thin zipped-up garment made of 'shell suit' material and his wrists were handcuffed in front of him. The space was about eight feet by twelve. It had no windows but there was a light built in to the ceiling behind a strong looking plastic guard. As Henry inspected his dream he noted two cameras built high up on the walls, also behind plastic guards. On the floor beside his bunk there was a plastic vessel with what appeared to be water and on the other side of the room there was another vessel into which the water could be placed once his body was finished with it.

Henry remembered the old TV series, 'The Prisoner', with the actor Patrick McGoohan. Each week McGoohan would be presented with the possibility of escape from 'The Island', but every time he would be thwarted. Henry wondered if this was the TV programme that was on in his bedroom, but as time passed he reckoned that his dream had ended and he was now in a conscious nightmare. Whatever the reality or the unreality, there was no further prospect of sleep.

Some hours later – how many it was impossible to judge – his cell door opened and three uniformed policemen entered. Without saying a word his upper arms were gripped firmly by two of them and he was walked out of the cell, along the corridor and down one flight of stairs. The third policeman knocked on the door in front of them and they were immediately ushered into a small room. There were two men in the room, both in plain clothes and sitting on one side of a small table set against the longer left hand wall. One of the men looked about forty and the other was more like sixty; quite old for a policeman thought Henry. Presumably he must be high ranking or he would have been pensioned off by now. On a shelf above the table there were some electrics, probably for audio recording. The right hand long wall was entirely black Perspex. Henry recognised this as a one-way-vision set up. There would be other police sitting behind the Perspex. So long as their room was in darkness and the interview room was bright they would be able to see everything but would be invisible themselves. Henry smirked; 'so they can't afford half silvered mirror glass, just the poorer quality black Perspex,' he thought.

Two of the uniforms stood on either side of the door and the other left the room.

"Good Morning Mr Doncaster" said the elder detective, ushering Henry to sit at one of the two chairs on the other side of the desk.

"I am Detective Chief Superintendent Roger Dingwall of the Specialist Crime Division and this is Detective Inspector Roderick Mitchell."

The senior policeman paused briefly until Henry was seated.

"You will understand that we need to ask you a number of questions. But first I have to inform you that you have been arrested under the Terrorism Acts of 2000 and 2006. You do not have to say anything, but it may harm your defence if you fail to mention something when questioned that you later rely on in court. Anything you do say may be used in evidence against you."

In a different tone of voice the Superintendent addressed the ether. "I am now switching on the audio recording... present in the room is myself Chief Superintendent Roger Dingwall, Inspector Roderick Mitchell, Constables Ritchie and Henderson, and the interviewee, Mr Henry Doncaster. Mr Doncaster has been cautioned."

Henry stayed calm though he wanted to scream. What was this about? The Terrorism Acts? How on earth?

Top Cop continued. "At this point I want to offer you your one and only escape from this situation. Please pay serious attention to what I have to say because it will give you the chance to work **with** me rather than against me. In fact, Mr Doncaster, I sincerely believe that you are a victim in this matter and I want to work with you on that basis. The last thing I want is for them to whisk you down to Paddington... you know about Paddington Mr Doncaster?"

"I know that Paddington police station in London is where many terrorist suspects are taken for interview," replied Henry.

"Yes, though it looks nothing like a police station as we know it; dreadful place in my view. Now, there is some urgency in this opportunity that I am giving you because the top brass from Paddington are getting into Glasgow airport as we speak. I only need one thing from you to enable me to hold on to you rather than give you up to them. Mr Doncaster, simply tell me who you have been working for."

Despite his barely restrained panic, Henry's mind was now working. But that did not materially assist him. Helping the Passport Office suits towards a convenient concept of reality was one thing. But these senior police; this was quite a different prospect. This was the real deal. Henry actually entertained the thought that, if he was truly guilty of something, he would positively grasp the opportunity to confess. In fact it was mildly attractive to confess anyway.

Henry could see that Top Cop was playing a game of 'Good Cop – Bad Cop'. He was the nice, even warm, fatherly figure really wanting to help Henry who would otherwise be thrown to the Paddington Gestapo. Henry reckoned that bit about the Gestapo already being at the airport was certainly inserted to induce hurried panic; probably they were watching this opening gambit from the next room.

Noting the fact that the audio and presumably video of his responses could be used at a later time, Henry decided to present the image of a poor old honest citizen not understanding why he was being so abused. He adopted the frail voice of an old man and said, in a polite tone, "I'm awful sorry Superintendent Dingwall, sir. I really want to help in any way I can; really I do sir...but I have no idea what this is about. All I remember is being dragged out of my bed by lots of police with guns and getting knocked out somehow."

Henry was pleased with this beginning; they wouldn't be able to use that recording against him, with the police being portrayed as abusing a frail old age pensioner.

Roger Dingwall looked back at Henry, feeling slightly irked that this old guy had reduced his rank from Chief Superintendent to Superintendent and wondering if there might be more to him than the way he portrayed himself. That fitted of course, because someone in Doncaster's position would be well trained in handling interrogation. Maybe the old guy was trying to play with him; perhaps he had reduced his rank on purpose. The Chief Superintendent continued, also 'playing to the camera' a little so that the Paddington boys could see his skill.

"I'm sorry that you are putting on this 'frail old man' act. We both know how accomplished you are in the world of international finance."

Henry reckoned that he was slightly ahead on points and might even win this first round, so he continued his act. "I'm sorry Superintendent; I really don't have a clue what you are talking about. I'm not in 'international finance'; I am a pensioner and I used to work for a haulage firm. The only 'finance' I get into is betting on the horses."

Someone watching from the darkened adjoining room behind the black Perspex screen let out a slight giggle that was heard by all inside. One of the Paddington officers in that room whispered at a level that did not travel, "Old Dingaling is getting beat up by a pensioner." Among themselves the Paddington police usually referred to Chief Superintendent Roger Dingwall as 'Dingaling' to mark their lack of respect for the man whose high rank they attributed to his Masonic Order connections.

"Get him out of there," instructed the senior Paddington officer, Chief Inspector Aldo Perretti.

Henry was surprised that the Chief Superintendent was called away so quickly, just as he was preparing for the second round. As he sat in silence looking around the interview room, Henry had a word with himself. 'What a silly man you are. You are in a dreadful situation here, but you are still playing games.' Henry often talked to himself and enjoyed the different parts of him that emerged, like the voice in reply, 'I'm not being silly...doing it this way helps me feel just a tiny bit of control...I need to feel that...it keeps me sharp... anyway, it's good fun.'

The door opened and an imposing figure walked in. He was tall and slim with short but styled black hair and dressed in a charcoal suit of expensive cloth and Italian cut. His shiny black shoes, also Italian, were of that fine calf hide that is illegal to produce in Britain.

"You won't be kicking me with those good shoes," thought Henry bizarrely.

The entrant switched on the recording and said, "Chief Inspector Aldo Perretti entering the room."

'Mmhm,' thought Henry '... hence the Italian suit and shoes.'

Perretti's studied entrance meant that he did not have to introduce himself to the criminal. He always found ways to avoid introducing himself to criminals because that falsely raised their authority. Perretti liked to keep thinking of them as criminals and the lowest of the low so that he would remember to treat them that way. He looked across the desk at Henry and said absolutely nothing.

Henry looked back but his damned eye flickered. He cursed it because that would have told Perretti that he felt frightened of him.

Satisfied that he had got the criminal where he wanted him, Perretti began to speak in a London accent with only a tinge of Italian from two generations back. "We have lots of time Mr Doncaster; lots and lots of time."

Perretti leaned back in his chair and folded his arms. Henry knew that it was time to stop playing games.

"I want to phone my lawyer and I want to phone one other friend," he said, looking seriously at his new and more dangerous adversary.

Perretti leaned forward and took a pen with his notebook out of his pocket. "What are their names, addresses and phone numbers?"

Henry gave details for Mr Macsween and also Roy, then paused. "I can't remember their phone numbers."

"No need," said Perretti. "We can track those down."

After a short pause the Chief Inspector looked long at Henry and spoke slowly. "I find it interesting to see that you know that our usual practice would allow you to contact your lawyer and also one other person. Normal citizens might know about the lawyer from TV shows, but not about the other person."

Henry tried to look strong. "I read books," he said.

Aldo Perretti gave the criminal his well-developed piercing stare. He had already found that this criminal was weak to the stare and confidently exerted its full power. Moving into his best funereal tone, Chief Inspector Aldo Perretti delivered his blow. "I need to make sure that you understand your position Mr Doncaster. You are arrested under the Terrorism Acts of 2000 and 2006. Under Schedule 5 of the 2000 Act, as amended by Section 26 of the 2006 Act, the local police obtained a warrant to enter your premises at 5.30 this morning to detain you and to seize and retain material that we have grounds to believe may be of substantial value to a terrorist investigation. I am having a list drawn up for you of what we have taken. We have searched you under the terms of Schedule 43 of the 2000 Act and we are considering charging you under Schedule 18 of that Act. Furthermore, under Section 23 of the 2006 Act, we may detain you for up to twenty-eight days before charging you. I am now going to allow you to return to your cell to have a rest and to think about your position for two hours before I interview you fully. Your lawyer will not be present at that interview, nor will we have informed your friend. In these circumstances we may deny these rights for up to forty-eight hours...though it might not take that long. Do you understand?"

"Yes," replied Henry softly.

Perretti leaned forward and emphasised his dominance. "I did not hear you Mr Doncaster."

"Yes," said Henry as loudly as his fear would permit.

37. THE INTEROGATION

On re-entering his cell Henry's first feeling was one of comfort; at least this was a familiar hellish place. He thought that if he had been trying to break a man down he would have put him into a new, but even bleaker cell. He lay down on what passed for the bed and considered his situation. Perretti was good; he had succeeded in making Henry scared of him. Henry knew that he had lost the first round with him. He had also lost a lot of his bravado. But the denial of his rights to support irked him seriously and helped him to get back on track. Henry spoke to himself sternly. 'Henry Doncaster, you are becoming a weakling. You want to roll over and show your belly when you should be using this time to get your act together; now concentrate for goodness sake!"

Then the bells came again to make Henry shiver. What did they portent? He smiled and shook his head at his frailty. The neighbouring church bells merely told him that it was a quarter past the hour and that he could use them to track time despite his confiscated watch.

 Henry addressed his task. His first consideration was the questions to which **he** wanted answers. Certainly there were the big questions like *Why am I here?* and *What do they think I have done?* This led him to a logical subsidiary question, *Have I in fact done something illegal of which I am not aware?* He was also interested in *Why did Perretti give me this two hours break?* He was strongly attracted to tackle these questions first, but he realised that they were not the priority areas in these first two hours of thinking. The urgent question he had to answer was *What position do I adopt in this next interrogation?*

Perretti had said that he would interview Henry fully. That might mean this would be a very long interview. Henry did not know if there were rules governing such interrogations, but he reckoned that they would want to make good use of the rest of these first forty-eight hours when his lawyer was not present, so perhaps he should prepare for a forty-four hour session.

Henry applied himself fully to his preparations, first deciding the orientation he would adopt, then testing it against the kind of challenges that Perretti might employ. With one roll of church bells left he felt satisfied that he was as prepared as he could be, given his lack of information and experience. He wanted to turn, in these last fifteen minutes, to the question, *Why am I here?* but his session was cut short by the arrival of his three guards. He needed to remember that while Perretti made the timings, he could also change them at will.

Henry sat in his chair, alone except for the two constables at the door, for twenty-five minutes before Perretti arrived, preceded by a new person to the scene. Perretti ignored Henry and spoke to the recording. "Chief Inspector Aldo Perretti and Detective Sergeant Joanna Henson entering the room."

Henry timed his opening gambit such that he spoke at the very moment Perretti sat down and turned to face him. "Excuse me Chief Inspector Perretti; may I ask a question?" Henry thought that it would not be a good tactic to reduce Perretti's rank as he had done with Dingwall.

"It sounds as though you are asking a question anyway, Mr Doncaster."

"Yes sir, sorry about that. Do you mind if I have a cup of tea and if that is not convenient, a cup of water? I am very dehydrated."

Perretti raised his eyebrow and wondered if it had been a mistake to give this criminal the usual two hours stewing time for first offenders; he seemed to have used it to compose himself and prepare.

"Of course Mr Doncaster; you should have been given a cup of tea in your cell."

Speaking directly to his table microphone, Perretti said "Bring Mr Doncaster a cup of tea with a biscuit and plenty water."

Henry found it interesting that Perretti had dispensed with the pretence that there was no one listening in the adjoining room.

Henry put in place the second part of his programme. "I have a second question, if that is acceptable."

Perretti had a fundamental confidence in his ability, which Chief Superintendent Dingwall lacked, so he was content to go along with what the criminal had obviously planned in his two hours. Indeed, the plan would tell him something about the criminal. In any case it was inconceivable that the criminal could win any advantage because his power in this situation was absolutely zero.

"Feel free," replied Perretti folding his arms across his chest.

Henry had asked the two easy questions that were only designed to get his adversary into a habit of acceding. Without them Perretti might have felt that he should think more carefully about his response to Henry's next question. Henry coughed slightly and asked his question.

"May I begin our session by making a statement on the record? I think that it may save some of our time."

Again, this seemed to be a small request in Perretti's view, though he did pause on it. Of course he had to go with the request; after all, the 'saving time' reference suggests that it may be at least a partial confession. Perretti knew that once a criminal gave some ground, then it was easy to pull him all the way.

"Of course you may; everything in here is on the record."

It may seem that Henry had made only small gains, but he knew that he could use this ground to protect the position he would maintain, perhaps throughout the next forty-four hours.

He began his discourse. "I need to explain my position. I have no idea what this is about and I had expected that I would be assisted in that ignorance by my solicitor. Finding that he may not be permitted to support me for forty-eight hours means that I have no alternative but to refuse to answer every question that is put to me. Of course, it would be impolite simply to ignore your questions, so I will acknowledge each one and refer you to this opening statement. I will maintain that same response through every single question, no matter how straightforward it may be. Even if you ask me my name, you will get the same answer. Only when you ask questions that relate to my present physical position, perhaps about a drink or food or sleep, will I give a different answer. Whenever I am able to consult my lawyer and when he is allowed to be present here, I will review this response policy. I need to emphasise that my position in no way reflects guilt. I know that your caution says that 'it may harm my defence if I fail to mention things under questioning that I seek to rely on later in court'. That is fair enough in normal legal circumstances, but my silence will simply denote the fact that I need legal support in this context and cannot help you without it."

Perretti smiled a genuine smile. In truth he considered that this criminal might be a worthy adversary. He knew what the criminal was doing; he was going to try to balk every single question over the next day and a half. Aldo Perretti knew how difficult it actually was to keep that up for so long and the various questions he had used in the past to weaken such resolve, like, 'Can you tell me your full name? Do you like dogs? I am told that you had sex with your sister, is that right? Are you a faggot?' Once the criminal had indignantly responded to a provocative question, and it usually did not take long, then he was on the way to being broken. But more subtle and effective than such provocative questions were acts of apparent caring such as, 'Henry, I really think that we have been giving you too hard a time; let's take a break for half an hour and have them bring us both a nice meal. We can have it in here together.' And there was always, 'Henry, I really think that we have got the wrong person, but to help me with that I just need a bit of information on...'

Perretti noted that the criminal had even thought about

how difficult it would be to survive by saying absolutely nothing; instead he had opted to refer questions to his opening statement. That was clever, because it is impossible to maintain a total silence to questions like, 'I'm sorry Henry, did you say something there?' So what had this told Perretti about the criminal? It had told him that he was up against a very intelligent and possibly well trained man.

The Detective Chief Inspector began the interview. "What is your name?"

"I refer you to my opening statement."

"Where do you live?" continued Perretti.

"I refer you to my opening statement."

"I'm sorry; what was your opening statement again?"

"You can get it from the recording."

Perretti smiled inwardly and did not say to the criminal. 'Continue as you please my clever friend, but I can outlast you, and I have some really tough questions for you in ten hours' time. Then in twenty hours' time you will be so weak that you will really need some tender loving care and I will be there to give it to you.'

38. CONFUSION IN THE CULLODEN

"But Henry definitely said that he would be in tonight," insisted Donnie. "I remember he said that we should be here to hear about his latest New Zealand plans."

Roy humped. "Him and New Zealand... I thought he had dropped that for good." Donnie continued. "There must be something wrong. Henry is reliable; he wouldn't just not turn up."

Roy silently agreed, but he was not going to be pulled into Donnie's anxiety. Instead he took out his phone and rang Henry's number. On the second ring a voice answered. "Yes? Who is this calling?"

Roy held the phone away from him, partly because he was startled by the strange woman's voice, but also to check that the number he had called was indeed Henry's.

The voice continued at considerable volume such that both Roy and Donnie could hear. "Who is this calling?"

Donnie's mild anxiety had now become an established fear. "Hang up Roy," he implored. The voice continued, "So your name is 'Roy'; and what is your surname caller?"

Roy glowered at Donnie for revealing his identity and closed the phone.

The two were in earnest discussion in an effort to make sense of this event when Maureen, aware that something was amiss, joined them.

"Henry has gone missing and there is someone in his flat...and they are probably after Roy now too," was Donnie's inadequate attempt to bring Maureen up to date with events. "Now Donnie, don't make it sound so bad." Looking at Maureen Roy explained. "All we know is that Henry was going to be in here tonight and when we phoned him someone answered the phone immediately and asked who we were."

"And you definitely dialled the correct number?" quizzed Maureen, opting for the logical explanation considering the age of the protagonists. Like two small boys being interrogated by the headmistress, Henry and Donnie nodded their heads in unison.

"Ok," said Maureen. "I'll try from the kitchen phone."

Maureen still thought that Henry and Donnie had probably called a wrong number, so she found Henry's number in the phone book and dialled it.

"Yes, who is this calling?"

"Who is this answering Henry Doncaster's home telephone?"

There was a pause, followed by the rebuttal. "I'm sorry; I cannot give you that information. What is your name caller?"

Maureen continued to assert her right to information. "Can you tell me if anything has happened to Henry? Is he all right? Has he been taken to hospital or anything like that?" Again there was a pause, followed by "No, he has not been taken to hospital. Now I need you to tell me your name?"

Maureen again countered. "Why do I need to tell you my name? By what authority do you require me to give my name?"

Maureen was pleased with this last challenge, though she was beginning to suspect that she knew the authority. Sure enough, the expected answer came.

"I am speaking on behalf of Police Scotland. We are conducting an investigation at this address. Part of that investigation is to make a list of Mr Henry Doncaster's associates. Now, you are required to give me your name and address."

Maureen put the phone down. It had been an instant decision, though she wondered if it had been a sensible one. She thought about ringing again and giving her details but instead she went back through to Roy and Donnie.

"Maybe we should leave the country; I could bring forward my Argentina trip, I have my ticket."

Donnie's panicked thinking was not helping in the discussion with Roy and Maureen. "But you do not have your passport yet," reminded Roy.

Maureen shook her head. "I definitely shouldn't have hung up on them. I think it will be better if I ring them up again."

Except when there was a premiership football match being screened, the Culloden television, though constantly switched on, provided interest only for one or two friendless customers. Hardly anyone was interested in the start of the national *News at Ten*, until one woman customer said in a raised voice, "That's here; that's just up the road!"

Heads were turned to attend to the narrative.

In a dawn raid by more than ten officers the door of the flat was broken down and the body of a white male dressed only in pyjamas was removed to a waiting van. Later the police also carried out a large quantity of electronic equipment including at least four computers. Here is a statement by Detective Chief Superintendent Roger Dingwall of the Specialised Crime Division with responsibility for Organised Crime and Counter Terrorism.

"At 5.30 this morning a man was removed to central police headquarters to assist police with on-going enquiries into activities of a terrorist nature. There will be no further statement on this matter until preliminary enquiries are complete."

As the national news switched to the next most dramatic event of the day, one of the customers was heard to say "Bloody terrorists...they're getting everywhere these days... even up our street."

Maureen's face puffed up in anger as she shouted, "That man is not a terrorist; that man is our Henry!"

At that moment the door of the Culloden was flung open and twelve armed police moved quickly to cover all parts of the pub.

39. THE POWER OF SILENCE

Henry was into the fourth phase of his plan. He had anticipated that it would not be easy to maintain a fixed response through lengthy questioning unless he could somehow switch himself off from what was happening. He had heard about terrorist suspects under interrogation finding something in the room upon which to focus and holding that object in the forefront of their attention while maintaining complete silence in the face of the bombardment of questions. Henry had elected not for complete silence but for a continual reiteration of, "I refer you to my opening statement." He had chosen this strategy for two reasons. Firstly it would appear to be a more positive response than blank silence if any parts of the tape were later to be used evidentially and secondly because he suspected that it would be more wearing on the interrogators to face this continually repeated response. But to be able to respond consistently in this way meant that he could not switch off completely. He had to at least know the points when he was expected to give his stock answer. Also, Henry wanted to catalogue the questions asked because they would certainly form the basis of later questioning when his lawyer was present. So Henry decided not to completely detach and focus on some object in the room, but instead to attend to the inside of his head. He had prepared a number of betting problems that required calculations. At this point, some twelve hours into the interrogation, Henry was working on the problem, *If a punter bets £10 on an accumulator across four horses at odds of 4/1, 11/4, 100/30 and 4/7, what does he get back if they all win?*

Meanwhile Chief Inspector Aldo Perretti was asking Henry about his finances.

"We find that you have a number of bank accounts Mr Doncaster, and not only in this country, but also in New Zealand, Canada and Gibraltar."

Henry's brain multitasked to think, 'Mmhm, funny

they haven't got Malta and Croatia,' then returned to his calculations.

"Why do you need so many accounts and in these other countries?"

Suddenly Henry blurted out, "£1276.79!"

"I beg your pardon" queried Perretti in genuine surprise.

"Sorry..." said Henry, blushing a little. "I refer you to my opening statement." He would have to try to dampen his enthusiasm when he found the solutions to his arithmetical problems.

The interrogation was not without breaks because Chief inspector Aldo Perretti was a careful and highly professional policeman. He did not get emotionally involved in cases so he was less in danger of exceeding boundaries. No one could review his cases and find examples of prisoner abuse or even harassment. Of course he harassed his 'criminals' intensely, but only within the boundaries set by interrogation protocols. Hence he would often check on the welfare of the criminal and make sure they had cups of tea, a constant supply of water, the regular availability of toilet facilities and even breaks. But he had no hesitation in asking them what their dead mother would say about their present behaviour and how far their criminality had contributed to their wife's suicide or their daughter's prostitution. He took it as a sign of progress in an interrogation when the criminal would jump to his feet and try to come across the table at him. If he had succeeded in harassing the criminal to that extent, then it would be a short time until he got them to make a fatal mistake. But terrorists were different from ordinary criminals. For a start they tended to be intelligent. Also, they were taught strategies, like how to detach emotionally.

Perretti had declared a thirty minute rest break and Henry was taken back to his cell. By this time Henry knew that he would be returned to the interview room ten minutes before the due time, but that Perretti would only come in later. Henry was making up some more problems for the next session, for example: *If I bet £3,000 on a horse at an average of 8/1 in order to force the price down, how much should I lay off at an average of 3/1 in order to balance my book such that I make exactly the same profit whether it wins or loses, and what will be that profit?* This kind of computation would challenge a maths teacher with a calculator, but Henry regularly solved it in his head while simultaneously operating four computers during his 'market manipulations'.

But Henry was becoming tired. Normally he would only put himself under stress a couple of times in a week, but this was intense and he felt the aging of his body and even of his mind as it would drift off into other perspectives on his present predicament. He had taken a stance over the issue of his lawyer not being allowed to be present. That was a principled stance but also it was a pragmatic one. He really felt intensely alone in an alien environment; he would dearly love to have some company. Also, he was having a great deal of difficulty in deciding on the right thing to do in these circumstances. Perhaps he should take the view that he was entirely innocent and therefore simply answer their questions and trust that 'right will out'. He was amused to realise that if it had been Perretti he had met at the outset, he might well have made that choice. Though Perretti was the enemy, Henry thought that he was probably a man of integrity, whereas that was not Henry's assessment of Chief Superintendent Roger Dingwall. In any case, by this stage in the process, Henry was more determined to hold on to his silence because he had been amazed at all the information the police had on him and how bad it could look from any perspective other than the truth.

Henry's tired mind drifted aimlessly in the way that prisoners' minds do. A prisoner has lots of time to think, and the subject is often one of freedom. His mind drifted to the Steve McQueen and Dustin Hoffman cult movie, *Papillon*. While the metaphor of the free to fly 'butterfly' must be an endearing one to most prisoners, Henry did not fancy years of solitary confinement eating insects. He was relieved to be taken out of his drifting state by the return of his guards.

Perretti entered the interview room in his usual way, ignoring all present and addressing only the microphone. Thereafter he sat down, tidied some papers in front of him, and, in a friendly manner, asked Henry a question. "Have you had a comfortable break Mr Doncaster?" Henry stayed true to his declared strategy by answering this question about his physical condition. "Yes, most relaxing. In fact I want to acknowledge how well my guards are treating me."

Perretti smiled – perhaps the criminal was showing a weakness – a need for relationship. "We aim to please Mr Doncaster. Now, perhaps you can help me with one little thing. It is of no particular consequence, but it is puzzling me. You see, my Glasgow colleagues are convinced either that you are the money man for a terrorist organisation or for the mob. For my part, I don't believe either of these. I think that you have become caught up in a series of circumstances that look bad when put together, but are entirely innocent. But just before I came in here my colleagues, they scoffed at me and they said, 'If he is so innocent, why was he hiding underneath his bed when we came to arrest him?' Now I am sure that there must be an innocent explanation for that Mr Doncaster. What is it?"

Henry smiled at his clever adversary.

"I refer you to my opening statement."

Perretti looked at the criminal and strongly resisted returning the smile. He liked this clever man but that would never be said in truth. Instead he would continue to wear him down. It felt slightly unsatisfactory that he could not trick the criminal but would have to physically and psychologically wear him down, but he would do that. Perretti opened his notebook and returned to his script of questions while Henry began one of his computations.

Four hours later the Chief Inspector paused and laid down his notebook.

"We have some of your friends in a room like this on

another floor."

Henry's mind stopped computing.

"They are being interviewed by Chief Superintendent Dingwall."

Henry desperately wanted to ask him the names of the friends, but he knew that this was precisely what the Chief Inspector wanted him to do, so he tried to go back to his calculations.

Perretti left a long silence, like a deep hole for Henry's fall; but eventually moved on. "Their names are Roy Fox, Donald Anderson and... now I don't seem to have the name of the woman in my notebook."

Perretti left another long silence.

"You bastard," thought Henry, imagining Perretti pulling the wings off butterflies.

Perretti continued, "It was interesting to see that there is indeed a person by the name of Donald Anderson, for that is precisely where I was next going to take this interview." Henry continued his head work, "$£k(x - 3) = £k(24 - 3x)$", while Perretti persisted.

"Mr Doncaster, can you tell me why you fraudulently sought to obtain a passport in a name other than your own, using your personal computer to make the online application and falsifying numerous statements in that application?"

"Investment of £6,750 and profit of £3,750!" replied Henry.

This was the point at which Perretti did something quite unusual. He looked at Henry Doncaster and stayed completely silent for a very long time. It was his personal invention, 'the power silence'. None of his colleagues could understand it until one day he had appointed one of them as the 'criminal' and subjected him to thirty minutes of silent staring while his colleagues watched from behind the screen. By the end of the half hour the young detective was crying and blubbering incoherently.

Similarly, Henry found the experience disturbing. He tried to stay as still as possible, simply staring at the table in front of him. He inwardly cursed himself when he took a quick glance up to find Perretti still looking at him. He tried to get back to the next problem that he had lined up, but he couldn't find it. He sought desperately to remember one of the others and even tried to make up a new problem. He reached a silent panic when he realised that his brain was fried. Perhaps it was time for a rest; maybe he should just answer all the questions they threw at him; Perretti didn't seem so bad; at times he had even showed kindness; better talking to Perretti than that Dingwall; maybe it was time just to get some sleep.

In the accompanying room Perretti's colleagues watched their boss and his victim, taking side bets on how many minutes it would take Henry to crumble.

After twenty seven minutes Chief Superintendent Dingwall entered the observation room. He watched the silence only for a few minutes before his patience was exhausted. "What on earth is he doing!" he asked too loudly.

"Shut up for God's sake!" whispered detective sergeant Joanne Henson, with no deference to the considerable difference in their ranks.

Dingwall stood up and glared at the offending officer. "How dare you speak to me in that fashion young woman!" he bellowed.

Henry jumped to a standing position at the dramatic intrusion into the silence. Then he looked into Perretti's dark brown eyes. He could physically see them change from those of the assured victor, first into anger, before finally wilting into the acceptance of defeat.

Henry smiled.

Perretti did not smile. He rose to his feet and addressed the microphone. "Interview terminated at seven forty-six." Looking at the policemen at the door he said, "Take Mr Doncaster to his cell. Make sure that he gets a meal."

After a particularly good dish of steak pie with chips followed by rhubarb crumble and custard, Henry waited a very long time to be recalled to the interview room. He did not know that things had changed. He did not know that he would now, on Perretti's instruction, be granted access to his lawyer. He did not know that Detective Chief Inspector Aldo Perretti and Detective Sergeant Joanne Henson were already on their way to Glasgow airport for a late flight to London. He did not know that Perretti had given his opinion to Chief Inspector Roger Dingwall that Henry Doncaster had nothing to do with terrorism. If he had known that Dingwall would ignore this advice and pursue the case under his own direction, Henry might have been very afraid.

40. MUCH ADO ABOUT SOMETHING

"You should be ashamed of yourselves, the lot of you. You are nothing but a bunch of Gestapo. That poor woman is recovering from major surgery and you are not showing any concern for her whatever, so you are. I am to be taking it to the newspapers; that is what I will be doing. Then the public can find out what it is that you are all like."

Donnie had never seen Roy as angry as this before; in fact he could not recall Roy ever being angry, apart from that time at the political meeting of course. Roy sat down beside him on the only other chair in the reception area of police headquarters. The duty officer who had been the beneficiary of Roy's tirade considered arresting him for verbally abusing a police officer, but decided that he did not need the paperwork involved. Anyway, the gentleman's face was between crimson and purple and he might not survive another bout of anger.

"It is not right Donnie. It is just not right. First they arrest Henry in his pyjamas and now they are keeping Maureen even longer than us. It is not right at all at all."

"No, you're right Roy; they should have let him put his clothes on."

Roy gave Donnie his usual look, not quite sure if he was taking the piss. "We are going to give them hell for all this, Donnie. They are going to be surprised at the trouble a couple of pensioners can create for them."

"Yes Roy," said Donnie.

Roy gave him that look again.

At that point Maureen came through to the reception area accompanied by a police woman. Roy moved on from crimson to purple as he saw from Maureen's face that she had been crying. Just as he was about to explode again, Donnie whispered, "Let it go Roy; it might make it worse for her."

Roy nodded, and invented an incongruent smile for his face as he greeted Maureen.

She smiled weakly back and said, "Let's go to the Culloden boys."

*
**

Amanda had been amazed to receive a call from Mr Macsween. She had no idea that he would still feel some kind of responsibility to her and that he would show her such concern. And the news that he brought...Henry arrested for questioning about terrorism...it was crazy. She remembered joking with Henry about him being a gangster.

Amanda recalled something on the news about an arrest and sat down to see what she could find on the internet. It did not take long for her to locate the story and various associated interviews on the BBC website. She could even download a podcast of a hastily made programme about Glasgow potentially becoming a centre for international terrorism. That's how it goes she thought; modern 'tabloid journalism' even taking over the BBC.

She sat down to think carefully about what she should do. She should certainly go to police headquarters right away. They probably wouldn't let her see Henry, but they might give him a message from her. And of course she was Henry's closest relative, so they should know that she was the person to contact about anything. Yes, she should go to the police station right away. Mr Macsween had said that he had just been contacted and was going down there; perhaps she would meet him.

Just as Amanda was leaving the house she remembered the sheet of paper with the numbers Henry had given to her. He had emphasised its importance and had said that she should keep it safe, perhaps in a bank safety deposit box and definitely not at home. Feeling somewhat guilty that she still had the paper on her writing desk, she retrieved it and headed first to her bank.

*
**

The Culloden was fuller than usual as the early evening television news time approached. Rosie had insisted that Maureen had a lie down on the sofa in the kitchen and Maureen was pleased that nowadays she could take suggestions like that. Roy and Donnie were sipping their beers slowly because it was unusual for them to be in so early and they had not had their tea. Donnie was still a bit worried about how Roy was taking things. They had compared notes on their interviews. Donnie had been interviewed by Inspector Roderick Mitchell and had found him OK, though he had spent a lot of time on the passport thing and said that they would likely want to talk with him again about that. But Roy had had quite a different experience with Chief Superintendent Roger Dingwall. "He kept shouting at me that I had been aiding a terrorist and that I would never see my grandchildren again as long as he had anything to do with it. He asked me how Henry got his money and I told him about Henry's horse betting. He laughed in my face and said that I must be a fool to believe that someone could make all that money off the horses. Then he asked how much money I had and where I had got it from. He even knew that I had been to Canada and asked where I had got my flight money from. He said that he knew the payment for the flight was from Henry's credit card. He kept sneering at me and standing over me, shouting. He was a real bully; I wanted to smash his face in."

"Good job you didn't," said Donnie.

"I'd still like to do it," Roy added.

At this moment a hush descended over the Culloden as two known men walked slowly into the pub and scanned it. Eyeing Roy and Donnie, Nicholas Andrews walked over to them, closely followed by Adonis who caught Rosie's eye, causing both to blush profusely.

"Good evening Mr Fox," was Finn's normal greeting, with a nod of acknowledgement shared with Donnie.

"Good evening to you Nicholas," replied Roy, "How are

things with you?"

Finn nodded slowly. "They are a lot better with me than I think they are with you. How was it for you at the police station? I heard it was not good for you."

Roy wondered how on earth Nicholas could get such information out of a police station and so quickly, but he let the question pass. Instead he re-told the story, only trimming it of the emotion he had felt. The last thing he wanted was for Nicholas to take out a contract on his behalf.

Nicholas shook his head and for the first time in Roy's recent experience of him he actually looked perturbed and not at all carrying his usual powerfully impassive visage. "You will have to be very careful of Roger Dingwall, Roy," advised Nicholas. "He is a real bad piece of work. Most of the polis are pigs, but they are not as bad as Dingwall. I know some stuff he's done in the past that I can't tell you. Just don't trust him with anything. Tell your Henry not to trust him with anything; that's really important to tell him. In fact, I'll get someone to let Henry know; you wouldn't be able to get in to see him."

Roy wondered how Nicholas could reach right into a top security part of a police station to get a message to Henry, but he thought that it might be improper to ask.

At this point the British early evening news began and Henry was the top item. Once again the Chief Superintendent was at the forefront. *"I can tell you that we are holding a local man for questioning in regard to an extensive, terrorist related, international money laundering operation. The investigation is under my direction. I will not be taking questions at this time."*

The item went on to name Henry Doncaster as the suspect and even show footage of the inside of his flat after the scene of crime officers had vacated and inadequately sealed it. There was virtually nothing left in the flat. Forensics had taken all the furniture and even the carpets had been removed. All that remained were a few pictures on the walls.

"I bet they stole Henry's big TV," whispered Donnie to no one in particular.

Maureen had come out of the kitchen to watch the news. As if by magic her make-up had been removed and perfectly re-applied. Roy looked at her; she was still not herself. Her surgery had taken a lot out of her and she did not have the reserves to handle this affair. She looked like the Maureen of old, but that was the make-up; in fact she was just a shell of her former self. That was why he had been so angry at the police for he knew that the harassment would hit her hard. The Maureen of old would have taken it in her stride, but not now.

Roy's attention was reclaimed by Nicholas, "What should we do to help Henry?"

It was an obvious question, but neither Roy nor Donnie expected it to come from Finn.

"I think that first we need to try to see him," suggested Roy.

Nicholas, perhaps not surprisingly, appeared to have greatest knowledge in regard to police matters. "Not easy; especially when they have him on 'terrorist related' stuff. Whenever they go for the 'serious crime and terrorism' label you lose a lot of the rights you would otherwise have, especially while the 'terrorism' thing is still open. Basically they have twenty-eight days to do what they want with him."

Roy was indignant. "But that is terrible so it is; we will have to make as much public noise as we can about them abusing a pensioner."

Nicholas looked at Roy and smiled. "Yes, that's a good idea. I think that you would be very good at that Roy!"

Donnie brought them back to the first question. "So, how do we make contact with Henry?"

Nicholas nodded. "The only person he may have contact with is his lawyer. And the lawyer will likely have contact with Henry's family."

Roy and Donnie looked at each other causing Nicholas to ask, "So, are there problems with the family? Does he not have **any** family?"

"Actually he does have one person, his sister," said Roy.

"And he loves her very much," added Donnie.

Nicholas continued the interrogation of ageing minds. "Do you know her name and how to contact her?"

Roy shook his head, but Donnie chipped in. "Her name is 'Amanda', but I don't know where she lives."

"Good," said Nicholas patiently, but not knowing if the information actually took them forward. "Now, how do we find her?"

*
**

While Henry's friends were feeling for him, Henry was feeling very alone. He had been told that he would not be further interviewed until he had seen his lawyer and that his lawyer would be able to be present during the interviewing. He was also told that the further interviewing would be conducted by Chief Superintendent Roger Dingwall. Henry asked what had happened to Chief Inspector Aldo Perretti, but was met with a silent stare from his informant, Inspector Roderick Mitchell. The Inspector was there to give information, not to answer questions. Henry felt uneasy. Aldo Perretti had been much more able than Dingwall but he felt safer with Perretti. However the good news was that he would have someone to talk to. He looked forward to seeing Mr Macsween. Now Henry reminded himself that, if he was going to survive like the butterfly, he needed to attend to his discipline. He had not been especially sleep-deprived during his initial interrogation but it had considerably worn him out. Now he needed to get a really good sleep. Funny, he thought as he lay down, a prison cell is probably only good for sleep. Nevertheless, he had difficulty getting all manner of betting calculations out of his mind. He was on the point of constructing a mathematical equation to analyse the speed of the clouds running around inside his head when sleep finally captured him.

⁎⁎

Amanda was being as polite as she could possibly be in discussion with the desk sergeant. Perhaps the fifteen year difference between them precluded the fluttering of the eyelashes routine, though she was tempted to try. There was also the sobbing possibility, which might engage the sergeant's fatherly feeling rather than manly feeling, but she couldn't bring herself to that. So, she simply sought adult clarification, but with a little understanding of his position thrown in – understanding could be the most powerful tool of all, simply because public servants seldom experience it.

"So, sergeant; I think I understand…it must be difficult for you to face the likes of me time and time again every day…you are very patient. If I have understood correctly, it is simply impossible for me to see my brother, even though I am his closest, indeed his only relative. I think I understand that… like, with such a serious charge as terrorism you wouldn't want any information coming out from the accused, or even going into him. I really understand that you would want to help me but it is simply impossible to allow me to see him. I wonder though, do you have any other ideas on what I could do?"

Amanda was very tempted to add an eyelash flutter to the last question but she realised that it would be more an experiment to see if she could still pull it off. In any case she was sure that the understanding of his position would already have nailed him. Predictably, Sergeant Dunlop came through. "Well…what I would do if I was in your shoes would be to see his lawyer. His lawyer would have access to him, at least from now on, and his lawyer would feel some responsibility to you as his next of kin. That's what I would do."

The sergeant looked around him in a sudden bout of anxiety. Amanda jumped in to make him feel good again. "Thank you very much indeed sergeant; that is extremely helpful." With a beaming smile and just the hint of a genuine tear in the corner of her eye she added, "You have been most caring towards me;

thank you very much. And...I will keep this between us."

Amanda marched out of the headquarters building with a smile on her face. She could have worked out the lawyer angle for herself but this confirmed that it was the only possibility. A bonus from the encounter was that she had made potentially useful contact for the future with a certain Sergeant Dunlop. Her smile broadened as she thought, 'I still have it!'

*
**

"I know how to find her," declared Donnie, having considered the Amanda question for some time.

"How?" asked Roy, not knowing whether to expect idiocy or genius.

In fact, Donnie's answer was somewhere between those extremes, though leaning towards the latter. "One of us can stand outside the police station with a placard saying 'Amanda, we are Henry's friends, Roy and Donnie. Contact us.' She is bound to be going to the police station to try to see Henry."

Nicholas looked at Roy and Roy looked at Nicholas as they both tried to work out the score on the idiocy – genius scale.

"Yes," Nicholas declared.

"Brilliant" added Roy, though he thought that his rating might be a trifle high. "But who would do it?" added Roy in fear that it might be him.

"I will," said Donnie, making Roy feel a trifle ashamed.

41. BETWEEN THE LAW AND A HARD PLACE

Henry was enjoying the visit of Mr Findlay Macsween. He was such a lovely man, and so caring of 'Mr Henry'. 'Boy,' thought Henry, with the sudden experience of emotion in his chest, 'I can do with caring right now.'

In the short preparation time given to him, Macsween had researched the Terrorism Acts of 2000 and 2006, with the considerable array of amendments attached, because these were troublesome pieces of legislation for anyone with an iota of concern for civil liberties. He had also researched the very thin case law that had derived from the legislation. It was amazing how little case law had actually been laid down. In what he considered to be unworthy scepticism, Macsween wondered if these enactments were not actually intended to bring people to justice but were more about police power. Because they were often cited alongside the 2000 and 2006 Terrorism Acts, Macsween also studied the Prevention of Terrorism Act of 2005 and the Serious Organised Crime and Police Act of the same year. Macsween had been interested in the frequent juxtaposition of 'Serious Organised Crime' and 'Terrorism'. His research revealed that several police forces had Units dedicated to 'Serious Organised Crime and Terrorism'. It sounded as though they might be getting extra powers in relation to serious crime on the back of the terrorism fear.

"You are sure that they won't have this place bugged," asked Henry with a smirk, but in complete seriousness.

"They just wouldn't do it; they couldn't use it in evidence anyway," replied Mr Macsweeen with as much conviction as he could muster. "Anyway," Macsween continued, "my advice is that, while I can handle these preliminaries, we should hire a lawyer who is a specialist in the terrorism legislation. The area is so new and so controversial that the law and its enactments are still at a formative stage. We need someone who is right at the forefront of practice in this area. Our research has revealed the perfect person for the task. She is based in London and she will not come cheap." Henry looked at him and answered seriously. "I can manage anything up to low seven figures."

Mr Macsween did not tell Henry about the work that had already gone on behind the scenes. His son Stewart had tried to persuade his father that, at eighty years of age, he was far too old to take on this case, even though it concerned his longest client. Findlay Macsween thought that Stewart would like such a public case for himself and his experience told him this kind of personal motivation was always dangerous for the client, so he had instructed Stewart to find the best specialist practitioner in Britain and hire them. Initially Stewart had protested, but soon realised that his father was correct, so he did the research and Nadira Khan, Professor at Oxford University and a Master of the Bench of Middle Temple, had been contracted on an emergency basis and with emergency fee note expectations.

Henry and his lawyer decided that, in relation to police questioning, they should steer a course that was not uncooperative, but was also careful, until their specialist lawyer was on the scene. On this basis they waited in the interview room for the arrival of Chief Superintendent Roger Dingwall. As usual, constables Ritchie and Henderson were waiting outside the door for the arrival of their superior. Henry wondered how much time police constables wasted while their superiors played silly time games. Twenty minutes late the Chief Superintendent made his entry followed by Inspector Mitchell. Unlike the impassivity of Aldo Perretti, Dingwall already looked angry. His look towards Henry inadequately disguised his underlying feeling that now was the time for revenge. After announcing those present for the sound recording Dingwall declared his agenda.

"Now that our London colleagues are no longer intervening, we will be able to make some progress. I do hope that you are going to cooperate fully in this investigation Mr Doncaster because we are aware that there are other very dangerous people involved in this affair and the longer you fail to help us the more chance they have of causing harm to this country. We already have enough evidence to charge you under Schedule 18 of the Terrorism Act of 2000, with aiding the resourcing of a terrorist organisation, in your case in respect of money laundering. The tariff for that is ten years and every bit of help you give that leads us to evidence against members of the organisation will improve my inclination to seek a reduction in that sentence. Mr Doncaster, you are not the kind of terrorist we want to put away for much of the rest of his life; please help us to catch the really evil ones."

Henry gave Dingwall a 'C minus' grade for this beginning. Obviously the Chief Superintendent had spent a long time preparing the text which contained a nice balance of threat and apparent concern. But the delivery had reduced the overall grade considerably. Perhaps Dingwall should have practised in front of a mirror because his non-verbals: his darting eye movements, self-centred tone, slight salivation in the corners of the mouth and his at times staring, vindictive eyes completely betrayed his emotion.

Henry and Macsween had also rehearsed their beginning, deciding that the latter would deliver their opening remarks. "Thank you for clarifying your position Chief Superintendent. We too look forward to offering as much clarification as we can because we are aware of how much police time this is taking up – time that might be spent apprehending just the kind of terrorists you describe."

Henry smiled inwardly; this old man was no push over. Macsween continued, "My client will shortly make a statement that should clarify matters to your satisfaction. But if you choose to continue with your investigation we will need a short pause while we bring a specialist colleague up from London and brief her so that she can lead our position. You will understand that this is such a new and tricky area of law that it is recommended by Supreme Court Judges Downing and Livingstone in a recent pronouncement, that specialist legal practitioners be employed from the earliest opportunity."

Dingwall's anger had been only just below the surface and this was enough for him to lose control. "We have wasted enough time; we have been days on this already and your client has done nothing but block things. No, Mr Macsween, you may not waste even more police time on this. If you want to replace yourself that's fine, but there will be no pause in the interrogation process!"

Macsween was ready for intemperate behaviour from the Chief Superintendent; indeed he had been looking forward to that possibility so that he could exercise his own implacable manner in response. "That is entirely your decision Chief Superintendent, but if you question my client while we are in our briefing process, then my instruction to him will be to decline to answer questions. I believe that he can do that rather well."

Dingwall's fists clenched and his teeth were bared. "Now listen here old man; this 'client' of yours is guilty as sin. I have never seen anyone so guilty. The evidence is overwhelming. He retired only a few years ago with a pittance of a pension after getting nothing from his father's estate, yet at the present day he has a total of eighteen bank accounts across four countries and assets totalling one and a quarter million pounds! How do you explain that?"

Macsween and Henry stayed silent because they knew that Dingwall had lost it and that they might learn something useful during his diatribe. In the vacuum that they created Dingwall's anger continued to flow. "We have evidence of his contacts with terrorist supporting organisations and of his attempt to obtain a false passport! We even have a statement from his former employer that he blackmailed them into giving him an enhanced lump sum payment on his retirement. Also he was hiding under the bed when we came to arrest him. Furthermore, he has state of the art security systems on his computers including an encryption system that the terrorism section has confirmed as comparable with those used by Al Qaeda. What do you have to say about all that?"

Henry reckoned that this was the time to respond, on the record. "As I told the police when I was first asked about my money, it has all been legally obtained as the result of my betting activities. Though it will take you some time, I am sure that you can obtain the necessary legal permissions to interrogate my banks and my routing banks internationally to trace the sources of the money. You will find that they are all either bookmakers or betting exchanges. Many of them will be names that you do not recognise from the high street, but they are nonetheless licensed betting organisations dealing internationally at the high end of the market. With respect to the passport thing, that was an innocent attempt to help a friend. We have already had it interrogated by Passport Office officials. As for contacts with 'terrorist supporting organisations' I have no idea what you are talking about. Yes, I dived under my bed; with all the crashing and destruction I thought the place was coming down around me. As to the matter of my previous employer...they simply gave me an enhanced final payment because they wanted my consultation services on matters where they had no continuing expertise."

The Chief Superintendent was still bursting with anger but he had started to function again. Pushing a pad and pen across the table Dingwall demanded, "Make a note of all your bank account details with logins and passwords; also the names of all your betting accounts, again with logins and passwords. Stay here and do it; you can have an hour."

"In your dreams..." replied Henry.

"I think that was a 'no'," clarified his lawyer who continued, "In any case you have normal protocols for approaching banks and any other organisations with that kind of request, and those protocols continue to preserve the security of my client's accounts." Chief Superintendent Roger Dingwall avoided exploding by striding out of the room and banging the door. Inspector Mitchell took up the microphone, "Chief Superintendent Dingwall leaves the room at 4.32pm. Interview suspended."

42. TELEVISION STAR

It was just past 5.30 pm and Donnie had been standing outside the police station since 9.00 that morning. He wore a large board on his front, tied with a string round the back of his neck. The board had been painted in white to create a background on which, over-painted in red, were the words. *Amanda, please contact Henry's friends, Roy and Donnie.* They were only eight words but their choice had been the subject of considerable debate. Donnie had wanted simply *Amanda, phone Roy* with Roy's number following. But Roy was worried about getting crank phone calls and even more worried when Rosie pointed out that he might get calls from a number of Glasgow's Amandas. They considered mentioning the Culloden as a place to contact them, but Nicholas pointed out that the police might think they were advertising the pub outside their headquarters. In any case, they were sure that Henry would have mentioned the Culloden to Amanda.

The day had not been uneventful for Donnie. Twice he had been taken inside by zealous young coppers knowing that 'friends' of Henry Doncaster were being sought for questioning. After the second arrest Donnie was given a typed letter on police stationery indicating that he was already known to police in regard to the Doncaster enquiry, and should not be further detained in relation to it, for the time being anyway. When he was challenged once more by a young policeman Donnie proudly showed his 'get out of jail free' card.

He was also accosted by four small boys who found it amusing to knock him over and see him struggle to his feet restricted by his board. They were coming in for a repeat performance when young Malcolm Jamieson appeared from round the corner eating an ice cream cone. Malcolm stood still, with his legs apart, and dropped his cone into a waste bin. He pointed to one of the boys with his left arm and with his right hand made a slashing action across his throat. The boys immediately ran, terrified, up the road. When Donnie turned to talk with him, young Malcolm was walking back round the corner.

Then there were the reporters, bored with nothing to do except wait for the terrorists hopefully to bust Doncaster out of jail in a daring raid right in front of their waiting cameras. It relieved the boredom for them to interview this strange little man with the board outside the police station. Donnie thought that his interviews got better as the day wore on. He was also pleased with the £65 he had in his pocket in unsolicited contributions from these press interviewers.

But no Amanda had approached him in the eight and a half hours, and he thought she would not likely be coming to the police station in the evening, so he put his board under his arm and got a bus to the Culloden to meet Roy and Nicholas.

"Never mind Mr Anderson, you put in a good shift; it was a long day," said Nicholas. "Yes," agreed Roy, "I couldn't have stood there all day."

"In fact," said Donnie, "Apart from not finding Amanda, I had a great day. I calculated that I walked back and forward a total of eleven and a half miles, got arrested twice, was given a free pardon in writing from the police, and I earned £65 from the reporters."

The Culloden customers had developed the habit of watching the early evening news together; a fact that led the owner to be present that evening to see why his takings had gone up so rapidly. There was nothing about Henry on the six o'clock British national news, but the Scottish news at 6.30 mentioned the case and how Henry was still being held in police headquarters for continued questioning. The news had nothing about Henry's lawyer who had used his local knowledge and the rear entrance to the building. Then, suddenly, Donnie and his placard were in full frontal to the camera. He was asked about the message on his placard.

"We are trying to contact Henry Doncaster's sister,

Amanda, to support her over her brother's imprisonment as a terrorist. We are friends of Henry Doncaster from the Culloden. Henry is a pensioner whose only sin is that he plays the horses and wins. He should be a hero to all pensioners in Glasgow, but they have made out that he is a terrorist and have locked him up. If he dies in jail they will not care. We want all the pensioners in Glasgow to rise up and show what they think of this being done to our Henry."

The interview ended there, with the interviewer perhaps getting more than she had expected. Roy thought that this might be why her donation was £40.

The cheers for Donnie filled the pub and the owner, delighted that his establishment had got publicity on prime time TV news, announced a free round for all present. Thirty minutes later Amanda walked through the door of the Culloden.

43. PREPARING

Henry was becoming used to jail food, finding it plain but acceptable. Previously his meal trays had been accompanied by two police officers but on this occasion only Constable Henderson entered and placed the tray on the floor between the door and where Henry was lying on his bed reading the one book he had managed to borrow. "Thank you Constable Henderson," said Henry without looking up from his book. Constable Henderson fidgeted but did not head for the door. Instead he said, "I'd be grateful if you would attend to your meal as soon as possible sir."

Henry's attention to his book was severed by this strange request. He sensed that there was no malice from Henderson, though there had been some concern in his voice. Henry closed his book, stood up and collected his tray. Returning to sit on his bed as Henderson left, Henry noticed a folded piece of paper held in place by his mug of tea. This was obviously the cause of Henderson's concern; it was important to him that Henry attended to it as soon as possible. Henry opened the paper and read the note.

Henry, you may remember me as an old friend of Roy. There is one important thing I have to tell you and I hope that I am not too late. Under no circumstances place any trust in Dingwall. He has built a good retirement pot out of theft. I can't say more here. Please find a way to destroy this note else others will get into trouble. Nicholas.

Henry guessed that 'others' would include Constable Henderson. It was interesting that Henderson sided more readily with Glasgow's most feared gangster than the Chief Superintendent. Henry remembered Dingwall's insistence that he give access details of his accounts when he must have known that there were protocols that would have given the police the information they required. Henry looked at the note and it's 'read and destroy' message, so he ate it.

***

Amanda enjoyed her visit to the Culloden. She had been feeling very alone with the situation and upset at not being able to see Henry. When Donnie's face and placard appeared on the News she had cried with joy at his 'free our Henry' speech. It had not been hard to drive around Henry's neighbourhood to find the Culloden but she had felt a little awkward, realising that it was probably thirty years since she had entered a pub on her own. She had approached the nice woman behind the bar, asking for Roy and Donnie. Maureen had looked her straight in the face and, with a big smile, said, "I bet you are Amanda."

Now Amanda was sitting in front of Mr Macsween's large desk. She had been taken aback at his considerable age and hoped that he was up to the task of defending Henry, but had been reassured when he told her about the appointment of Professor Nadira Khan. Now Amanda was telling him about her visit to the Culloden the evening before.

"I spent a couple of hours with Roy and Donnie. Roy is an old fashioned perfect gentleman and Donnie is quieter but I know that they both love Henry and they are making big plans. I liked them both immediately. There was also a younger man there by the name of Nicholas. He seemed to know Roy from a long time ago and he had a lot of knowledge about the police and the law."

"Do you know his second name by any chance?" asked Macsween.

Amanda thought hard. "Now, he did introduce himself, but I can't remember..."

"Was it 'Andrews' by any chance?" asked Macsween.

Amanda's face lit up, "Yes, it was; such a nice young man. Do you know him?"

"Not exactly, but I know **of** him," replied Macsween.

***

"Roy, there is a journalist from the local paper wanting to talk to you," declared Maureen down the phone. "I wasn't going to give him your number but I said that I would phone you," she added, looking at Sam Hunt with suspicion. Maureen did not like journalists, but then she remembered that she had never met any. Putting the phone down, she passed on Roy's message. "He says that he'll be right over. Would you like to buy a drink?"

Sam ordered a half pint and took it to a corner table where he could survey the whole pub. Sam was a writer; in his mind he was a great novelist, though his success had not yet arrived. The job with the local rag was temporary, just until he got his breakthrough, though it had been temporary for the last eight years. He had three novels in various stages of development and he was beginning to entertain the unpleasant thought that what was stopping his success was himself. He had just read a book called *The Courage to Write* and had uncomfortably recognised himself as the writer who does not have the courage to finish the manuscript and risk rejection by the publishers. Half way through his beer Sam Hunt was wondering if this realisation would kill him or cure him, when Roy Fox came through the door with his too small cap pulled tight on to his head and carrying his shopping bag. Sam waved to him and Roy nodded in acknowledgement before purchasing his beer and coming over to the reporter. They introduced themselves and Roy sat down.

"How did you know it was me?" he asked.

"I've seen you before," said the reporter. "I was at that hustings where you ended Robin Fairweather's career."

Roy's face broadened into a smile. "So you were that journalist! I read the piece you wrote in the paper; it was that piece that ended his career!"

Their conversation ranged across a number of topics before Sam Hunt asked a probing question. "So, are you going to follow through on what Donnie was talking about on the news – to organise a 'Free Henry' campaign."

Roy sighed. "Well, we were talking about it the other night.

We had lots of ideas, like a march from Glasgow Green to George Square, but we don't really know how to get it started."

"Use the papers," said Sam simply. "I can do a piece for our local paper with others for the main Scottish papers coming out the following day. My paper would be happy with that. The big papers would pay for the piece, but I don't want the money. We could use it for any expenses the campaign had. I would be happy to get people that would organise the march. The earliest we could have it would be Saturday week because I would have to lodge a 'Notification of Public Procession' form with the police a minimum of six days in advance. Shall we do this thing?"

Roy looked at the younger man and let his mind wander into all the possibilities. His smile beamed and his eyes twinkled with mischief. Putting his hand into his shopping bag he pulled out a brown paper bag and said, "Have a nice bunch of freshly dug carrots Mr Hunt."

*
**

Nowadays Mr Findlay Macsween OBE was not usually going to Glasgow airport in a chauffeur driven limousine at eight o'clock in the evening. He had even put on his best pin stripe suit and a somewhat daring pink tie. He wasn't sure about the tie, but it seemed to reflect his bouncy mood. He was working again and he was pleased to find how sharp he still was. At the airport he asked the chauffeur to wait with the vehicle in the limousine parking area. He hadn't used the car firm for years and he had been impressed that they had remembered his name and account details. When he got out of the car he made to retrieve his cane and decided that he did not need it.

Professor Nadira Khan was the first passenger to come through her gate. Findlay Macsween looked at her in admiration, though somewhere in the back of his mind was the awareness that in his earlier years there would have been something stronger than admiration in response to this beautiful and manifestly capable thirty-three old woman. He recognised her from photos on her website but in person she was all the more impressive in her 'power dressed' black trouser suit.

Nadira Khan saw the old gentleman make towards her. She had also done her research on him. Her contacts in the profession in Scotland had spoken highly of him. He was regarded as the leading criminal lawyer of his generation and one of only a few who had not sold their integrity for public fame. She was slightly taken aback to see how old he was, but nonetheless he did not hesitate, after greeting her, to take her bag as would a gentleman of his generation.

"Thank you very much for taking on this case and at such short notice," declared Macsween as they were being driven out of the airport.

Nadira Khan nodded her head. "I was initially reluctant because I have so much on right now. But your son presented the case very well. I was intrigued because, from the papers he forwarded, it is difficult to imagine our client as a terrorist. Also, I liked the fact that you both recognised the need for specialist assistance on a case under the Acts. Too often local firms press on into the case, often in the hope that it will make their name. By the time they realise the need for specialist assistance they have conceded so much that the opportunity for early closure is lost."

As their car pulled up at the Hilton, Macsween gave the Professor a sheet of paper. "This is a list of all the addresses and phone numbers you are likely to need while you are with us. Most important is the number for this car firm. Call them any time you want to go anywhere; even if you want to find a particular shop, they will know of it. The firm will always have a car available for you and it will usually be Max here who is your driver. Max took me home from my retirement dinner many years ago...and had to put up with a crying old man."

Max smiled at the memory but did not look round and Nadira Khan's heart warmed to this old man.

Macsween continued, unaware of the emotion he had inadvertently aroused. "Max will pick you up here at 8.40 tomorrow morning to get you to our meeting with our client at 9.00. Good night Professor Khan."

"Goodnight to you Mr Macsween," replied Nadira Khan, feeling pleased with another experience of Scottish hospitality and the grace of old Findlay Macsween.

44. A BRIEF MEETING

Professor Nadira Khan was as familiar with police stations as she was with high table at Trinity College. Indeed there were interesting symbolic similarities between the two institutions. Both relied for their existence on the establishment and maintenance of a culture of subordination. The Oxbridge colleges sought to achieve that aim through language, dress and spatial design, with the 'masters' expected to wear gowns to dinner and high table being set on a stage four feet above the domain of the underlings. Police stations maintained their authority by means of the same kind of symbols but also through their control of time. By any measure Nadira Khan would be the most distinguished visitor this police station would have had in the month, but she knew better than to expect respect and was prepared to be kept waiting as a deliberate policy that emphasised the power of the police. She sat alongside Findlay Macsween on two straight backed chairs in a draughty corridor outside the room that was given for their meeting with her new client. Thirty-five minutes after the appointed time the door was opened and they were admitted. As Nadira Khan and Findlay Macsween entered, nothing was said as the two officers made to exit through the back door of the room leaving sight of the crouched figure of a man sitting on a chair set at a work table. His hands were on his lap and obscured by the table.

"I don't suppose there is any chance of some tea?" asked the professor of the departing officers.

"There's a machine down the corridor," was the cryptic response.

Findlay Macsween walked round the table and put his hand on Henry's shoulder. "I am sad and angry to see you still here Mr Henry."

Henry gave him a weak smile in return, saying, "And it is good for me to have your friendship and support Mr

Macsween. I never imagined that I would ever be in a place like this and with these on." Henry raised his hands to reveal the handcuffs binding his wrists.

In these situations Nadira Khan was always slow to speak; instead she wanted to observe her new client. She wanted to see who he was before she spoke with him; speaking is a distraction to seeing. Looking across the table, she saw two men of dignity. She also saw their relationship of fifty years and their affection for each other. She looked at Henry's eyes and he returned her gaze as Mr Macsween introduced them. The words of introduction were unimportant because Nadira Khan and her client were meeting through their eyes; neither blinked nor looked away. 'Yes,' thought Nadira to herself; 'I can work with this man.' Henry felt deeply relieved to meet Nadira Khan. He had not allowed himself to feel his full fear, but seeing the strength in her eyes allowed him to symbolise just an edge of that fear and he shivered.

"Good Morning Mr Doncaster," was Nadira's conventional greeting.

Henry replied. "Call me Henry...I am very pleased that you are going to help me Professor Khan."

Nadira Khan smiled and nodded. "Call me Nadira, Henry."

Mr Macsween took a small plastic bag out of his pocket. The bag was full of coins of various denominations. "I took the precaution of bringing change in case we had to use the machine. Would you like tea or coffee?"

During the next hour Nadira Khan interrogated her client. At first it was difficult for Henry to speak openly, so firmly had he established his resistance to previous questioning. He became distracted and examined all corners of the room for possible cameras and microphones.

"The room is clean," Nadira assured him. "I can't see any cameras and there is definitely no sound recording which is more important."

"How do you know?" Henry queried.

Nadira reached into her handbag and removed a small

electronic device about the size of an iPhone. "Because I swept the room as soon as we came in."

Henry relaxed in the realisation that his lawyer's paranoia could allow his own anxiety to subside.

After her interrogation of Henry, Nadira put down her pen and sat back in her chair. She looked at Findlay Macsween and shook her head. "Something stinks about this, Findlay. I know Aldo Perretti very well; we have been adversaries on other cases. He would not give up so easily and go back to London unless he was sure that there was nothing in the case. The man is relentless in his work; once he has his teeth into a suspect he does not let go. Also, if he judged that there was nothing in the case, he would report that to the local senior officer. I cannot understand why Dingwall is continuing."

Henry told his lawyers about the message from Nicholas Andrews.

"It sounds as though we will have to be extremely careful in regard to Chief Superintendent Roger Dingwall," concluded Nadira Khan.

Findlay Macsween left to inform the officer outside that they had concluded their briefing meeting and were ready for further interviewing. After another thirty-five minute wait they were led to the interview room to meet Chief Superintendent Roger Dingwall.

45. DINGWALL'S REVENGE

"So, can we take it that Professor Khan has taken over from you as the representing lawyer for Mr Doncaster?" As he asked the question of Macsween, Chief Superintendent Dingwall looked unusually calm.

'He's up to something,' thought Henry, more alert to Dingwall after the note from Nicholas.

Macsween replied. "That is correct Chief Superintendent, though I will continue in a junior capacity, as the local brief, so to speak."

Dingwall paused and stretched his upper body to add a little to his already considerable physical presence. "You may continue in any role you like, but you will not be present at these interviews."

Nadira Khan knew that the Chief Superintendent had the right to make that decision, but she must challenge it. "Chief Superintendent that is most unreasonable; what harm can be done by allowing Mr Macsween to support me in here?"

Dingwall was enjoying this; he liked it when he was on top and other people had to squirm or beg. "In law it would be quite inappropriate for Mr Macsween to continue to be present here, because he is likely to be a material witness in this case."

Nadira Khan never lost her cool and that would not happen now. "How could he possibly be a material witness? He is the client's lawyer."

Dingwall was at his supercilious worst. "I am afraid that I cannot divulge aspects of the police investigation. Constable Ritchie, escort Mr Macsween elsewhere."

Findlay Macsween looked instantly older as he slowly got to his feet and walked to the door. He said nothing to Professor Khan or to Henry because that would not have been appropriate. It had been deemed that he should not be present in that room, so he should not communicate in any fashion. Even in these circumstances Findlay Macsween knew the correct way to behave and would not deviate from that.

Constable Ritchie led Macsween silently down the basement corridor and up the stairs, but instead of heading towards the reception area he turned the other way down the corridor. Macsween stopped and pointed in the other direction

"Isn't this the way to the entrance?"

Constable Ritchie looked slightly embarrassed. "We are not going to the entrance sir; I have been instructed to take you to another room. It's just down here."

Macsween was puzzled, but he followed the constable until they came to a room at the very end of the corridor. The constable knocked and they were bid to enter.

Inside, seated at a table, were Inspector Mitchell and a detective constable. They stood up and Inspector Mitchell uttered the dreaded words. "Mr Macsween, I have to inform you that you are arrested under the Terrorism Acts of 2000 and 2006. You do not have to say anything, but it may harm your defence if you fail to mention something when questioned that you later rely on in court. Anything you do say may be used in evidence against you." Holding up a document, the Inspector continued, "I have here a search warrant issued under Schedule Five of the 2000 Act allowing us to search your business premises and your home and to seize and retain material that may be of value to an on-going terrorist investigation. Do you understand what I have said?"

"Yes," said Findlay Macsween, now a critically deflated old man.

The inspector continued, "You will be kept in the cells on these premises until we have made the searches and interrogated you, but we will inform your son at the first opportunity."

Chief Superintendent Dingwall continued his interview with Henry. "You have not been exactly frank with us about your finances Mr Doncaster. In an earlier interview you led us to understand that your liquid assets totalled one and a quarter million pounds, but it is considerably more than that is it not?"

Henry looked at his lawyer with a raise of his eyebrows asking if it was OK to respond. She nodded and Henry answered. "In fact I did not mislead you. It was you who stated that my assets totalled one and a quarter million across eighteen accounts, but you had missed some accounts. If you listen to your recording you will find that you did not ask me if one and a quarter million was the correct figure or what the total actually was." "And what is the total Mr Doncaster?" asked the smiling policeman.

"When I came in here it was two million four hundred and forty four thousand pounds, give or take a little."

"And what have you been contributing to Her Majesty's Revenue and Customs Mr Doncaster?"

Dingwall had a way of saying 'Mr Doncaster' that made Henry squirm. It took him all the way back to school when the hated masters would refer to him as 'Doncaster' before they satisfied their lust by flogging him. Forcing himself back from that old place which might make him too emotional, Henry answered. "I don't have those figures in my head but it should be easy for you to check with HMRC. If you need an authorisation to look at my tax account I will be happy to give it. But I have been paying quite a lot really, mainly on bank interest."

Henry enjoyed offering Dingwall easy access to his tax records because it was really a meaningless offer; he could easily have got the cooperation of HMRC without permission.

"And you have paid no tax on your other earnings?" continued Dingwall.

Henry sighed. "We have been over that before. I have paid tax on my pension but not on my earnings from betting. You well know that those are tax exempt." Henry used a 'talking-down' tone of voice designed to rile the easily riled policeman.

"It's a shame that the government takes no tax from the degenerate gambler but other working people have to pay tax on their honest earnings."

Henry looked at Dingwall. Was he really that stupid or was he trying to return the riling?

"No, the tax man is cleverer than that because he knows that if he taxed the better's winnings he would have to make his losses tax deductible and since more betters lose, he would be in deficit. Unlike some other public servants the tax man is indeed clever!"

Dingwall did not show that Henry had riled him even more; he knew that he was taking revenge on him in another part of the building. He moved the interrogation on. "We have been having a great deal of difficulty with your computers Mr Doncaster. It seems strange that a retired man needs to disguise his internet identity to such an extent that he routes his communications through false servers in countries such as The Netherlands, Switzerland and Canada. Why do you need this sophisticated system of deception Mr Doncaster?" Henry shook his head slowly to reflect his disdainful tone of voice. "They are not 'false servers' – they are 'proxy servers' – normal ways to disguise one's identity in order to stay safe on the internet. Oh, and you missed Romania and South Africa." Henry enjoyed talking down to Dingwall, even giving him information that was not endangering his security.

But Dingwall was not fazed as he continued. "I am told that you do not use the USA Mr Doncaster. Most proxy servers are in the USA yet you use these other countries to hide your activities. Are you scared to use the USA because your terrorist activity would more likely be detected there?"

Henry saw that Dingwall had been well briefed, but not by someone who knew the international betting industry. "I do not use the USA because online betting is prohibited in that country; bets coming from a USA IP address would be blocked."

Dingwall paused briefly but tried not to show the exasperation he felt at the ease with which his target was fielding his questions. He switched the direction slightly.

"There also seems to be a highly sophisticated encryption system disguising the important banking and betting details within your computers. We sent it to experts in London and a specialist even came over from Washington but they could do nothing with it. Washington says that the only encryption system they have seen that was as sophisticated was one which stored information about networks of Al Qaeda cells. The Washington expert was trying to find the agency from which you purchased the random numbers upon which the encryption is based, but it seems that you have erased all possible clues. His conclusion was that no innocent citizen would know about this 'back door' as he called it."

Henry smiled, but only briefly, as Dingwall continued. "I would like you now to give me the codes for the encryption system or tell me where we can obtain them."

Henry did not pause to check with his lawyer. "I will not give you the codes because I do not trust the security of your use of them. If what you are trying to find are my bank accounts I will give you a list of the banks and also the routing banks I use, in Britain and abroad. If the courts deem it appropriate you will then be able to get sight of my balances and the records of transactions while the security of the finances will not be jeopardised. If you win your case against me, then you may well be able to have these funds sequestered. That approach follows due process, but you wanting my encrypted banking and betting access codes is not due process and would lay me open to theft."

Henry dwelt on the 'theft' word, staring straight into Dingwall's eyes, and seeing the flutter and the anger.

Suppressing his desire to shout, the policeman continued. "Very well; it would have been faster, but now you will have to stay in custody for much longer. I think we will send you to Barlinnie, though I must warn you since you have never been in prison, that it is not a nice place and they are not very nice people."

"Are you threatening my client Chief Superintendent?"

asked Professor Khan.

His broad senseless smile returned. "Not at all dear lady, not at all!"

Nadira Khan had been around too long to accept the sexist comments of a policeman. "You will address me as Professor Khan and not as 'dear lady' or any other sexist term, or, believe me you will find yourself in serious trouble."

Dingwall, still feeling that he had won, raised his arms, palms to the front, and said, still with the same inane smile, "Oh I **am** sorry, Professor Khan."

The Chief Superintendent rose and turned around, as if to end the interview, then turned back and asked, "Do you have a will Mr Doncaster? We did not find one in your flat." Henry looked to his lawyer who firmly shook her head. "I refuse to answer that question," he declared.

Dingwall smiled again. "Oh, how tiresome; that means we will have to look for it elsewhere."

46. FIGHTING BACK

The first article in the local newspaper had been its best scoop in years, but it raised little in the way of waves. However, when varieties of the story came out in the national papers the next day, with front page headlines, inside features and editorial leader comments, a tsunami ensued. All the papers carried interviews, mainly with Roy. Under his own by-line *The Voice* 'Special Reporter', Sam Hunt, quoted Roy Fox, pensioner friend of Henry Doncaster.

> *"It is a matter of concern to our whole nation that a pensioner like Henry Doncaster, who has been in no trouble all his life and has contributed to the country throughout his working years, should have his home trashed by the police in the middle of the night and should be dragged outside, to be incarcerated for weeks and denied the support of a lawyer. Then when he is allowed to have his lawyer present, the well-respected Mr Macsween OBE a retired gentleman of eighty years of age, that old man himself is arrested and thrown into the cells. Is this how pensioners are to be treated in our country? We think not and we believe that the people of Scotland and our friends in other parts of Great Britain will want to show what they feel about this outrage. Next Saturday we want all pensioners, and younger people who feel strongly about this, to meet on Glasgow Green at twelve noon to march on George Square. We expect that there will be a hundred thousand people marching."*

Some papers also carried a briefer interview with Donnie, including the following extract from the *The Globe*.

> *"The police are out of control in this country. Poor*

Henry is just the first pensioner victim. Others will follow. So if you don't want to become a pensioner victim of police brutality and have your television stolen, join the march."

The morning newspaper revelations were picked up by the evening television news broadcasts throughout Britain. The item carried an interview with Roy and Donnie, where they managed to advertise the March, and also a press conference led by Chief Superintendent Roger Dingwall where he was anything but apologetic.

"I think that it is appalling that a few misguided members of the public should seek to interfere with an on-going police investigation of such a serious nature. They are in danger of making it difficult to take this case to court because it might be impossible to get an impartial jury. For this reason the court will be asked to grant an injunction against the proposed march and any other activities of this ill-informed group."

Chief Inspector Aldo Perretti was enjoying an early evening glass of a good Chianti with his wife, Lucia, in their designer London apartment when the item came on the News. He shook his head and said, more to himself than his wife, "Dingaling you really are a plonker!"

Lucia tutted at his coarse language.

Amanda was watching the small television in Stewart Macsween's office along with him and Professor Nadira Khan. "Could he get such an injunction?" she asked the experts. They nodded their heads simultaneously, with Nadira replying. "Yes, I imagine that he could. The courts are very strict about any public events or press interference that might prejudice a trial. Given this notice of the demonstration they might feel that they have to act to prevent it."

It was late morning in Vancouver as the Edwards family poured over the screen of their PC watching the item on BBC World. Paul and Clara screamed and clapped their hands at the sight of their grandfather while Emily was so proud of her dad.

Mrs Jamieson could not remember her son Malcolm ever switching on the television news and sitting glued to it. When Donnie came on he pulled his mother in from the kitchen. "See...that's ma friend Donnie. Didnae he dae great!"

In the Culloden, now established as campaign headquarters, every table was given over to the manufacture of banners. The owner, rapidly becoming a regular early evening visitor, was intently using all the primary colours in his own creation. Maureen and Rosie looked down on the workers, with Maureen observing, "I have never seen so many customers in this early." Rosie commented, "Yes but the buggers are so busy they aren't buying any drinks!"

In Assynt, Anthony and the regulars of the Crannog had also been in front of the TV, cheering Roy and Donnie and booing the Chief Superintendent. They were having a meeting to organise their bus down to Glasgow for the March. Jock leant over to Duncan, "Agus, am bith thu tighinn còmhla rinn a Ghlaschu air an caismeachd a Dhonnchaidh?" (And will you be coming with us to Glasgow for the march Duncan?) Duncan replied, "Bithidh gu cinnteach Iain, tha mo bhratach ullaichte agam mu thràth!" (Of course Jock, for I have already made my banner!)

47. THE DEFENCE DOES NOT REST

"What in hell's name is this? Dingwall bellowed as he looked at a sheet of numbers. Inspector Mitchell had expected the response. "Well, it appears to be his will, sir. Or at least it is what he is leaving in his will to his sister. We got it from his lawyer's office. There was a rudimentary statement with it that he was leaving all his estate, including the proceeds from these numbers, to her. We sent it to the London boys who say that it is probably a full statement of Doncaster's accounts, but it still lacks the key to open it." "But where is the damn key?" shouted Dingwall in his usual belligerent manner.

"Probably the sister has it."

Dingwall spat out his invective, "Bring her in and don't make it nice. I want you to frighten the hell out of her. In fact, send an armed response unit. Also, have our anti-terrorism boys put taps on her phones and also on those belonging to Stewart Macsween.

Roderick Mitchell knew he would be breaking the law. "Don't you think…I mean…shouldn't we get judicial approval for phone taps on a lawyer?"

His superior sighed, "That is the kind of wishy washy thinking that will prevent you ever getting a proper promotion. There is no time to bother with the niceties; we need to get the key to the code."

Inspector Mitchell tried again to speak, "Yes sir… although…I mean…"

But he was cut off by his superior leaning right into his face and spitting out his words, "Is that you beginning your resignation speech Inspector?"

Roderick Mitchell thought about his pension, shut his mouth and left to do his master's bidding.

*
**

The defence team was somewhat depleted. With Henry Doncaster in prison, Findlay Macsween in a police cell and Amanda sent away for safe keeping, only Stewart Macsween and Nadira Khan remained. Amanda's departure had been on the suggestion of Nadira after Amanda had told them about Henry's will and the sheet of numbers she had deposited with her bank.

Nadira explained, "Henry has his systems well protected against crooks, but what he never reckoned on were police crooks. Having a man like Dingwall at that level of rank is dangerous. He will be able to get the code out of Amanda's bank and while Henry is held in Barlinnie he won't be able to move his money anywhere. It will be easy for Dingwall to move a million or so somewhere off shore. No one is going to bother about the difference between Henry's stated two and a half million and a found one and a half. I think that you should get the code out of your bank and go away somewhere we don't know about, at least until after Saturday. My sense is that Saturday is going to be a big day in this affair."

So Amanda had retrieved the code and gone to her favourite hotel in Perthshire, reducing the defence team to three: Stewart Macsween, Nadira Khan and, at this moment, Nadira's driver Max, who had come to the office to have a word with them.

Maxwell Forbes took up his story. "Well, it's like this, ma'am. About a year ago I had a regular client who turned out to be one of Glasgow's finest. I mean that ironically of course!"

Max smiled at his own humour and Nadira wished he would hurry up.

Max continued, "It turned out that my man was into the drugs big time. Eventually I told my bosses that I wanted off him in case I got done as the car man. Anyway, there was this one time, see. There was him and another guy in the back. They thought I couldn't hear them because my window was up, but I could still hear clearly. They was talking about this cop who had done over two guys they knew. He had locked them up, questioned them and then took their money. The two in the back talked about croaking the cop, but he was too high ranking they said, and anyway it wasn't their money. Anyway, When I saw that Chief Superintendent on the telly – the one that has our client banged up – he fair reminded me of the cop they were talking about. And then when I heard you two talking about Mr Henry's money, well it all seemed to add up so it did."

"Did they mention the name of the policeman?" asked Nadira.

"Well, that's another thing see." Max was now very excited. "They didn't, but they had a nickname for him...they called him 'Dingaling'."

Nadira did not often smile, but this was worth the deviation from normality. "Thank you Max; this might prove to be very important indeed."

*
**

Derek Smallwood had not been watching a television programme about earthquakes and he wasn't even sleeping, but he had the same reaction as Henry to the breaking down of his front door; he dived behind the couch.

"Your wife, Amanda Smallwood; where is she?" shouted the policeman, adorned in helmet and bullet proof vest, and holding an automatic rifle two inches from Derek's left ear.

"I don't know. I really don't know," whimpered Derek Smallwood who was not a brave man at the best of times.

"Tell me your wife's mobile number!" was the policeman's next instruction.

"It's 07802 81177222" stuttered Derek.

"That's too many numbers. Think again."

"There is only one '2' at the end," said Derek, frightened to try to reproduce the number again.

"Search the place for the paper and take the computers," said the policeman to his underlings and throwing a search warrant at Derek's feet. "When do you expect her back?"

"I don't know. I really don't know."

Derek wondered if ignorance was a criminal offence, perhaps even a capital offence with these 'commandos'. In a bizarre turn of his mind he also wondered about their weapons procurement contractor because they had state of the art stuff. Usually older models were off loaded on the police who did not know any better.

The policeman growled at Derek and spat out his instructions like a machine gun. "You will stay here with two of my men. You will not answer the door or the phone unless instructed to do so. You will not to go to the window. If you go to the toilet you will have company. And give me your mobile."

The policeman instructed the curtains to be pulled and the door to be repaired; then he and most of the police left. One of the two remaining officers looked at Derek and, developing a smile as he chewed his gum, appeared to Derek almost certainly like a homicidal maniac. The officer said, "Would you like a cup of tea Mr Smallwood?"

*
**

Nadira Khan knew exactly what to do. "What is the best private detective agency in Glasgow?" she asked Stewart.

"We have used *Donaldsons* since they opened fifty years ago. In fact it was my father who used to fish with old Mr Donaldson and helped him to get contacts when he started up."

"Is everything in this country done around fishing?" she joked.

"No," said Stewart with a smile, "There is the golf as well."

"Get Donaldsons," instructed Nadira. "We can go to them ASAP."

Fifteen minutes later they were having tea with old Mr Donaldson's grandson. He knew, of course, about the incarceration of his grandfather's friend and said that they had the full use of all the firm's resources and he would be insulted if they asked for an invoice at the end. Nadira told the story of the dealings with Chief Superintendent Roger Dingwall in the fashion of the expert lawyer that she was. There were no frills, no value judgements, and every fact that was relevant was described accurately.

Before she started on the account given by Max she said, "Doubts about the Superintendent's veracity were first expressed by a friend of Roy Fox. This 'Nicholas Andrews' said that they should warn Henry about Dingwall. He said that Dingwall had a reputation for theft."

Young Mr Rory Donaldson looked at Nadira. "I know of Nicholas Andrews; he has an interesting reputation. Nevertheless, I suspect that he would not be exaggerating."

After the half-hour briefing, Rory Donaldson rose to bid them farewell. Looking at Stewart he said, "You can be sure that you will get very special service from us. We will not only turn over every stone but, in the words of another idiom, we will cut every corner. There are things that we can do for which the police need terrorism legislation. Also, we will keep your name out of it as much as we can. I will report to you every six hours at worst."

When they were out of the room Rory Donaldson spoke through the intercom to his personal assistant. "Get everyone off what they are working on and in the conference room for a briefing in forty-five minutes time."

48. NOTHING IS THE SAME

On the evening before the March Roy and Donnie were sitting in silence in their usual position at the bar. Eventually Roy broke the silence. "What are you thinking about Donnie?"

"That it is only a year since Robert Alexander died in here and we three got together."

"That is exactly what I was thinking about. A lot has happened in a short time."

"It has," agreed Donnie. After a pause he continued, "I think that more has happened to me in this last year than in the whole of the rest of my life." Donnie sipped his beer. "I am an entirely different person than I was this time last year. I would not recognise myself if I met me."

Roy was still trying to work out this last sentence when Donnie continued in full flow.

"I wish I could have my life again. Like I wish I could go back to when I was young, but as the person I am now. Everything would be different. I wouldn't be scared like I was… I could climb the mountains."

A tear came to Roy's eye and, unusually, he did not wipe it away. His silence in response to his friend honoured the gravity of what had been said. This was not the time to lighten the conversation; that was one of the things that Roy had learned in the past year.

After a while Donnie continued. "I wonder who I would have become if I had climbed Suilven that day."

"That day?"

"That day when I was fifteen."

"And what about the rest of your life?"

"What do you mean?"

Roy explained, "Well, who do you intend to be for your life that is to come?"

Donnie paused a long pause, and then declared firmly, "The mountaineer of Assynt."

*
**

Maureen had invited Rosie to gin and tonic in the kitchen after closing.

"A double or a triple?" queried Maureen.

The women had developed their own measures and there were no half measures.

"A triple, but I'll only have one, for it will be a long day tomorrow," was Rosie's reply. She continued, "What do you think will happen tomorrow?"

Maureen considered her response. "I don't know, but I have a feeling that everything will be different after tomorrow."

"Everything is different for the two of us anyway," said Rosie, pausing only slightly before she continued, "Look at you Maureen; you are quite different these days. You are thinking a lot more, or maybe you always did but you are showing it much more. Yes, that's it; you are not hiding who you are, even if it is not easy."

Maureen nodded and smiled. "You know me better than I know myself. You are quite right. I am not able to 'pretend' any more. It was a big effort to come back to work and I am glad that I did. But I can't keep up the same pretences as before. Life is too serious for that...my death walks with me, probably for ever."

"And your life too? Does your life walk with you?"

"It is the same thing, my life and my death. Everything else is just pretence. The main thing is that I can't pretend anymore."

"How is that for you... that you can't pretend anymore?"

Maureen paused. "I probably will have less fun than before...but it might mean that people will see me better and I will see them better."

"Are you looking forward to the future?" asked Rosie, surprised that she had taken such a risk in asking this.

Maureen looked at her and smiled. "Yes, if it is filled with people like you."

*
**

Henry was alone and lonely again; his most uncomfortable configuration. Barlinnie was not a nice place. His previous police cell had become a 'place of power' for him as he took on his aggressor, but this prison cell felt quite different. He was a man who had no power. He had to address the screws as 'Sir' and think first what they wanted of him rather than what he wanted. He could see that already he was becoming depersonalised and that was what the prison system primarily sought. He was frightened by how fast it was happening. What happened when you were in here for years? He remembered Jimmy Boyle's book, *A Sense of Freedom.* He had found it poignant when he first read it, but it was even more powerful to remember it here. Boyle had been in Barlinnie, and also Inverness, Peterhead, and Saughton prisons. The thing that was strong in the book was Jimmy's fight against the depersonalisation that was already happening to Henry. He remembered Boyle's smearing of his faeces around the cage he was kept in; the smell would keep the screws out. Jimmy Boyle survived a life sentence in prison, with seven years in solitary confinement, to become a renowned sculptor among other things. 'Hell', thought Henry, 'and I can't even survive these few days.'

*
**

Findlay Macsween had dropped like a stone from his 'pink tie' evening to this moment when he was lying curled up on his bed in the police cell. His guards had not been unpleasant to him; they had even looked uncomfortable about him being there. As the days wore on he found the remains of his spirit depleting. They brought him food that he could not eat. They brought him fresh clothes that he could not put on. He lay, curled up in the foetal position from which he had emerged eighty years ago. Findlay Macsween died that night.

49. THE GATHERING

'Campaign Headquarters', previously known as The Culloden Bar, had never in its eighty years been open to the public at 7.30am. Though no alcohol was for sale, anyone could come in and they did. Most of the regulars and the irregulars and those who used to be regulars before their lives changed with marriage and children were there by 8.00am. They enjoyed meeting each other again, but there were no smiles on their faces, for they were here to prepare for serious business.

At 8.15 a caterer's van arrived to deposit freshly made sandwiches, cold chicken, warm pies and an array of soft drinks. There was enough to provide a hearty breakfast for the sixty people present plus those who were to come. The delivery note indicated that the purvey had been provided by Sam's paper.

Two teachers had taken over the pool area and were in charge of banner making. They had a plentiful stock of white cloth, sticks, gaffer tape and an array of spray paints, as well as a team of eight final year school students. Banners with a range of pre-prepared slogans were coming off the production line at a rate of one a minute.

Donnie and Roy arrived at the same time. Donnie walked straight through the front door without his former hesitancy. They greeted Maureen and Rosie, but with atypical serious expressions. Maureen gave them both a hug and Rosie thought about doing the same until the moment had passed. Everyone in the pub turned to look at the superstars who were so absorbed in their own solemnity that they did not notice.

The next principal to arrive was Sam Hunt, in a hurry as always and carrying a dozen folders spilling contents on the floor. Donnie picked up a fallen file and glanced at it. "This is from something called *Events Maestros*. Who on earth are they?"

"They are helping us on Glasgow Green and in George

Square. They are supplying the staging and the sound systems as well as stewarding."

Donnie looked perturbed. "That must cost a packet."

Sam smiled. "Donnie, what they are supplying would cost £30,000 minimum."

Now Roy looked perturbed. "But how can we possibly pay for that?"

Sam realised that a more detailed explanation was required. "Remember that you put the organisation into my hands. Events Maestros is doing the gig for free, partly because they want to support the cause, but also because it is going national as far as the press coverage is concerned. They will get so much good exposure I even thought about charging them."

Sam changed the subject. "Roy, when you are speaking at the gathering you will have to go slowly and with regular pauses. The reason is that, while the sound system has plenty volume, it has to cover a big distance. Now sound is a slow traveller over a distance so you need to give everyone the chance to hear each thing you are saying before you move on to the next bit, otherwise your audience will all be responding to different parts. Some will be trying to listen intently to one bit while others will be cheering another. That's why *Flower of Scotland* never works as an anthem. In big events people are all at different parts. Oh, and be ready yourself for the delayed feedback. Some of the speakers will be so far away from you that you will hear your own words coming back at you half-a-second later. It can be disorienting if you are not ready for it."

Roy looked at Sam. "You sure know how to terrify a pensioner. Suddenly, at sixty-six, I've got to become a pop star."

Sam did not relent. "Yep Roy, that's about the size of it. Are you prepared?"

While Donnie thanked his earlier reticence over taking a speaking role, Roy replied. "Let's say that it is a work in progress. I wanted to leave a bit of scope for improvisation."

Sam nodded. "Improvisation is good; it lets you speak from

the heart in the moment. How long is it?"

"Between seven and eight minutes like you said."

"That's good, but slow down your delivery so that it extends to ten or even twelve minutes. I will be standing right in front of you in the first row and I will be wired into four Events staff at the extremities of the Green. They will give me feedback and If you need to slow down I'll give you hand signals."

Roy used humour in an effort to salvage his last vestige of bravado. "And if I get pissed off with your signals I'll give you a hand signal!"

But Sam had a last word that only intensified Roy's anxiety. "Don't do that while the world's press is filming you Roy."

Next to arrive was Nadira Khan to whom Roy had taken an instant liking when they first met. Donnie also liked Nadira, but for him she was in the same category as Rosie; she terrified him. They were surprised that she was on her own, a fact she explained as soon as she reached them.

"Stewart won't be with us today; his father died in his police cell last night."

Roy's rage was countered by his shock and he could not speak. It was Donnie who asked the 'how' question.

To her own surprise Nadira's eyes filled up. "No one really knows...perhaps the lovely old man just ran out of spirit."

Their little group fell silent together.

Nicholas Andrews came down the street whistling a tune that had been in his head all morning. He did not know that this song he had picked up from his politically militant grandfather featured the words, 'We shall overcome'. As they approached the pub, Adonis paused to check his reflection in a shop window, using his fingers to spike up his gelled black hair before they entered.

Rory Donaldson needed to ask directions to the Culloden. Unfortunately his first consultant had either finished his imbibing late or, more likely, he had started early.

"Oh so it ish the Culloden that you ish looking for ish it. Well, it ish very straightforward so it ish. You just carry on this road until you get to the motorway east towards Edinburgh, then you take the other motorway north to Stirling and beyond. Then, when you get just short of Inverness, you take a right to Culloden. But you are late, for the battle finished in 1746!"

By this time Rory had wound up his window and was cursing all Glasgow drunken wits. Much later, as he parked his sparkling new silver Porsche near the pub, another local wise guy, this time aged ten, approached.

"Look after your car for you Mr?" came the age-old offer that Rory remembered using himself when he was aged ten outside Glasgow football grounds on game days.

"How much?" he asked.

"Two quid an hour," came the instant reply.

Rory knew that the price had been doubled by the gleam of the Porsche, but that was the way of business. "Ok, a quid now and the other when I come back."

The young entrepreneur nodded and sighed at the same time. Obviously the Porsche guy knew the score; now he would have to stay around for the balance of the fee.

From the quiet of the street outside, Rory was taken aback by the throng of humanity inside the pub. It took him some time to find Nadira and be introduced to Roy, Donnie and Sam.

Nadira jumped in, "Have you heard about Findlay?"

Rory made a pained expression of genuine grief and his voice was choked. "Yes, a friend in the police knew I was involved and left a message on my mobile first thing. Miss Khan, could I have a word with you? I'm sorry to be rude gentlemen." Rory won the privacy without offending anyone and made for the quietest part of the busy bar with Nadira following.

It was only while they were away that Roy found his voice after the shock he had felt about Mr Macsween. "You know, this sickens me. I just want to give it all up. Old men are not supposed to die in police cells Donnie. It's not what we are about."

Donnie's response was not the quiet one that Roy expected.

"Then you have to really give them hell Roy. You have not got to hold back anything. This is the one chance we have to draw the country's attention to what is happening. Tell them about men dying in police cells under the pretence of protecting democracy."

Roy and Sam looked at Donnie with similar surprise. "Maybe you should be doing the speech Donnie," suggested Roy.

But Donnie was clear. "No Roy, this is your thing – you are the man – today is your day."

Sam looked upon these old men and wondered why his father was not like them.

Nadira led Rory back to the group. "Roy, you have a friend called Nicholas Andrews. Is he reliable?"

Roy took a deep breath and looked squarely at Nadira. "On the street Nicholas Andrews is called 'Finn' on account of the fact that he uses a twelve inch Finnish blade to do serious harm to anyone who gets in the way of his criminal empire. His main business is money lending, but I don't know what else he is into."

Nadira shook her head. "That is not an answer to my question Roy; is he reliable?"

Roy did not pause. "I would trust him with my life Ms Khan."

Nadira smiled. "From what Rory and you have said, this 'Finn' seems to be an interesting character. Can we contact him?"

"Yes," said Roy, "For he is standing right over there."

Roy pointed to a part of the bar that had been automatically cleared by those locals who knew of Finn. Nicholas stood there with Adonis, both sipping their tonic waters.

"Roy," said Nadira, "Can I ask you to do an unusual thing? Can I ask you to introduce me to Nicholas in such a way that he will do anything for me that he would do for you? And...can you leave us together so that you do not hear what I ask him?"

Roy smiled and mentally thanked Sheila for sending

them Ms Khan as he took her over to Nicholas and Adonis. Roy introduced Nicholas and Nadira then paused awkwardly wondering how to introduce Adonis whose name he did not know. Nicholas supplied the solution. "It's OK Roy; he is just part of me."

Roy did not understand, but nodded. Nadira understood perfectly because in her dealings with the underworld she had come across that concept of the bodyguard not being a person in his own right but simply an extension of his boss. The ethic was to allow the bodyguard to be present at all times, but never to acknowledge his presence.

Roy completed the introduction. "Nicholas, Professor Khan has something to ask you and she does not want me to hear it. Would you treat her request as though it was coming from me?"

"Yes," said Nicholas Andrews with convincing finality.

No one knew why a fleet of twenty black cabs arrived at 9.30 until Sam explained. "The Taxi Owners Association was desperate to help the cause, so they came up with the idea of providing our transport to Glasgow Green. The whole of Glasgow wants to support The Pensioners March."

One of the taxi drivers spoke to the company. "We were going to come at 10.30 but the streets are congested around the Green and the police told us to come early. Just spread yourselves around the taxis and we'll be off."

Roy, Donnie and Sam were ushered into the first taxi, a 'black cab' but in bright silver. Shortly, the whole fleet took off as one to make its way across the city, preceded by a police escort of five Yamaha FJR1300 motorbikes. One bike kept a steady pace at the front while four others rushed forward in pairs to cut off the intersections ahead. When one intersection was cleared by the fleet the two bikes that had closed it would speed two intersections ahead to close that one off. The pairs worked in tandem in this way just as they normally escorted heads of state to and from the airport.

Roy sat back in his seat. "Yes, this will do me fine... and we don't even need our bus passes."

Donnie wasn't so sure and begged the question, "Do these police know that we are going to try to destroy a Chief Superintendent?"

"Probably not," said Roy, "But even if they did know, it is in the nature of the great British police not to allow it to matter."

Donnie looked doubtful; he was not accustomed to entertaining any positive thoughts about the police. "Don't let them butter you up Roy," he said. "Give it to them good!" Roy smiled back at Donnie while Sam made mental notes about their conversation for inclusion in the syndicated articles he was going to sell around the world.

As they passed close to George Square the fleet was slowed by the throngs of people who realised that the cabs carried the VIPs for the march. They waved, clapped and cheered. One elderly black man stood with one leg stiff in front of the other, stretched his black gloved clenched fist above and in front of him, giving the 'Black Power' salute. A woman of about fifty stripped off her jacket to reveal a T shirt declaring, 'I love you Donnie'. Donnie blushed.

Roy was anxious. "But they have got it the wrong way round. We are going to start at the Green and end at the Square."

After a police outrider spoke with their taxi driver he was able to clarify matters. "These people are trying to get to Glasgow Green but it is like this the whole way. The city is gridlocked. The police are going to change our route to take us on a loop round to enter from the other side of the Green."

**

Inspector Roderick Mitchell rushed into Chief Superintendent Roger Dingwall's office. The Chief was standing in front of his full length mirror flicking minute flecks of detritus off his dress uniform. He barked, "Well, have we got it?"

"Not yet, but we have been promised that it will be at the

Green before noon."

Dingwall smiled. He had been sure that his Masonic friend, Judge MacDonald, would come through with his much needed injunction. It had simply been a matter of asking the right judge.

Mitchell interrupted his superior's train of thought. "But there has been another development. The sister is on the move; her credit card has been used an hour ago at a hotel in Perthshire!"

Dingwall saw that there was still an opportunity to move from a defensive strategy to take up the offensive. "She will be coming to the March! Get the Stirling boys to check the trains."

"I've already done that sir," reported Mitchell, proud of his initiative.

"Good," said Dingwall. "And get our boys to rendezvous with them between here and Stirling. Now here are my explicit instructions on how she is to be handled…"

*
**

Amanda was looking at her watch every thirty seconds, wishing that this slow train from Perth to Glasgow would get a move on or she would be late. She knew that she should have stayed in her hotel but she simply could not resist coming to the March, so she had quickly settled her bill but asked the hotel to hold on to her luggage for the time being. The earlier train that she had aimed for would have given her plenty time but it was completely full with even the standing room taken. The Aberdeen and Dundee pensioners on board had been singing protest songs from the 70's and trying to wave their banners out of the too small windows of the modern train. A Perth station announcement had said that the train was completely full and even if some people disembarked at Perth no one would be allowed to board. All the platform guards were on duty to enact the dictum. So, Amanda was on the later train and anxious. Her anxiety increased when her First Class front carriage passed at least a dozen uniformed police spread along the platform at Stirling station. Amanda cursed herself; how could she have been so stupid as to use her credit card? They would have been monitoring it and it would not have taken them long to work out where she was going. Her distress increased and she felt beads of cold sweat running down her back when she realised that the code sheet was in her hand bag. Being in the front carriage gave her just enough time to locate the slip of paper, fold it twice and press it down the back of her seat. She made a mental note of her seat number before jumping across the aisle to another.

Within seconds of the train's stopping two police constables jumped on board her carriage and ran down its full length. They grabbed Amanda and pulled her to her feet. She was genuinely frightened by their roughness. "What are you doing? You have no right to manhandle me like this! You are hurting me."

The two male officers said nothing and immobilised her with minimal bodily contact by extending each of her arms to the side and holding them while they called in. A woman police officer arrived and even more brusquely searched Amanda before pulling her hands behind her back and handcuffing her. Another officer searched around Amanda's seat, completely ripping off the cushion and shaking his head to confirm that he had found nothing. Amanda was as frightened as she had ever been; the reality of a rough arrest is worse than a person could ever imagine. She thought about her brother being dragged from under his bed and Tasered. That thought gave her the strength to function and she noted the number of the carriage as she was led out.

*
**

As the fleet entered Glasgow Green from the James Street direction a hundred thousand people roared.

"Oh my God," said Roy, his face adopting a paler pallor. "Oh my God... Oh my God."

Simultaneously Donnie was bouncing up and down on his seat. "They've come...they've all come...all the pensioners have come!"

"Oh my God," added Roy.

*
**

The prisoner hand-over took place outside Cumbernauld police station. The three Glasgow constables said nothing to Amanda as they helped her into the back seat of the BMW pursuit vehicle. The woman officer shared the back with Amanda while the two men were in the front. Amanda screamed at them. "But I need to go to the toilet!"

The driver smirked, switched on the blue light and siren and said, "Don't worry, we'll be there in no time," as he accelerated to 90mph in the four hundred yards between the two town centre roundabouts.

*
**

The Green was unlike anything ever seen in Glasgow. Even the big 2003 gathering that had vainly thought they could stop Tony Blair entering Britain into the Bush crusade to improve upon his father's work in Iraq had been nothing like this. The whole Green was a mass of colourful, cheering humanity. There were five motorised large screens, two of which displayed a massive image of Henry in hill walking gear and sitting astride a rock. The picture had not been doctored, but it had been very well chosen; there was a bit of the ageing hippie look about Henry. Donnie remembered that it had been taken on one of their Assynt walks, just a moment before Henry had taken off his sock to have treatment administered to his troublesome blister. The other screens displayed the live music act that was playing on the main stage.

Sam explained. "They are 'The Sweaty Band' from the seventies. They are all pensioners and have re-formed just for this one event. Look at the pensioners in the crowd going wild about them. Also there are two other groups from the seventies and one from the sixties that have already been on. I was a bit worried about 'The Dream Sniffers' from the sixties because I think they may have been sniffing ever since. I made them sign waivers."

Roy and Donnie were peeking out from behind the backstage curtain with Roy repeatedly mumbling, "Oh my God."

"Look at all the TV cameras," exclaimed Donnie. "I can see STV, BBC, Channel 4 News, Sky News, CBC, NBC, Australia Channel 9, Channel One – I think that's a New Zealand flag they have up. And look over there, that crew has the Argentina flag!"

Sam expanded the list. "And there are also News crews from Japan, Spain, Sweden, Russia and, of course, Canada."

"Oh my God," said Roy.

*
**

Amanda had not heard about Findlay Macsween's death in his cell in the same police building she was approaching at speed. She was to think about that sometime later and wondered how the knowledge might have changed things for her. Would it have made her more frightened, more despairing, or perhaps just even more damned angry? The woman constable took her by the arm out of the car with the two men bursting ahead and up to the desk sergeant. Amanda was crying, but it was the kind of crying that little girls develop when their tears have been more accepted than their anger. She looked up and cried even harder, for it was her nice Sergeant Dunlop who was behind the desk.

One of the male constables reported. "Her name is Amanda Smallwood. She is a suspect in the Doncaster terrorism case. She is to be strip searched immediately and not allowed to use the toilet except in the presence of a woman police officer – orders of Inspector Mitchell relayed from Chief Superintendent Dingwall."

Sergeant Dunlop had not been so angry since that morning many years ago when he had found a young girl raped, beaten near to death and left in a Glasgow lane. He put on a steely tone of voice. "You forgot something at the end of your statement Constable."

The constable looked lost as did his male colleague, but the woman police officer chipped in, "He forgot to say 'Sir'...sir."

"Precisely, Constable Shaw," agreed the sergeant trying to slow his speech down in order to increase its power. "And why is she back cuffed? You know that it is only the violent ones we back cuff because it is brutally uncomfortable on a car journey."

The second young constable was happy to answer this one because he was absolutely sure that they had not done wrong. "Instructions of the Chief Superintendent sir – in case she tries to hide vital evidence she has concealed about her person...sir."

The other male constable nodded in agreement, but Constable Shaw, brighter than the other two, did not join in.

Sergeant Dunlop raised himself to his full height behind the desk. "Constables Burke and Dawson, have you heard about the Nuremberg trials after the war?" Dunlop did not wait for a response but continued. "The officers had done inhuman things to their prisoners and their defence was that they had been under orders from superior officers. They were executed."

Only Constable Shaw understood the point, but none of them dared to respond to an angry Sergeant. Having established control, Sergeant Dunlop continued. "So, I am the senior officer present in this room and I instruct you, Constable Dawson, to unlock this poor woman's cuffs, and you, Constable Shaw will escort her to the ladies washroom where you will leave her in peace. You will then guide her back here and I will brief the three of you on your further duties this morning. Mrs Smallwood, on behalf of Police Scotland I apologise for the dreadful treatment you have received this morning."

As she led Amanda down the corridor Constable Shaw was trying to think her way through the sergeant's argument. There was definitely a flaw in it somewhere. She wondered if Nuremberg meant that she should disobey the Chief Superintendent's orders or the Sergeant's orders or both. She shrugged her shoulders; in the Force you could get executed either way.

Amanda, walking slightly ahead of the constable, was smiling to herself. What a hero was her Sergeant Dunlop!

On her return to the desk Amanda had fully regained her identity as well as her appearance, but she resisted a smile to the desk sergeant in case it weakened his credibility with the constables. Sergeant Dunlop looked to the constables and gave what he knew would be his last command as a serving police officer. "This has gone on too long. It is time that we took a stand. You will escort Mrs Smallwood to meet her friends at the front of the March. I imagine that it will be in progress by the time you get through the city crowds." Amanda could not resist throwing Sergeant Dunlop a big smile, but she did resist a peck on the cheek.

*
**

"So, are you ready for it Roy? You will be on in twenty minutes." Sam was feeling just slightly worried about Roy's catatonic state.

"Oh my God," replied Roy.

As well as Roy, Donnie and Sam in the space behind the stage curtain, there were Nadira Khan and Rory Donaldson. Nadira was nervously looking at her watch when Nicholas, flanked by Adonis, burst in. They had obviously been running hard because both had difficulty retrieving enough breath to speak.

Seeing his lost prodigy was enough to spark Roy out of his stress induced psychosis. "Not as fit as you used to be, Nicholas."

"Every bit as fit Mr Fox," Nicholas replied with a smile. "We've just done five miles in thirty minutes through the crowds. You and I will have to train a team together after this; you'll do the thinking and I'll do the running."

"It's a deal," Roy replied.

Nicholas turned to Nadira. "It's all fixed...everything you wanted."

Nadira looked him in the eyes. "And there has been no... no...collateral damage?" Nicholas returned her look. "None, they wanted to help."

Nicholas, with his hands behind his back, felt the bulge down the back of his trousers. Adonis chipped in, "Yes, they were fine about it." He still had his gloves on.

Everyone looked at Adonis because he rarely spoke. He looked apologetic and added, "Sorry Boss."

Nadira still wondered whether the reported cooperation had involved any aspect of a filleting knife, but decided to take the risk. Taking Roy's arm and moving towards the far corner of the backstage space, Nadira said, "Roy, I want a word with you in private."

Donnie looked across at the one-sided conversation between Nadira and Roy. She sure was impressive he thought. As the two re-joined the company, Nadira was saying to Roy, "Now, Roy, as a lawyer I must tell you that you could be in serious danger of civil litigation if you use what I have told you. The whole thing could be brought down around you."

"It's all right Ms Khan," said Roy. "I've made my decision; sometimes you've just got to do things because they are right."

Donnie decided to try to remember Roy's statement; it sounded good.

The police did not really 'burst in', for their intrusion was quieter and reflective of their confidence. Chief Superintendent Dingwall had in fact delayed the intrusion to the last possible moment, only carrying it out after the Chief Constable of Police Scotland criticised him for delaying and making the crowd situation potentially more dangerous. The second most senior police officer in Great Britain had made it his priority to supervise the March. The London, Birmingham, Liverpool and Bristol riots had never come north of the border but the Chief Constable was worried about this event, especially when his ninety year old mother had berated him for not releasing 'poor Henry'.

Inspector Mitchell moved forward, holding out a document folded long ways and tied with a thin red ribbon. "This is an injunction set to Messers Fox, Anderson and Hunt as well as any others involved in the organisation of this March. The courts have declared that the event must not be undertaken as it would seriously prejudice future court proceedings against Mr Henry Doncaster and cohorts."

Donnie screamed. "You bastards; you murdered the old man you said was a cohort."

Mitchell wondered if he should arrest this wild man, but was pre-empted by Chief Superintendent Dingwall standing behind him and saying, "Serve the injunction Inspector Mitchell."

Mitchell handed the paper to Sam Hunt and added, "You are immediately to vacate this place through the back of the stage where police officers will take you to you're a police station for questioning. We will explain to the public."

The document was grabbed out of Sam's hand by Professor Nadira Khan. There were twenty-two pages, but Nadira knew where to find the points of importance. Two minutes later her face broadened to a smile and she said, "In my experience the police often make mistakes with injunctions and then take them to tame judges who do not examine them critically but only sign them. The same is true here. Throughout this document all the references are to 'The March' but the injunction does not cover the meeting here on the Green. There is nothing in here that can legally prevent this meeting."

Dingwall moved forward and grabbed the document from Nadira, flicking through the pages, giving only a few seconds to each. He threw the document down and ground his teeth in the face of Roderick Mitchell. "I want your resignation on my desk in the morning you incompetent moron!"

The Chief Superintendent swept out of the backstage area only realising too late that he had gone through the curtain on to the stage. Though a dozen ice creams and five bottles of water were immediately thrown, only two ice creams reached their mark, but these were sufficient to undo Dingwall's self-preening in front of his mirror earlier in the day. He retired back through the curtain and the police, except for Roderick Mitchell, withdrew through the back exit.

Nadira called their whole backstage group together. "They will not interrupt the event here but they may well try to stop any March thereafter. Strictly speaking, the Chief Superintendent's snatching back the injunction and throwing it to the ground could reasonably be taken as indicative of its withdrawal, but that would have to be an argument in court and not here. Roy, you must be sure that you inform the crowd that they may be seen to be in contempt of court if they go from this meeting on to March."

A face above an Events Maestros T shirt poked through the curtain saying, "Mr Hunt, Mr Fox, it's time."

50. ROY'S SPEECH

The police intrusion had taken the time Roy had wanted to take a final look at his notes, so he just dropped them in a bin and sat for a moment on a back stage chair. He allowed his mind to drift to the people he felt close to. There was Henry in his Barlinnie cell: Henry, a man from the other side of the tracks from himself; someone he would never have expected to even know, never mind care for; Henry who had worked hard to help Roy to connect with his family; Henry who had always been there for both Roy and Donnie in this past year. And there was Donnie, dear Donnie: timid as a mouse and fierce as a lion; Donnie who had lost his way in life a long time ago, but was now finding it again and with a vengeance; Donnie the Mountaineer of Assynt. Roy next remembered Maureen: brave Maureen; lonely Maureen; Maureen who laughed and cried at the same time; Maureen who so craved love that she had had to hold herself back from loving. And Rosie, who was like a new sister for Maureen: Rosie who was Maureen's rock; Rosie who terrified Donnie because she looked so hard; Rosie who had to look so hard because she felt like a jelly inside; Rosie who was just realising that the most important person she had to love was herself. Roy called up each of his Canada family in turn and spent moments with them before joining Sheila. "Well, here we go girl. Will you stand by my shoulder as I do this thing?"

Sheila smiled back at him and took his arm. Together they walked through the curtain.

It was like walking through a portal from one world into another. He passed from the quiet solitude behind the curtain to the explosion of sound from a hundred thousand cheering, screaming people. The sound hit him like a wall; he had to push to get through it to the microphone. He looked below him to Donnie standing with Sam in the front row; Sam now adorned with earphones and giving him the best hand signal, the thumbs up. The crowd fell silent. Roy paused, slowed down time and began to speak.

"Ladies and Gentlemen, my name is Roy Fox and I am not accustomed to speaking in public...particularly so much public!"

Roy paused and smiled as the cheers rang out. "I am a retired toolmaker and I spend my time at my allotment or with my friends. One of these, Mr Donald Anderson, is here with me."

The cameras picked out Donnie in the front row and there were squeals in a house in Tigre, Argentina.

"We are just two men who have lost our dear friend, Mr Henry Doncaster, currently jailed without charge in Barlinnie. Like many old Glasgow gentlemen Henry enjoys a punt on the horses...I am sure that there are a few here..."

Roy paused and smiled during the confessions and laughter. Several confessors were battered by their wives' handbags.

"The difference between Henry and the rest of us is that Henry is a genius with his computers and he wins. For that reason and that reason alone Henry Doncaster was dragged from his bedroom at 5.30am one morning. When he tried to stand up the police gave him an electric shock of fifty thousand volts. Imagine how that would feel for an old man... to be given a shock that is two hundred times normal domestic voltage Records show that only five men older than Henry have been Tasered by the police and three are dead. To pass fifty thousand volts through the body of a sixty-four year old man is the morals of a police state."

Roy delivered the last sentence very slowly so that the whole crowd could join in the crescendo of shouting at the end.

"For weeks now..." In delivering this sentence Roy turned to look directly into the lens of the front camera, to the delight of the TV director in the transmission van. "...in the name of you, the citizens of this country, Mr Henry Doncaster has been held without being charged. Initially he was not even allowed legal representation. Ladies and gentlemen this is all being done under the pretence of protecting you from terrorism. When his lawyer, the reputed Glasgow solicitor Mr Findlay Macsween OBE, was eventually allowed to be with Henry in interviews, eighty year old Mr Macsween was then also arrested and thrown into a police cell."

Roy left a long pause during which the murmurings of discontent were considerable.

He raised his voice and perfected his diction for the next sentence which he delivered slowly. "Ladies and gentlemen, it is with enormous sadness that I have to tell you that, in your name, Mr Findlay Macsween died in his police cell last night."

In the long pause left by Roy the crowd grew wild in their anger and five hundred police officers around the perimeter drew their batons. The Russian RT news presenter provided an editorial comment for their viewers. "The Police State that is Great Britain has murdered an 80 year old lawyer in his police cell and now they have drawn their batons to club the Pensioners to death!"

Roy held up his arms. "Dear friends I know that you are angry. We are all angry, but we are also dignified citizens who can express our anger in dignified ways."

In his Holyrood office the First Minister of Scotland looked up from his TV and said to his aides, "This guy is good."

The aides nodded their agreement; they were still relieved that they had managed to talk the First Minister out of joining the March.

Roy, still with his arms held aloft, continued. "I am looking here at some young members of our police force. These are not heartless, cruel young men and women. They are also victims. They are victims of a system that has got out of control. These young police officers in front of you are victims of an authority structure within the police that punishes honest questioning. We have evidence of officers being uncomfortable with what is happening but being put in fear of losing their pensions. Some of them would prefer to be over here supporting you."

'Too true,' thought former Inspector Roderick Mitchell, still sitting backstage with his head in his hands.

Roy continued, "We are all victims of the disease that has been around in various forms for many years. The American war strategist, Thomas Schelling, in a book called 'The Strategy of Conflict', wrote about it in 1960 when he said that the best way for a nation to get control over its **own** people was to strike **terror** into them. From a hundred years ago that terror was conveniently obtained by the First and the Second World Wars. Thereafter our fear was maintained by the so called 'Cold War': a wonderful conspiracy that met the same need for fear in the Western and the Eastern bloc countries. More recently the terrorism threat has comfortably kept us in fear and maintained our unquestioning obedience to authority.

Roy paused at this point because he knew that this was heavy stuff. The pause gave space for huge cheers and cries of 'Yes! Yes! As well as others that were more militant.

Roy continued. "We have not seriously challenged the six major Acts of Parliament in the past fifteen years that have dramatically increased police powers in relation to suspected acts of terrorism and serious crime. The result is that in the present day it is possible for a rogue senior police officer simply to apply the label 'terrorism' or even 'possibly terrorist related' in order to gain complete control over his victim. Once the label is applied, the rogue officer simply relies on the unquestioning authority structure within the Force and indeed the country to do his bidding.

Roy pointed to all points of the Green and implored his crowd, "Before you go from here today, please give a friendly smile and a wave to the policemen and policewomen around you, because they are victims as well as Henry. Henry's aggressor is a certain rogue officer by the name of Chief Superintendent Roger Dingwall whose only concern has been to gain access to Henry's bank accounts. We have this morning obtained statements and documentary evidence that Henry is not the first of Dingwall's victims. If our police friends care to examine the case two years ago involving John Bethel and Luigi Lugano and compare the banking records of each of them in relation to those of Roger Dingwall, they will find that the Chief Superintendent confiscated nearly £150,000 from their accounts to his own."

The Chief Constable of Police Scotland was firing instructions to all around him. Even the young man delivering complimentary Silvios ice creams got a command.

Roy moved towards the end of his speech. "In a few moments I am going to begin to march towards George Square. I need to tell you that Chief Superintendent Dingwall has just served us with an injunction against the March, so anyone who joins me may be arrested. Ladies and gentlemen, thank you for listening so patiently to me today."

Later folklore described the cheering at the end of Roy's speech as being so loud that it spooked horses at Hamilton Racecourse, some eleven miles away. Roy was joined by Donnie's big smile and a firm handshake from young Sam as they moved towards the exit to the Green. In the early hours of the morning in Vancouver, Emily, John, Paul and little Clara were watching the newsreel and dancing about their living room with the banners they had made up.

Because they had prior orders from Chief Superintendent Dingwall, three officers moved to arrest Roy, Donnie and Sam. No one had heard the normally quiet Chief Constable shout before, so they had no idea he could be so loud.

"Are you crazy? Get back here!" he bellowed.

When the officers came back alongside their Chief Constable he posed a question. "Have you not been listening to a word that man has been saying?"

The officers did not get the point at all, so their superior gave them chapter and verse. "A good police officer has to think for themselves. Following orders is important but so is weighing up the issues. You had been instructed to arrest them if they started marching so that is what you were blindly going to do, regardless of the issues. Here we are with five hundred officers and they are a hundred thousand. At one moment in his talk he had them so enraged against the police that they would have torn us limb from limb. But he controlled them; God, he even got them to smile and wave at us! Being a good officer is not simply about obeying orders; it is also a matter of reasoning and conscience. We should put an examination of the Nuremburg judgment into the police training manual." For some weeks thereafter the Nuremberg judgment was frequently googled on Police Scotland computers.

51. THE PENSIONERS MARCH

As Roy, Donnie and Sam left the Green, some young people in light blue jump suits bearing the motif 'Aqua Scotia' gave them bottles of water while others dressed in orange and labelled 'Silvios' plied them with ice cream cones.

Roy looked at Sam. "Another of your ideas Sam?"

Sam nodded. "The water was my idea; I thought it would be a nice touch for the pensioners and Aqua Scotia jumped at the chance to donate twenty thousand bottles. That was too few as it turned out, so they have sent to their Perthshire factory for more. But the free ice cream was an offer from Silvios. As the oldest ice cream maker in the city they thought that it was appropriate. They have ten vans turning out as many cones as they can all day. There is another van going back and forward to their factory for extra supplies. But I never thought about the cones being used as missiles against a Chief Superintendent!"

The principals moved fast down London Road to the Gallowgate in order to allow the massive crowd behind them some space. This was the part of the old city where public hangings used to take place. Someone had made a giant effigy of a senior policeman and hung it from a top floor window. Despite much of the population being on the March, all the tenement windows had someone waving and cheering. One rather heavy looking woman leaned out of her top floor window and bellowed above the din. "Donnie, here's yer jeelie piece!" A knotted Tesco bag parachuted down from the window and Donnie moved swiftly to his left to grab it just after it had landed. He opened the bag and shouted back. "Thanks missus, blackcurrant's my favourite!"

Sam was bemused. "What was that about?"

Roy explained the old tradition of Glasgow mothers making up a jam sandwich, putting it in a bag and throwing it down to their playing child in the back court of the tenements.

Three helicopters hired by TV companies wheeled high over

the March, with the reporters giving their commentaries. The most under-stated report came from the BBC correspondent, but even he was excited by the event. "You can see that the March is snaking about half a mile from the Glasgow Green and still only a small proportion of the people have got out of the park. In front of every group are the pensioners. Most of the Mobility Scooters in Scotland must be here! Inside the Park those waiting to join the March appear to have organised themselves into their own March that goes round and round the park before it exits. At the very end of the March are the pipers. Evidently there are a hundred of them playing every conceivable reel and jig. That must be some noise; how is it down on the Green Bob?"

Bob replied, not from the Green but from within the outside broadcast van where he could scan the feeds from fifteen cameras and coordinate the commentary with the Director. "You're right about the noise Harry; those hundred pipers are sure belting it out. Evidently they wanted the pipers at the end so that they would encourage any marchers who were flagging; some of them are a fair age after all!"

Bob moved to the prepared link. "Talking about age, Mandy, I believe that you are with someone who could give us all a few years?"

The Director shifted to a close-up of the smiling blond reporter Mandy; then panned out to show that she was walking beside a very old lady on a Mobility scooter.

"Yes Bob," said Mandy. "I am with Mrs Jessie MacTavish who is one hundred and one years old. How are you getting on Mrs MacTavish?"

Jessie, still as sharp as she had ever been, was used to the ageist way that the young talked to her. Generally she would destroy the perpetrator, but today she was trying to be on her best behaviour; she nearly succeeded.

"I'm getting on just fine, except for this damned scooter... oops, sorry dear! It has a mind of its own on these cobbles. It needs bigger wheels. They made me use it, but I'm going to ditch it half-way and jog the rest."

Mandy might have picked up on the jogging thought the Director, but instead delivered the prepared question. "Is this your first March Jessie?"

"No," replied Jessie. "I was on one a wee while back, in 1936 it was. It was like this one…an anti-fascist demo. The coppers were against us then as well. Maybe this time we should string a few of them up from the lamp posts to teach them a lesson for good."

The Director's normal diligence would have had a finger hovering over the time delay button that gives a few seconds grace for a switch away from toxic content, but he had completely underestimated Mrs Jessie MacTavish and the feed had all gone to air. He switched back to Bob who was nearly caught laughing but got it together in time. "Thanks Mandy. Let's use some of our roving cameras to pick out people and their banners. There's one over there that says 'BRIGADOON SWINDON PENSIONERS'. I spoke with them this morning. Evidently they were passing through Glasgow on their 'Brigadoon Tour' to the Highlands. They kidnapped their bus driver and bartered his release with the Tour Company which then had to allow the driver to bring them to the March."

The cameras then scanned some Trade Union banners, always the most ornate and generally the oldest. They paused only briefly on the Socialist Workers Party banner 'PIGS PERSECUTE PENSIONER' that was also the title of the lead article in their weekly paper, liberal quantities of which were being sold as they marched. Historically, 'Red Clydeside' had been strong for the predecessors of the SWP. There was also a wide range of banners representing the views of smaller groups of people, 'DIGNITY FOR PENSIONERS'; 'THE PENSIONERS OF SLOUGH SUPPORT HENRY'; 'PAKISTANI PENSIONERS FROM POLLOKSHAWS'; 'SCOTTISH BOOKMAKERS ASSOCIATION SUPPORTS HENRY'. The cameras alighted on one young man who walked on his own and held a small banner, with one pole in each hand. The banner read, 'HENRY IS INOCINT'. Young

Malcolm Jamieson was on his first March. Anthony Mason walked with a dozen friends under the banner, 'LOCHINVER SAYS FREE HENRY', closely followed by Jock and Duncan, with their banner declaring, 'GAEL ASAINTE AIRSON EANRAIG' ('THE GAELS OF ASSYNT SUPPORT HENRY')

Staying well away from old people, Mandy moved to interview two younger men holding a banner with an unusual motif, 'COMPUTER GLEN **KNOW** THAT HENRY IS INNOCENT'. Amjad and Mohsin were delighted to be interviewed. But, as Mandy leaned the microphone towards them, Mohsin thought she was handing it to him. He took it out of her hand and declared to the camera. "We are Henry's computer suppliers. We regularly work on his hardware; we know everything on it and there is nothing bad. We went to the police to tell them but they weren't interested. COMPUTER GLEN is your friendly local computer shop – we mend so that you don't have to spend!" With big smiles from Amjad and Mohsin, the microphone was returned to Mandy.

The Director was a broken man. "Did you miss the button again?" asked his assistant, seeing the possibility of her promotion. Lifting his head from the table in front of him her superior replied. "I got out in time to cut the advert, but I missed the first part. We could be in serious trouble having put that out while the case is sub judice. I need to hit someone... where's Mandy?"

Roy, Donnie and Sam were well up the High Street, nearly at the Ingram Street left turn towards George Square, when a police car came down the road towards them at speed. Donnie thought that it was Dingwall at the wheel and that he was going to wipe them out. As he made to jump towards the pavement the pursuit vehicle braked violently to a stop thirty yards in front of them. Amanda jumped out and ran towards them with arms open ready for big hugs. Roy caught her and got the first hug, followed by Donnie and Sam. As they walked, she first told her story then Sam gave his journalist's account of the day thus far.

As they turned into Ingram Street Donnie's phone rang. His jumping into the air was indicative of the fact that incoming calls were rare. After a scramble to find the instrument, Donnie pressed the green button and indicated his presence. "Hello, Donnie Anderson here. Who is that?"

From eight and a half thousand miles away came the reply. "Hi Dad. We are watching you on television. Give us a wave."

Donnie lifted his head, smiled and waved into the ether at a son he had not seen for twenty-five years and a daughter in law and two grandchildren he had never seen, but today had seen him for the very first time. As he smiled and waved he started to cry unfamiliar tears...not tears of sadness, fear or anger, but tears of joy.

Donald said, "Love you dad; see you soon," and hung up.

*
* *

Henry glanced across the table at an evil looking inmate who had ignored the vacant tables and sat at his. The man was about forty, only five foot seven, but at least eighteen stones in weight, distributed more or less equally between fat and muscle. His distinguishing feature was a scar that crossed his face diagonally from above his left ear down to the right side of the chin. It had been a deep cut and badly stitched. Luckily, or perhaps it was the skill of the user, the blade had missed the left eye, but a portion of the nose was missing and the top lip existed in two separate parts.

Henry was trying to be his 'cool' self, but he had become so diminished by the prison experience that he could not access 'cool Henry', only 'frightened Henry'. His fear was intensified by the knowledge that regular inmates usually completely ignore remand prisoners like him. Henry was trying not to look at the 'The Beast', but he sensed the man's constant gaze.

Finally The Beast spoke. "Ur ye 'enry?"

"Yes" replied Henry, and, completely forgetting the

context, offered a handshake.

The Beast looked at Henry's outstretched hand but did not respond in kind. Instead he said, "Leave ere three minutes efter me and go tae the toilets. Go intae the last cubicle oan the left."

The Beast devoured his mince, potatoes and peas in ten seconds, taking his plate and plastic fork to the clearing up area before exiting. Henry looked at the clock to count down the rest of the last three minutes of his life or his homosexual virginity, he knew not which.

The toilets were just outside the canteen and, as Henry entered, there was loud shouting behind him. Someone was threatening to rape someone else's mother and the respondent was going to cut his f.....g balls off; normal prison stuff Henry imagined. But it was enough for the officer stationed in the toilets to run out to assist his colleagues in the canteen. Henry was going to pop back to have a look until the chilling realisation dawned that this was probably a cover for his visit to the cubicle. Having lost all strength to do anything different, Henry walked the length of the toilets and entered the last cubicle on the left.

With The Beast already sitting on the toilet it was a tight squeeze. Henry was understandably flustered. That flustered state was not remediated by The Beast's next suggestion. "It'll be easier if ye sit oan ma knee."

Henry thought that this was the very last thing he wanted to do in his life, but he did it nonetheless. And so, Henry Doncaster was by now as far away from his normal life as he could be. He was in a prison toilet sitting on the lap of The Beast. At this very point of ultimate surrealism The Beast took a mobile phone from his top pocket and said, "Call fir ye."

Henry turned round to look in the face of The Beast from a distance that was far too close. "What?" he cried.

The beast simply held up the phone, which Henry took and said, "Hello."

The reply was instantaneous. "Hello Mr Doncaster, this

is Nicholas Andrews. We have very little time, so I will speak quickly."

Nicholas quickly recounted the day's events as he rushed to the head of the March. "I will now pass you to someone important; you only have one minute." Nicholas handed the phone to Amanda.

A minute later The Beast made a signal to end by silently running his finger across his throat. Henry said goodbye, pressed the red button and handed the phone back. The Beast ended the relationship with, "Noo get aff ma bloody lap an dinnae tell onywan aboot this."

Henry struggled to get his old knees to straighten and actually fell back on The Beast's lap, an event that led to some swearing. Henry left the cubicle and strode down the length of the toilets with his old swagger restored. The Beast switched off the phone, put it into a water-tight plastic bag and returned it to the cistern. He then waited one minute before pulling the flush and exiting the cubicle.

*
**

And so it was in high spirits that the head of the march, with Roy, Donnie, Sam and Amanda in the front line followed by Maureen, Rosie and other Culloden regulars, turned right on to South Frederick Street, only a hundred yards from the south east corner of George Square. The police had kept the Square and the adjoining streets clear for the marchers, but still a huge cheer went up as the March crept into the empty square because office buildings had been opened to allow access to staff and their families and every roof top was covered with a mass of people. Even the turreted roof of the impressive Victorian City Chambers Building was crammed with people cheering and waving.

It took an hour for the Square to fill with marchers. There were still many who had not reached the end point, but the police, realising that their original prediction of twenty-five thousand for the march was way off the mark, had arranged for Events Maestros to move three of the large screens and speakers to points along the route such that everyone could hear and see the ending. In the middle of the square was a six foot high stage, about the size of a boxing ring. The only object on the stage was a microphone on its stand.

When Roy got a sign from the police that everyone was in place he slowly walked up the fourteen steps to the stage and made his way to the microphone. Standing erect with his arms by his side, Roy looked as though he had been doing this all his life. He did not have a smile on his face because, although there was much joy on the March, its purpose was serious. He said simply and slowly. "Thank you for coming."

If he had intended to follow this with any other words it was impossible, because more than a hundred thousand people in the centre of Glasgow went into massive and lengthy cheering. Eventually Roy raised his arms and a silence gradually formed. He continued, "On February 15th 2003 there was a March as big as this in Glasgow to tell the Government that Prime Minister Blair should not be allowed to take our country into a war against Iraq. The banner at the front of the March said 'NOT IN OUR NAME MR BLAIR'. I am sure that there are many people here who were also on that March."

Roy left a moment for those people to declare themselves noisily before continuing. "Your voices were ignored that day and some of your children lost their young lives in that war."

Roy had not meant to leave a pause at this point, but he heard a mother cry, so he gave her a moment's silent hearing before continuing. "This March today could as easily be for those children. It is not only about Henry Doncaster. It is about people. It is about valuing our people and not treating them as dispensable. Roy paused again, because he was miles away from his intended script and did not know where he was going. But he was thoroughly inside the feeling of the event, so he allowed that feeling to dictate his speech. "We invite political and social leaders to carry out executive actions on our behalf, but we and they must remember that it is humanity they serve. We must remind them that they are there principally to honour the people they serve and only secondarily to protect political ideologies. Nearly a hundred years ago in 'the war to end all wars' children were thrown in their millions to their deaths to protect alternative political ideologies against each other. They were cannon fodder; their humanity was discounted. If they had feelings that were too powerful to let them continue, they were shot. We have moved on as a nation since then but we still need to ask our executives to mature as leaders. We need to ask them to think about people as well as policies. We need to ask them to think ethically; always to weigh the policy against its consequences. We must help them to remember that accountability does not only come at the ballot box, accountability means listening... listening to the people...listening to you."

Roy had to pause to allow the cheers; then he continued. "Today our society has been given a rare opportunity, an opportunity to see what is happening to us. The future will record that a small part of what we did this day was to draw attention to the predicament of current victims like Henry Doncaster and Findlay Macsween. The larger part was to see what was happening to Britain. Ironically, the errant actions of a rogue police officer have given us a window on the soul of our society to see how it is drifting into inhumanity. We should be grateful for that glimpse and act on it by asking questions of our police and also our political representatives. We must be patient with them because it is difficult for people in authority to retain perspective on the consequences of their actions. We must help them with that. Ladies and gentlemen, I believe that today you have spoken so loudly that you will have helped them to hear. I thank you for Henry Doncaster and for Findlay Macsween and for our society to come."

Roy bowed in farewell, made his way slowly across the stage and down the fourteen steps. Thousands of people cried as he made his exit. The pipes broke into a loud rendition of

'Scotland the Brave' and a hundred thousand people stayed on to live the last minutes of 'THE PENSIONERS MARCH ON GLASGOW'.

52. AFTERWARDS

Maureen unlocked the door of the Culloden and entered the unfamiliar bar. It was unfamiliar because it was a deserted campaign headquarters rather than her familiar neat and tidy territory. The early departure of the fleet of taxis had caught everyone out, so nothing had been cleared. The banner-making area had been abandoned even with one product declaring 'FREE HEN…' There were plates of untouched and partly eaten sandwiches on every table and an array of unfinished soft drink cans and bottles. Roy's cap was hanging on the back of his chair. Maureen picked it up and brushed it off. She smiled at its owner in her mind. "Dear Roy, you sure did good today. You took my breath away. I had no idea you could do that. You had all those people in the palm of your hand. People cried real tears Roy. Where did you get all that from?"

Maureen looked again at Roy's cap. "Unlike you to forget your cap Roy…or did you leave it on purpose? Did it not fit with your image today?"

She smiled at her Roy, then she looked around at the mess and gave herself a challenge. "Well Mo, I dare say we will be busy at the evening opening and they will all be expecting their usual clean place, so we had better roll up our sleeves and get stuck in."

*
**

At the end of the March Rosie had been invited by Nicholas to have tea in one of Glasgow's famous old tea rooms. Of course, if Nicholas was there, then Adonis also had to be present. They were drinking tea from fine china cups and sampling the delights from all three levels of the cake stand situated in the middle of the table. There were sandwiches on the bottom level, three kinds of fruit cake on the middle plate and exotic cream cakes on the top level.

"My mother used to love this place," declared Nicholas. "She would come every Thursday with three of her cronies and they would spend two and a half hours. The waitresses knew her so well that two of them came to her funeral. This was her special place; I come once a month."

Both Rosie and Adonis looked at Nicholas, surprised that he was speaking so personally. Looking at Adonis, Nicholas continued. "Do you have a special place?"

Adonis was caught in the middle of a cream cake, some of which ended up on his nose. Rosie skilfully removed the cream with her serviette. Adonis made to start to speak three times before his muteness was finally overcome. "I used to go to my father's betting shop after he was killed. As a boy I would be in the shop with him at weekends and during the week if he let me skip school. He would let me pin up the racing papers on the walls in the morning and I would sweep up the spent betting slips in the afternoon. He would say to me. 'Enjoy it more if there is a lot to sweep up because every crunched-up betting slip on the floor is a profit for us!' After they killed him and we lost the shop I went in a few times a week and just sat about. I remembered the times with him."

Rosie could hardly speak. She wanted to know why his father had been killed, but it did not seem right to ask. Instead she asked a different question. "You said that you 'used to' go to the shop; what made you stop?"

Adonis smiled – Rosie always melted when he gave that smile – then he explained. "The owner asked me not to come in again, for every time I came in, half the punters left!"

"Ha!" Nicholas chuckled. "So they were our customers as well as the bookie's!" Turning his attention to Rosie he asked her the same question. "Rosie, what about you; do you have a special place?"

"Recently it has been the kitchen in The Culloden, with Maureen. We have perfected the triple gin and tonic as well as the talk. She is like the best sister a girl could have and the kitchen is our space."

Nicholas nodded and used his finger to mop up the bits of cream that had dropped on his plate. He called for the bill and said to Adonis, "I won't need you from now until Monday noon. I'm going down to London to spend a couple of nights with Everton's team; he will supply the cover."

Nicholas looked at the bill and left the cash including his usual large tip. He rose and bid them farewell. "Enjoy yourselves you two; I'm off to the airport."

'Nicholas, you are a cunning pig,' thought Rosie, looking across at Adonis with his sheepish grin.

*
**

Donnie needed to go for a walk; that was the only way he could get back to any kind of normal life. Straight after the March he set out from George Square to head north, knowing that at some point he would intersect with the Forth and Clyde canal and take the towpath home. He had worn his walking boots for the March, so he was well equipped. Every step refuelled him; this was what he needed to be the person he knew he was. Roy could do the talking and, by God, he did it well. But Donnie knew that he was not that kind of man; he had to be climbing mountains. Donnie revised his plan and hailed a black cab.

"Take me to the Arrochar Alps."

The taxi driver was cautious. "Are you sure? That's a big fare."

Donnie looked in his pockets and found the money from the journalists. "I have £65; is that enough?"

"Yes, with a discount, but not to wait and take you home again."

"There's a bus service back to Glasgow," said Donnie, "And I have a bus pass."

The driver nodded. "Fair enough my friend; it is to the Arrochar Alps that we go."

If Donnie had climbed his mountain all those years ago as a boy he might have gone on to become one of Scotland's famous establishment of mountaineers. He would have been a regular on the winter ice climbing in Glencoe and a summer visitor to the French Alps. He may even have gone on to the Himalayas and Aconcagua in South America and the rest. But, as Aonghas had observed, "He was a little late." The taxi driver took him to the point, a little beyond Arrochar, where the track to ascend 'The Cobbler' begins. The Cobbler is the focal mountain in 'The Arrochar Alps'. Generations of Scottish 'weekenders' had based their life on the Cobbler, ending work in the shipyards at noon on the Saturday and catching the bus to that far extremity of Loch Long. They would climb the Cobbler that evening and spend the night in a well-known overhang near the summit. The stories and the whisky would go on late into the night, but the following day would be filled with specialist rock climbs in the area. The Sunday night would usually be 'dry' only because all the whisky had been drunk on the previous evening. But, instead of the whisky, the Primus stoves would come out and strong tea would be brewed. Whether it was whisky or tea that was imbibed, the result would be the same – severe intoxication in the mountains. Thus Scotland won many world class mountaineers, and lost some of the most notable in the Himalayas. Donnie ascended the mountain like a man obsessed, because that was his condition. The early part is a steep incline that is boringly stepped by logs. The few late walkers would not be going to the summit and Donnie passed them at pace and without comment. He reached what he thought was the summit, but the top is confusing, with two peaks, so he also did the other one, just in case. Donnie jogged down the mountain, mostly in the dark, and realised that his change of plan would make him late for meeting Roy in the Culloden, especially since he had no idea of the bus timetable except that there were two busses a day. He was just resigning himself to hitch hiking when he saw that the taxi was still in the car park below.

"You were quick," greeted the taxi driver. "I thought that I would wait and give you a lift home. Oh, and here is your £65 back. We've got to look after the organisers of The Pensioners March after all!"

*
**

Roy needed to be alone and the best place for that was sitting beside Sheila's grave. He picked up his lifetime conversation with her. "I have had a bit of a day Sheila, but you know that already, because you were with me. You were on my arm as I walked out that first time. I could not have done that without you beside me. I kept fairly close to what I had prepared, though, as I got into it I had the strange experience that all I had to do was to stay connected with *the feeling* of what I was talking about and that closeness would give me the best words. It was as though time had slowed down and it was easy for me to find the words. The second time was even easier because, from the beginning, all I did was to feel what I was trying to say, and the words came out. The first time I was nervous before you took my arm and you settled me. But the second time I could do it myself; I was not nervous at all. But now, after it is over, I just want to curl up and sleep with you to comfort me. Will you do that Sheila? Can I sleep here with you? I am so tired, so very tired."

Roy Fox, hero of Scotland, curled up on his wife's grave and slept with her.

*
**

Henry walked towards the dining room for the evening meal, served at 5.00pm for the convenience of the staff who needed their evenings, and the prisoners who did not care. Henry was still feeling buoyed by his one minute talk with his sister. As he approached the dining room entrance, he wondered if The Beast would be there. He pushed the door open and the place erupted in cheers of 'ENRY, ENRY, ENRY!' accompanied by the clatter of tin plates against the tables. He noticed that the prison guards were also clapping.

53. COMING TOGETHER

Maureen had cleared the mess by 4.40pm which gave her precisely twenty minutes to wash and put on her face. In fact, she decided to do better than that and, from the clothes she kept in a wardrobe, she selected a red dress and her red satin shoes. People, especially women of a certain age, always admired those shoes. At precisely 5.00pm she opened the doors of The Culloden.

The first person in the lengthy queue was the owner who declared, "First drink free for those in the queue apart from the journalists, Maureen". Maureen loved him for being so involved with all this. She knew that The Culloden must be a marginal financial venture for him, for the regulars were not exactly big spenders. But she also knew how connected he was with the area. His father had been part of the Glasgow Jewish community who had established a business interest in this pub and several retail outlets in the locality. Historically, the Jewish community had been badly treated in Glasgow, as in the rest of the world, and the present owner had been amazed when twenty Culloden men and women had attended his father's funeral. He had been moved by how they quietly accommodated themselves to the Jewish funeral tradition that separated men from women. For ever he would continue to honour them in return.

There were forty people in the queue to enter The Culloden. Thirty were regulars and ten were journalists asking for Roy. Maureen tried to call Roy to warn him, but, as usual, his phone was switched off, so she phoned Sam.

Sam had spent the past hours selling his pieces to the world's press. In advance of the day he had engaged three agents to lay the groundwork for the worldwide sales on a 15% commission. During the afternoon he had begun to churn out the pieces but he had also fielded calls from the agents on things like exclusives and photo opportunities, the latter which meant that he had to meet Roy and Donnie. The last call he had received before heading for the Culloden was a request for Roy and Donnie to appear on *Newsnight*, the main BBC news analysis programme. This was an impossible decision for him to make without consultation, but he had to do it. He sat for a moment and thought of Roy's speeches. Then he said to the producers of Newsnight, "Roy and Donnie could not possibly appear on Newsnight without their friend, Henry Doncaster. Perhaps you could exert some influence in that regard."

Roy wandered slowly up the road towards the Culloden. Part of him would have preferred to stay at home alone, but he knew that others would be there and it was right to meet them. As he reached the entrance a taxi swept up at speed and Donnie jumped out with a farewell wave to the driver. Roy, who himself was washed and dressed in his second best clothes, looked at Donnie in muddy boots and dirty trousers.

"I see that you have dressed for the occasion Mr Anderson," was Roy's greeting.

Donnie looked down at himself and back at Roy's apparel. "I can't change a habit of a life time even if we are rock stars."

Roy smiled. "OK, let's go in together, but don't get too close to my nice clothes."

Donnie held up his hand to pause Roy from pushing the door and said to his friend, "You know that nothing will ever be the same anymore?"

Roy smiled and contradicted him. "One thing that will always be the same is you, me and Henry."

The two men hugged as they were not supposed to do in the working class Glasgow subculture and entered the Culloden together. As if it were an ordinary evening, they made their way to the other end of the bar, nodding to Maureen, Rosie and also Adonis as they gained their normal bar stools which were unoccupied despite the full pub. The regulars had helpfully protected the seats from infrequent visitors with whispers of, "That's Roy's/Donnie's seat."

Roy's request was simple as always. "Rosie, could I have a

pint of heavy and two packets of smoky bacon crisps?"

Donnie added, "And could I have a pint of heavy and a packet of smoky bacon crisps." "But I've got you a packet!" said Roy.

Donnie explained. "Yes, but I've got one for Henry in case he comes."

At this point the national television news began and the whole pub fell to be silent witnesses. Much later, grandchildren would be told of this experience in The Culloden Bar in Glasgow. The Pensioners March was the main feature and Roy's speeches were well represented. But the newsreel did better than that, for it also showed the reactions of people in the crowd. It recorded the anger, the grief, the tears of sadness and joy, and the huge impact of Roy's speeches. The commentator said, at the end of the event, "We are witnessing the power of humanity over autocracy." That sentence would be replayed for many years in the annals of newsreels.

The reportage shifted to an interview with The First Minister of Scotland. It was mentioned that the British Prime Minister had been invited on to the programme, but neither he, nor a representative, was available. The First Minister was asked what he thought about the day's events. His reply re-wrote the textbooks on 'political speak'. "I applaud all of them. I am annoyed that I was not marching with them. I was not marching with them because I was caught up in that dreadful political presumption that we should not declare our support for a movement if it may appear to be anti-establishment. I curse myself that I fell into that old trap. But, we should turn that around and ask why did the First Minister of Scotland feel that he could not give this protest his full support? Why did he feel that he had to be deferent to Westminster? Why is it that the public in Scotland, as represented by 'The Pensioners March', had to tell us what was right, while the government of Scotland had to remain silent in fear of the very laws on terrorism that may have been abused. I am sad and I am apologetic to the people of Scotland that I failed them in this matter. I allowed myself to be silenced by the legislation that required these matters to be deferred to Westminster. There will soon come a time when that feudal tie to the demands of the Westminster establishment will end. Until that time I can only apologise to the people of Scotland."

Everyone in the Culloden cheered as the politics of Scotland took another lurch. The Prime Minister of Great Britain held his head in his hands. Donnie looked at Roy and said, "He is good, isn't he?"

"Well, he's clever, I'll give him that," Roy replied. "He knows how to use events to his own political ends. But in this situation the people of England, as well as Northern Ireland and Wales, are just as oppressed as us; it is not really a Scottish issue."

Sam entered the pub loaded with his usual bunch of files and made his way to the other end of the bar where Roy and Donnie resided. He stopped, put his files on the bar, and asked Roy an unusual question for both of them. "Roy, you were wonderful today; can I give you a hug?"

"It seems as though this is the way things are going, so let's do it." Roy reckoned that he had hugged the first two men in his life in the past half hour.

Sam began his report and consultation. "I'd like to talk you through our situation in regard to the financing of the March."

Roy's heart sank; he had forgotten that they would be responsible for the costs.

Sam continued. "I should have talked with you about the financing in detail before. I was so excited about it all I just kind of went ahead, expecting things to balance up…but they haven't. Let me take you through it. We were helped by the fact that the staging, the sound system and the screens were given free, as were the ice creams and the water. There were some small things we had to pay for, but the only large cost was for emergency medical cover. That used to be given free by Greater Glasgow Health Board for events like this but it is just one of the many cuts they have made."

Roy was worried. "So, what did it all cost us?"

Sam took out a sheet of paper. "The medical cover was £11,000 and the rest looks like it will be about £2,000."

Roy's worry was not diminished. "So we need to find £13,000," he concluded with a heavy tone.

Donnie took a wad of notes out of his pocket. "I've got £65 here and I can bring another £825 that was my winnings from the horseracing and from a football match I bet on with Henry. But that only comes to £890. I was going to use some of it for clothes for Argentina, but all I really need is my walking boots." Donnie put the crumpled pile of notes on to the bar in front of them.

Roy shook his head. "That is very good of you Donnie, but you should not have to pay your Argentina money; it was me that made the agreement with Sam after all." With a sigh he added, "I've got £2,000 in my savings. It will take me about four days to get it out in cash. We still need a lot of money." He smiled. "Perhaps Nicholas will give us a preferential loan rate!"

Sam shook his head. "But it's not as simple as that, because we also have some earnings, though they are difficult to tie down precisely."

Roy asked, "How can we possibly make earnings?"

"Well, the TV companies contributed for their pitches and I have written and sold a load of articles worldwide. Also Newsnight will pay for you two and Henry to appear if he gets released, though they don't pay much."

Roy held up an arm. "Wait just there; what is this about 'Newsnight'?"

Sam explained the background and his semi-commitment to the producer.

Now Roy held up both hands and demanded of Sam, "So how much of the £13,000 will we recoup in earnings?"

"Well", said Sam, "That's the problem I did not anticipate, because we are likely to make a profit of about £107,000!"

The evening continued with the journalists gradually

exiting as they realised the exclusives were already tied up. One photographer darted forward at the bar to snap Roy and Donnie without their permission, but unfortunately Adonis got in the way and the man's camera fell. Adonis accidentally stood on it, then picked up the terminated instrument to return it with apologies. The photographer knew better than to challenge the rippling muscles. Rosie purred.

Rory Donaldson had gone to his office after the March to tie down the witness statements of John Bethel and Luigi Lugano and completely forgot about his brand new Porsche parked at The Culloden. As his taxi approached the pub at speed Rory dreaded to see his beautiful car damaged or stolen. But it was still there and a quick circuit of the car revealed that it was undamaged.

"It's OK mister; no one's touched it" came the voice of a small boy seated in the nearby close. The boy added, "I make it twelve hours at £2 per hour, that's £24, less your £1 deposit. You owe me £23."

Rory gave the urchin three ten pound notes and told him to keep the change. The boy pocketed the wealth and skipped down the road saying, "Nice doing business with you Mister."

Amanda and Nadira had spent much of the afternoon in legal consultation about the next steps they might take in relation to Henry. As a result they had gone to the police station in the early evening with two purposes: to arrange a visit to Henry in Barlinnie and to keep the pressure on the police. As Nadira had explained, "I suspect that the Chief Constable is desperate to find a way to end this as soon as possible. He will have known for at least this afternoon that he likely has a rogue senior officer. He will also know that his office has been lax in allowing the senior officer so much latitude." Nadira had phoned ahead of their visit, asking for a meeting with the Chief Constable. She had been told that he was not in Glasgow so she asked for a meeting with the highest ranking substitute.

The respondent had sounded nervous. "Well, none of the

Deputy or Assistant Chief Constables is available, so that would be Chief Superintendent Dingwall…"

"Perhaps that would be inappropriate under the circumstances," Nadira suggested.

"Yes," came the reply, "suppose you come along in two hours and I'll see what I can arrange."

Thus it was that Nadira and Amanda entered the station and walked towards the desk sergeant. Sergeant Dunlop was in the process of gathering his things into a satchel as Amanda approached with a smile and an explanation to Nadira. "Nadira, this is the nice sergeant I told you about, who let me go to the March instead of having me strip searched."

Nadira knew what this would mean for Sergeant Dunlop. "That was an honourable thing you did sergeant; you would have known what it would mean for you."

The sergeant nodded. "Yes, but sometimes you just have to say 'no more'."

Amanda did not realise the significance of this interchange and asked, "Is this you finishing your shift, Sergeant Dunlop?"

The sergeant smiled weakly. "I'm finishing more than my shift; this is me out."

Amanda was shocked. "You mean out of the police force?"

He nodded. "A sergeant cannot countermand an order from a senior officer and get away with it. I've been suspended pending an investigation. If I'm lucky they will just let me retire; I've done my years and I'm ready to go. If I'm unlucky, they will have my pension."

Amanda's anger was compounded. "But that is not fair – that is so unfair – you are better than any of them!"

Sergeant Dunlop smiled just a little more strongly. "Thank you ma'am; it will be nice for me to remember that in the years to come."

Nadira dipped into her document case and handed Sergeant Dunlop her business card. "Make sure they know that you will be represented at the Disciplinary Hearing by Professor Nadira Khan. If they have any intelligence they will realise that my involvement will create a huge amount of publicity that they do not want. My bet is that they will drop the Disciplinary. Phone me directly on my mobile as things develop Sergeant."

Five minutes later Nadira and Amanda were ushered into an office where the Chief Constable offered a hand shake in greeting.

Maureen had asked the owner if she might use the premises for a small private party after closing time. He had readily agreed. "Of course, the law will not allow us to sell liquor after closing time without a special licence, so this should balance the stock." He had handed her five twenty pound notes.

So, after the pub emptied and the doors were locked, seven seats were gathered into a circle for Donnie, Roy, Sam, Rory, Maureen, Rosie and Adonis. Maureen invited orders. "Rosie and I normally have our triple gin and tonic; perhaps you gentlemen would also like something a bit special. For instance, I have a twenty year old cask strength Glenfarclas. The Scotsmen's eyes opened wide and they smiled. Most of them rarely drank malt whisky but that was to do with cost rather than taste. Maureen poured four large whiskies, two gins with tonic and a tonic water for Adonis, bringing them on a tray along with a small jug of water and the instruction, "Remember that you will have to add water to the whisky, partly to open it up but also because it is 56% alcohol rather than 40%."

They chatted about the events of the long day, about the fleet of taxis, the March and Roy's speeches. Adonis, in the absence of his boss, was more forthcoming than usual. "Your speeches were great Roy. At first I got so angry I wanted to fix the cop myself, but by the time you finished I was crying."

Rosie glanced at Adonis in considerable surprise and wondered again if earlier decisions might have to be reviewed.

They all jumped when the loud knock came to the door; no one in Glasgow would seek entry to a pub after closing time. Adonis nodded to Maureen to suggest that he cover for her and went to open the door. Maureen liked having his strong presence around. He opened the door and in walked Amanda, Nadira and Henry.

"We saw the lights on and reckoned you were having a party," said Henry in his re-found ebullient manner.

Through the mixture of screams and greetings, Maureen asked, "What would you like Henry?"

His reply was instantaneous. "A half-pint of beer, dear Maureen. Oh, and I would kill for a packet of smoky bacon crisps!"

54. NEWSNIGHT

Donnie had gone along with all the suggestions thus far. He had donned a smart light blue rather than white shirt because he had been told that blue comes over better than white on television. He had bought a flash tie that cost more than he would normally pay for a jacket since his only other tie was the black one he had bought for the funeral of Robert Alexander and that had not seemed appropriate. But he was digging his heels in as they were ushered into the make-up room. Of course, the make-up artist was well used to male resistance to such self-adornment and immediately decided that it would be Donnie who would be third in line, in order to give him time to get used to the idea. She rightly selected Henry as the first choice.

"Delighted my dear," he declared in response to her invitation. "I've always wanted to have a reason to try make-up. Will there be mascara?"

Roy and Donnie looked at each other with the same unvoiced question about whether Henry was putting on a show or if he was serious.

"No sir, there will be no need of the mascara, just a light dusting will be enough to take the sheen off your faces."

Roy felt reassured, not by the promise of a 'light dusting' whatever that was, but by the realisation that the young woman was from Lewis in the Western Isles. His nerves might now be forgotten by a little local banter. "So is that the west of Harris I hear in your voice my dear?"

"No, but it is the east of Lewis that you hear."

Roy was ready. "Oh, but I am sorry for you, ochone, ochone."

"So it will be Harris that you will be from?" she continued.

"Yes, from near Leverburgh," replied Roy, unwittingly falling into her trap.

She applied the finishing touch. "Oh, yes, I know

Leverburgh. I used to step out with a boy from Leverburgh, but my father made me dump him; he said that the folks from Leverburgh had very questionable genetics."

Roy fell silent, reminding himself that he should stick to bus drivers rather than taking on a woman from Lewis.

Their Newsnight slot was the main piece that evening and the production had been relocated to the Glasgow base, a decision that reflected the pressure on the national broadcaster to be less London centred. Roy, Donnie and Henry were seated in the studio in advance of the programme with the presenter seeking to put them at their ease by telling them the order of events. "We will begin by showing clips of the March and of both your speeches Roy. The clips will be short, just enough to inform people who have been living on the planet Zog for the past few days. Then we will show an interview I did this afternoon with the Assistant Chief Constable. He won't be applying for any promotion after this interview. Only after that interview will we switch to the studio. Henry, I thought that it would be best if I began by asking you about the experience you have been through. Is that all right?"

Henry nodded. "Yes, that makes sense as a place to begin."

The presenter turned to Roy and Donnie. "Then, later I'll invite you both to give your views on what happened."

Roy and Donnie nodded silently.

It was a strange experience for Henry to watch clips of the March. He had seen some of the recordings that afternoon, but it was a different experience to see it on the large studio screen. When it came to Roy's second speech Henry turned to look at him and winked in the minimal way men do to show their respect for the other.

The red light of the front camera facing the studio presenter came on and he addressed it. "We invited the Assistant Chief Constable with responsibility for Organised Crime and Counter Terrorism to join us this evening, but he declined on the grounds that a live broadcast ran the danger of encroaching on matters concerning one of his senior officers that are sub judice. Instead, we agreed that I would pre-record the interview this afternoon. Here is that interview."

The screen showed the Assistant Chief Constable seated behind his desk with the presenter on the other side with his back to the camera. The presenter asked his first question with no intention of taking prisoners. "Assistant Chief Constable, earlier today you suggested that we could not invite Henry Doncaster to take part in our programme this evening on the grounds that proceedings might still be taken against him despite his release last evening. You later recanted that suggestion, thus allowing tonight's programme to go ahead as planned. Assistant Chief Constable: is this yet another example of the police, in this case YOU, seeking to misuse power for your own ends. Did you want to block the programme because it would be embarrassing for Police Scotland?"

The Assistant Chief Constable nearly choked. Later the presenter admitted to his studio guests that this first question was quite different from the one he had earlier intimated as his starting point. Trying to recover, the Assistant Chief Constable resorted to what he thought was safer ground. "No...not at all. It's just that we have to be very careful where matters may be subject to legal proceedings."

The presenter continued. "But Henry Doncaster was not subject to legal proceedings. That was ended with his unconditional release by the Chief Constable last night. But today you sought to re-open a case against him. I put it to you Assistant Chief Constable: did you try to re-open proceedings on the authority of the Chief Constable or was this an attempt on your own part to block our programme tonight?"

The Assistant Chief Constable had lost all perspective on what was happening. "Look here, we will have to end this interview. This is not at all what you said we would be talking about."

The interviewer tightened into the doomed fish. "Assistant Chief Constable, if you want to withdraw from the interview that is your prerogative, but we will broadcast it as it is and let the public decide."

"No, no, that is not necessary…not necessary at all," said the Assistant Chief Constable with pleading in his voice.

The interviewer removed the hook, only to sharpen another. "Assistant Chief Constable, I will not be asking questions about your Chief Superintendent Roger Dingwall, because that matter is certainly sub judice. I simply want to establish the current position before moving on. Am I correct that the Chief Superintendent has been suspended and that he is being questioned in regard to the arrest of Henry Doncaster and also one earlier matter, about a year ago?"

"That is correct," replied the stricken policeman, pleased that it was an easier question than the first one and not realising that, if he had not already lost his way in this interview, he would have deflected the question rather than concede on it.

The presenter continued. "Turning to the arrest of Henry Doncaster; am I correct that this sixty-four year old gentleman was Tasered in his own bedroom?"

The new hook had set into the Assistant Chief Constable who vainly tried to wriggle. "Only approved restraint procedures were used in response to resisting arrest."

"So, is it 'approved procedures' that when you have ten armed officers restraining a naked sixty-four year old man they will need to run 50,000 volts through his body?"

"He wasn't naked," squealed the soon to be demoted policeman. "He had his pyjamas on!"

In a comfortable residence in Stirlingshire the Chief Constable of Police Scotland shook his head.

The red camera light came on and the studio presenter offered the link to the studio. "Sometimes in broadcasting it is sufficient to show an interview and make no comment. But we are pleased to have Henry Doncaster here in the studio after his ordeal. We also have Henry's friends, Roy Fox and Donnie Anderson who so ably led The Pensioners March that showed the strength of feeling in Britain. First, Henry, what are your thoughts on your experience?"

Henry had prepared only the first part of his response. "The first thing I want to do is to acknowledge the death of my dear friend and my lawyer, Mr Findlay Macsween."

The presenter interrupted. "Just to remind viewers that Mr Findlay Macsween OBE died in Police custody and the First Minister of Scotland has asked the Metropolitan Police to lead a major enquiry into the circumstances of his death."

Henry continued. "I just can't believe that they arrested him...an eighty year old man. Surely someone must have known that this was a wrong thing to do."

The presenter developed the point. "I suppose that that is what we are learning from this case and a point which you, Roy, made in your speech on Glasgow Green: that there probably were police officers who did not like what was happening, but there is such a culture of fear and blind obedience in the Force that no one took a stand against it." Henry nodded. "That was my experience. Most officers treated me extremely well, even with caring. I got a sense that many were uncomfortable with what was going on, but were afraid to question it. Some even undermined the system in small ways to do me kindnesses, but I won't be giving details on that."

The interview with Henry progressed to explore other details about his experience, before the presenter turned to Roy.

"Roy, we have seen portions of your speeches on Glasgow Green and in George Square. Those speeches were very powerful, but I imagine that you haven't done anything like that before. How was it to speak to all those people?"

Roy thought that it was a good first question and tried to answer it honestly. "I was speechless with nerves beforehand, but when it came time to walk out I was perfectly calm. I just wanted to tell the people what was happening as honestly as I could."

"We didn't show it on the clip, but there was a point where you had got the crowd so angry that there might have been a riot. The police even drew their batons. But then you backed the crowd off. People have remarked that that took some skill..."

"It wasn't 'skill'," interrupted Roy with a touch of impatience in his voice, "I was just being honest with people and telling them how I saw things. Yes, I had been angry at the police, and I was furious at the death of Mr Macsween, but it wasn't about ALL the police, just one. As I said on the Green, most of the police who had found themselves tied up in this were also victims; victims of a system that had no means of monitoring and challenging itself."

The presenter spent most time on his interview with Roy and ended it with the comment, "Well Roy, you may have added something important to British politics, the notion that the most important thing is humanity!" Turning to Donnie he apologised. "Donnie, I've spent so long talking with Henry and Roy that we don't have much time left..."

Donnie interrupted. "That's fine; it was Henry who went through the bad time and it was Roy who spoke so well."

"Yes," added the presenter, "but you also stepped out of your normal quiet life and stood up for what was right. Where did you get the courage to do that?"

Donnie paused, looked at the interviewer, and with extreme gravitas said, "Sometimes you've just got to do things because they are right."

That offered the presenter a wonderful point at which to close the piece. Roy looked at Donnie wondering why his closing statement had sounded familiar. Donnie avoided looking at Roy.

In the Crannog in Lochinver Jock said to Duncan, "Agus sin againn streapadair beanntan Asainte." (*And there is our mountaineer of Assynt.*)

55. A DISTINGUISHED VISITOR

Professor Nadira Khan switched on her mobile as she exited Chambers. She was back in her familiar London/Oxford circuit, but often she thought about her time in Scotland. It had reminded her of what it was like to be fighting in the trenches of the civil liberties war. The satisfaction was not measured by the amount of remuneration but by the integrity of the case and the people around you. She felt like the actor, Peter Reigert, playing the character 'MacIntyre' in the Scottish film '*Local Hero*', when, at the end of the film, he was whisked back from the Scottish Highlands to his Houston apartment, still with the Scottish sea shells in his coat pocket. He had realised the difference between a community that was defined by the humanity of the people within it and the life he customarily led in Texas. Nadira entertained the thought of taking a flight north, just to pop into The Culloden that Friday evening and to meet Maureen, Rosie, Roy, Donnie, Henry, Amanda, Sam, Rory, Nicholas and that minder of his... whatever his name was. She also thought of Stewart and spent another tear on his father who had contracted her, dear Mr Findlay Macsween of the pink tie. She had submitted her fee note to Henry, through Stewart Macsween. It had been for £1 inclusive of expenses. She did note that she might seek their permissions in regard to a book she was writing on 'Policing in the Tabloid Society'.

Nadira noted seven messages on her phone but returned the call of only one. The respondent answered a trifle nervously. "Hello, this is George Dunlop."

Nadira smiled; she had not known his first name. "George, this is Nadira Khan. What can I do for you?"

George cleared his throat nervously before he answered. "You have done enough by allowing me to use your name in regard to my Disciplinary Hearing. They dropped it immediately and gave me my retirement and my pension."

"That's great George; now are you really wanting to retire or would you like an interesting job?"

Nadira informed George Dunlop that Mr Rory Donaldson, of the long established Glasgow private detective agency Donaldsons, would like him to make contact because he was particularly interested in employing experienced former police officers of special integrity. The former Sergeant Dunlop was so excited that he called his wife Elaine to the phone to share the moment. Professor Khan closed her phone with a smile.

*
**

Donnie had worked out that the best place to stand was at the very beginning of the platform at Stirling station. That way he could check the numbers of all the carriages as they passed him. When Amanda had told them about her cache he had immediately volunteered to seek out an acquaintance in the train-spotting community to track the whereabouts of the carriage in which she had hidden the encryption code. His friend had assured him that it should be on this train from Inverness through Stirling to Edinburgh. As it happened, the very first carriage, in First Class, bore the correct number, which required Donnie to sprint the length of the platform to board it. He walked down the carriage to seat 32 and his heart sank when he found it occupied by a very large and fierce looking woman. Donnie had hoped to find the code and get off at the same station, but that was not going to be possible. He sat down across the aisle from seat 32 and contemplated the woman as the train moved off.

He was still wondering how to get her off her seat when the conductor came to ask for tickets. "Can I have a single from Stirling to the next station please?"

"Yes, a First Class ticket from Stirling to Falkirk will be £8, plus a £20 fine," replied the guard.

"Why is there a fine?" asked Donnie.

"Because there are adequate ticketing facilities in Stirling and you failed to use them," was the institutionalised reply.

"But I didn't intend to travel," replied Donnie.

"Then why did you board the train?" came the obvious reply.

"Because my friend left something important down the back of this lady's seat," was Donnie's innocent response.

The lady whom Donnie feared looked at him and the conductor. She then felt down the back of her seat and withdrew the folded paper. "Is this it?" she asked Donnie. "Probably," was his measured response.

The lady handed him the paper which he unfolded to find the rows of numbers. "Yes, this is it; thank you ma'am."

The lady addressed the conductor. "Under the circumstances I think that the gentleman has given a perfectly reasonable explanation of his failure to purchase a ticket. Perhaps his offer to pay the first class fare from Stirling to Falkirk is sufficient?"

"Yes your Ladyship," agreed the conductor and did the business with Donnie.

For the remainder of the ten mile journey Donnie kept looking at the lady he feared and smiled incompetently. Who on earth was she? Donnie got out at Falkirk Grahamston station to make his way to the bus station in order to use his bus pass for the journey back to Glasgow. As he exited the train the Lady he feared gave him a smile and a wave. 'Weird,' he thought, as he waved back.

*
**

That evening Donnie, Henry and Roy were in their usual positions at the bar. They had been joined for the session by Maureen, Rosie, Sam, Nicholas and Adonis. Sam had wanted to discuss what they should do with the £107,000 surplus. They agreed that it should be used for some purpose that would benefit pensioners, but no definite ideas had been forthcoming.

Donnie proudly passed over the sheet of numbers to Henry who turned the paper round in his hand, saying, "All that trouble for this little sheet of paper. Maybe I should have just given Dingwall the money and saved old Mr Macsween's life."

Roy's question was telling. "What do you think Mr Macsween would have thought about that?"

Henry looked back at Roy. "Yes, you're right; he wouldn't have liked that idea at all. But I still crack up every time I think about him lying in his cell and dying alone."

The eight people were silent. Perhaps the spirit of Mr Findlay Macsween OBE could feel their presence.

At this moment the front of the pub also fell into a silence that spread throughout the establishment like a Mexican Wave. Three men and one woman moved across the bar from the entrance. The first man smiled broadly and held out his hand to Roy. "It is a pleasure to meet you Roy," he declared.

Roy returned the handshake. "And you too, First Minister."

No one in the pub quite knew how to deal with this situation of an unannounced visit from the First Minister of Scotland. It should be explained that although half the population of the pub, including Roy, had voted at the last election for a party other than that of the First Minister, he was personally held in high regard throughout the country. The populace knew an accomplished politician when they (rarely) saw one.

The First Minister spotted Donnie and Henry, introducing himself to both and then asking Roy, "Will you introduce me to your other friends, Roy."

Thus The First Minister of Scotland was introduced to Maureen, Rosie, Sam and Nicholas. Adonis had quietly drifted out of sight. Rosie smiled as she thought about the fact that the First Minister had just been introduced to 'Finn', arguably Scotland's most feared gangster, who had his twelve inch 'persuader' in its sheath down the back of his trousers as they shook hands.

The distinguished visitor to The Culloden reflected on the March. "OK, I played things up a little in my newsreel piece, but everything I said was genuine; I wanted to join the March, but I let myself be persuaded otherwise. You were absolutely right to do what you did, but it must have taken courage… courage more than I had."

Roy interrupted what was beginning to sound like a political speech. First Minister, can I buy you a drink?"

The First Minister responded, "No Roy, I don't."

"Perhaps a pack of crisps?" queried Roy.

"Yes," declared the First Minister, "Smoky bacon if you have them please Maureen." "Oh, we have plenty smoky bacon crisps in this pub sir."

The First Minister was not just on a flying visit, for he stayed until Maureen tinkled her bell. By this time he had taken Roy aside and engaged him in a conversation that he began boldly. "You should be in Scottish politics Roy."

Roy did not respond, so the First Minister pressed his case. "Roy, you are a natural. No one in the country could have addressed a hundred thousand people the way you did. And you did it twice. The people loved you Roy. And they believed you. They believed you were telling them the truth, because you WERE telling them the truth…well, apart from once.

"Once?" queried Roy.

"Well, there was that thing when you told them that only five people older than Henry had been Tasered and three of them were dead."

"Yes?" continued Roy in non-committal fashion.

"Well," continued the First Minister, "I got our researchers on to that statistic, and they found that what you had said was accurate…up to a point."

"And the point is?" queried Roy.

"The point is that, of the three who died; one of them died of cancer and another in a car accident."

"Still leaves one," said Roy.

"See what I mean Roy, you are a natural politician!" declared the First Minister in an irony they both understood. "Seriously," he continued, "Your talks were powerful because they were from the heart and they were honest. Scottish politics needs that. I would be proud to have you in our party."

Roy looked The First Minister of Scotland in the eye. In truth, he respected the man and believed that British politics had been much improved by his participation. "But I have never even voted for your party," Roy declared. "I always have voted Labour until the last time I voted for those Lib Dems."

The First Minister stifled a disrespectful smirk that accurately mirrored Roy's view. "OK Roy, you are right. You know, Scotland has done a lot to broaden political thinking in Britain since devolution. First we overturned the myth spawned by the tabloids that the Scots would be too stupid to govern themselves. Second, we opted for a powerful system of proportional representation that Westminster politicians said would be unworkable. Third, we have successfully managed an electoral system that has demanded constructive dialogue among parties rather than the Westminster adversarial system that can only entertain a single victor over the majority of the populace. You know Roy; perhaps our new political system in Scotland may also be able to develop politics beyond the political parties. For example, I wonder how Roy Fox would fare in the next Scottish Parliament election, standing as an independent candidate for this constituency, promising only an unpartisan appraisal of every issue. Seriously Roy, this might be a major development that could resonate more widely throughout the country. Imagine a Scottish Parliament where, as well as the party politicians, there were perhaps thirty independent MSPs. It would change the dialogue completely. With thirty independent judgments being thrown into the mix on every issue the only way that the parties could get their wishes would be by putting up a genuinely good case. And imagine what it would mean for the people of this country to be able to rely on an honest, largely unpartisan appraisal from their politicians!"

Roy turned to an obvious argument. "I am sixty-six years old; far too old to become a politician."

But the First Minister of Scotland was not so easily deflected. "Roy, the age demographic has changed a lot in the last thirty years and will continue to change. Thirty years ago you would have been right; sixty-six would be too old. Men did not even expect to live much beyond retirement. But things are totally different now; people, like yourself, are much sharper at sixty-six than thirty years ago. Also, a larger proportion of the electorate is over sixty-six. They might prefer their MSP to be someone who has experience of their own times and culture rather than a thirty year old career politician."

Roy was moved by the First Minister's argument, but he was enough of a politician not to declare that fact. Instead, he changed the subject. "First Minister, I wonder if you could help us with a slight predicament we have encountered, for we have unintentionally made a profit out of the March of £107,000 and we would like to use that to support some future initiatives involving pensioners. But we need someone of status to approve our use of the funds for such purposes."

The First Minister of Scotland looked at Roy and said something unusual. "Roy, sometimes when I look at you it is like I am looking in the mirror, but looking at my best self in that mirror."

Roy interrupted. "That feeling is entirely mutual sir."

The Culloden emptied without its customers knowing that the future of British politics had been changed in their presence that night.

56. MEETING UP

Three months had passed since 'The Pensioners March'. The media circus around Roy and Henry had subsided. The Assistant Chief Constable (Organised Crime and Counter Terrorism) of Police Scotland had been allowed to retire. The sacking of Inspector Roderick Mitchell had been rescinded by the Chief Constable but he had been reduced in rank to Sergeant and lectured on his failure to stand up to Dingwall's tyrannical regime. Chief Superintendent Roger Dingwall faced four proceedings. The first was as a result of the Metropolitan Police independent investigation into the death in custody of Findlay Macsween. The second was a hearing which he faced along with Sergeant Mitchell on their failure to obtain judicial approval for phone taps. The third was a lengthy enquiry into his handling of the case against Henry. The Chief Superintendent's case had not been helped by a phone call to the Chief Constable in which Chief Inspector Aldo Perretti informed him that early in the investigation he had strongly recommended to the Chief Superintendent that terrorism related proceedings against Henry Doncaster should be dropped. Perretti's official letter to Dingwall to that effect could not be found in police files. The disciplinary hearing that followed these three investigations dismissed Roger Dingwall from the Police Force. The fourth proceeding was a criminal investigation into the events a year earlier in relation to John Bethel and Luigi Lugano. That led to Roger Dingwall being committed for trial and receiving a ten year jail sentence. Under a new arrangement with the Swiss banking system, his assets totalling a little over £150,000 in Hyperswiss Privatbank were frozen pending sequestration. Having read all the reports of the investigations, the Chief Constable instructed that the retired Sergeant George Dunlop, now working as a private investigator, should be invited to the next police awards ceremony to receive a commendation.

*
**

Maureen and Rosie were sprucing up The Culloden during the afternoon closing in preparation for the last evening of the year – Hogmanay. The Culloden was adorned in its usual decorations, but it also had several lines of greetings cards strung from wall to wall. The cards were from all around the world including one was from the office of the President of the USA.

For Maureen, much had happened in these last months because nothing had happened. She had had no symptoms that would have heralded the possibility of her cancer returning and the tests had also revealed nothing. On her last hospital visit she had met her surgeon; he who had sought to represent her in theatre. "Well Maureen, it looks as good as it could. We will need to keep a close eye on it for a wee while yet, but we may have got off with it."

Maureen began to ask him the questions that had always been on her mind. "How can you do this? How can you work this way? How can you think of me, as a person, in the operating theatre? How can you do that for every patient?"

He answered only her last question and that merely served to leave her with a further question. "In truth, I can't. I would like to and I try to, but it only sometimes really happens. With you it was important for me, so it happened. I'll see you in three months." He smiled and swept out of the room before she could ask another question.

*
**

There had been a lot for Rosie to talk about with Maureen and most of it concerned Adonis.

"But he really has feelings!" Rosie had declared soon after the March.

Maureen had been cynical. "Since when did a man with a body also have feelings?"

"I know," replied Rosie, "That's why I dumped him. But

there is more to him."

Maureen played the big sister strongly. "Rosie, you know that there are a million Scottish women saying the same thing as their man is in the betting shop in the day and down the boozer at night. They are so sure that there is a loving person in there if only he could come out. Someone even wrote a book about it once. It was called *Women Who Love Too Much*, though it should have been called *Men Who Cannot Love At All!*"

They laughed together and Rosie continued, "Maureen, It is as though you are speaking for a part of me, for I have always walked into that trap of falling for a man like that. But perhaps that caution is also a trap for me; maybe it means that I always play too safe." Maureen looked at her sister and shivered. "That feels far too close to me."

The sisters laughed together.

*
**

Donnie had been to Argentina to meet his family. He had enjoyed the whole of the seventeen hour British Airways flight from London to Buenos Aires, though he had not been paying attention to the announcements and had actually disembarked the plane during the brief runway stop in Sao Paolo, Brazil. Nothing had indicated a stop in Brazil, though it was the normal British Airways route, and Donnie had presumed that the thirteen hours to that point had taken him all the way to Buenos Aires. After causing a considerable flutter in the airport Donnie was led all the way back on board and to the seat that he had carefully tidied before disembarking. The other passengers gave him a look.

On arriving at Ezeiza airport in Buenos Aires Donnie had been surprised that he was not at all nervous or embarrassed about meeting the family he had ignored for a generation. Donald had run across the concourse to be the first to greet him. Without hesitation he had hugged his father warmly and strongly, in the manner that men do in Argentina. Donnie did his best to step out of his Glasgow upbringing that prohibited such contact and hugged his son as strongly as he could. The important thing for Donnie was that he meant it. Angela arrived next and, also in South American fashion, she kissed Donnie on both cheeks. His grandsons, Mark and James, came forward more hesitantly, but the elder Mark broke the ice by saying, "You were great on TV grandad!" Mark and James shook hands with their grandfather for the first time.

*
**

Donnie described his time in Argentina to Henry and Roy on Hogmanay in Henry's flat before they went to The Culloden. "We had a few days in the Buenos Aires area, staying in their home in Tigre, a huge old wooden house built on stilts in the river delta. Donald works in the centre of Buenos Aires and commutes from his home by powerboat. It takes him fifteen minutes rather than forty-five by car. I love Buenos Aires; the people are so friendly. But the most powerful experience was on Thursday afternoons in the Plaza de Mayo in central Buenos Aires, when Las Madres…they are the mothers of the 30,000 children who were 'disappeared' in the 'Dirty War' thirty years ago…march in a never ending circle. Every Thursday, for all these years, they have marched in the Plaza, in front of the pink Government Building asking for information about their disappeared children. Now they are joined by 'Los Hijos' who are the children of the lost generation. Roy, <u>we</u> have politics, but nothing like those politics."

Roy nodded and continued to listen to his friend who carried on. "Later we flew south to San Carlos de Bariloche, in the foothills of the Andes. Wow, that is a beautiful place. They have a lakeside house in a place called Llao Llao. You two would love it for the fishing. I walked out on their jetty and watched two huge trout cruising about. We spent a week walking and riding horses. There were gauchos who took us out on the horses. Our main trip took us for three days up into the high Andes, to the border with Chile. I want to go to Chile someday, and also to Peru and to Bolivia."

Henry raised an eye at the mention of Bolivia.

Donnie ended his account and turned to his friends. "But, enough of me and my holidays; how has it been for you two here? Henry, I see that you have got the flat back to the way it was, or even better...?" Donnie's pause accompanied his nod to the opposite wall that was entirely covered by a plasma flat screen television that must have been eight feet long by four feet deep.

Henry explained what had been happening to him in these recent times. "I took a bad turn soon after I got out of prison. I think that the experience finally got through to me and in a bad way. I would never come out of the flat, and I never really fixed the flat either. I was living in a stripped place with only a bed. I stopped cooking and seldom ate out either. Amanda would phone me and Roy would phone me and I would say that I was OK. Then they got together and came round. It was only when I was talking through the locked door to two of the people in this world that I love that it finally got through to me. I opened the door and cried with them. I cried for a long time. I don't think that I would have come out of it without them."

Roy continued, "Henry breaking down helped me in a way I don't understand. During the March and with the visit of the First Minister and all I was 'flying high'. I had found myself doing stuff that I never would have dreamt I could do. I was in real danger of 'losing it'. But when Amanda and I got together to be with Henry, it brought me right back down to earth. It reminded me that this thing was not about my fancy speeches, but it was about people being abused by those who should be protecting them. I had to have a long talk with Sheila in order to sort my head out. What is important is not speeches, it is people."

Donnie looked at his friend. "That is also a great speech, Roy."

Roy launched a pretend punch at Donnie but managed to just miss.

Henry ended the meeting. "My last batch of cakes is ready to take out of the oven. Let's get them all together and go to the Culloden."

Roy said, "You two go ahead of me for there is something I have to do before the end of the year."

Henry and Donnie knew what this meant and they accepted it in silence.

*
**

"So, are your intentions entirely honourable?"

The question, coming as it did from a gangster, should have sounded bizarre, but Adonis knew exactly what his boss meant. He replied, "I love her so much that I nearly told her." Nicholas exploded with laughter, for this was an age-old Glasgow expression that well depicted the temerity of men in love.

"Well it is maybe time that you really did tell that lovely woman that you love her," said Nicholas. "Don't tell her that I said that of course."

Adonis fell silent for a moment and his boss filled it in. "Of course, you will not be able to continue to work for me. I could not live with the possibility that such a beautiful woman could be widowed just because you were protecting me."

Adonis knew that his relationship with his boss was closer than that expression. "But you will not manage on your own… and you will not find someone like me…and others will know that."

Nicholas wondered if he would say the next bit. He had tried to say it several times to himself, but had never quite managed to complete it. "Anyway, I am thinking about getting out of the business." He said it without emotion, but he also knew that his friend would not miss its implications.

Adonis did something that he could never before have

conceived. He stood up in front of his boss and stretched his fingers forward to touch each shoulder. "But they will not accept that...they will kill you...you will have to go to London."

The concept of 'going to London' has always been around the Scottish criminal fraternity. The best place to hide is always among lots of people and London has lots of people.

Nicholas continued, "I don't really want to do that. I'd prefer to stay here."

Adonis knew his boss well enough to know that he had chosen his path, but he already grieved for him.

**

Amanda would never have contemplated the possibility of her seeing in the new year in a Glasgow pub, but she had promised to meet Henry in The Culloden, so that was where she would go. But Derek had phoned her begging that she come to the house for a talk. He had been crying and slurring but she felt that it would do no harm to see him. It was not as though he could change her mind for she had already moved out and into a flat of her own. The house was in her name, having originally been purchased with her money from her father's estate and she had arranged for it to go on the market in January. She had taken all the furniture that was her own, which was most of it, but she allowed Derek to continue to stay in the house until the middle of January under a contract established between their lawyers.

To his credit Derek had arranged the remaining furniture to bring together armchairs and a small table such that they could sit comfortably to talk. He had opened a bottle of very good wine for Amanda but he was drinking whisky. Amanda declined the wine, but she did so graciously, reminding him that she was driving.

Their talk went reasonably well at first, though Amanda found it irritating when he slurred. He accepted that she was gone and he said that he respected that, even apologising for some of his earlier behaviour. He even asked her about her Cochabamba project and seemed to show an interest. It was only when he realised that she was going to invest a lot of money in the project that his behaviour changed. He raised his eyebrows and declared, "Well I suppose you can have your playthings as long as you don't affect the business."

Her response was not revengeful, though Derek experienced it thus. "I will be selling the business. If you get together the finance I will sell it to you at a reduced price."

Derek clenched his fists and exploded. "But it is **my** business; your father only put the shares in your name for tax purposes!"

"No Derek," replied Amanda, "My father put the shares in my name because he did not trust you."

Derek stood up and strode over to stand above Amanda. Then he hit his wife full in the face with his fist for the first and last time. Amanda had not at all anticipated that he would do this and was unprotected, which meant that she was severely hurt. She grabbed her bag and coat and ran out of the house holding her broken nose streaming with blood and frantically searching for her car keys.

*
**

Sam was sitting on their living room rug with his wife Katie in his arms in front of him. They were enjoying a glass of a twelve year old Chateau Siran Margeaux, a special treat on this Hogmanay. Katie broached the question that she had harboured for a long time. "But I don't understand why you couldn't keep the money you made from all the articles you sold?"

Sam had been waiting for this question. The answer had been so clear for him, but he wondered if it would be as clear for Katie. "I felt that it was not really my story; it was Roy's story and Donnie's story and Henry's story and the marchers' story. I didn't think that it was right for me to take the money for their story. My thinking was that if my actual writing was good, then I would gain out of that through my 'by-line' being attached to the pieces. And that has happened; the new job with *The Voice* has come from that. But I felt that the income from the story belonged to them."

Katie put down her wine glass and stretched up to kiss her wonderful husband.

*
**

For only the second time in his life Rory Donaldson pulled his Porsche up near the Culloden. As he got out and locked his dream machine a small voice chipped up. "Look efter yer car mister?"

Rory turned round to look at the familiar urchin. "What are your terms?"

"Well," came the reasoned response, "This is Hogmanay and that is special rates. It is £3 an hour, but, since you are a reliable customer, a deposit is not required."

"It's a deal," agreed Rory, "but even a minute after midnight on such a special evening merits a £10 bonus."

"Agreed," confirmed his contractor, offering a handshake to seal the deal. Rory returned the handshake and tried to resist the smile that might have devalued it.

*
**

Henry was on the walk with Donnie to The Culloden when he got Amanda's phone call. "The bastard!" he cried, and nearly dropped the platter of cakes he was carrying. Quickly he told Donnie about Amanda's call and asked him to take both platters to The Culloden while he went to the hospital. Donnie would have preferred to ditch the cakes and go with Henry to be with his new friend Amanda, but he knew that the Hogmanay cakes for The Culloden were important for Henry.

Thus it was that, instead of a united Culloden entry of

Henry, Donnie and Roy, it was only Donnie who struggled through the door with Henry's platters of cakes. Maureen, Rosie, Rory, Nicholas and Adonis soon gathered round Donnie who told the whole story. Adonis stepped back and looked at his boss. Nicholas returned the eye contact and nodded in a fashion imperceptible to anyone else. Adonis left the pub.

*
* *

Roy was with his wife. "So, here we are Sheila, at the end of another year. But this year has been pretty different. I was amazed at what we could do with you by my side during the speech. But it changed nothing that was important, because when I got home it was missing you that I felt even more strongly...what it would have felt like to have had you really there with me. I wonder if things are going to change even more for me next year; I have a feeling that they will. But then is then and now is now and I really need to be with you before I can go back to them. They are my dear friends, but they are not like you." Roy curled up with Sheila.

*
* *

George Dunlop had not expected that he would want to visit The Culloden on that Hogmanay. He knew of the place and that it would be the likely venue for the principals of the March. He had felt uncertain when he broached the question with Elaine, but she was sure. "Of course you should go George, for you were a part of all that; you were an honourable part of all that."

Thus it was that the former Sergeant George Dunlop sidled into The Culloden without being noticed. He recognised his new boss, Mr Donaldson, and he also remembered Maureen whose distress in the police station had first begun his questioning, but he slipped around the bar unnoticed and ordered his beer from Rosie.

Henry and Amanda arrived together, just after eleven, with Amanda sporting a huge dressing on her nose as well as blotched black eyes. Donnie crossed the bar to kiss both her cheeks and embrace her. This was exactly what was best for Amanda; a full South American greeting from a person that she knew really cared for her. Her tear filled eyes were not improved, but her mood was. She felt part of a 'family'.

Rosie came over to the developing group and spoke to Donnie. "There is someone outside asking for you."

Donnie made his way to the door with no idea what to expect. He stepped out into the street and an almost unrecognisable short haired and seemingly taller young man in an army uniform stood before him. Young Malcolm Jamieson stood upright, stamped both heels and saluted Donnie. A world of abuse and retribution passed through Donnie's mind in an instant, but he knew that he must leave that behind to meet his young friend. Donnie stood up straight and saluted. "Good to meet you Private Jamieson".

Young Malcolm smiled broadly, but not in his former child-like way. He had been through 'boot camp' and had gained adulthood from it.

Donnie asked, "Would you like to come inside with me for a drink?"

Private Jamieson's response was quick and clear. "No sir... with respect sir. It would be OK for me to do it, but, as a fairly new recruit, I don't want to do that in uniform. I just wanted you to know."

Donnie was in a mixture of delight and dread for his young friend and he sincerely hoped that he had not been an influence towards Malcolm joining the army and all that that might mean. But he knew that it was important to meet the young man exactly as he presented himself; that is the way every human being should be met. Donnie said, "Malcolm, thank you for showing me. I am delighted that you have got what you wanted. It is a pleasure to know you and I would like you to feel free to come to me...whatever happens in your life."

Private Malcolm Jamieson straightened once again and saluted. "Thank you sir, that is much appreciated." He swivelled, in a military way, and marched down the street.

As Roy made his lonely way to The Culloden he noticed the young man in army uniform across the street but did not recognise him. He was surprised when the young man saluted him.

Roy was feeling a weight...what was that weight about? He had never felt 'weight' when it was just him and his allotment. Even in his earlier days in work he had never felt this 'weight'...except one time when he had to sack a young and promising apprentice who had been systematically stealing. So the weight was...? He recognised that the weight was the feeling of 'responsibility' which is forever the other side of the coin from standing up for something. A familiar part of Roy again wanted not to enter The Culloden but just to go home to bed but another part pushed the door open.

*
**

Adonis looked at his watch to check that it was a few seconds after midnight. He wanted to be Derek Smallwood's 'first foot'. He pulled on his thin black leather gloves and fastened them with the press studs at the wrists. He rang the bell. There was no response, so he rang it several times more because he knew that his victim was inside. Eventually a drunken Derek Smallwood was roused and opened the door. There has always been a conundrum in Glasgow culture where women are beaten but there is also a powerful imperative against men who commit such violence, within the working class sub-culture at least. Adonis entered and gave Derek a cross-cultural lesson that he would never forget.

*
**

Planes never behave themselves on Hogmanay but thank goodness for Mr Macsween's reliable limousine firm thought Professor Nadira Khan as her car drew up outside The Culloden shortly after midnight. Although the hire was pre-paid, she gave Max a £20 tip and a kiss for the New Year. Max was more delighted with the kiss. Nadira Khan entered The Culloden with her metaphorical sea shells in her pocket and was greeted with rapturous cheers. Rory Donaldson came forward to kiss Nadira and take her to join the company.

57. MOVING ON

"So, remember that we leave for our trip next Tuesday" said Henry.

Donnie and Roy looked at him blankly. They were enjoying their usual evening drink together on a Monday in early January. The conversation had been about Roy's Skype call with his daughter and grandchildren and Donnie's plans to do some serious walking in Assynt in April.

Roy asked the obvious question. "What trip is that?"

"Our New Zealand trip of course," replied Henry in a matter of fact fashion. "Remember that I said to keep this time of year free."

Neither Roy nor Donnie spoke, but both looked at each other.

"Oh, you old geezers haven't forgotten, have you?" queried Henry in pretend annoyance. "But..." said Roy. "But..." echoed Donnie.

Henry continued, "Remember that the trip to New Zealand was my choice of a new thing to do and you both agreed. It was always the responsibility of the chooser to make the arrangements, so I've done that. We leave a week tomorrow. The limousine will pick us up from our flats around noon."

"Limousine?" echoed Roy and Donnie simultaneously.

"But that discussion about New Zealand was just pretend," said Roy.

"Yes...pretend," added Donnie still echoing.

Henry shook his head in pretend solemnity. "Not to me. I paid attention to all our plans and I have booked exactly what we wanted – a week in the North Island staying in nice hotels and three weeks in South Island where we will pick up our motorhome in Christchurch then drive north to the wine country before moving across and down the West coast, eventually to the Fjord region. I've booked us a nice two day cruise in Doubtful Sound and a helicopter trip over the glaciers. Here are your plane tickets by the way."

Henry withdrew two airline tickets from his inside pocket, checked the names and passed them over.

Roy opened his ticket and noted, "This says 'Business Class' on it."

"Yes," said Henry, "We agreed that the trip was too long for old people like us to travel 'economy' because we might get deep vein thrombosis. We agreed on First Class, but this airline only has Economy and Business on this flight, no First Class."

Donnie had so many 'buts' that he could not get them into a sensible order. "But I won't have time to get my trousers."

Roy and Henry looked at him, wondering not for the first time how his mind worked. Donnie tried again. "But it will cost a fortune...I've only got £890."

Roy nodded and took over the echoing. "Yes...a fortune."

Henry knew that this question would arise and had thought about how to respond. Roy and Donnie were proud men who might feel uncomfortable with everything being paid by him.

"Look guys, when I was lying in my prison cell the only pleasure I got was to make these plans. They had given me pen and paper to write down the details of my accounts and I used them to make notes. They confiscated them and sent them to a code breaker! Every day I would work on these plans and my depression would gradually lift and I would start laughing as I imagined this very meeting and the looks on your faces. This kept up my spirits and I really hope that you will accept it as my gift. I know that it would be a lot of money on your budgets, but...really...it's small change to me."

Henry looked at his friends, anxiously hoping that they would feel comfortable in accepting his gift.

Donnie nodded. "Fair enough by me; thanks Henry."

Henry was pleased to see the genuine look of acceptance on Donnie's face, but was alarmed to see Roy's serious expression and the slow shaking of his head as he said, "Well, it's not really OK with me Henry."

Henry's heart sank; he had feared this possibility. In a much smaller voice and with his head slightly bowed, he said, "I'm really sorry if I have offended you Roy."

Roy's serious expression continued. "You have indeed offended me Henry...if this airline does not have First Class, why did you not pick one that did?"

Henry raised his head and with a broadening smile he said, "Roy Fox, you are a very bad man; you really had me going there!"

The friends shared a laugh and Donnie said, "OK, now I want to break with tradition and buy our last drinks for the evening. Maureen, can we have two pints and a half pint please? I'm paying."

*
**

The limo collected Roy first, then Henry, before pulling up outside Donnie's building. Although it was a freezing January day Donnie was wearing shorts with knee length socks. Roy and Henry got out of the car to greet him as the driver lifted his case into the generous car boot.

"Are you not cold in those?" asked Roy nodding towards Donnie's shorts.

"No, not really...the socks are warm" Donnie replied.

"So this is what you were meaning by 'needing time to buy your trousers'?" queried Henry.

Donnie nodded. "Yes, I read a book once about New Zealand and it said that the men wore shorts and long socks."

Roy probed further. "How old was this book Donnie?"

Donnie thought for a moment. "It was quite old."

*
**

During the walk from the Executive Lounge to board the Boeing 777 the three men each had pause for thought. Henry was full of pure joy at the thought of their adventure together, though he was also conscious that the trip was effectively postponing his decision about joining Amanda on her project. Donnie was thinking about how much life had changed for him in the last sixteen months. Back then he could never have envisioned that he would now be embarking on his second long haul air trip and that he would have found his family. Roy had a lot to think about for he had a sense that more change was to come for him. He had summarised his feelings the evening before when he had been talking with Sheila. "Before this all started I was slowly dying. I had stopped living and was letting go. I had forgotten what living was about; it was easier just to let things go. It wasn't that I was depressed, it's just that I had stopped finding the edge of life."

They were welcomed into one of the three Business Class compartments and seated in the central section that gave them three seats together. Immediately a stewardess offered glasses of champagne or orange juice. All three calculated that it would be impolite to decline the champagne. As they sipped delicately but casually under the pretence that they were accustomed champagne drinkers, a new set of passengers began to board. The eyes of the newcomers opened wide in delight at the sight of the champagne. But quickly they would look at the low seat numbers compared to their own and their hearts would sink as they realised there would be no free champagne at the back of the plane. Donnie decided to promote the distress of the newcomers by taking out the large dinner menu whose cover displayed a sea food platter worthy of their status. Inside the menu each dish had its formal title but also carried a simple English description as well as a photo of the dish. This was the moment that Donnie discovered the provenance of 'escargots'. He looked at the description and photo of 'Escargots de Bourgogne'. Turning to Henry, Donnie asked, "Henry, what are escargots?"

"Snails," replied Henry and looked back to his own menu.

Donnie turned to Roy and gave him a look.

"What?" asked Roy.

"Nothing," replied Donnie.

Henry turned to the 'Healthy Meals Options' and selected just a main course of 'Steamed fillet of garoupa topped with julienne of vegetables served with a light basil sauce accompanied with nutmegged broccoli, turned carrots and tagliatelle noodles.'

Roy scanned the menu, sighed and put it away. Summoning a stewardess with the call button, he smiled broadly at her and asked, "Excuse me dear, do you have any smoky bacon crisps?"

Printed in Great Britain
by Amazon

81573349R00197